Praise for the Inspector Anjelica Henley series

"Well-written and engaging... The twists and turns are excellent, and the author ratchets up the suspense with every chapter."

—**NPR**

"Expertly depicted... A heartpounding work of suspense."

—*Booklist*

"Matheson has a keen instinct for keeping the pages turning."

—*New York Times Book Review*

"Fiendishly clever."

—*CrimeReads*

"A taut and addictive thriller."

—*PopSugar*

"Crime fiction has a significant new star."

—Sarah Hilary, author of *Someone Else's Skin*

"Excellent... It's the small things in Matheson's work that add up to the unforgettable. Definitely a new writer to watch."

—*Globe and Mail*

"A thrilling story that starts out strong and never lets up."

—*Red Carpet Crash*

"[A] complex mystery with plenty of twists."

—*Novels Alive*

"Matheson has given us a smart, modern heroine. I hope this is only the first of many adventures fo

—Tami Hoag, #1 *New York Times* be

T0054507

"Elegantly grim and irresistibly gruesome... This is a page-turner of the highest order."

—Hank Phillippi Ryan, *USA TODAY* bestselling author of *The Murder List*

"Smashing!"

—J.T. Ellison, *New York Times* bestselling author

"Nadine Matheson knows how to grab her reader's attention from the opening page and doesn't let go. *The Jigsaw Man* is smart, deftly plotted, and expertly paced... With a tale that's dark, devious and deliciously twisted, Matheson brings a fresh new voice to crime fiction that I can't wait to hear more from."

—Hannah Mary McKinnon, author of *The Neighbors*

"*The Jigsaw Man* is so tense and dark. It has a real *Silence of the Lambs* vibe, and Peter Olivier is my new Hannibal Lecter. Brilliant."

—Lisa Hall, author of *Between You and Me*

THE
BINDING
ROOM

Also by Nadine Matheson

The Jigsaw Man

THE
BINDING
ROOM

A NOVEL

NADINE
MATHESON

HANOVER
SQUARE
PRESS

**HANOVER
SQUARE
PRESS™**

Recycling programs
for this product may
not exist in your area.

ISBN-13: 978-1-335-45504-8

The Binding Room

First published in 2022. This edition published in 2023.

Hanover Square Press
22 Adelaide St. West, 41st Floor
Toronto, Ontario M5H 4E3, Canada
HanoverSqPress.com
BookClubbish.com

Printed in U.S.A.

To Mum (best reviewer in the world) and Dad.
Love you and thank you. x

THE

BINDING

ROOM

…do not believe every spirit, but test the spirits to see whether they are from God, for many false prophets have gone out into the world.

1 John 4:1

PROLOGUE

A shrapnel of rib bone pierces the thin, slippery membrane of his right lung. Yellow pus, carrying the pungent stench of rotten meat, leaks from the broken and infected skin on his back. The jagged rusted spring from the mattress has embedded itself just below his shoulder blade.

Distorted voices drift in and out as though someone is messing about with the volume on a cheap radio. He screams, but there is no sound. The parched muscles of his throat have trapped the broken notes of distress.

"You need to stop."

"What the fuck are you doing? I told you to stop."

His body contorts, his toes stiffen, and the blisters burst as scalding heat spreads across the bottoms of the feet. The rope tightens and cuts farther into the exposed flesh on his wrists. Blue veins push and glow against the translucent skin as his blood struggles to flow freely.

Heavy footsteps make their way toward him. He painfully turns his head toward the wall.

"What are we going to do? We can't... What are we—"

"Stop talking."

Seven words are on repeat in his head. *I don't want to die. Please* stop.

He hears a whisper as a spasm rips through his body and his head thrusts back against the bloodstained, moss-covered wall. The force creates a second fracture in his skull. He feels the warm heat of someone else's skin on his chest. A brief respite. Hot air cloaks his ear. He hears a whisper.

"Leave."

Hands push hard against his chest and a third rib cracks in half and pierces his left lung, cutting off his breath.

Tears soak the cloth that covers his eyes.

"You're going to kill him."

Please.

He dry heaves and inhales the smoke of heavily perfumed incense. The cough rattles the broken bones in his chest. Rotten phlegm fills the back of his mouth and coats his tongue.

He tries to kick out. A second pair of hands pushes down on his thighs which compresses the lateral femoral cutaneous nerve against coiled and thick scar tissue and ignites a torrent of pain. He feels as though he's being burned alive from the inside.

"We need to go."

"Look at him. Lying there like a dog."

A hand grips his jaw and squeezes.

"I told you that he had the devil inside of him."

1

Henley stared at the calendar on the desk. It was one of those feel-good calendars. *Enjoy Every Moment* was emblazoned in gold against an abstract print in bright primary colors while the date stared back at her. Monday 17 February. There was nothing special about the date. No landmark occasions, not even a dentist appointment. It was just a day.

"Are you OK?"

Dr. Isabelle Collins stopped pouring green tea from a glass teapot as Henley placed her head between her knees.

"I'm fine," Henley replied. She closed her eyes and waited for the familiar but uncomfortable moment to pass.

"Are you sure?"

"It doesn't happen all the time. It doesn't mean anything."

"It all means something. Would you like to tell me what it was that set you off?"

"No," said Henley, straightening herself up.

"I've been telling you that these sessions usually work best when you talk," Dr. Collins replied as she continued to pour herself a cup of tea into a porcelain cup. "It's 7:43 a.m."

"And you're disappointed that I haven't opened up in the past twelve minutes."

"A watched pot never boils, Anjelica."

"God, you sound like my mother."

"Hmm, that's the first time that you've mentioned her in five months. In fact, that's the most that you've said in the first fifteen minutes of a session."

"I thought you said that a watched pot never boils."

"That's true, but the second that you take your eye off the pot, it's bound to spill over. I told you in our very first session that I had no intention of wasting your time or mine. I would get a cat if I was looking for non-verbal company."

"You're a bit snappy this morning," Henley said with a raised eyebrow.

Dr. Collins shrugged. "As I said. It's been five months. I want to be in a position to satisfactorily send you on your way, knowing that you've done the work, reached a place where you're able to accept what happened to you and live your life without the fear that you're going to implode. You need to talk honestly about what's happened to you, and that includes the loss of your mother."

"Just because I mentioned my mum's name doesn't mean that there's suddenly going to be an outpouring of grief," Henley said. She ran her finger round the collar of her polo neck and pulled it away from her skin.

"I'm not asking for the wailing and gnashing of teeth, but perhaps some recognition of the fact that it will be a year since your mother passed?"

"I'm aware of that."

"And it doesn't concern you? That sense of cold detachment."

"It's not detachment. I can't detach myself from my mother like she's an investigation that I'm working on, but I can compartmentalize so that it doesn't keep me up at night."

"'It'? The fact that it's not keeping you up at night or that you're not thinking about her during the day, right now, in this moment. You're dismissing her."

Henley stared back at Dr. Collins. She had lost count of these moments. The challenges that she couldn't defend herself from. Dr. Isabelle Collins didn't subscribe to the touchy-feely practice which Henley's previous therapist, Dr. Afzal, had used. Henley had suffered through three sessions with Dr. Afzal before she threw in the towel. Dr. Collins stabbed, provoked and then sat back and watched. Henley still hadn't worked out if this was how Dr. Collins treated all her patients or if Henley's mere presence wound her up every second Monday morning. Henley shuffled in her chair and resisted the urge to take off her jacket, even though Dr. Collins had made sure that the temperature of her office was near tropical.

"It concerns me that you're still not willing to talk about your mother or your old boss, DCS Rhimes," said Dr. Collins.

"I don't need to talk about Rhimes, and my mum is not the reason why I'm sitting in this chair," said Henley. "I know where she is. She's in an oak casket, six feet underground at Brockley cemetery. Plot number 19R5QA."

"But you don't know where Olivier is?"

Henley stiffened at the sound of his name. She'd done her best to forget about the man who'd intended to add her to his long list of murdered victims, not once but twice. Henley had spent too much energy trying to convince herself that Peter Olivier was dead and that he couldn't touch her, but there were days when she swore that she could feel his breath on her neck.

"I know that we've been through this, but we're five months in. Logically, what does your brain tell you? Imagine yourself talking to a victim's family."

The knots in Henley's shoulders tightened. She breathed in and thought back to what Pellacia, her boss and ex-lover, had told her from his hospital bed.

"I would tell them that no one could survive that water,"

said Henley. "He'd already been injured before I even...before he attacked me."

"But you're still doubtful that he's dead?"

"I'm not doubtful."

"You told your husband that Olivier was dead."

"It's what he needed to hear. How would that have helped us if he believed that Olivier was still out there?"

"But how is that helping *you*?"

"What do you mean?"

"You still haven't let go, Anjelica. There won't be any room for anything else in your life the longer that you hold on to the notion that Olivier is still alive."

"Maybe it would be easier for me to let go if I'd seen Olivier cut into bloody pieces, with his intestines all over the carpet like his copycat, Dominic Pine, but that didn't happen."

Unfazed, Dr. Collins picked up the hardback notebook which she'd tucked down the side of her chair and opened the pages. "I prescribed you a lower dosage of Zopiclone last month. Is that not helping?" she asked.

"Oh, it helps all right," said Henley. "It knocks me right out, but I can't function when I wake up. I feel like I'm moving about in a fog."

"So, what you're telling me is that you've stopped taking them?"

"I need to do my job."

"Which job is that? Wife, mother, or detective?"

Henley felt a flush of anger wash over her. "Is that a criticism? Are you suggesting that I put my job over my...my duties at home?"

"I can't answer that for you. You can make that your homework. Be honest with yourself about what you want."

"I know what I want. I want to be able to wake up and not have the feeling that someone is crushing my chest. I want to not end the day in an emotional mess."

"That's not going to happen until you finally decide what

it is that you really need to come to terms with. Olivier is a trigger but you and I both know that you're holding on to a lot more than that."

The snow began to fall. Henley zipped her coat as far as it could go and pulled her hat firmly onto her head, stepping out of the converted warehouse on Shad Thames, where Dr. Isabelle Collins lived and worked, and onto a cobbled street slick with black ice. Icicles hung dangerously from the iron gantries that connected the buildings on both sides of the street. Henley chastised herself as she walked toward her car. She'd been the one to ask for help. She'd handed Dr. Collins's creased business card to Rob and begged him to make an appointment for her. An appointment that Henley had canceled twice. She had promised herself that she would bare her soul, convinced that it would be easier to talk to someone who had no attachment to her. The minute she had sat down on the pale green sofa she had clammed up, spilling the steaming hot coffee from her overfilled cup onto the scarred skin of her right hand. Henley felt like a fraud.

"Oi. Step away," Henley shouted out, spotting a traffic warden approaching her car. She tried to run but stopped and grabbed the lamppost when she lost her footing on the icy pavement.

"This is residents only," the traffic warden said as he took out his handhold computer.

"Not on this side of street. Mate, do not start with me," said Henley. She reached her car and pulled her car keys out of her pocket. "Controlled parking doesn't start until 8:30 a.m. and it's only…" she checked the time on her phone, "8:29 a.m. Step back."

Henley resisted the urge to flash her warrant card in the traffic warden's face as he reluctantly stepped back, and she opened the car door. She turned on the engine and waited for the car to warm up as the snow fell onto the windscreen and the pavements began to fill with people begrudgingly making their way toward their jobs in the city, and she made her way back to the Serial Crime Unit.

2

Uliana Piontek held on tightly to the handrail as the double-decker bus suddenly hit the brakes at the bus stop opposite Deptford DLR station. She craned her neck to check the time—13:32 flashed on the digital display. Road diversions and an accident on Blackheath Road meant that the 53 bus, and Uliana, was late.

Uliana pressed the stop button and uttered excuse me's as she forced her way through the large cluster of passengers standing unnaturally close to each other. Trapped, she leaned over the head of an overweight woman in a puffa coat, pushed the red emergency button and jumped off the bus, leaving the cursing driver behind her.

Neon blue flashing lights reflected off the shopfront windows and the sharp sound of sirens pierced the cold air. Uliana didn't bother to stop. She kept her head, burying her face in her oversize purple scarf as she made her way toward the Art Deco building that was once a cinema, bank, a Vietnamese restaurant and was now Deptford's first megachurch, the Church of Annan the Prophet.

The agreement was that she would clean the church at 8 p.m. on Saturday evening and at 1 p.m. every Monday and Wednesday. Ninety pounds. Cash in hand. The pastor had said that she would be richly rewarded in heaven, and then he had put his hand on her knee when he had agreed to the arrangement. Whatever the pastor may have been thinking, the only thing that Uliana was initially prepared to do on her knees was pray or plug in the vacuum cleaner, but that had been before he had offered her another hundred quid. She turned up the volume on her phone, hoping that the enhanced bass would force out the mental image of the pastor grabbing her hair and forcing her to her knees.

Uliana ignored the catcalls from her eastern European compatriots who were working on the building site on the other side of the street. She waved at one of the employees of the graphic design agency that occupied a small unit next door to the church as he stood outside smoking.

"Shit," said Uliana as she spotted the pastor's car, a brand-new silver Range Rover Discovery, in the makeshift car park. The winter sun bounced off a tarnished gold crucifix that was hanging from the rearview mirror. Uliana inserted the key into the lock, but only had to turn it once before she felt the door give way. Something wasn't right. She stepped into the darkened foyer and blinked twice as her eyes adjusted. A thin stream of subdued light crept through the office door to her right.

"Caleb," Uliana called out as she turned on the foyer light and made her way toward the office. The room was empty save for Caleb's coat on the armchair. The only sound came from the filter in the small aquarium in the corner. She went up the stairs for the vacuum cleaner and dragged it back down, silently cursing why no one had the good sense to put the cleaning equipment in the cupboard on the ground floor. She plugged in the vacuum, turned up her music and began to clean, pushing the Hoover through the double doors that led into the church.

Uliana Piontek smelled Pastor Caleb Annan before she saw him, and she recognized the scent of blood that had been spilled by force.

3

"We all lost," said DS Paul Stanford as he held out a Quality Street tin in front of Henley.

"What on earth are you talking about?" Henley asked as she took off her coat and flung it onto a spare desk. "Are there any toffee pennies in there?"

"You might want to keep your coat on. The heating's on the blink again. Either that or they've forgotten all about us and haven't paid the bill. There's a hundred and forty pounds in the pot and no toffee pennies."

"Why is there a hundred and forty quid in there?"

Stanford rolled his eyes in mock exasperation. "Remember our bet?" he said. "On him. Our illustrious fully fledged Detective Constable Ramouter."

"What have I done?" Ramouter asked from his position in the kitchen where he'd been eyeing the bottom of a mug with disgust.

"This is ridiculous," Henley said. Her ears picked up the whirr coming from the electric fan heaters and the ice-fueled wind whistling outside and rattling the glass.

"You lasted, Ramouter; that's what you did," said Stanford. "We had a bet on how long you would last in the SCU."

"And you didn't think that I would last six months?" asked Ramouter as he picked up another mug.

"Mate, I didn't think you would last six days. I'll have a coffee if you're making."

"You shouldn't be so mean to him," said Henley as she took off her scarf and pushed it against the rotting frame of the window to block the icy draft that was sweeping across her desk.

"How am I being mean? I'm paying him a bloody compliment. After everything that happened, no one would have blamed him if he'd bolted for the door."

"Well, he didn't. He's stuck with it. So, what are you going to do with the money?"

"I could give Ramouter the money. He could spend it on a train ticket to Bradford or something."

"Now who's getting soft?" Henley said. The phone on her desk started to ring.

"Or I could book a table at the curry house down the road. It will be teambuilding."

"Or a normal Friday night out with you falling asleep in your chili chicken."

"Rude," Stanford replied as Henley picked up the phone and Ramouter appeared by his side with a mug of steaming coffee for him.

"Right. I see," said Henley, reaching for the pad of blue Post-it notes on her desk and a ballpoint pen with a chewed cap. "I didn't realize that we were still on duty. Can you send me the CAD details? No, I can't get it myself because the system has crashed again. Thank you. Who found the body? Right."

Henley pulled off the Post-it note and stuck it to the side of Ramouter's mug. He peeled it off and looked at it quizzically. "Depending on traffic, we should be there in fifteen minutes."

"You're not going to have time to finish that," said Henley, putting the phone down and grabbing her scarf.

"There's a body in a church?" Ramouter said as he read the note. "Seriously?"

"That's what it says."

"Why are we dealing with this?"

"We're dealing with it because the borough commander decided that the Serial Crime Unit should be helping out Homicide and Serious Crime with their caseload," Henley replied wearily.

"Anyone would think that we were just sitting here watching Netflix all day," Ramouter moaned. "Is it even a murder?"

"We won't know until we get there, will we?"

"Can I say it?" asked Stanford, a grin spreading across his face.

"No, you can't," Henley replied. She picked up her bag and headed toward the door, with Ramouter in tow. She knew Stanford well enough to know exactly what he was going to say.

"I bet you a tenner that it was the Reverend Green with a candlestick in the library," Stanford shouted out as Henley slammed the door shut behind her.

"I'm not telling you again. Step away from the tape."

"What's going on?"

"If I knew I was going to spend the afternoon standing out in the freezing cold I would have stayed in bed this morning."

"I bet that they've found a body or something."

"Look, those CSI lot have turned up."

"I only popped out for a coffee and now the old bill are saying that I can't go back into my own office."

"F this. I'm going home."

"I'm telling you that they've found a body."

"Wouldn't be the first time."

"I don't understand these kids. Too busy stabbing each other up. No value for life."

"You can dress it up as much as you like. It's Deptford innit."

The murmurings of the curious and disgruntled crowd met Henley and Ramouter as they walked toward the scene of the crime.

"This is a church?" Ramouter asked as he looked up at the

cream-colored facade of the brickwork. "I was expecting something a bit more… I don't know, church-like. Maybe a steeple. This looks like a bank."

"It used to be a NatWest when I was seventeen. The space was once cheap to rent. Not so sure now," Henley replied.

"I did a quick Google search—"

"Of course you did."

"And there's another seven churches on the Broadway."

"I'm not surprised," said Henley. "Betting shops, churches and chicken shops on literally every London high street."

Henley and Ramouter held up their warrant cards to the officer behind the police tape. Henley scoped the gathering crowd. Nothing about them raised any alarms, but she knew from experience that some murderers were voyeuristic by nature.

"Look likes Dr. Choi is here," Ramouter said, pointing out the car of Henley's friend and the Serial Crime Unit's favorite pathologist, parked between a police motorbike and small white transit van that had 'Forensic Services Crime Scene Investigation' marked in black font on the side.

Henley stopped and looked around the small car park. There were no security cameras. She felt a sense of calm as she walked closer to the crime scene. It was a welcome emotion and a respite from the anxiety that was usually coursing through her veins, which she could keep at bay if she bothered to take her prescription to the chemist. She spotted the police officer that she was looking for leaning against the side of a police car, flipping through the pages of his notebook with a pen in his mouth.

"PC Tanaka? DI Henley from the SCU."

PC Tanaka looked up and then stood to attention a little bit too quickly as Henley walked toward him.

"Ma'am," said PC Tanaka.

"This is my colleague, DC Ramouter."

"Shit," said PC Tanaka when he dropped his notebook. "Sorry." He brushed off slush from the cover. "It's bloody freezing."

"You were first on scene?" Henley asked.

Tanaka nodded. Henley could tell that he wanted to get it right. Giving a senior officer information about a murder scene was a lot different to dealing with burglaries, domestics and breaking up a fight between a couple of crackheads at the bottom of the high street.

"We, that's the sarge, Sergeant Rivers, and I were driving back to the station. We're based around the corner at Deptford station. We had just finished our shifts and was coming back from the McDonald's up the road…"

PC Tanaka paused and took a breath.

Henley felt sorry for him as nerves or possibly shock overtook him. She saw a look of sympathy on Ramouter's face as they both waited for PC Tanaka to continue.

"Sorry, guv, I mean ma'am," said PC Tanaka straightening himself again and lowering the volume on his crackling police radio. "As I said, we were heading back to the station and one of the guys who works in the design agency practically threw himself onto the bonnet of the car. He was screaming about a body. We found the cleaner in hysterics in the staffroom of the agency. She refused to leave and take us to the church. I left her with the sarge and I went into the church and yeah, I won't forget what I saw."

4

Henley stepped around the remains of PC Tanaka's McDonald's lunch. Inside, the church felt sterile and unwelcoming, but the familiar scent of incense and holy anointing oil reminded her of her uncle's church services. She could also smell blood. The scent of death anchored itself to her nostrils and tickled the back of her throat as she entered the church's inner sanctum.

Henley stopped at a life-size cutout of a well-dressed black man standing with his arms outstretched, with what Henley could only describe as something reminiscent of a halo over his head. *All who enter my Church of Annan the Prophet will be saved.* Farther along the wall was a gold-framed photograph of the same black man next to a black woman.

"'The Prophet, Pastor Dr. Caleb Annan, and First Lady, Serena Annan'? I don't get it," Ramouter asked.

Henley sighed and watched her breath escape into the air and then evaporate. "That's what they call the pastor's wife. It's an American thing."

They were a good-looking couple. More glamorous than spiritual and, in Henley's opinion, more high maintenance than charitable.

"Does she do anything? The first lady?" Ramouter asked.

"Depends. Sometimes, they're just a face, a trophy to parade, but more often than not they're just as active as the pastor."

Henley was aware that they were both doing the same thing. Delaying the inevitable.

"What sort of church is this anyway? It doesn't seem like your usual songs of praise." Ramouter paused at a mock scroll that was nailed on the door that led into the church itself. "'We are a lively and welcoming church and will always receive those who are ready to be saved,'" he read, before pushing the door open.

"Come on," Henley replied, readjusting the elastic bands of her mask that were cutting into the skin behind her ears. Hazy winter light streamed through the gaps of the heavy red velvet curtains. The church auditorium was vast. There were at least three hundred chairs separated by an aisle. Henley looked up at the balcony which she guessed housed another hundred seats. The church hadn't been cleaned. Empty water bottles, coffee cups and sweet wrappers littered the ground.

Pastor Caleb Silas Annan was forty-three years old and lying in the fetal position on his left side underneath the altar. His long legs were bent underneath him, but his left shoe was missing, revealing a mustard-colored sock with a small hole on one heel. The first row of chairs, which had once been arranged meticulously to face the raised stage where the altar stood, were scattered across the floor. Henley spotted a black suede loafer underneath a chair.

"They're Gucci, in case you were wondering. Not my thing at all," Anthony Thomas, the senior crime scene investigator, said as he followed Henley's gaze from the lone shoe to the white cloth that was half hanging from the altar and covered in bloodied handprints like a crude child's painting. Two brass candlesticks were on the floor next to the pastor. A large Bible covered in faux brown leather, with a broken spine, was by his head. The pathologist, Dr. Linh Choi, was crouched down next to him, deep in concentration as she placed a gloved finger on a wound in his neck.

"I didn't think that you would be gracing us with your presence," said Anthony as he made his way toward Henley.

"I didn't realize that we were on duty," Henley explained. "You're lucky that you got us. How are you?"

"Same shit, different toilet. Overworked, underpaid, underappreciated and it's absolutely cutting in here. Anyway, I've got a little present for you." Anthony unclipped an evidence bag from his clipboard and handed it to Henley. After twenty-five years working in the forensic services, Anthony was reluctant to give up his trusted old clipboard and hard copy reports in favor of the temperamental cheap tablets that had been issued by his department. "I see that you're still with us, DC Ramouter? We haven't chased you back to the moors yet?"

"You say that every time you see me," said Ramouter.

"Consider it a sign of me taking a vested interest in your emotional well-being."

"I appreciate it. Thanks," Ramouter replied as Henley handed him the evidence bag. He squinted at the photograph on the light pink UK driving license that was due to expire in three weeks' time.

"How long has he been dead?" Henley called over to Linh.

"Anywhere between twelve and eighteen hours." Linh groaned as she stood up. "God, my knees. You all right?"

"Not bad," Henley replied, kneeling next to the body. "He was stabbed?"

"Multiple times, in the chest and in the back. His very expensive cashmere jumper is soaked through."

"What do you reckon?" Ramouter asked as he joined Henley; his oversuit rustled when he clasped his hands behind his back. "Burglary gone wrong?"

Henley shook her head. "From what we've seen so far, all of the struggle has taken place right here. It doesn't feel like a burglary unless CSI find signs of a disturbance taking place in here.

PC Tanaka said that the cleaner was late for work and when she arrived, realized that the door hadn't been deadlocked."

"It could have been opportunistic if the door wasn't locked."

Henley shook her head again as she stood up and pointed at the large candlesticks on the floor.

"Those candlesticks are brass and cost, at a minimum, three hundred quid. Why not take those? And did you notice the pastor's car outside?"

"That massive SUV?" Ramouter answered. "Would be hard to miss it. It's straight out of the showroom brand-new."

"Well, I did. You're going to check out the registration details when we get back. I wouldn't be surprised if he bought it outright and claimed it against the church."

"A bit cynical, isn't it?"

"You've still got a lot to learn, Ramouter, but the point is, if this was an opportunistic burglary, why not take the car and all the candlesticks? Nothing of value has been taken; well, not from what I can see," Henley said, walking around the altar. Linh sat back on her haunches, tapping her pen against her notebook.

"So, the cleaner, Uliana, thought that the pastor had come in early, but that wouldn't make sense if he's been dead for up to eighteen hours," Henley mused. "He either opened the door to someone he knew last night, or maybe an unhappy parishioner stayed behind, or..."

"It could still be a burglary gone wrong," Ramouter said again with a shrug. "Whoever it was might have been caught by surprise. This guy here confronted them, they killed him and ran."

"From what I can see," said Linh and she stood up, stretched and stood almost protectively next to Henley to absorb the impact of Ramouter's unwarranted bout of mansplaining, "this is frenzied and vicious. If it was a surprised burglar, I would expect maybe one or two stab wounds and that would be it. As far as I can see, he's got wounds on his hands, on his shoulders, his back and his face."

Henley leaned in closer to the pastor. A thick gold chain holding a large diamond-encrusted and bloodstained crucifix nestled in the creases of his neck. Henley's cheek flinched at the gaping hole in the pastor's own cheek. The open wound exposed his jawbone, molars and a mottled tongue nestled amongst the congealed blood. The pastor's right eye was open. The pupil was fixed and dilated. Dried blood coated his eyelashes like poorly applied mascara.

"Let's look around," Henley said to Ramouter. She shivered as a chill ran down her neck. The walls were covered with either gilded framed extracts of Bible scripture or photographs of Caleb captured in animated preaching.

"Oh, for crying out loud," Henley muttered as she paused at the large photograph of Pastor Caleb preaching next to a quote from the Bible.

"'But the Lord said to him, Go, for he is a chosen instrument of mine, to bear my name before the Gentiles and Kings and the sons of Israel,'" Ramouter read out. "Is our dead pastor saying that he's God's chosen instrument? A bit full of himself, isn't he?"

"Don't speak ill of the dead. At least not yet," Henley said as she pulled back the heavy faux-velvet curtains. The floor-to-ceiling windows needed a clean and were incapable of being opened. Henley looked up to see large air-conditioning vents on the ceiling. It was an improvement on the churches from her childhood where you were either freezing your arse off in the winter or wondering if some unholy deal had been made with the devil as you sweltered in the summer.

"Why don't you go and see how forensics are getting on in the offices?" Henley said to Ramouter as they walked out and entered the foyer. "I want you to make sure that all documents, laptops and tablets are seized."

"Will do."

"And ask them if there's been any sign of the murder weapon. I doubt that the killer would have been stupid enough to leave it behind, but you never know. I'm going to look upstairs."

5

The large space upstairs had been converted into a series of rooms, each separated by partition walls that looked as though they'd once been part of a conservatory. Henley stood in the doorway of a makeshift television studio and watched as a CSI officer took photographs while a second carefully dusted for prints. The rear wall had been painted green and in front were two brown leather armchairs with a glass coffee table in the middle. A large crucifix was on the table next to two glasses of water and a half-empty jug, all covered with black fingerprint dust. In the corner of the room was a tripod stand with a video camera. The camera hadn't been turned off and a light flashed red and blue intermittently, presumably signaling that the battery was dying. Henley thought that it was likely that someone may have forgotten to turn the camera off, but she would have been an idiot to ignore the possibility that the pastor may have been operating the camera but was disturbed by his killer. Henley made a mental note for the camera to be sent to Ezra, the SCU's forensic analyst, to check if anything had been recorded. On the right side of the room was a large table which had been set up to record podcasts. Two microphones, headphones, an audio interface and a laptop had been abandoned next to a new iMac computer that, thanks to Ezra, she knew would have cost in the region of five grand. There were no signs of a disturbance taking place upstairs.

Henley moved toward the storage room, and stepped in. There was a shelving unit at the back, covered with a sheet. She pulled the sheet aside, and saw there was a door behind the unit.

"What the hell?" Henley said to herself. The door was bolted shut, with a padlock. The shelving unit was empty and Henley pushed it aside with ease. She placed her finger under the shackle and felt it give way. It hadn't been locked. Henley opened the door and the nauseating smell of urine, feces and damp ambushed her senses, and she began to cough uncontrollably. Henley's eyes failed to adjust to the darkness as she brushed aside tears, but her ears picked up the sound of scurrying in the corner. She pulled out her phone and turned on the torch. The light illuminated white pools of hardened wax on the floor and candles that had burnt down to the wick. Water trickled down moss-covered walls, and the tail of a dead rat hung from a red bucket in the corner. It had been years since Henley had been sick at a crime scene. She had hardened herself to not be overcome by disgust when she saw a dead body, but sometimes it was the little things that turned her stomach. She couldn't find the words as she turned her phone to her left, illuminating the edge of a stained mattress on an old bed frame. Broken rusty springs protruded from the cheap, fraying material. A thick, metal chain, secured around a pipe, bound the ankles of two dirt-streaked skeletal legs. The skin on the bottom of the feet was a patchwork of blackened blistered skin. A dead cockroach and rat droppings covered a sunken stomach. The light from the torch bounced against the hard shape of ribs pushing against thin, purple-veined skin that was covered with dried scabs and burns. Red rope, encrusted with dried blood, had been tied around his wrists. He was completely bound.

"Ramouter!" Henley shouted out as she leaned in closer toward the man's wrists. The skin had been worn away; the tightened rope had cut him to the bone. "Ramouter!" she yelled again. "Linh, Anthony! I need someone up here now."

Henley leaned in closer to the young man. Death cemented the pain that was deeply etched in his face. His cheekbones were sharp. Dried vomit caked the edges of his cracked lips. Overgrown and damp brown curls hung limply across a forehead that was smudged with dirt. A thick rosary hung from a nail on the wall behind him. A small Bible was on the mattress, on the right side of his head; the pages opened to Revelations 20:10:

And the devil, who deceived them, was thrown into the lake of burning sulfur, where the beast and the false prophet had been thrown. They will be tormented day and night forever and ever.

"What the hell?"

Henley stumbled back at the sound of Ramouter's voice. She tripped over the bucket and fell onto the dead rat. "Don't do that! You scared the life out of me."

"Sorry, guv. Are you all right?" Ramouter asked as he rushed to Henley's side.

"I'm fine. Where's Linh?" Henley quickly scrambled to her feet and brushed down her body. She looked up and saw a light switch with a black fingerprint on the panel. There was no way that she could turn on the light without destroying what could be crucial evidence.

"Coming," Ramouter said slowly as he stood unmoving at Henley's side, his eyes transfixed by the body. "She was just about to drive off when you called. Is he dead?"

Henley nodded.

"Why on earth would anyone… This is…" Ramouter stammered. He held his hand to his mouth and stepped closer to the body. "It's fucked up."

"I need some air," Henley said, overwhelmed by a wave of

nausea. She made her way to the door and bumped straight into Linh who had a CSI investigator behind her.

"Hey, what is it? Are you all right?" Linh asked Henley. She placed her black case onto the ground and pulled on a fresh pair of latex-free gloves.

"I'm fine. I just need to step out for a bit. He's over there."

Linh pulled down her glasses from the top of her head and walked toward the body.

Henley drew back the hood of her oversuit as heat swept over her. She welcomed the sharp shock of cold air as she stepped out into the corridor. She'd seen dead bodies before, so there was no reason why this one should have shaken her up so much. After a few minutes she made her way back into the room, watching from the doorway as Linh assessed the body. Ramouter looked on quietly as the CSI officer gently lifted the man's body and Linh inserted a thermometer into the man's rectum.

"Hmm," Linh muttered as she pulled it out and read the temperature.

"Why are you hmmming?" Henley asked, stepping back into the room.

"Shh." Linh reached into her case, pulled out a stethoscope and leaned over the body.

The only sounds came from the passing traffic outside and the dull activity from the church downstairs.

"Anjelica," said Linh, "we need an ambulance. He's still alive."

6

He should have been dead. His pulse was weak. His blood pressure low. He was dehydrated and all twenty-four of his ribs were broken. His skull was fractured, and he had a subarachnoid hemorrhage. His kidneys were damaged with a lower bronchial viral infection in his lungs. His body had violently convulsed when the paramedics had pierced the top of his left hand with a catheter, inserted a saline drip into his veins and placed an oxygen mask over his face.

"He looked dead," said Ramouter as the ambulance doors closed, the blue lights started to flash, and the sirens wailed. "He smelled dead."

"He must have been there for weeks." Henley took off her blue overshoes and oversuit, threw them into a black bin bag and quickly put on her coat.

"Do you think the pastor knew? A motive for killing him, perhaps?" Ramouter asked.

"I would be surprised if he didn't, but if he did, whether that was the motive for his murder? I don't know, but one thing I'm sure about is that whoever killed the pastor had no idea about that poor boy imprisoned upstairs."

"We don't actually know that. What if the killer knew and just left him? It could be as simple as that."

"It could be, but…" Henley checked the time on her watch. It was after four o'clock and she knew that there was no way that she would be making it home in time to give her three-year-old daughter, Emma, her bath and put her to bed. "Nothing is ever simple."

"So, we've got a murder and an attempted murder to investigate?"

"Let's just hope that it stays that way," Henley said as the church doors opened and a body bag containing the pastor was wheeled outside in the waiting private ambulance. Its windows blacked out and its occupant encased in anonymity.

"So, our victim…"

Det. Supt. Stephen Pellacia paused and looked up at the ceiling as the sound of ancient pipes rattling violently against each other reverberated throughout the building.

Twelve seconds later, DS Stanford placed his hands against the radiator next to his desk and shouted out, "We've got heat."

"Yay," DC Roxanne Eastwood responded sarcastically as she pulled down the sleeves of her jumper and pulled her hoodie over her head.

"As I was saying," Pellacia said. "Our victim. Who is he, Henley?"

Henley tried to catch Pellacia's eyes as he spoke her name, but he wouldn't look directly at her. Instead, he focused on the space just above her head.

"Which one?" Henley responded in such a way that it forced Pellacia to look at her. He rubbed away at the bags under his eyes.

"The dead one."

"The dead one is Caleb Silas Annan."

"But he calls himself *The Prophet* Dr. Caleb Silas Annan," Ramouter concluded.

"The Prophet?" Pellacia asked disbelievingly. "How do you know that?"

"It's written on the posters and the newsletters that were in the foyer and it's all over the church website," Ramouter explained. "He actually named the church after himself, and he's definitely not a doctor."

"And you know that how?"

Henley smiled as Stanford gave her a knowing wink. He knew that she was feeling a bit proud of Ramouter at this moment.

"I checked with the General Medical Council and he's not on the database as either a registered or unregistered doctor. In fact, from a quick Google search, I don't think that he's a doctor of anything, but he is known," said Ramouter.

"Known to us?" asked Pellacia.

Henley nodded as she handed out copies of Annan's criminal record. "We haven't formally identified him, but he's on the police national computer. The PNC search shows that Caleb Silas Annan has three aliases: Kaysen Abani, David Onyeka and Edward Silas Annan. In 2008 he was convicted of fraud at Southwark Crown Court and received a prison sentence of three and a half years."

Stanford let out a low whistle from his corner of the room. "Must have been a big one. You don't get three and a half years for having a dodgy driving license."

"No, you don't," said Pellacia, turning the pages of Annan's record. "Whatever he got convicted of had to be high value. It says here that he was bailed to return to Stoke Newington police station on the twenty-first of February."

"Well, he won't be making that date," said Stanford.

"Do we know why they were investigating him?" Pellacia asked, ignoring Stanford.

"The system is down, so I've no idea," Henley answered. "I've asked Joanna to contact the custody sergeant at Stoke Newington to find out who the officer in the case is and why he was arrested. In terms of next of kin, he appears to be married to Serena Malikah Annan who, unlike her husband, doesn't have a criminal record."

"Has anyone told her that her husband is dead?"

"Not yet."

"What do you mean, not yet?" Pellacia's lips silently moved as he counted. "It's been almost five hours since his body was found."

"I know that." Henley tried to keep her voice level and calm. "But I didn't want a couple of local PCs to do the job and Serena Annan wasn't at home when Stanford and Eastwood went round earlier. Ramouter and I are going round there later to try and deliver the news."

Ramouter's head swiveled around with surprise. "We are?"

"Yes, we are. The last thing I want is a couple of green PCs to tell Mrs. Annan that her husband has been murdered and then for her to just be hanging around waiting for us and the family liaison officers to turn up."

"Have you at least managed to sort out the FLOs?" asked Pellacia.

"I've managed to grab Bethany Stewart and PS Levine. Bethany wasn't exactly over the moon about it."

"She's never over the moon about anything."

"You can hardly blame her. She's the FLO on three murder cases and a missing person's investigation. We'll be on our way, as soon as she texts me with their ETA."

"And the other victim? Any idea who he is?"

"None at all," said Henley. "He's been admitted to intensive care at Lewisham Hospital. The last I heard, the doctors weren't even sure if he would make it through the night. Hopefully, he will."

"Attempted murder or murder, doesn't make any real difference," said Pellacia. The phone in his office began to ring and Henley's phone pinged with a text.

"It makes all the difference," Henley said, and indicated to Ramouter to grab his coat. "At least for one family there may be a bit of hope."

★ ★ ★

The closure of the Rotherhithe Tunnel earlier in the day meant that the traffic now snailed along the A2. As the lights turned red on Blackheath Hill, Henley kept her eyes focused on the road. Across the dual carriageway, and in the middle of the heath, was the place where Olivier had stabbed her nearly three years ago.

Ramouter let out a low whistle next to her as he tapped away on his phone.

"What are you looking at?" Henley asked.

"I wanted to see how much the Annans' house is worth. They bought it a couple of years ago. Guess how much it sold for?"

"It's Blackheath. Probably something ridiculous. One and a half million."

"Nope. Two million. Six bedrooms, four bathrooms, roof terrace. Do you know what I could buy in Bradford with that amount of money?"

"The entire city of Bradford," Henley replied with a smirk as the traffic finally began to move.

"Wow, that's just... What would you call it?"

"Rude. But on a serious note, why are you checking?"

Ramouter shrugged. "You said that he had previous for fraud. I wouldn't have thought that he would have been earning that much on a pastor's salary, even with a sixty grand SUV parked outside the church. How do you even make money from running a church?"

"You'd be surprised."

"He could be responsible for our other victim being locked up and tortured half to death. You can't have someone locked away in the church that you named after yourself, and not know about it."

"You've got a real bee in your bonnet about the fact that he named the church after himself."

"It just seems a bit pretentious."

Henley sighed as she took the second exit on the roundabout and drove onto Shooters Hill.

"If, and I mean if, it turns out that Caleb Annan knew about the man in the locked room, then we will deal with it, but remember, Caleb Annan will always be our murder victim. Nothing changes that."

A crescent moon hung above a three-story house freshly painted in pebble gray. Henley was silently impressed as she drove across the graveled driveway.

"How many of these have you done?" she asked Ramouter.

"What do you mean?"

"How many times have you had to knock on someone's front door and tell them that their loved one is dead?"

Ramouter placed his scarf around his neck but kept his eyes down. "Never," he replied, opening the door.

"Have you even been with another officer—"

Henley was cut off as the sharp cold air squeezed through the crack of the door and brushed against her face.

Ramouter shook his head. "You're not going to make me do it, are you?"

Henley didn't get a chance to reply as a motion sensor was activated and placed the pair of them in the spotlight.

7

The woman who answered the door didn't fit the house. She was in her mid-twenties and she wore no makeup. Her hair was covered by a tightly wrapped navy and white headscarf, but loose strands of black hair escaped from the sides. Henley couldn't place the woman's ethnicity, but she looked as though she'd done everything to conceal her beauty. Henley held up her warrant card.

"Good evening. My name is Detective Inspector Henley, and this is my colleague, Constable Ramouter."

Henley's introduction didn't act as an incentive for the woman to fully open the door.

"What do you want?" The woman's tone was gentle and soft, but with a slight musical lilt. She pushed a hand through the crack and took hold of Henley's warrant card.

"We're here to speak to Mrs. Serena Annan. Is she in? It's important that we—"

The door slammed in her face.

"Not very hospitable," said Ramouter just before the door opened again.

"Is Mrs. Annan expecting you?" the woman asked. "She usually lets me know if she's having visitors."

"This isn't a social call," Henley replied, irritated. "Who are you?"

The woman shrank back as though she was a child being chastised by her parents.

"Dalisay Ocampo. I belong to the family. I'm sorry. Come in."

Henley maintained a poker face as Ramouter flashed her his familiar *What the hell was that?* look.

Henley and Ramouter stepped into the hallway. The house looked and smelled expensive. The air hung heavy with the scent of spicy fruit, similar to the glass bottle of her mother-in-law's favorite bath oil, that Emma had helpfully thrown down the toilet. Henley should have been sorry, but she wasn't. She had realized a long time ago that the only thing that would make her mother-in-law happy would be if Henley divorced her son.

"Are these the Annans' children?" Henley asked, stopping at a mahogany side table with a photograph of two smiling children. A boy and a girl in their Sunday best. Staged and perfunctory.

"Yes," Dalisay replied, almost conspiratorially, as though she was revealing information that she wasn't supposed to have. "Maliah is seven and Zyon is five."

Above the table hung a large picture of Serena Annan and her husband. On the left, a gold crucifix had been placed on the wall. It looked more decorative and opulent than a sign of religious acceptance. If it wasn't for the photograph, Henley would have been hard pushed to conclude that this was a family home. No toys, odd pairs of shoes, or Lego on the staircase. No clothes drying on the radiator. No parcels sitting by the door. It felt clinical, as if the protective plastic had just been taken off the furniture.

"Please," said Dalisay. "If you wait here, I will get Mrs. Annan."

Henley watched Dalisay place a hand on the stripped wood of

the banister and carefully walk up the carpeted stairs as though she was afraid to leave an imprint.

"This is unnaturally clean," said Ramouter. He stood to the side, his feet firmly placed on the wooden floorboards, careful not to step on the fuchsia-colored rug in the middle of the room. There were more pictures on the wall. Weddings. Christenings. The standard school photographs of young children missing their front teeth. A white-bound Bible was laid out on the coffee table in the middle of the room next to an opened laptop. Henley didn't have a chance to check what was on the screen as a woman had entered the room.

"Dalisay explained that you're from the police." Serena Annan was taller than both Henley and Ramouter. Henley guessed that she was close to six feet in her slippers. Her hair had been pulled back into a loose bun. She closed the door behind her.

"That's correct, Mrs. Annan. I'm Detective Inspector Henley from the Serial Crime Unit at Greenwich police station."

"And who are you?" Serena turned around and faced Ramouter as though she had just become aware that there was someone else in the room and they smelled.

Ramouter introduced himself. He was polite, but Henley could see the slight etches of anxiety in his forehead. Something in her gut told her that Serena would not be surprised at the news that she was about to deliver. Three minutes had passed, and she had not yet asked about her husband. "Mrs. Annan. I'm afraid that I have some very bad news to tell you. Your husband—"

"Has something happened to him?"

"I'm very sorry to inform you that Caleb has died."

Henley waited for the usual protestations of *You're lying. You're at the wrong house. You have made a mistake. I just spoke to him this morning, but he never came home.* But there was only an unspoken and unnerving acceptance.

"What happened to him? Was there an accident?" Serena finally asked.

"No. He wasn't involved in a car accident."

There were rules. There was protocol as to how you should inform the next of kin that their loved ones have been killed. There had been training about the appropriate language to use. Gentle language. Empathetic, but sometimes you just had to rip the plaster off. Something told Henley that Serena Annan could handle it.

"He was killed, Mrs. Annan."

"What do you mean, killed?" Serena asked as she sat down on the sofa. She placed her hands on her laps and adjusted the large diamond ring on her finger. The skin of her forehead creased slightly as she focused on Henley.

Henley scanned Serena's face for any signs of shock, denial or anger, but there was nothing. Serena's lack of emotion made Henley uncomfortable.

"Your husband's body was found in the church by the cleaner, Uliana Piontek, at one fifty this afternoon," Henley said slowly.

"Are you sure it's Caleb?"

"Well, he hasn't been formally identified."

"And you said that the cleaner found him?"

"Yes."

"She could have made a mistake. She's not very reliable."

"We need you to formally identify Caleb," Henley said carefully.

"You want me to do it?"

"Unless you don't feel able to—"

"I'm more than capable," Serena said forcefully.

Henley continued to feel uneasy. She waited for any sign that Serena had been impacted by the news. There was nothing. No protestations. No murmurs of disbelief. No tears.

"When do you want me to identify this...man that you found?" Serena asked.

"You don't have to identify him right now and I wouldn't

ask that of you. This is a shock," said Henley. "You don't need
to do it alone. You could—"

"I will have to let the family know," Serena said in a busi-
nesslike tone. "And the pastoral board, and…oh my God…the
children…"

It was only then that Serena Annan showed any signs of
cracking as she bit her lower lip and bolted out of the room.

"Is it me or did she not seem that surprised?" whispered
Ramouter.

"No, she didn't," Henley said quietly. The doorbell rang
sharply and she turned around and saw Dalisay, the woman
who'd opened the door to them earlier, move swiftly through
the hallway. There was the sound of a door opening and then
Henley heard the familiar gravelly voice of Bethany.

"Sorry we're late," Bethany said as she and PS Levine were
shown into the room.

"It's fine," Henley replied. "It's always hit or miss, coming
up these sides. Sergeant Levine, I don't think that you've met
DC Ramouter."

"Haven't had the pleasure yet," PS Levine said as he shook
Ramouter's hand. Levine was past retirement age and should
have been sitting at home, planning his golf trips, but he
couldn't handle the boredom. He had been one of Henley's
favorite custody sergeants when he used to work at Walworth
police station, but she knew that people were easily fooled
by the grandfatherly appearance. He was warm and empathic,
but he was sharp, perceptive and would call you out on your
bullshit within a second.

"Oh, more of you," Serena Annan said as she walked back
into the room. Henley looked for signs of distress; red-rimmed
eyes or a snotty nose, but there was nothing. Her hair was
neater, and her lipstick had been reapplied. She sat back down
on the sofa, crossed her ankles and patted the diamond-encrusted crucifix hanging from her gold necklace.

Serena didn't ask any questions while Bethany explained who she and PS Levine were and their roles as family liaison officers.

"I've forgotten my manners," Serena said. "Would you like tea or coffee? I can arrange for Dalisay to bring it through."

"No thank you. Ramouter and I are fine," Henley replied. "I've just got a few questions before we leave. When did you last see your husband, Mrs. Annan?"

"Yesterday evening about 6:30 p.m. The last Sunday church service finished at 2 p.m. We came home and had dinner. Afterward he watched a film with the children while I did some work in the study. He then left at 6:30 p.m. to go back to the church for his Bible study classes."

"Why would your husband be at church so late?"

"My husband is a well-known and respected pastor. *We* are well respected," Serena said a little more forcefully. She didn't elaborate. "After service, members of the congregation still want to have meetings with him. Private Bible study, counseling, prayer, confessions."

"Confessions?"

"People tend to talk if they feel that they're one step closer to God. No matter how flawed the messenger."

Henley had to stop herself from immediately asking "What do you mean by flawed?" Serena's demeanor was so controlled that Henley was 100 percent sure that calling her husband flawed was intentional.

"When did you next hear from Caleb?" Henley asked.

"He texted me after Dalisay had put the children to bed, telling me he was going to be late. It was about quarter to midnight." Serena got up and walked over to the mantelpiece to where her phone was charging. She scrolled through the screen before handing it over to Henley.

Won't be home until late. Lincoln was late and have to sort out a few things for tomorrow.

"Who's Lincoln?" Henley asked as she returned the phone to Serena.

"Lincoln Okafor is one of the pastoral assistants. He's been with the family for many years. He is devoted to us."

"Weren't you concerned when your husband didn't come home?" Henley asked.

"No. As I said, he texted me and told me that he was going to be late. I was asleep and when I woke up this morning, I assumed that he'd left for his session with his personal trainer. I asked the housekeeper, Dalisay, if she had seen him—"

"Housekeeper? My mistake. I thought that she was a friend of the family?" Henley asked purposefully.

"Definitely not," Serena smiled tightly. "She's the help."

Henley decided not to push the point. "So, you asked Dalisay if she'd seen Caleb?"

"That's correct. She said that she hadn't."

"And you didn't attempt to contact him?"

"There was no need, because he texted me after I took the kids to school."

"This morning," Ramouter asked. "Your husband sent you a message this morning?"

"I just said that," Serena huffed. She held her phone to her face to unlock and then handed it to Ramouter.

"Nine thirteen this morning." Ramouter showed the phone to Henley.

Sorry I didn't see you last night. Didn't want to disturb you. Slept in the spare room. Left early to meet KJ. Promise to make it up to you later. Love you.

"Did Caleb usually send you messages like this?" Ramouter asked.

"Yes. He would always tell me if he was going to be late," said Serena.

"Who's KJ?"

"Kareem Jarret. He's a personal trainer."

"Do you have his details?"

"He wasn't *my* personal trainer," Serena replied frostily. "I'm sure that you can find his details online."

"Dead men can't send messages," Ramouter said, opening the passenger door of Henley's car. "There's no way that Caleb Annan texted his wife at 9:13 a.m. It's impossible."

"I know," was all Henley could say as she settled into the driver's seat. "That completely kicks out the opportunistic burglar angle. Whoever killed Caleb Annan knew him and they know his wife."

"Are you saying that this was premeditated?"

"Maybe not premeditated, but someone is definitely trying to cover their tracks."

8

Ramouter picked up the cup and placed it back down on the table without taking a sip. He never drank the tea, coffee or water when he sat down for an hour of avoiding and finally answering therapist Dr. Mark Ryan's questions.

"Sorry, again, that I'm late," said Ramouter as he tried and failed to relax in the chair.

"That's fine," said Mark. "Luckily for you my eight o'clock canceled. So how have things been since the last time we met?"

"Bad," Ramouter admitted. "Lately, it's been bad. There were a couple of weeks when I came back from Bradford where I was sleeping OK, eating OK... I was doing the right thing." He stopped as his breath caught in his throat.

"It's all right," said Mark. "Take your time."

"I thought that I wouldn't be calling you again, but then about two weeks ago..." Ramouter paused as he ran his hand across his beard, sniffed heavily and brushed away the tears. "Bloody hell, this is embarrassing... Sorry. I'm sorry."

It had been weeks since he'd broken down and cried. The first time had been a month after he'd left the hospital following Olivier's attack. There had been a power cut on Ramouter's street, and he'd found himself standing in the shower in the darkness as the water had run from hot to cold. He'd heard noises but couldn't be sure if it was his own breathing or someone else's. He slid down on the shower floor and cried until the power returned.

"Salim, you've got nothing to be embarrassed about," Mark said, handing over a box of tissues.

"I go to sleep. That's not a problem. I can go to sleep OK but then I wake up at two or three o'clock and that's it. My brain starts working away and I can see him, smell him and feel him all over me."

"I can prescribe a short course of sleeping tablets."

"No, no drugs," said Ramouter. "I know what I'm like. I've got… I've got an addictive personality."

"You've had addiction problems before?"

Ramouter took a deep breath. "I got a bit carried away with pills, skunk and then it was cocaine for a bit, but I sorted it out. I'd rather try something a bit more natural before I start with the chemicals."

"Let's go back to your addiction problems," said Mark. He rearranged himself in his chair. "How long ago was this?"

"It started when I left uni. I hadn't even thought about joining the police at that time."

"What were you doing?"

"Working for an insurance company. I started working there after I graduated. The money was good, but I hated it. It sounds a bit stupid to say that there was a lot of peer pressure when you're in your twenties, but that's how it started."

"We can be subjected to peer pressure at any age."

"Well, I thought that I had more sense than that, but it was just a couple of lines on a Friday night when we went out for drinks. Friday nights then turned into Saturday nights, and then Monday mornings before I even had my morning coffee."

"How long did this carry on for?"

"About eighteen months. I didn't think that I was an addict

because it wasn't as if I was doing it every single day. It was just a case of work hard, play hard. I was an idiot."

"So how did you stop? What made you reach the point of no more?"

Ramouter leaned back in his chair and twisted his wedding ring. It'd been years since he'd thought about that moment when he'd decided to quit. "I saw someone overdose in the toilets at a club in Manchester. It scared the shit out of me because I'd just bought a bag from the same dealer. It was as if someone had turned the lights on in my life. I stopped using that night."

"Did you get any help? Counseling? Rehab?" asked Mark.

"I called Narcotics Anonymous a couple of times and went to a few meetings, but I didn't like being around so many... I know it sounds bad."

"You didn't want to be around other addicts. It's not unusual to think that."

"But it's a shitty way to think. It's like I'm looking down on them, thinking that I'm better than them when I'm not."

"Of course, but it's moments like that which force us to focus on who we are and the things that we've done."

"I suppose so," Ramouter said sadly.

"Let's put things into perspective. You made it through a challenging time. There aren't many people who have the self-awareness to be honest about the person they're turning into."

"I didn't plan to turn into a police officer, though."

"So how did it happen?"

"Well, it wasn't a spur of the moment decision. I must have filled out the application and deleted it about six times and then I just thought, I don't care what the family will say; I'm going to do it."

Ramouter sat back in his chair and felt a small release of tension in his body after holding onto the weight of undeserved guilt for so long.

"Thank you for sharing. I know that it couldn't have been

easy for you," said Mark as he picked up his cup of tea from the table.

"It helps that I trust you."

"I know that we spoke about this before, but it's going to take time for you to first accept and then move on from what Olivier did to you. You suffered a trauma."

"Aye, but it's part of the job, isn't it. It's not as if I signed up for a cushy job in financial crimes. This is part of it."

"No, it's not," Mark said determinedly. "No one signs up for nearly getting themselves killed, and the truth is that there's nothing in your police training that would ever have prepared you for that."

"Maybe if I was more experienced."

"What difference would that have made?" Mark said with a shake of the head. "Whether you'd been working for the SCU for two weeks or twelve years, there would have been nothing that would have prepared you for being attacked by a...well, a raging psychopath."

Ramouter sat back and scratched the scar that Mark couldn't see under the sleeve of his jumper.

"Do you know what it's like not being able to move?" Ramouter said softly. "You can see everything, hear everything and you can smell your own fear, but you can't run away from it."

"Did you think that you were going to die?"

"Going to die? I thought that I was dead until I saw Henley staring down at me."

"Have you shared this with her?" asked Mark. "How you felt and what's happening now?"

Ramouter shook his head. "She's supposed to be teaching me, not carrying me."

"Do you blame her?"

"No, no. It wasn't her fault. I knew that something wasn't right in that house, but I wouldn't have been doing my job if I'd run away and the team wouldn't have respected me."

"What about your wife, your family, your friends? Are you sharing this with them?"

"I can't put this on Michelle," Ramouter said. "She's dealing with so much. It's one thing being diagnosed with early onset dementia, but actually living with it is something different. There are no good days for her. How could anyone enjoy a fleeting moment of normality when you know that one day, you'll forget your own name? It's bad enough that Michelle and Ethan are living two hundred miles away in Bradford and I'm here. I should be home, but it's—"

Ramouter stopped.

"It's what?" Mark asked, leaning forward.

Ramouter couldn't say it out loud; that he didn't want to go home. But the truth was that it was easier to battle through the sleepless nights and memories of Olivier invading his daydreams, than it was dealing with the living nightmare of watching his wife disappear right in front of him.

9

Dead men can't send messages.

Ramouter's words were still rattling around Henley's head as she pushed her key into her front door. Caleb Annan had been dead for a minimum of twelve hours by the time Henley and Ramouter had arrived on the scene, eighteen hours at the most. The latest that Henley could estimate death was 2:30 a.m. Even if Caleb had messaged his wife to say that he was working late at midnight, was it possible he had sent that message while he was with his killer?

"Close the door. You're going to let all the heat out," Rob shouted out from the kitchen.

"Sorry," Henley shouted back, and hung her coat on the banister as Luna the dog, wagging her tail in excitement, approached her. "Hello, gorgeous," Henley said as she stroked Luna's head and looked at her home, trying to imagine how a stranger would view it if they walked in for the first time. A blast of radiator heat, her daughter's favorite blue boots on the floor next to her small, purple rucksack covered with unicorns. The sounds of the TV in the background, the cupboard door under the stairs slightly ajar, and the spicy and sweet scent of

Caribbean cooking. Unlike the Annans', there was nothing artificial about Henley's home, except maybe the affection between herself and her husband.

"You all right?" Rob asked as Henley joined him in the kitchen. "You were miles away."

"New case, that's all. I had planned to be home earlier, but the day ran away from me. I'm sorry. Where's Ems?"

"Already in bed. She had a playdate and it knocked her out."

Rob's stubble grazed her cheek as she kissed him. She placed a hand on the right side of his face. "You're not planning on growing a beard, are you? That's at least three days' growth."

"Don't worry. I'll shave in the morning. You better be hungry because I've been cooking up a storm."

Henley put a hand to her stomach. The last thing she had eaten was a Twix and half a packet of crisps before she and Ramouter had headed off to the Annans' home.

"I'm starving, actually." She lifted the tea cloth and inhaled the scent of spiced ground split peas from the pile of rotis on the plate. "You made proper dhal puri roti?"

"Yeah. Your aunt Celia talked me through it. We've got curry goat too."

"I couldn't love you more right now," said Henley as she picked up a roti skin from the plate, ripped a piece off and put it in her mouth. The words sounded false in her ears. She'd been making an effort to put things right over the past six months, but it'd been difficult. Maybe her words would have sounded authentic if she'd actually felt guilty about sleeping with Pellacia last year. She sometimes felt that if she spent too much time with Rob he would eventually smell the betrayal seeping from her. "Just give me twenty minutes," she added. "I need to wash the day off me first."

"Cool. I'll set the table."

Henley couldn't shake the heaviness from her shoulders as she walked up the stairs to her daughter's bedroom. She stopped at Emma's door. The room was bathed in soft rotating blue and pink beams from the night-light in the corner. Henley entered the room and picked up the blanket that Emma had kicked to the floor. She didn't want to touch Emma or kiss her forehead until she felt clean. It was as if she was faking the role of the wife committed to making her marriage work. She didn't need a therapist to tell her that there was something very wrong with treating her relationship with Rob like a school project that she had to pass, but she felt worse about failing as a mother.

"How did it go this morning?" asked Rob.

Henley wrapped the last piece of curry goat with her roti and placed it into her mouth. Buying herself a piece of time. *Help. I need help.* It was what she had begged Rob for when she had broken down on the steps of the SCU six months ago. *Help. I need help.*

"Same ol', same ol'," she said.

"You've got to want therapy to work, Anj," Rob replied as he picked up the bottle of red wine and filled Henley's glass.

"I do want it to work, and it is helping a bit, but she wants me to talk about Mum, and Mum isn't the problem."

"But you not talking about her is a problem. It's going to be a year on Saturday."

"I know."

"And your brother Simon has organized the memorial celebration for her on Saturday afternoon. Everyone will be talking about your mum."

"I know," Henley said again through gritted teeth.

"So, maybe it will be a good idea to talk about her with someone. Perhaps we can go to her grave as a family on Saturday morning and then go on to your brother's for the memorial celebration."

"I don't want that," Henley said, shaking her head.

"But you haven't been since the funeral."

"I don't see the point. I can't stand the idea of knowing that she's down there. Alone."

"It's just a shell. She would have been the first one to tell you that."

"So why do you want me to go? What good will it do, to visit a cold grave?" Henley picked up the empty plates and carried them to the sink.

"I just think that it would probably be a good idea for you to spend time with her for yourself before you're in a house where everyone will be talking about her. You don't know how you're going to react. It could be overwhelming for you."

"Why would you want me to go to Mum's grave and relive those memories of the day we buried her? That day was awful."

Henley thought back to the irony of the occasion. A sea of family and friends dressed in black in unseasonably warm weather. Henley could remember the feeling of sweat dripping down her back as her cousin Gayle read the eulogy in the church. The sickly scent of lilies, which triggered Henley's allergies, had made her throw up at the graveside.

"I'm not asking you to relive the—"

"No, Rob," Henley said firmly. "Just no."

"I didn't mean to upset you," said Rob as he followed Henley and leaned against the counter. "I just want you to be you again."

"I am me!" Henley snapped back. "I'm not a broken doll being held together by cheap Sellotape."

"That's not what I meant," Rob said with clear frustration in his voice. "I want us to be the 'us' we were before that entire mess with…with him."

Henley turned and faced Rob. Searching for clues as to which "him" Rob was talking about. Olivier or Pellacia. She thought about kissing Rob right then. It seemed the right thing to do, but she couldn't.

"We are us," she said instead.

"There could be more of us though. Not just you, me, Ems and Luna. Look how close you and Simon are."

"We fought like cat and dog when we were kids."

"But at least you and I had that. I don't want Emma to grow up with just the dog and the school hamster during the summer holidays for company."

The baby talk. It had started just before fireworks night, with the news that Simon's wife was expecting their third child. A big family was something that Rob had wanted, and he wasn't placated by Henley's first response that Emma had enough cousins to keep her busy. She hadn't told him the truth: she didn't want a second child.

"Look, we didn't plan for Emma. She just happened. A very happy accident, not that I would ever tell her that, so why don't we just see what happens?"

"Fine. Fine."

Henley couldn't ignore the disappointment that tainted Rob's words.

"I'm not fobbing you off."

"I know you're not. I just don't want us to wait too long. We'll both be forty soon." Rob pulled out another bottle of red wine from the rack. "Anyway, how was work? Something must have kicked off to keep you out so long."

Henley didn't miss the flash of annoyance. She knew that he was trying to be understanding about her commitment to the job, but she also knew that her breakdown last year was like unloaded ammunition in his *Leave the job* argument.

"Someone killed a pastor."

Rob stared back at Henley. "Wow," he said. "You don't have to sound so cold about it."

"You know what I'm like. It's as if my brain automatically compartmentalizes itself when I'm talking about a case."

"Well not everyone works with the dregs of society. The way you talk about your cases, it sounds like you're talking about a shopping list. I should be used to it by now but..."

"Sorry," Henley replied as she kissed him on the cheek and hoped that Rob could sense that she was genuine.

"What happened?"

"Absolutely no idea. It's frustrating," Henley continued, her tone warmer. She opened the cupboard door and pulled out a bag of popcorn while Rob picked up their wineglasses, and thought back to the broken body of the young man they had found.

"So, who is he? Your dead pastor," Rob asked following Henley into the living room. He placed the wineglasses on the coffee table, picked up the remote control and turned the channel over to *MasterChef.*

"I don't want to say just yet. I'll tell you as soon as he's formally identified."

"Well, I can say with a hundred percent certainty your dead pastor was probably up to no good if someone's knocked him off."

10

"*The death of a forty-three-year-old man whose body was found in the Church of Annan the Prophet in Deptford is being treated as murder. A second man, in his twenties, was found seriously injured.*

"*Officers cordoned off the area around the building while investigations were carried out. Police said there would be a postmortem to ascertain the cause of death after the discovery at 1:50 yesterday afternoon and that his family have been informed.*

"*A murder investigation has been launched by the Serial Crime Unit, and a crime scene remains in place. No arrests have yet been made. Detective Superintendent Stephen Pellacia said that 'Although cause of death has not been determined, the man who was sadly found deceased had injuries suggestive of third-party involvement. We have yet to confirm the identity of the second male, and request that anyone who has information should contact us. To confirm: this is not a serial crime, but it is a murder investigation that the Serial Crime Unit have agreed to undertake in order to assist the South London Homicide and Major Crime Command.'*"

It was the lead article on the news that morning. Henley had heard the same report at least three times before she'd left that house earlier. She looked around the coffee shop to see the reaction of the "general public" who had been asked to give information anonymously. But they were too engrossed in the nuances of their own lives captured in the LED screens on their phones to pay any attention to what was going on around them.

"What about that boy we found in the other room?" Ramouter asked as they walked out of the coffee shop and made their way toward Greenwich mortuary where Linh had been completing her autopsy of Caleb Annan's body. "Aren't we going to work hard to establish the circumstances of how he ended up half dead?"

"Of course we are," Henley replied, sipping her coffee. "Did you get anywhere with missing persons?"

"Nothing yet. Do you know how many white males in their early twenties have been reported missing in the past six months?"

"You know full well that I have no idea."

"Loads—33,862, to be exact, and seventy-five percent of those missing are found within twenty-four hours, eighty-five percent in forty-eight hours. Our boy had to have been missing for more than a week."

"And what are the odds on someone being found after a week?" asked Henley.

"Five percent, and let's be honest, guv, people tend to make a lot of noise when young white men go missing. What if he was never missing?"

"What are you talking about?" Henley handed over her coffee cup to Ramouter as they approached the security gate and she keyed in the code.

"What if no one reported him missing because he'd been kidnapped or he'd agreed to be kept there?"

"You're asking me to consider the idea that this may have been consensual?" Henley said very slowly, staring at Ramouter.

"Don't look at me like that."

"Ramouter, you saw the state of that place and you saw the state of him."

"I'm just trying to determine why no one matching his description has appeared on the missing persons' database."

"There could be a hundred reasons for that. He may not be from this country, so no one has reported him missing here. Or he has no family."

Ramouter shook his head. "Everyone has family."

"Well, let's hope that someone might have claimed him by the time we visit the hospital later."

There was a look that Henley hadn't seen before on his face. One of defiance.

"What's wrong with you?" she asked.

"What do you mean?"

"This is an investigation, no different to any that we've conducted since you started working with me. Why have you got your hackles up about this one?"

Ramouter shrugged and pulled his collar up against his neck as the flakes of snow began to fall.

"I haven't got my... It's just... There's just something about it, all of it, that doesn't sit right."

"The murder or our kidnapped victim?"

"We've got a murder victim and we found someone who was almost dead, hidden in a back room in his church. I'm just finding it a bit hard to have any sympathy for the pastor."

"That's not like you," said Henley. "I'm used to constantly reminding you to keep your emotions in check."

"Maybe you're finally rubbing off on me," Ramouter said with a grin.

"In that case, it won't surprise you when I tell you that I don't need your sympathy for the pastor. I just need you to do your job. Emotions don't come into it. OK?"

"Aye."

"Come on, let's get inside."

★ ★ ★

"Forty-eight times," Linh said as she pulled back the plastic covering from the body of Caleb Annan.

"Excuse me? How many times?" Henley asked. She joined Linh by the examination table. Ramouter was standing in his usual spot, midway between the autopsy table and the door. The room softly hummed from the motors of the refrigerators containing corpses.

"Caleb Annan was stabbed forty-eight times," said Linh, poking her gloved finger into a stab wound in Caleb's left arm. He didn't look like a man who had worked out, and there was no definable tone to his muscles. Two days of death had made his body limp and his mottled dark skin had taken on a greenish tint. His eyes were open, fixed and staring at the ceiling. Stab wounds covered his thighs, his chest and his abdomen.

"Forty-eight?" Henley stepped closer to his body.

"Yep. Do you want a pair of gloves, Ramouter?" Linh said with a grin.

"No thanks. I'm good where I am," Ramouter replied.

"Well, I'm not," said Henley. "Get over here."

Ramouter let out a sigh like a petulant schoolchild, and walked over to the table. He stood opposite Henley.

"Which of the stab wounds killed him?" Henley asked as Linh handed her two sheets of A4 sheet of paper with a predrawn outline of the front and back of the pastor's body. Linh had placed on the body map a neat and precise series of red circles and crosses, each with a number, indicating the location of every stab wound.

"I know that it looks bad," said Linh ushering Ramouter to move around the other side and next to Henley, "but the forty-one wounds to the front of his body are mainly superficial. The deepest ones were about 6.5 mm and those were the defensive wounds to his hand, and to his arms. Amazingly, none severed any of his arteries, and the ones to his chest and abdomen weren't life-threatening at all."

Henley saw the color disappear from Ramouter's cheeks as Linh inserted her fingers into the gaping wound next to the shoulder blade.

"This is the stab wound that killed him. It's deep. Seven inches," said Linh. "The knife was thrust into his back with so much force that the tip broke off. I've bagged it up to send to forensics. Not sure how far you will get with it, to be fair."

"Is he missing the top off his ear?" Ramouter asked as he leaned in closer to the body, despite his earlier protestations to stand as close to the door as possible.

"Didn't you look at the body map?" Linh shook her head as she stepped away from the body, and then peeled off her gloves and dropped them into the yellow clinical waste bin. "Top of his left ear and his right index and middle finger have been cut off." Linh switched on an overhead light and pulled it downward. "There's bruising at the base of his back," she said. "Just between the T12 and L1 vertebrae. There was enough pressure asserted to cause a contusion to the right kidney and some bleeding inside the kidney and, if you look close enough..."

Both Henley and Ramouter leaned as Linh traced a marking on the back that had been molded into the flesh like Plasticine.

"That's a footprint?" said Ramouter. "How hard do you have to stand on someone to leave an actual footprint behind?"

"That's a lot of force, to push down on him and to pull out the knife as it became stuck between the vertebrae," said Linh. "Have you got any suspects yet?"

"Not yet," said Henley, rattled by the footprint.

"I wouldn't be surprised if it's a long list," said Ramouter. "He wouldn't be the first representative of God to be knocked off his pedestal. Look at all of those priests who got away with abusing children, or those hate-preaching imams. It's not such a leap to think that someone may have had enough."

"The question is, enough of what?" Henley challenged. "I know that I said to put sympathy aside, but what could he possibly have done to deserve being stabbed forty-eight times? You need to focus on the facts."

"Before I forget," said Linh. "Your dead pastor's wife is coming in at midday to formally identify him. Are you staying?"

"No. The FLO is coming in with her, but I've asked Eastwood to be here. Any idea when you'll get a full post-mortem report to me?"

"Because it's you, I'll try to have something tonight. Worst-case scenario, tomorrow afternoon, but unless toxicology turns anything up, it looks like a good old-fashioned murder to me. You just have to find out who did it."

"Don't you dare, Linh." Henley knew her friend well enough to know exactly what she was going to say next. Linh was as bad as Stanford.

"I'll put my money on Miss Scarlett in the billiard room with a dagger."

11

"Do you have any idea how he's doing?" Ramouter asked Henley as they walked through the intensive care unit of Lewisham Hospital. The only sounds came from the barely audible conversations of hospital visitors, family and friends gathered around bedsides, unsure if their words were being understood or evaporating into the sterile air.

"No, not a thing," Henley replied.

"They say no news is good news, I suppose."

"Crap," Henley muttered under her breath as they reached the empty nurses' station and she read the whiteboard of patient and room names.

"What's wrong?" Ramouter asked.

"We don't have a name for him," Henley replied.

A male nurse appeared from a side door. "Oh, we've called him Mr. Question," he said after Henley had explained who they were. "We couldn't keep calling him the bloke in bed number eight and we've already got a patient Smith."

"Is it possible to speak to the doctor who's been dealing with him?" Henley asked as she and Ramouter were handed disposable plastic gowns by the nurse and directed to use the hand sanitizer.

"If you're good to wait for about half an hour. Dr. Chaplin should be coming down to do his checks. One of your colleagues came in this morning with a photographer. Have you got a name for him?"

"No. Nothing yet. There should be an article in the early edition of the *Evening Standard*, so you never know, we may get an ID on him by the end of the day."

"I hope so. He looks so young. He has to be someone's baby," said the nurse as a bell went off in the ward and he left Henley and Ramouter to wait.

"We almost lost him at quarter past five this morning," said Dr. Chaplin standing at the foot of the bed with his hands clasped behind his back. "He stopped breathing and he went into cardiac arrest. It took us nearly twenty-five minutes to resuscitate him. We were just about to declare him dead, when he came back. His pulse is still weak, and his blood pressure is not where I would like it to be, but he's still here."

Still here. Henley repeated the words in her head as she stared down at him. How would anyone be able to identify him? His brown eyelashes briefly fluttered against the swollen yellowing and purple skin under his eyes. The clear breathing tube in his mouth had pushed his tongue out grotesquely to the side, with saliva dried to a crust. A thin yellow tube joined the breathing tube and had been taped against his neck. Henley could make out the bruised imprints left behind by cruel fingers on his scratched skin. His white and blue checked hospital gown covered half of the ECG sensors on his chest. How would anyone recognize him as belonging to their family?

"We had to remove his right kidney," said Dr. Chaplin as Henley's gaze followed the urine that flowed from the patient's bladder into the catheter and drainage bags. "We also found fluid, well, water to be exact, around his lungs and heart."

"Water?" Henley's mind flashed back to the bucket and plastic jug that had been found in the room with their unknown boy. "How would he get water around his heart and lungs?"

"We usually see that amount of fluid in the lungs of drowning victims, but I've also seen it with a patient who had an epileptic fit and nearly drowned in the bath."

"We found him tied to a bed," said Henley as she looked over at Ramouter and then at the thick bandages around the patient's wrists. "And he was nowhere near a bath, but there was an empty bucket in the room where he was found."

"Waterboarding?" the doctor said with a shrug. He walked over to the right side of the bed and checked the contents of the drainage bag.

"Waterboarding?" Ramouter repeated. "I've only ever seen that in episodes of *24*."

"It wouldn't be the first time that I've dealt with something like this," said Dr. Chaplin. "But it's usually been a prank gone wrong."

"Jesus Christ," Henley muttered, raising her eyes to the ceiling.

"Well, whoever it was really did a number on him," said Dr. Chaplin as he walked over and checked the monitors. He pulled out the chart attached to the side of the bed and made a note on the page. "If he makes it through the next few days then I would say that his chances of survival are reasonably good."

"What do you mean by 'reasonably'?" asked Henley.

"I don't like to give odds. Let's see how he does over the next twelve hours or so."

"Do you think that he will be able to talk to us if he does wake up?" Ramouter asked.

Dr. Chaplin scratched the top of his head, like a mechanic about to give you an unwelcome estimate. "His heart stopped beating when he was in the ambulance. He was technically dead when he arrived here yesterday afternoon. It took us eight minutes to restart his heart, which means that his brain was starved of oxygen for that entire time. I'm not saying that it's impossible, but you need to be prepared for the fact that he might not be able to tell you anything if he does wake up."

12

Uliana Piontek was searching the kitchen for a clean mug, while Henley and Ramouter stood trying not to touch the countertops. A pile of dirty dishes filled the sink. Bulging rubbish sat on top of the already overflowing bin in the corner. Uliana was renting a room in a three-bedroom flat on the fourth floor in a council estate in Crofton Park. The flat was worse than any student digs that Henley had stayed in back when she was in university. Her nose tickled with the lingering scent of fried food and stale oil.

"There is nowhere else," said Uliana apologetically. She gave up looking for a clean mug, picked up a damp dishcloth and wiped the small kitchen table. Her lank hair was piled up in a loose ponytail. She rubbed her fingers across the puffy skin under her eyes. She looked so much younger and more vulnerable than her twenty years of age.

"We could talk back at the station," said Ramouter, trying not to lean against the grease-stained worktop. "It may be more comfortable."

"No," Uliana said quickly. "No. I don't want to. Here is fine."

Henley didn't say anything as she watched Uliana pick at the cuticles of her bitten-down fingernails.

"Are you having trouble sleeping?" Henley already knew the answer. She sat down at the table with Uliana, who put a hand to her face to stifle the yawn and looked around the small kitchen.

"I don't want to be here anymore," Uliana said. Someone in the flat above walked noisily across their own kitchen floor, which was accompanied by the sound of banging. "I want to go home."

"I understand that you've been through something terrible. Are you planning to return home? Back to Lithuania?" Henley asked, hoping that the answer would be no.

"I want to, but I have uni. Work. I don't know. Why have you come to see me?" Uliana's tone switched, as though she'd just become aware that she was talking to two detectives. "I already spoke to the police."

"You had a shock yesterday, and you can miss out on little things when that happens. We just need to ask you a few questions about your relationship with Caleb Annan and your interaction with his wife and any other church members."

"Why?" Uliana kept her gaze focused on a tomato ketchup stain that she had missed with her cloth. "All I did was clean."

"What else did you do?"

"What do you mean?" Uliana's words were rushed, her tone high-pitched and wary. The switch wasn't lost on Henley.

"Sorry," Henley said. "I only meant that you told PC Tanaka that you cleaned the church three days a week. I wouldn't have thought that would be enough to support you. I remember what it was like being at uni; living in halls and trying to have a life."

Henley knew that Uliana had to be paying a minimum of £600 for whatever hovel of a room had been allocated to her by her landlord.

"I have my student loan and I work in a coffee shop in Victoria," Uliana said cautiously.

"What are you studying?" Henley was trying anything to make Uliana feel comfortable.

"Mechanical engineering. I'm in my third year."

"And how long have you been working at the church?"

Uliana's eyes filled with tears. She sniffed and wiped her nose with the back of her sleeve. "Nearly a year. Easy money. I clean and then go to uni. It's local."

"And how did you get the job?"

"A friend of mine used to clean there. She lived here once, but she moved and got a job in Hammersmith. I took her job."

"What's your friend's name?" Henley asked as she took out her notebook and a pen.

"Why?" Uliana's eyes flashed with anger, and then fear. "You don't need to talk to her. She will know nothing."

"But she knew the pastor," said Ramouter. "Any information that she can give will be helpful. Sometimes it's the small things. Her name and number would be good. We won't say that it came from you."

"Her name is Nicole Fleming," she finally said as she reached for her phone, scrolled through her contacts and read out the phone number.

"So, you worked for Pastor Annan's church for a year," Henley clarified. "What was he like?"

"Fine. He was fine," Uliana replied as she kept her eyes downcast. "I hardly saw him. He was never really around when I cleaned but he was...fine when I saw him."

"Did you ever go to any of his services?"

Uliana looked at Henley as though she'd lost her mind. "What for? No, I didn't."

"Did you have any reason to think that the pastor would be in danger? Anything that you had seen or heard during your—"

Henley stopped as Uliana's head bowed, her neck seeming to disappear into her shoulders, and she began to cry. Loudly. Ramouter tore the last two sheets from a roll of kitchen paper and handed it to Henley.

"It's OK. I know that it's hard," Henley said as she gently lifted up Uliana's head and wiped the tears from her face. "It's going to be hard for a while, but it will get better."

"He was just there. On the ground. There was so much blood," Uliana said, her words strangulated as she attempted to talk between the tears which were catching her breath. "I, I... Everybody liked him, I think."

"You can't think of any reason why anyone would want to hurt him?"

Uliana vigorously shook her head.

"And his wife? Did you know her?"

Henley caught the scent of paranoia in Uliana's demeanor as she looked up at the kitchen door as if she expected Serena Annan to be standing there.

"I had nothing to do with her," Uliana said, turning her attention back to Henley.

"OK." Henley motioned to Ramouter to pull out his phone. "Uliana, this may sound like a silly question, but how did you get into the church?"

"I have my own keys."

"And that is for the front and rear entrance of the church?"

"Yes. I have keys for everywhere."

"And did you clean the entire church?"

"No, I didn't get far because I found Caleb."

"I'm not talking about the day that you found Caleb," said Ramouter. "I meant in general. The church is a big building. Three floors. Did you clean all those floors? All of those rooms?"

"No, only the ground floor and the first floor."

"By yourself? That seems like a lot for one person."

"It is. Caleb was supposed to get another cleaner, but I think some of the women from the church helped."

"Did you ever go to the other floors in the time that you've been working there?"

Henley watched Uliana as she went quiet for a second.

"Maybe once or twice," she finally said. "But that was it."

"When was the last time that you went up to the third floor?" asked Ramouter.

"I... I can't remember."

"Could you have gone up there in the past few weeks? Did you go into any of the rooms on that floor?"

"I don't know. I don't think so." Uliana shook her head, her eyes darting nervously between Ramouter and Henley.

"What about the meeting rooms?" asked Ramouter. "Did you go into those rooms?"

"No. No," Uliana replied quietly.

Henley placed Ramouter's phone in front of Uliana. "There's a storage room on the third floor at the end of the corridor. In that room was another room, where this young man was found bound and dying." Henley enlarged a photo she'd taken of the young man in hospital.

"What do you mean?" A tortured grimace spread across Uliana's face as she zoomed in on the photograph and then pushed the phone back toward Henley. "This man was there... when I was there? In the church?"

"Exactly what I said," said Henley. "He was found in a concealed room in the storage cupboard."

"I don't know about that room."

"Take another look," Henley said as she pushed the phone back in front of Uliana. "Do you recognize him at all? I know that it's a bit hard with the bruising and the tubes but try and think back if anytime over the past few months you may have seen someone, even vaguely matching his description, in the church or around the area."

"I'm sorry but I've never seen him before," Uliana said as she handed the phone back.

"There's just one more thing," said Henley. "PC Tanaka said that you refused to provide the crime scene investigators with a sample of your DNA or your fingerprints."

There was a clear panic in Uliana's voice as she became tearful.

"I didn't... I haven't done anything wrong," she said, her voice strained. "They made me feel like a criminal. I didn't hurt Caleb."

"Uliana, we wouldn't be talking to you in your kitchen if we thought that you were involved in Caleb Annan's murder," said Henley.

"I don't want to give you my..."

Uliana's voice grew quiet as she looked down at the kitchen table.

"Uliana," Henley said firmly. "I really don't want to arrest you, bring you to the station and put you into a miserable cold cell unnecessarily."

"What? Arrest! But I didn't do anything," Uliana said as she shot up from her seat. "I just found him."

"And that's why we need your prints and DNA, so that we can eliminate you as a suspect from the investigation. The samples will be destroyed once the investigation is over."

Uliana was silent for a moment. "Can I think about it?"

"Sure," Henley replied, taking out her card and a pen. "Here's the details of the CSI investigator who will take your samples *when* you change your mind."

"I'm really tired now. Is there anything else?" Uliana asked, reluctantly taking the card from Henley.

"No, there isn't," said Henley. "But one of the officers from my team will be in touch over the next few days, just to confirm the contents of your statement. Hopefully you wouldn't have booked a ticket home to Lithuania before then."

"I haven't seen that boy before," Uliana said defiantly, "and I don't know who would want to kill Caleb."

"To say that she was cagey is an understatement," said Ramouter as he and Henley walked along Marnock Road.

Henley suddenly stopped as an intense rush of heat washed over her. The beads of sweat pricked her forehead, fusing with the cold air. She leaned against the railings that bordered the community garden behind her.

"What is it? Are you OK?" Ramouter's voice was filled with concern as Henley wiped her brow with the back of her gloved hand. The winter air, cut with polluted diesel, only intensified her nausea. The railings began to vibrate as the incoming train into Crofton Park station grew closer.

"I'll be fine," Henley finally said, pulling herself away from the railings.

"You don't look fine," Ramouter said. "I thought that...the PTSD."

It was easier for Henley to talk about her PTSD when it was a remote, abstract notion, but it was the last thing that she wanted to talk about when she was in the middle of a panic attack that felt like red-hot barbs clawing at her chest.

"It doesn't just go away. It's not like having the flu," said Henley. "Anyway, what you said about Uliana being cagey."

"She didn't even flinch when you showed her the picture of..." Ramouter paused, unsure what to call the man.

"We need to get him identified," Henley said as she opened the car door. "He deserves the basic dignity of having a name, and you're right, Uliana is hiding something."

"You don't think that she's involved, do you? I mean, I know that she found the body and she had twenty-four-hour access to the church."

"My gut is saying that she's definitely not telling us everything."

"I wonder which victim she's keeping quiet about?" said Ramouter as Henley started the car.

13

Serena Annan pulled up the sleeve of her navy coat and checked the time. The subdued lighting of the mortuary viewing room still managed to capture the intricate diamonds that graced the circumference of the watch face.

"Do you need me to say anything?" Serena asked, pulling out a packet of tissues and wiping her nose, as if she was allergic to the space that her dead husband now occupied. "Is there a certain protocol?"

"We simply need you to confirm if that is your husband, Mrs. Annan," said Eastwood, glancing over at Bethany, the family liaison officer, who was sitting on a chair in the corner with her head cocked to the side as though she was analyzing an actor's performance at an amateur play.

"Do I need to touch him?" Serena asked.

"As I said," Eastwood explained cautiously, "we just need you to identify him. If he's not your husband, then all you have to do is say so."

Serena sighed and bowed her head. Her lips moved silently and then she crossed herself, her perfectly manicured fingers touching her head, middle of her chest and just above her left and right breast. "I'm ready."

"Would you like to take a step forward?" Eastwood asked gently. She pulled the cord and the thick gray velvet curtains obscuring the glass parted. Eastwood kept her gaze firmly on Serena's face as she stepped forward. Eastwood waited in the brief interlude for Serena to react upon seeing her dead husband, but there was nothing. Serena's face remained impassive, as if she was just reading a poster in the doctor's surgery.

"That's Caleb. That's my husband."

"Thank you, Mrs. Annan," Eastwood said. "I understand that this would have been—"

"Do I need to sign something?" Serena pulled her phone out of her bag and switched the ringer back on.

"No, you don't have to sign anything."

"So, I can go. I have a lot going on today."

"Of course you can."

"I'll walk you both out." Bethany stood up with a grimace and grabbed the left side of her lower back. "Sciatica. Hurts when I sit down, hurts when I stand up. Can't win."

Serena placed her hand on the handle, then turned around. "When do we get him back?"

Eastwood hated this question. There was never a satisfactory answer. No one ever responded well to being told that the body wouldn't be released until the pathologist had finished their post-mortem, and even then, that wasn't guaranteed, especially if someone was arrested for the murder and then the defense solicitors decided that they wanted their own pathologist to examine the body.

"I'm afraid that I can't tell you that. It all depends on—" answered Eastwood.

"What do you mean, you can't tell me? What could it possibly depend on?"

"Serena—" Bethany began.

"It's Mrs. Annan. We're not friends."

"It's as I explained to you, Mrs. Annan." Bethany's voice was gentle, as though she was telling a five-year-old why it was a good idea to eat their vegetables. "There are so many reasons why there could be a delay. But we will do our best to make sure that Caleb is returned to you."

"What about his things?" Serena turned toward Eastwood. "His watch, his chain, wedding ring."

"If there's no evidential need for them, then they'll be returned to you as soon as possible."

Serena opened her mouth as if to say something and then decided better of it as her phone rang.

"And the press conference. When will that be?"

"Press conference?" Eastwood asked.

"My husband was an eminent member of the community. I'm expecting there to be a press conference so you can make an appeal to find my husband's killer, and of course I would be there."

"I'm not the one who..." Eastwood paused as the air in the room suddenly felt colder. "We will keep you informed on any developments; including a press conference."

"You have my details. I expect it to be held promptly." Serena walked out of the viewing room.

"Dad, turn the camera round. You're showing me the cooker," said Henley as she sat down at her desk.

"Oh, am I?" said Elijah. "Simon got me this new phone and I don't know what's going on with this thing. Can you see me now?"

"Yes, Dad, I can see you." Henley felt a warm flush of relief as her dad's face filled the screen. She could make out new creases under his eyes and there was a bit more gray in his hair, but it was a complete contrast to the man who'd been in the grips of a deep depressive episode last year and pleaded that he didn't want his children to see him broken.

"So, you're checking up on me, daughter?"

"Of course I am. Have you eaten lunch yet?"

"I was just about to but then you called. Rob came over with Emma earlier and dropped off the curry and roti."

"And what about your medication?"

Her dad rolled his eyes. "You forget that I'm the parent and you're *my* child?"

"Don't start," said Henley. "I'm just being... I just want to make sure that you're OK."

"Are *you* OK?" Elijah asked in a tone which meant that there was no way that Henley could avoid the question.

"I had a moment this morning, but it passed. I'm OK."

"OK, if you say so. By the way, Rob said that you were going to the..." Elijah let out a deep sigh and looked away from the camera. "Going to the cemetery to see your mother."

"He said what?" Henley asked, stunned.

"Yes, he said that he would pick me up after I go swimming on Saturday morning."

"Rob told you that we were going to Mum's grave?" Henley asked as the door opened and Eastwood walked into the room. "Are you sure that he wasn't talking about the memorial celebration at Simon's?"

"No. Rob definitely said the cemetery. I think that your brother is coming too."

"Right," Henley said slowly.

"Anjelica, it's a good thing."

"I didn't say a word."

"You didn't have to. I know that face of yours too well."

"Listen, Dad, I've got to go. I'll give you a ring later."

"All right, baby girl. Love you."

"How did it go?" Henley asked Eastwood as she ended the call.

"I'm telling you, guv, it was weird. She was weird." Eastwood pulled up a chair and sat down in front of Henley's desk.

"What do you mean, weird?" Henley asked as she updated the CRIS report for the investigation.

"I don't mean, 'No one wants to be looking at a dead body,' sort of weird. I mean, I have no idea how I would react if I was in that situation, but Serena Annan acted as though it was just business; actually, scratch that, she acted like it was an inconvenient interruption of her day."

"How did she respond? Did she cry? They usually cry." Henley moved her computer monitor to the side so that she could take a better look at Eastwood. The frown line in Eastwood's forehead had deepened as she opened a packet of chocolate digestive biscuits.

"Nothing. Not a single thing."

"You were asking her to identify her husband's body, maybe it was just—"

"The whole thing just felt off," Eastwood said through a mouthful of chocolate biscuits. "I didn't expect her to be wailing on the floor, but there was absolutely no emotion. Not a single tear. She just wanted to know when we would be holding a press conference. I'm thinking that she should be put on the suspect board."

"We can't just add her to the suspect list because she acted a little weird during an identification viewing."

"Well, I know that."

"So, she identified him. Anything else?"

"She asked when we would be releasing the body, which is to be expected, but she was more interested in getting his jewelry back, if you ask me."

"What did she ask for?"

Eastwood listed the items of her fingers. "Watch, chain and wedding ring. She said that it was for the children. If you ask me, that was a load of bollocks."

"Ramouter," Henley shouted. Turning her attention back to her computer, she opened the search report and the crime scene photographs that Anthony had emailed earlier. "The pastor's body. You remember seeing a watch, right?"

"Yeah," Ramouter said. He picked up his takeaway cup of

soup and walked over. "Even with all that blood, you couldn't miss it. It was a Tag Heuer."

"You couldn't wait to get away from the body, but you're able to remember the watch brand?" said Henley.

"I've got a thing for watches. Can't afford them, but nice to look at."

"Grab the search record off the printer."

"What am I looking for?"

"Any personal effects recorded as being on the pastor's body."

Ramouter placed his soup down on his desk and walked off to the printer. He leaned against the table as he thumbed through the pages.

"'Twenty-one-inch gold chain with diamond-encrusted crucifix. Gold bracelet. Signet ring on his right little finger,'" Ramouter read out loud. "Tag Heuer watch, told you." He let out a low whistle. "It's a Carrera. They're worth about five grand."

"No wedding ring," Henley said, enlarging the photograph of the pastor's body in situ. It was no help. The photographs showed the pastor's body in the fetal position, his head laid on top of his arms, his fingers curled around the edge of a table-cloth.

"What's the issue?" Ramouter asked as Henley picked up the phone on her desk and dialed the number for Greenwich mortuary.

"Serena Annan apparently asked for his wedding ring to be returned to her, but I don't remember seeing it on his body and there's no sign of it on the report." Henley raised her hand as the call connected.

"Hey, Linh, quick question. Did you remove any rings from the pastor's body? Was that it? Well of course you would know. Thank you." Henley hung up. "Linh confirmed that she re-moved a gold signet ring from the pastor's right hand. There was nothing on his left hand, but there were deep indent marks on the left ring finger and also scratches from the base of the finger up to the knuckles," said Henley. Her computer pinged with an email alert. "Take a look. Linh's sent photographs."

"Someone forced the ring off his finger?" asked Ramouter, peering at the zoomed-in image of the pastor's left hand.

"Linh said that the scratches were fresh."

"That doesn't make any sense," said Eastwood. "Why would the killer take his ring but leave behind, if our resident watch specialist is correct, a five-grand watch, a gold chain covered in bloody diamonds and his other ring?"

"And there's his sixty-grand car that was parked outside," Ramouter chimed in.

"It makes perfect sense," said Henley. "A wedding is a sign of commitment and it's supposed to mean something. Whoever killed him must have known the pastor, and personally enough to take something from him. How angry must you be to rip a wedding ring off someone's finger after you've stabbed them forty-eight times?" Henley pulled at her own wedding ring, which she'd only removed twice in her life.

"I would put money on his missus," said Eastwood.

"Maybe she caught him doing something that he shouldn't," said Ramouter.

Henley held up her finger as she scanned through her emails and stopped at one from DS Rickman at Stoke Newington police station. She felt the sharp prickles of anticipation as she realized that this could be the result of Joanna's task to find out why Caleb Annan had been arrested and released on bail last year.

Tuesday, 18 February 2020 at 13:07
From: Mason Rickman, Met Police, Sapphire Unit
To: Anjelica Henley, Met Police, Serial Crime Unit
Subject: Caleb Silas Annan

Afternoon, DI Henley
Caleb Annan was arrested on Tuesday 12 November for an allegation of rape. There is one complainant, Raina

Davison, 28 years old, who alleges that Annan raped her in October. Could you confirm if Annan's body has been formally identified?

I've attached the CRIS report which contains up-to-date contact details for Davison.

Regards,
DS M. Rickman

14

Henley stood with Stanford at Pellacia's office door. There was a time where she would have brazenly walked into his office but there was now a caustic edge to him as he deliberately kept his distance from her. Henley wished that she could put the hostility down to Pellacia's regret that they'd slept together last year, but she knew that it was more than that. Three years later and she herself was still coming to terms with what Olivier had done to her. She would be naive to think that Pellacia had moved on emotionally from Olivier's attempts to kill him six months ago. She wondered if Pellacia traced the scars on his chest with his fingers when he stood in front of the bathroom mirror or whether he refused to look. If he had been able to block out the memory of Olivier carving the crescent and the double dagger into his chest while he lay naked on the ground, meters from the river's edge. Henley knocked on the door twice and waited.

"It's not as if he's not in," Stanford said as he shook the snow off his coat. "He's been a right moody twit recently."

"He probably heard that," Henley replied.

"What have I said that's wrong?"

"Absolutely nothing."

"Well, there you go. By the way, your brother texted me this morning. He wanted to check if Gene and I were still coming to your mum's memorial celebration at his house on Saturday."

"You are still coming, aren't you? She adored you and I'd like it if you were there."

"Of course I'll be there, and Gene will definitely be there. He's just itching to see what Simon's missus has done with the renovations; I should never have married a bloody architect. Anyway, you got time for a quick drink later?"

"Yeah, why not," Henley said as she raised her hand to knock on Pellacia's door again, changed her mind and opened the door.

Inside, Pellacia didn't raise his head as he tapped away at his computer. "You couldn't have knocked?"

"I did knock. Twice."

"What do you want?"

"Seriously, is that the way you're going to talk to me?" Henley asked as she turned to close the door, ignoring Stanford who mouthed *"Told you."* He stood overprotectively, outside the door.

"Well?" Henley asked.

"I haven't got time for you to stand there and throw a tantrum because I didn't hear you knock. I'm assuming that you're here about the investigation so far."

Henley pulled out the chair and sat down. She opened the copy of the *Evening Standard* in her hand and flipped to page eight.

"Firstly, our boy in the room has made the paper," said Henley.

Pellacia's face softened slightly as he skimmed the article. "Poor kid," he said. "Have there been any responses?"

"Not yet, but it's only been an hour since the papers were published in print and this went online. The local news channels have already started running the appeal for information."

"Did our CSI team find anything that could give us an idea about who he is?"

"Not a thing. He was tied to that bed stark naked. There was nothing in that room except a Bible, holy water, a bucket and a couple of dead rats."

"But you and Ramouter are suggesting that he was tortured?"

Henley folded her arms. It felt as though Pellacia sucked all of the oxygen out of the room. "You didn't see the state of him."

"I saw the photographs."

"But you didn't *see* him or smell him," Henley said firmly as she sat up. "You were here. Pushing paper."

Pellacia shoved back his chair, the legs scraping against the cheap parquet flooring. Henley saw it. A flicker of pain in Pellacia's eyes as he stood up and opened the window, letting in a sharp wind that bristled across her cheek. She knew that it was a sore point, the fact that he was stuck in the office, glorified admin instead of a true detective.

"What about the priest?" Pellacia asked as he lit a cigarette.

"He's a pastor. Not a priest. A Pentecostal Christian. They don't have priests." Henley wasn't sure why she needed to reiterate the point.

"Same difference."

"You're Catholic. You know better than that."

"So are you, not that you've paid much attention to the commandments."

Henley didn't respond. They'd made an agreement. Not to talk about what had happened between them last year and not to repeat it. She'd been fooling herself that Pellacia was content with the status quo.

"Speaking of the sixth commandment, which is 'thou shall not commit adultery' for the Catholics amongst us and the seventh commandment for everyone else, Caleb Annan's wife made a positive identification earlier, and he's also been accused of rape. DS Rickman gave me the basic details. A twenty-eight-year-old woman called Raina Davison has made three allegations dating back to October last year. He was interviewed, denied rape and said it was consensual."

"Rape? That's a motive for murder. What about witnesses, CCTV, anything like that? The church is on the main road. Someone must have seen something."

"Not if our killer used the back entrance, which it looks like he or she did. Also, it was late on a Sunday night. I doubt that we're going to find any witnesses."

"You've got one witness."

Henley's mind flashed back to the young man in the hospital, his broken body on life support. As far as she knew, the only person praying for him was her.

"And I told you that he's still in critical condition. I doubt very much that he heard anything. I thought that he was dead when I found him. We all thought that he was dead. Hopefully, he doesn't die on me."

"So, what next?" Pellacia asked, keeping his gaze focused on the papers on the desk. "You seem to be stagnant with this investigation. It's not what I want to hear in the first forty-eight hours."

"Don't start with me," Henley snapped back, unable to sustain Pellacia's hostility for a second longer. "You know full well that some cases are like this. Slow. No momentum, but we're doing our job, and it would be easier if you weren't sitting in here sulking and making little digs just because you can't put your personal feelings to one side."

"You can't talk to me like that, Anjelica," Pellacia replied as his face flushed red. "You can't talk to me as though I'm nothing and not your boss."

"Well, do better. Whatever happens... I expect you to do better, Stephen."

"I don't know how you can—"

"We've already spoken to Uliana," Henley said, cutting Pellacia off. "She's the cleaner who found the pastor. Ramouter's leaving in a bit to interview members of the church and I'll be making a start with Raina Davison. Hopefully, that won't be too stagnant for you."

15

"What are you doing about it? He was murdered in his own church and so far, nothing."

The woman who spoke was sitting on the edge of her sofa. Anger, not sorrow, was etched in her face.

Ramouter wanted to say, give us a chance. This isn't a TV show. We don't solve a crime in an hour.

"I'm very sorry for your loss," he said instead. He couldn't bring himself to be cruel. "Kristen Palmer," he said as he pulled out his notebook. "You're listed as being on the church board of trustees."

"Yes," Kristen sniffed. She pulled out a tissue from the packet on her lap as her husband, Gordon, came into the room and placed a cup of tea on the coffee table in front of Ramouter.

"Yes, there's seven of us," said Kristen. "We've been there since day one."

"Actually, that's not correct," said Gordon. "There's only five of us, well, I suppose that it's four what with Caleb being... Anyway, Derrick and Tameka Sullivan resigned from the board, a couple of months ago."

"Oh yes, that's right," said Kristen. "I still can't believe it. I thought, well I didn't know what to think when Serena called me last night."

"She called you last night and not this morning?" Ramouter asked. It was a bit strange that Serena was spreading the news of her husband's death when she hadn't yet identified his body.

"Yes, she called me about nine last night and then we saw the news this afternoon," said Kristen. "Do you have any idea who did it?"

"I can't believe that anyone would want to hurt Caleb. It must have been some crazy crackhead or something," said Gordon.

"We don't know at this stage, it's still early in the investigation," Ramouter explained as he took a sip of his tea, which had far too much milk. "But I did want to ask how many people had access to the church?"

"What do you mean by access? It's a church that's open to everyone," said Kristen, exchanging a look with her husband.

"Sorry, I meant who had keys to the building?"

"Oh. The keys. Only Caleb and Serena had keys."

Ramouter looked up from his notes and hoped that his face didn't betray what he was thinking. Uliana Piontek had confirmed that she'd had a set, too.

"No one else had keys?" asked Ramouter.

"No. Just Caleb and Serena," said Gordon. "They owned the building, but as my wife explained, we were always open for church services and if we weren't, Caleb or Serena would buzz us in."

"Mr. Annan's body was found by the cleaner, Uliana Piontek. Have either of you met her?"

"No," Kristen said with surprise. "I wasn't aware that Caleb or Serena had already employed a cleaner. Volunteers from the church were helping to clean after services, while we are getting quotes for a cleaning service. He could have just forgotten to tell us."

"Right," said Ramouter. "There's something else that I need to ask about."

"The young man who was found in the church building?" Gordon asked cautiously, taking hold of his wife's hands. "We don't know anything about him. I saw his photo in the paper earlier and we don't recognize him."

"When was the last time that you were at the church?" Ramouter asked.

"Sunday afternoon for service and we're supposed to be there tomorrow evening for our weekly meeting," said Gordon.

"That's great. You've both been really helpful. A member of the crime investigation team will be in contact with you."

"What for?" asked Kristen, looking at her husband with concern.

"It's nothing to worry about," explained Ramouter. "We'll be asking all of the church board members for samples."

"It's probably just so they can eliminate us from their investigation, so that they can find Caleb's…killer," said Gordon to his wife. "Isn't that correct, Detective?"

"I still can't believe it," said Kristen as she began to cry. "I just can't."

"Well, I'll be going," said Ramouter. He finished his tea. "You've got my number if anything comes to mind and just a word of warning, now that Caleb's name has been released to the press, the reporters might come knocking. This is one of those cases that tend to generate media interest, so let me know if anyone starts hassling you."

Gordon nodded. "We'll do anything to help," he said. "We're just praying for the family."

Ramouter double-checked that the Palmers' front gate was secure before he walked away from their house. He'd been expecting Gordon and Kristen to be just as hostile as Serena Annan, only to be surprised by their openness and naivety as they spoke about their limited but committed role in the church.

Ramouter braced himself against the cold and started to head toward the direction of the train station. He'd been walking for less than a minute when the full beams of a police car's head-lights hit his face. He caught the eye of the officer sitting in the passenger seat as the car drove past him. Ramouter quick-ened his steps, but he couldn't escape the crushing, inevitable screech of car tires, and the street was suddenly illuminated by the flashing blue lights.

"Oi, mate. Stop," shouted out the first police officer. Ra-mouter put his hands into his coat pockets and fished around for his warrant card as he walked. He pulled out half a packet of fruit pastilles, a loyalty card, but no warrant card.

Ramouter felt the muscle in his arm clench as the officer grabbed his elbow and turned him around.

"Didn't you hear me? I said stop. What's your name?"

"Why do you need to know?" Ramouter asked as he mem-orized the officer's shoulder number. Both looked as though they were the same age as Ramouter, but there was an air of arrogance and entitlement around them.

"He asked you a question," said the second officer, who had concealed his shoulder number with his hand, whilst reaching for his radio. Ramouter checked the body-worn video cam-eras that all uniformed officers wore on the chest. The two small lights that usually flashed red when they were record-ing were dark.

"I can't believe that you two are actually doing this," Ra-mouter said, trying to recall where he'd placed his warrant card.

"We asked you to stop, but you didn't, and we're now ask-ing you for your name and you're refusing," said the first po-lice officer, who was now reaching for the left side of his belt where he kept his baton.

"And what's your name?" Ramouter asked as he unbuttoned his coat and put his hand in his inside pocket.

"Take your hands out of your pockets." The officer spun Ramouter around. "I'm going to search you. There's been a robbery and you match the description of an IC4 male acting suspiciously in the area."

"Name!" shouted the second officer as he stepped in front of Ramouter's face. He was so close that Ramouter could smell the stale coffee on his breath.

"Detective Constable Salim Ramouter, attached to the Serial Crime Unit. Now get your hands off me and you, get out of my bloody face."

Ramouter clocked the hesitation on the first officer's face. "He's talking bollocks," he said to the second.

"I've already memorized your shoulder number, mate," Ramouter said as he thrust his hand into his inside coat pocket and rummaged around. He felt a sense of relief as he grasped the lanyard attached to his warrant card. "EP 2816, which means that it's not going to be difficult to work out the name of your idiot partner."

Ramouter could hear the sounds of the double-decker bus pulling over. He could imagine what was probably happening inside, passengers wiping away the condensation from the windows and holding up their phones to film.

"Shit," said the first officer as he released his grip on Ramouter and stepped back.

"Now what's your name?" asked Ramouter.

"Constable Douglas," he said. His tone was far from conciliatory, which angered Ramouter even more.

"You've broken every single rule in Section A of the Codes of Practice," said Ramouter. "And you wonder why people have a problem with the police."

"Mate, listen, it's—"

"Don't 'mate' me."

"Look, there's no harm done. We were just doing our job."

"And don't give me that shit that you were just doing your job. Neither of you even bothered to turn on your body cam. The last thing that you were doing was your job. Now piss off."

Ramouter was still bristling as the officers got back into their car and drove away. He was still undecided about whether to make an official complaint, but then he thought about the times when he'd been stopped by the police and hadn't had his warrant, the protection of his status as an officer. There were many young black and Asian men who weren't that lucky and whose loud voices of protest had been ignored, ridiculed or written off as an overreaction. Ramouter knew that he would be betraying each and every one of those young men if he walked away and said nothing. The decision should have been an easy one, but Ramouter was still wrestling with the possible consequences as he entered the train station.

16

Henley was sitting in their regular booth at the Tavern, waiting for Stanford. She took a seat facing the door. It used to be the seat which her old boss and first head of the Serial Crime Unit, Rhimes, would occupy. His explanation was that he didn't want to be caught unawares by having someone stab him in the back. Henley could feel tears prickling her eyes. She was still waiting for the grief to ease, but Rhimes's death still felt raw. The pub regulars knew Henley and the SCU team and kept well away from them; not wanting to be seen interacting with the police.

"Double vodka and tonic for you, because you look like you need it," said Stanford as he placed his pint and Henley's drink on the table.

"Thanks." Henley picked up her tall glass and took a long sip.

"From the look on your face, I should have made it a triple." Stanford ripped open a bag of cheese and onion crisps. "What's wrong?"

"I'm pissed off with Rob."

"You've got my full attention," said Stanford, sitting up straighter. "Why are you angry with your betrothed?"

"He's just… I know that he thinks that he's doing the right thing, but…"

"But what? What has he done?"

"He's arranged for us to go to Mum's grave on Saturday morning."

"Why would he do that?" asked Stanford as his tone switched from jovial to a mixture of concern and anger. "You're not ready. And if I know that, then, surely, *he* must know that?"

"I'm probably overreacting. Maybe Rob doesn't know," said Henley.

"Why are you making excuses for him? He does know, and he's choosing to ignore it. This isn't about him. He needs to let you handle your grief in your own way and in your own time."

"But I'm not handling my grief," she said sadly.

"Stop doubting yourself," Stanford said definitively. "Do you want me to have a word with Rob? I'll be more than happy to."

"No, don't do that. I don't need the headache."

"The offer is there whenever you want it," Stanford replied. He put his arm around Henley, and she laid her head on his shoulder.

"Where are the others?" she asked as the pub doors opened and two young women walked in, dragging the winter winds with them.

"Eastie is finishing up a call, Ezra said he'll be in here in ten minutes, Joanna has taken herself home for her old man's birthday and Ramouter is on his way."

"You didn't ask Pellacia?"

"No, he's behaving like a twat," Stanford said firmly.

Henley didn't disagree. "I'm trying to give him a bly because he just wants the job done. There's a lot of pressure on him. He's running the SCU on his own and he has to fight to get a single penny from the bosses."

"Why are you being so protective?" said Stanford, sipping his pint. "It's almost as if you feel guilty about something."

"Oh look," Henley said, grateful to see Ramouter walking into the pub, followed by Eastwood and Ezra.

"You got lucky." Stanford grinned. "But you're not getting out of it that easily."

"My auntie Maureen went to your victim's church," said Ezra as he wiped away his foam mustache left by his pint of Guinness. "She called me after she saw the news earlier."

"What did she say?" asked Henley. "Is she a regular?"

"Nah. She's always looking for spiritual enlightenment. She was a Buddhist for about five minutes last summer."

"But what did she say about the church?" Henley repeated, nudging him with her elbow.

"She said that it was the first church that she's been in where they handed out the cash card reader with the collection plate."

"Are you serious?" Stanford asked, tapping his own debit card against his empty pint glass.

"Auntie Maureen said that she was just going to put in a couple of quid, which is a lot coming from her because she's stingy, but people were putting in twenty and fifty quid notes or paying by card."

"Why is that such a big deal?" Ramouter asked. He looked around at the surprised faces of his colleagues.

"Haven't you ever been to a normal Catholic or Anglican church? People just throw some change in the collection plate or, at a push, a fiver," said Eastwood. She grabbed Stanford's card from his hand. "You're so lazy and annoying," she said as she stood up and went to the bar.

"I haven't been to the gurdwara for ages," said Ramouter.

"What's a gurdwara?" asked Ezra.

"The Sikh temple. We give offerings like food, and you can give money, but no one is going around with a card machine. I don't recall any cash being found in the church. It could have been stolen by whoever killed Annan."

"I don't think so," said Henley, lowering her voice. "Stabbing someone forty-eight times is a bit extreme if all you want to do is steal some cash. This killing seems motivated and it would explain why the young man upstairs was undisturbed if the killer's only target was Caleb Annan. We just need to work out *what* that motivation is. Anyway, how did it go with the board members?"

"Gordon and Kristen Palmer. They were fine. Completely clueless, but fine," Ramouter replied flatly.

"What happened?" Henley asked, noting the dark look that crossed Ramouter's face. There was a subtle shift in the atmosphere when he spoke. In the six months that they'd been working together, Henley had learned to recognize the transitions in Ramouter's moods, but the sight of him visibly holding on to something that was gnawing away at him was new to her.

"What did I miss?" Eastwood asked as she returned with their drinks.

"It's nothing," Ramouter said, taking his pint from Eastwood.

"There's clearly something going on," Henley insisted. "You look upset, and I doubt that meeting the Palmers would upset you."

"There's definitively something," Ezra whispered to Stanford.

"Fine," Ramouter said, his voice low and angry. "A pair of overzealous PCs tried to stop and search me."

"You!" said Ezra. "They stopped you?"

"Aye."

"And you're just being polite. By overzealous, you mean racist," Ezra replied matter-of-factly. "What did they come out with? I bet you matched the description of someone acting suspiciously."

"Apparently, there was a robbery in the area."

"It's London. When aren't there robberies?"

"I'm sorry about that, mate," Stanford said.

"What are you apologizing for?" asked Ezra. "You're not an idiot like some of them out there. I've quit calling it a stop and search and renamed it a stop and dash because that's what they do. Dash you over the car hood. Twenty-six times and counting so far. They even tried when I was coming into work one morning. To a police station. You should have seen their faces when Rhimes pulled up."

"Did he make them apologize?" Henley asked as the table grew silent.

"Of course he did," Ezra said with a smile. "Bunch of muppets."

"So, are you going to do something about it?" Henley asked.

"I've been thinking about it," said Ramouter.

"Just don't think about it. Do it," said Henley.

"It's not an easy thing to do; grassing up your colleagues."

"Those two who stopped you are not your colleagues," Stanford said sternly. "You don't owe them anything. We're your colleagues—actually, no, we're your friends."

"Hey, Ramouter. I think that's Stanford's way of telling you that he likes you," said Ezra.

"Wind your neck in," Stanford said affectionately. "All I'm saying is that Ramouter doesn't owe them idiots anything."

"Do you remember when I got stopped?" Henley asked Stanford, who pursed his lips at the memory.

"You'd just passed the sergeant's exam," Stanford said.

"Yep, and I'd just spent four hours in Tottenham with witnesses watching ID parades when I got stopped about a hundred meters from the station." Henley could still picture the faces of the officers who stopped her. "Firstly, they accused me of driving without due care and attention. And then they said that my car was associated with firearms."

"Did you tell them that you were a police officer?" Eastwood asked, unable to cover up the look of shock on her face.

"Of course," answered Henley. "They then accused me of attempting to impersonate a police officer. I was furious and told them to check my name and my car details."

"It was the Lewisham CID pool car," said Stanford with a grin.

"Absolute bastards. They gave me a weak-arsed apology and drove off."

"Did you put a complaint in?" Ramouter asked.

"No," Henley replied. She could still feel the hot flush of shame after all these years. "I should have done but it was that fear of rocking the boat. Could you imagine the labels that they would have at me? A black female detective sergeant accusing two white male police officers of racial profiling? They would have called me angry, oversensitive, precious and a grass. Who would want that?"

"Bloody hell. No pressure on Ramouter then," Ezra said as he dramatically slammed his empty pint glass on the table. "So, are you going to do it?"

"Aye. I think that I will," said Ramouter.

"Good. So, back to the Palmers," Henley said in an effort to bring back some normality to the evening.

"Kristen and Gordon Palmer did say something interesting," said Ramouter. "They mentioned that Caleb and Serena were the only ones who had keys to the building. None of the other board members have a set."

"Why is that an issue?" asked Stanford.

"Because in her first statement, and to us, Uliana said that she had her own set of keys," Henley explained.

"It may be nothing, but why would you give keys to someone that you've only known for a few months, even if they are the cleaner, when everyone else has to be buzzed in?" asked Ramouter.

"Maybe she's more than just the cleaner," said Ezra.

"What do you mean?" asked Henley.

"It's just common sense. The majority of people who were actually in charge of the church weren't allowed into their own building unless their pastor let them in," Ezra continued, "but he's going to trust someone who he's only known for five minutes with a set of keys just so she can run a Hoover around the place a couple of days a week? Nah."

"Maybe, and I'm playing devil's advocate, Caleb Annan just wanted to make life easier for her," said Eastwood.

"But he hasn't given her the run of the place," said Ezra confidently. "It's all about control, innit. He gives her a set of keys and makes her feel that she has the power but really he's the one pulling all the strings."

"He's got a point," Henley said as she sat back.

"Thank you, boss," Ezra replied proudly. "All you need to do now is work out why Caleb Annan would want to be pulling his cleaner's strings."

"So, you thought that you would go straight to my dad and make it impossible for me to say no?" asked Henley as Rob walked into their bedroom. She stripped off her clothes and threw them into the clothes' basket.

"What are you talking about?" Rob replied.

"The cemetery. I told you that I didn't want to go but you went to my dad."

"It wasn't like that. We were just chatting, and he said that he wanted to go."

"You could have spoken to me first," Henley said in a low voice, not wanting to wake up Emma. "Have you told Simon? Because Dad's under the impression that he's coming as well."

"No, I haven't," Rob admitted. "But I've spoken to Mia and—"

"Well, that's great. Give her your dirty work to do."

Henley sat on the edge of the bed and waited for the anger to dissipate.

"Not everything is about you, Anj. You have an entire family who have lost your mum. Even Mia agreed that you need to—"

"Don't talk to my sister-in-law about what you think I need. You have no idea," Henley said, storming into the bathroom. She turned on the shower and let the room fill with steam as she sat on the toilet seat. Henley waited to cry and let go of the grief that felt like a permanent dead weight in her gut, but the tears never came.

Stepping into the shower, she caught sight of her reflection in the mirror. She could see that the fine laughter lines on the right side of her mouth had deepened. The small scar on her cheek almost looked like an arrow pointing to the dark circles under her eyes. Henley allowed the scalding water to wash over her. She needed to feel anything else but anger and to calm the revolving door of thoughts in her head. All of her frustrations were because of the men in her life. She was angry that she couldn't have done more for Ramouter. It wasn't good enough for her to just give advice, but she wasn't sure what else she could do to help him combat the inherent prejudices that were still so prevalent in their personal and professional lives. Henley was also angry that she still wanted to reach out to Pellacia in this moment, who had always been there for her in moments of crisis. And then there was her husband. Henley couldn't shake off the feeling that Rob's determination for her to visit her mother's grave was an attempt to exert some form of control over her. She knew that this was always the first step toward coercive behavior, and that scared her. She needed to find a way to regain control over her marriage and herself.

17

They'd told her that the blindfold would help to calm her, but there was no peace. She was in pain. She'd welcomed the darkness when they'd first wrapped the blindfold around her eyes, but her tears and the salty sweat that had poured from her scalp had dampened the cheap material. She had twisted and turned so much against the dirty pillow that the blindfold had loosened and now her left eye was exposed. The yellow crust in the corner of her eyes had almost welded them shut. She could feel her thin eyelashes tearing from the roots as she forced her eye open, but still couldn't adjust to the darkness. She struggled to follow the flickering shadows that had been cast by the candles in the corner of the room.

Every muscle in her body was stiff and there was the overpowering stench of soured milk that wafted up from the stained sheets underneath. All she'd needed was help.

Why aren't they helping me? Why are they hurting me?

There was a fluttering of panic in her chest as she felt something scurry across her legs and then bite into the sores on her calves. She tried to move but the rope cut deeper into her swollen ankles.

"Where is he?"

She tried to turn toward the voices but the chips of bone from the fracture in her neck pressed and pinched against the nerve in her spinal cord. She cried out, her voice hoarse, as a sharp pain like red-hot needles ran down her back and across her buttocks. She couldn't stop her body from contorting as though she was possessed. Her weakened muscles couldn't hold back the torrent of watery excrement that escaped from her bowels. The searing pain locked her muscles, and her body was fixed like a broken puppet that had been set in cement.

"Oh my God. It's disgusting. Look at this."

She tried to scream "Get away from me! Don't touch me!" when she heard the voice that penetrated her nightmares. The voice was always present. Haunting and threatening her even when she was alone.

"I told you to wait for me. You shouldn't have started without me."

"Oh stop. You act as if you're the only one who's capable. It would be too late if we waited any longer."

Her skin pricked with sharp goose bumps as the window behind her head was cracked open and the harsh air swept over her almost naked body. She couldn't fight against the hand that gripped her jaw. Another ripple of pain traveled down the right side of her body as her head was turned to the left.

"You will thank me."

The blindfold was pulled back over her eyes. She didn't fight against it. She wanted the darkness, but it didn't stop her from feeling what happened next.

18

Seven o'clock on a Wednesday morning and Marcia Whittaker stood in the kitchen with a bottle of vodka in one hand, a box of cranberry juice in the other and year eleven's mock history exam papers on the counter. She had tried to drink the coffee that she'd made earlier, but it wouldn't settle in her stomach. She held up the bottle of the vodka to the light. It was a liter which she had bought on Sunday on her way back from church. Marcia emptied what was left into her glass of cranberry juice. She pushed aside the guilt and there was a feeling of relief as she drank, avoiding her reflection in the sparkling glass of the kitchen cupboard.

"Right. Pull it together," Marcia said out loud. She rinsed out the glass and placed it on the draining board. Then she picked up the rest of the bottle of Smirnoff and emptied it into her glass, cringing as she threw the empty bottle into the bin and heard it crash against the two empty wine bottles. She knew that she was drinking too much, but what else could she do? She needed peace. Even if the peace was only temporary.

She walked barefooted into the living room and turned the television on. Avoiding the photographs on the mantelpiece,

Marcia turned the volume up as the national news ended and the local news began. The image of a bruised young man, covered in tubes but still identifiable, filled the screen. The newsreader appealed for anyone who knew the young man, who was currently in intensive care at Lewisham Hospital, to come forward. Marcia's screams sounded alien to her ears. The glass fell out of her hand and splintered into sharp shards on the floor. She didn't feel a thing as she walked toward the television and broken pieces of glass pierced the flesh on her feet. Marcia screamed again and fell to her knees and began to pray.

It was him.

19

Pellacia sat impatiently on a chair outside the borough commander's office in Lewisham police station. He was unable to push aside the confusion of annoyance and hurt as he reread the text messages on his phone.

Mum's memorial is on Saturday and the SCU will be there.

The invite is open, but I don't think that it would be a good idea for you to be there.

I don't want you to feel excluded, but it will probably feel that way.

That was one thing that he couldn't fault Henley for, her brutal honesty, but he couldn't help himself from reading between the lines. She hadn't said that she didn't want him there, but only that it wouldn't be a good idea. Pellacia couldn't lie to himself. The rejection hurt.

He tried and failed to stifle the yawn as the tiredness itched away at his skin. He hadn't slept through the night once in the past six months. The nightmares of Olivier, carving symbols into his naked chest as he slipped in and out of consciousness, still disturbed his sleep.

The streets were talking loudly about the murder of Pastor Caleb Annan, and the noise had reached the ears of Laura Halifax, the MP for Lewisham and Deptford.

"The last thing I wanted to do was drag you here. Neither of us have time for this," said Chief Superintendent Geraldine Barker, the borough commander for the southeast command unit who had taken over after the sudden resignation of Chief Superintendent Larsen.

"That's all right, ma'am," said Pellacia.

"Please," Barker said dismissively as she pushed back a strand of gray hair and sat on the other side of the small table in her office on the fifth floor of Lewisham police station. "You can save the ma'am for when our *esteemed* MP arrives. She's been making a lot of noise about the progress of your investigation."

"Which one?" asked Pellacia. "We've got two investigations ongoing. The murder of Caleb Annan and the attempted murder of the young man that was found."

"Has he not been identified yet?"

"Not yet, but the appeal went out yesterday so hopefully we'll get a lead by the end of the day."

"Well, I hope that something comes up soon, but that's not the reason for you being here this morning. Laura Halifax only appears to be interested in Caleb Annan."

"The investigation is only two days old. We've got nothing so far except a cold body in the morgue."

"What's DI Henley's line of thinking? Crime of passion? Burglary gone wrong?"

"Well, she's firmly ruled out burglary gone wrong, and I agree with her. Someone being stabbed forty-eight times would suggest a crime of passion, but you know what Anj—sorry, DI Henley, is like. She won't be pressured into going down a particular alleyway if the evidence isn't taking her there and she definitely won't take too kindly to, well, whatever this is," said Pellacia.

"Yes," Barker replied as she checked her watch, "which is why I thought that it was best to keep Henley's attention focused on the investigation instead of—"

Geraldine was interrupted by a soft rapping at the door before it was gently pushed open. Pellacia smoothed down his tie and stood as Laura Halifax was escorted into the room.

"Chief Superintendent Barker," Laura said as she took a seat at the table. "I am grateful for you agreeing to meet me so early. My morning surgery with my constituents starts at nine thirty and I make it a policy of never being late for them."

"That's fine," Barker replied, her tone more clipped and reserved than five minutes earlier. "This is Detective Superintendent Stephen Pellacia."

"You're in charge of the Serial Crime Unit," Laura said as she smiled at Pellacia and shook his hand. "I don't think that I've ever seen you at any of the community policing meetings since I became an MP."

"No, you haven't," Pellacia replied. "Conflicts with the timings."

"Right," Barker cut in. "Pastor Caleb Annan. That's the reason why you're here."

"Yes," said Laura as she opened and pulled out her iPad. "As you're aware, the news about the awful circumstances of Pastor Annan's murder has spread like wildfire, and I'm afraid that the local community, which includes the family of Mr. Annan, have expressed their dissatisfaction."

"Pastor Annan and his family live in Shooters Hill," said Barker. "That area is not part of your constituency."

"You're absolutely right," Laura replied without breaking her smile. "But the Church of Annan the Prophet and a lot of the congregation are in my constituency, and they're not happy. Mrs. Annan especially, and I can't say that I blame them, or her."

Pellacia leaned back in his chair, grateful that he hadn't told Henley about the meeting. She would have been giving sharp and pointed responses. "Mrs. Annan only identified her husband yesterday morning, and an official statement was made by Inspector Henley later that afternoon. We're depending on the local community to help *us* at this early stage."

"What about the witnesses? Surely they could have given you some headway into the investigation?" Laura asked.

"What witness are you referring to?" Pellacia asked cautiously.

"The report said that a woman found Mr. Annan and that there was another man on the scene. I understand that he was found in the church by the senior investigating officer and now he's at Lewisham Hospital."

"Well, firstly, the woman was not a witness to Caleb Annan's murder, and it would have been impossible for the young man who was found to have played any role in Mr. Annan's murder."

"But—"

"I'm sorry, but I'm not prepared to go into any further details about the status of the Annan investigation," Pellacia said, keeping his voice steady. "All you need to know at this stage is that until the evidence tells me otherwise, that young man is a victim and we're doing what we can to identify him."

"See, that's the problem. No, sorry, problem is the wrong word," said Laura in a tone of voice that indicated she wasn't prepared to sit back and play games. "That's the concern."

"Why would you be concerned about the young man, a victim, being identified?" asked Pellacia. He shifted in his seat.

"Well, it appears to be the focus of your entire investigation," said Laura as she leaned forward and helped herself to a cup of coffee. "Mrs. Annan is concerned, deeply concerned, that not enough is being done for her husband, since her—"

"So Mrs. Annan called you and complained," Barker interrupted.

"I've known the family for many years," Laura explained.

"And due to my position, it was completely understandable that she would come to me."

"What exactly is Mrs. Annan's issue?" Pellacia asked, locking eyes with Laura.

The smile disappeared from Laura's face as she took a sip of her coffee and wrinkled her nose in disgust, turning her gaze toward Barker. "Can you imagine how she felt last night, hours after identifying her husband's body, when she turned on the local news and opened her papers and was literally bombarded with images of the young man who was found in the church, and requests for information, and absolutely nothing about her husband? Her *murdered* husband. I'm not here to tell you how to do your jobs…"

"Of course you're not," Pellacia muttered under his breath as he watched Barker sip her own coffee slowly.

"What she's going through is traumatic enough, but to feel that your husband's case, a murder investigation no less, is secondary or not deemed important—"

"It's been two days and we've kept Mrs.—"

"There's been one statement. Only one," said Laura, turning her attention to Pellacia. "And that's not enough. Pastor Annan was a respected member of the community and his family, and my constituents would like something done. I'm actually surprised that Inspector Henley is not here."

"She's busy investigating a murder and an attempted murder," Barker snapped. "Look. Let's cut the nonsense. What exactly are you suggesting?"

"I'm suggesting that you, the local police and the SCU need to think very carefully about not inflaming tensions in the community."

"What tensions? It's been two days. Look, Laura, this isn't a black-and-white thing. This is an 'I've got an unidentified half-dead man in a hospital bed who was found in a locked room in your very dead pastor's church,' sort of thing," said Barker.

"I didn't suggest racial tensions," Laura replied, unflinching.

"I'm just stating facts. That there's a clear and obvious disparity, even at this early stage, in how you're conducting your investigations, and Mrs. Annan is distraught."

"I think that's exactly what you're suggesting," said Barker. "That Detective Superintendent Pellacia and the Serial Crime Unit are giving priority to the unidentified man because he happens to be white, and Mr. Annan was a black man."

"A black man who had made six complaints to the Independent Office for Police Conduct because he'd been stopped a total of thirty-five times in the past three years. Annan made complaints to the IOPC, and absolutely nothing was done about it," said Laura.

"Are you seriously suggesting that my team are not fully dedicated to the investigation because of a complaint that he made to the IOPC?"

"I have not suggested that at all," said Laura. "But what's distressing for Mrs. Annan is that DI Henley seems more concerned about the boy than someone from her own community, and—"

"Do not make the mistake in thinking that DI Henley is not committed or is biased in any way. She would not give preferential treatment because of race." Pellacia tried to keep his anger at a simmer. He felt a responsibility to protect Henley in her absence. There was no way that she would have put up with what Laura Halifax was insinuating.

"I won't have that at all," agreed Barker. "Those suggestions do more harm to the community than your perceptions of how you think the SCU are conducting their investigations."

"I'm just telling you the concerns of my constituents and of the Annan family," said Laura with a look of genuine surprise. "A family man has been brutally murdered and the Annans feel unsupported."

"The Annans have the support of a family liaison officer and direct contact to DI Henley," said Barker.

"But we don't have media exposure," explained Laura. "Instead it's being given to a young white man, like always."

Pellacia wondered how passionate Laura Halifax would be about media exposure if she knew that Caleb Annan had been arrested for rape.

"You of all people should know how both fickle and dangerous the media can be," said Barker sternly. "Especially when it comes to a man like Annan."

"Look, I'm not here trying to throw my weight around."

"You could have fooled me," said Barker.

"And this isn't even a matter of politics," Laura said with a straight face.

"Everything is politics," said Barker. "I have absolutely no issue with us working together and doing the best for everyone involved but I won't allow any of my officers or any investigation to be used as a political football."

Barker stood up, signaling that the meeting was over.

"I'm hoping that we'll see you at the next community meeting," Laura said to Pellacia as she handed him her card. "Hopefully DI Henley will attend too."

Chance would be a fine thing. Henley will hate you, Pellacia said to himself.

"My personal mobile number is on the back of the card," said Laura as she gathered her belongings. "We'd just like to see more done. Visibly done and not just a passing soundbite on the six o'clock news."

"You're going to have to keep an eye on her," said Barker as she stood in her office doorway and watched Laura Halifax being escorted to the elevators by Barker's assistant. "She's the type of woman who would politicize a criminal investigation for her own advantage. Maybe it would be a good idea to introduce her to Henley, just to appease her."

"I'm telling you now, ma'am, that Henley will not be jumping up and down about that proposal," said Pellacia as he picked up his coat from the back of the chair.

"I know, but let's face facts. Relations between us and the local community are tense at the best of times. I remember what it was like being a mixed-race Asian woman as a young constable and being called all sorts of names. It's hard enough building and keeping the trust of people when all they're seeing on the news is the worst of us."

"I'll talk to Henley," Pellacia replied wearily.

"Good, and see what you can do about organizing a press conference. The sooner the better."

20

"Baby girl, Mummy is so sorry that you're not well, but I've got to work," Henley said as she tried to peel Emma's small arms from around her neck.

"No," Emma wailed as she squeezed tighter. "Don't go to work."

"Daddy will be here."

"I don't want Daddy. I want you."

"Rob," Henley pleaded as she glanced at the clock on the living room wall. It had already gone 9 a.m. and she should have been sitting at her desk at the SCU. "I'm going to be late. In fact, I'm already late."

"You heard Ems. She doesn't want me. She wants you." It was the most that Rob had said to her since last night. He picked up the remote control and turned the channel over to the financial news. "And you're not the only one who has to go to work—I've got a meeting, with the newspaper's new business editor, this afternoon in Holborn. Can't you take the day off?"

"A meeting. You didn't mention anything about a meeting last night."

"That's because you were too busy biting my head off last night."

Henley pursed her lips to stop herself from swearing as Emma tightened her grip around her mum's neck.

"I'm at the start of an investigation," said Henley. She managed to prize Emma off her, placed her on the sofa and covered her with a blanket. "I just can't take a day off when I feel like it."

"But you expect me to give up my work just to suit you," said Rob as he picked up the cushion that Emma had kicked to the floor. "You don't think that me not turning up to meetings doesn't affect my career as a journalist? Or do you think that my work is not as important as what you do?"

"Whenever have I said that to you?" Henley snapped back. "It's not a bloody competition."

"You can keep telling yourself that, but I'm the one who's always giving something up because Ems is sick or there's a delivery or the plumber is coming round. I told you last night, that it's not all about you. Try being a proper mum for once. I've got to go."

Henley was stunned and at a loss for words as Rob walked out of the room. Luna barked in protest as the front door slammed shut. She wasn't sure if the hot tears that had started to fall were because of anger or Rob's cutting questioning of her ability to be a mother.

"Mummy," Emma whined. She jumped off the sofa and clung onto Henley's legs.

Henley groaned as she wiped away the tears from her face, picked Emma up and pressed her palm against her forehead. "You've got a bit of temperature, baby. Looks like it's going to be just me and you today."

"And Uncle Paul."

"No, Uncle Paul will be at work, but we'll give him a call later. Let's change your clothes; you're all clammy."

"Mummy."

"Yes, baby."

"My tummy hurts."

"Oh God," Henley said as Emma threw up all over her chest.

★ ★ ★

"Where's Henley?" Ramouter asked, checking the time on his phone. "It's after ten. It's not like her to—"

"Emma is ill," said Joanna, the SCU's office manager, as she dumped a file on his desk. "I'm sure that you'll be able to cope without her for one day."

"I don't need my hand held, Joanna," Ramouter snapped back.

"Oi, watch the tone," Pellacia said, walking into the office and taking off his scarf.

"How did it go with the chief?" Joanna asked. "And her royal highness, Laura Halifax?"

"Who's Laura Halifax?" asked Ramouter as the sound of the intercom began to buzz.

"Local MP who wants us to do more with the Caleb Annan murder investigation. How did you know that I was meeting Laura Halifax?" Pellacia asked.

Joanna tutted. "What don't I know about what's going on in this job. So, what did the right honorable MP for Lewisham and Deptford have to say for herself?" Joanna's voice was dripping with sarcasm.

"You don't like her?" Pellacia asked.

"Nope. One of those women who thinks that all she's got to do is flash a bit of leg and she can get what she wants. If that doesn't work, then she'll fling her weight around. I've heard some stories."

"Of course you have."

"And I bet that when it came to you, she fluttered her eyelashes and said that she was protecting her constituents."

Pellacia's face reddened with embarrassment.

"What exactly does she want us to be doing? And no disrespect to the victim," Ramouter said carefully, remembering Henley's words to show empathy. "What has this murder investigation got to do with this MP? Do you know how many people were murdered in her borough last week?"

"I'm sure that you're going to tell me," said Pellacia.

"Five murders in the past seven days," said Ramouter. "So why is she so concerned about this one?"

"She knows the family and she's concerned about inciting racial tensions because right now it looks as though we're focusing all our energies on the case of an unidentified, still breathing white man and not a murdered black man."

"What?" Ramouter exclaimed. The intercom buzzer went off again. "But that's ridiculous."

"For God's sake. Don't all rush at once," said Joanna as the intercom buzzed again. She grabbed her shawl and walked out of the office.

"I know it's ridiculous, but there's the danger of it looking that way right now," Pellacia replied as he walked off toward the kitchen. "We need to make some progress with the investigation."

"What is it?" Ramouter asked as Joanna reappeared. He saw the look of bewilderment on her face. "What's happened?"

"There's a girl downstairs," said Joanna, each word followed by the small, misty clouds of her breath as the temperature dropped in the room. "She says that the man that was found tied up in the church is her brother."

A young woman sat shivering in a room that was previously used for interviewing vulnerable witnesses. Victims of sexual assault and children had been invited to sit comfortably on the burgundy sofa, in a warm room, that had been painted blush pink. A reproduced painting of the sun setting over Waterloo Bridge hung on the walls, while the red lights of the three-camera video blinked repeatedly as they told their story. The walls were now covered with the gray film of neglect and the stained blue carpet tiles had lifted at the corners. Ramouter placed a milky cup of tea, with two sugars as per her request, on the chipped coffee table and switched on the fan heater.

The woman pulled her gray bobble hat off her head and shook out a mass of unruly auburn hair as the heating in the building finally kicked in. She unhooked a strand that was caught in her silver hoop earring. Ramouter guessed that the woman was in her late twenties. There were dark circles under her red and puffy eyes. She looked as though she'd spent the past twenty-four hours crying. The room was now warm but with a strange smell of old carpet and the acrid scent of burning rubber, as the cheap fan heater worked overtime.

"I hope that the tea is all right," said Ramouter.

"It's good. You make it like my gran. I saw you on the TV earlier with that other detective. I didn't catch her name."

"Detective Inspector Henley."

"I wasn't sure if the station was even open, when I came here, but I saw that there were lights on."

"Technically, we're not open. I didn't catch your name."

"Amy. Amy Whittaker. Brandon is my brother."

Amy placed her mug down and pulled out her mobile phone from her bag. "This is Brandon. My little brother. He hates it when I call him little, but he is."

"How old is he?" Ramouter asked. He took the phone from Amy. It was him; the boy who had been tied to a bed in a rat-infested room and left for dead. He didn't look that much younger than Amy. He was leaning back on a deckchair in a garden. A Scottish terrier sat on his lap. Ramouter zoomed in on his green eyes and his tanned skin. He recognized the shape of his mouth and his nose. He had a bright smile. He had the same unruly hair as Amy.

"He's twenty-three. Twenty-four in May," said Amy. "I went to the hospital first thing this morning. The nurse in the hospital wouldn't let me see him. She was so rude. She said that I could be anyone." Amy sniffed and pulled a creased tissue from her pocket. "I came as I soon as I found out. I only saw the paper this morning. I didn't even get a chance to brush my hair, I just got dressed and came here. I don't want you to think that I don't care."

"Why would I think that?" Ramouter said as he handed the phone back and picked up his notebook.

"Because the paper said that he was found on Monday and he's been alone in the hospital for two days."

"Don't worry about that, but I do have to ask if you have anything to prove Brandon's identity and yours. I know that you say that you're his sister, but I need to be sure."

There were a few seconds of silence as the fan heater whirled. "I suppose that people will try all sorts," said Amy. She pulled out her purse from her bag. "I've got my driving license, but it's got my old address on it. I haven't got round to changing it."

"That's fine," Ramouter said as he took the license.

"I've also got this," said Amy, opening up her bag again to pull out an A4-sized envelope. "It's Brandon's birth certificate and his passport. It's expired. He left it at my flat the last time that he visited. He was supposed to send it off to renew but he can be so scatty, sometimes."

Ramouter took the passport and opened it to the photograph page. There he was again. He looked as though he was trying very hard to stop the grin from spreading to his face.

"Can you just give me a sec? I'm just going to step outside and make a very quick call."

Ramouter closed the door behind him to stop the heat from escaping. He called Joanna at her desk and asked her to check if Amy Whittaker was who she said she was, and to also run a search on the missing persons' database to see if Brandon had been reported missing.

"Nope. No sign of him," Joanna had confirmed. "I even did a Google, Facebook and Twitter search for anyone asking if he had been seen. Nothing."

Ramouter took a moment before he went back into the interview room. Amy was who she said she was, but why hadn't she reported her little brother missing? She looked innocent enough and genuine, but she could just be covering her tracks. It wouldn't be the first time that someone had played the role of distraught family member who pleaded for the police to find the person who'd killed their family member, only for it to be revealed that they were the ones who strangled them to death.

"Is that the most recent photograph that you have of your brother?" Ramouter asked Amy when he returned to the room.

"Yeah, we had a party for my granddad's eightieth birthday at his house in Eastbourne back in the summer. That was at the end of July. I went traveling in August and came back in December to start my new job."

"When was the last time that you spoke or saw him?"

"It was a couple of days after Christmas. Maybe the 27th."

"That's more than six weeks ago."

"I don't live with him. I live in Leytonstone."

"And where does Brandon live?"

"In Isleworth with my parents."

"You can probably tell from my accent that I'm not from around here," said Ramouter. "Where's Isleworth?"

"The furthest part of West London," said Amy. "It's an absolute mission to get there, which is why it doesn't make any sense that my brother was found in Deptford. I don't understand." She pulled her sleeves over her hands and folded her arms. "It doesn't make any sense. What was he doing there?"

"That's what we're trying to find out," Ramouter said gently.

"What happened to him? The paper said that he was found in a church."

"That's correct."

Ramouter puzzled over how he would explain the conditions in which Henley found Brandon. It was a quality that he admired in Henley. Her ability to adapt her approach to each witness so that they didn't feel like another cog in the investigation wheel. Henley could make you feel that she was 100 percent invested and cared about you, and made it crystal clear that she was the one who was in control.

"What happened to Brandon?" Amy asked again, but more insistently.

Ramouter instinctively knew that he would have to tread carefully, but it wouldn't help to leave any details out. "Inspector Henley and I attended the scene because a body had been found in the Church of Annan the Prophet. Have you heard of it?"

"No, never. So, someone found Brandon?"

"Not exactly. The body that was found belonged to Caleb Annan. You may have read that in the newspaper article. Caleb Annan was murdered."

"You don't think that Brandon did it. He couldn't. He—"

"No, it would have been impossible for Brandon to be responsible. DI Henley found Brandon locked up in a room," Ramouter explained.

"A room. What sort of room?"

"It was a room in the back of a storage cupboard in the church building. We don't know how long he'd been there."

"Did that man… Caleb. Did he hurt Brandon? He had so many tubes in the photograph."

"We're still trying to find out what exactly happened, but your brother did have numerous injuries and was malnourished."

The tears started to flow freely from Amy's eyes as she wiped her nose with her barely useable tissue.

"Sorry, I'm sorry," she said.

"No, you've got nothing to be sorry for," Ramouter said as he rummaged in his pockets for tissues. Henley would have been prepared, he said to himself.

"How long was he there for?"

"We're not sure," Ramouter admitted. "But he was definitely there for a significant period of time. Maybe as long as six weeks."

Amy's face paled, but Ramouter could clearly see the anger in her green eyes. Then, just as quickly, it was replaced with an eerie composure that came when someone had just connected the dots.

"They lied to me," she said.

"Who lied to you?" Ramouter asked.

"My parents. They're the ones who lied."

21

"Brandon hasn't been well for a long time," said Amy sadly as the radiators rattled with the sound of trapped air. "He started self-harming when he was fourteen, and he was fifteen when he first tried to kill himself. Mum found him lying in his own sick in the bathroom. He first tried with pills and then he tried to hang himself."

"What made him want to take his own life?" Ramouter asked gently.

"He was bullied in school but I'm not sure if that's what started the anxiety and depression," Amy said. "The doctors referred him to CAMHS—"

"That's the Children and Adult Mental Health Services?" said Ramouter.

Amy nodded. "He had a really good community psychiatric nurse. He was put on antidepressants and had CBT."

"What's CBT?"

"Cognitive Behavioral Therapy."

"I see. Did it work?"

"Yeah, it did, but then we moved to a new house when Brandon was nineteen and his therapy stopped. His GP was registered in one borough, but he was living in a different borough and then he started uni. It became a nightmare because the local authorities were arguing over who was financially responsible."

"So, he slipped through the system?"

"Completely. He was fine for a little while but then in his final year of uni, Brandon started hearing voices and seeing things. He was convinced once that there were spiders living in his hair. He was scared. I was scared. One night I got a call from Brandon's housemate—he had broken into the neighbor's house and stolen a dressing gown, of all things. They found him half an hour later, running around naked in the street. Luckily, they didn't arrest him. Brandon was diagnosed with schizophrenia and a psychotic disorder. He was in hospital for about a month. They changed his medication, and he was having regular therapy. He left and somehow managed to graduate with a first in history and then he went back to Mum and Dad's. I say somehow, but Brandon has always been very smart. He was one of those annoying kids who could mess around all term and then still pass all his exams."

"You said that he went back to his parents'. When did he go back?"

"Last June. It's the same address that's on my driving license. He went back to save money but then he got ill again. My parents told me that he'd stopped taking his medication."

"Did you believe them?"

"No," Amy said as she put her coat back on. The temperature seemed to be dropping in the room.

"Why didn't you believe them? I mean, if he'd stopped taking his medication then it would make sense that he would become ill."

"Brandon was obsessive about taking his medication," said Amy. "He hated that feeling of not being in control. I can't believe that he would have stopped taking it. When we last spoke, he said that he was going to the doctors about his prescription, because he didn't like the side effects, but he wouldn't have just stopped taking them. He knew better than that."

"What do you think happened?" asked Ramouter.

"A couple of months ago he said that Dad had started talking about people being misdiagnosed and treatment resistant."

"Treatment resistant?"

"Some stupid theory about someone's body being too strong for medication. He also mentioned something about Dad looking into alternative treatments."

"Did you speak to your dad about what Brandon had told you?"

"No, we weren't exactly on the best of terms, my parents and me."

"You said that your parents lied to you. What exactly did they lie about?"

"I haven't heard from Brandon since Christmas. I knew that he was ill, but he would always talk to me, even if it was absolute nonsense, so I called my mum and dad. I asked to speak to Brandon on FaceTime, but my mum told me that they had taken him to a private hospital for treatment. Which was a shock, as my dad is a tight-fisted git at the best of times."

"Did they say what hospital?"

"The Webster Clinic in St. Albans. I called but they gave me the client confidentiality rubbish. All Mum and Dad said was how well he was doing at the hospital and to keep praying for him. I should have known better. I let him down. I'm his big sister. I'm supposed to look out for him."

"When did you last speak to your parents?"

"Last week, and they said the same thing." Anger flashed across Amy's face. "I called them and asked how Brandon was. Dad said that he had seen him earlier in the afternoon, but that was a lie, because you're saying he was locked in that room for six weeks?"

"What do you think happened to your brother?"

"All I know is that it's something to do with my parents," said Amy. "They've always been religious, but it was more only going to church for Christmas, Easter, christenings, weddings, funerals and to make sure that we got into the right schools."

"Are you religious?"

"I believe in God, but I couldn't tell you the last time that I went to church. My parents became born-again Christians, and I don't mean the happy-clappy songs of praise type."

"Did your parents try and convince you to go?" asked Ramouter.

"Not at all. That would have been a complete waste of time. I haven't lived at home since I was eighteen. But as I said, my parents have always been religious, and my dad had a tendency to get a bit preachy about certain topics, including Brandon's mental health."

"Was there anything that he said that caused you concern?"

"Only that the doctor didn't know what he was doing; but he always said that."

"When did they become born-again?"

"They started going to a new church in Acton last May. It had to be my dad's idea. My mum doesn't know how to make a decision," Amy said bitterly.

"Did Brandon go to this church with them?"

"Not as far as I know, but I wouldn't have been surprised if they'd managed to convince him to go. Brandon is not much of a fighter. He doesn't do well with confrontation. He would have gone with them just to keep the peace."

"Do you know the name of the church?"

"No, but what I do know is that it wasn't long before they were both saying that mental illnesses were man-made constructs and a vehicle for pharmaceutical companies to make money out of people who have not accepted Jesus as their personal Lord and Savior."

"So, what exactly did they think was wrong with your brother?"

"You wouldn't believe me if I told you," Amy replied as she looked down at the specks of dust on the carpet.

"If it goes some way to explaining why your brother was locked up and abused in a church, then you need to tell us."

Ramouter slammed his mouth shut. If Henley had been in the room, she would have given him one of her looks.

"You never said that he'd been abused," Amy said frantically, standing up. "The photograph in the newspaper... I thought that he'd been in the accident, but you're saying that—"

"I'm sorry," he said. "I didn't mean for it to sound so hard."

"I want to see my brother. I can't be here. I need to see him."

"Amy, I'm really sorry. I really am," said Ramouter. "Why don't you just sit back down and tell me what your parents thought was wrong with Brandon?"

Amy eyed Ramouter suspiciously.

"We just want to find out what happened to your brother," Ramouter said softly. "He's not in a position to tell us, so whatever you tell me, I promise you, I will take it seriously."

"Will you?" Amy asked as she remained standing.

"Try me."

Amy sat back and took a deep breath. "They believed that the voices that he was hearing was because he had neglected his faith. They believed that the devil had taken over."

"She told you what?" Henley said over the phone as she sat on the living room floor watching Emma play.

"Possessed," said Ramouter. "She told me that her parents believed that Brandon—"

"Is that his name? Brandon?"

"Aye. Brandon Christopher Whittaker."

Henley felt a small sense of relief at the realization that the boy in the room now had a name. "Did she actually use that word—'possessed'?"

"Well, not that exact word," Ramouter admitted. "But I think the words 'the devil has taken over' is close enough."

"Shit," Henley said.

"Mummy, bad word," Emma squealed.

"She sounds better," said Ramouter.

"If she hadn't thrown up all over me, I would have been

convinced that she'd been putting it on. So, do we have contact details for the parents?"

"Aye. Marcia and Patrick Whittaker. They live in Isleworth and there's nothing known, other than the fact that Marcia is a teacher and Patrick works in marketing."

"Isleworth? Do you have any idea how far that is from Deptford?"

"I do now. Seventeen miles, door to door. You might as well take your passport."

"So, how on earth did Brandon end up in a back room in Deptford, all the way from Isleworth?"

"No idea, and the sister is just as clueless."

"Where is she? The sister?" Henley asked as her phone beeped with the arrival of a text message.

"Still here. I left her with Ezra. I thought that it would be better than having her freezing to death downstairs."

"What is she like?"

"She's nice, upset and confused. She's desperate to see her brother, so I said that I'll take her to the hospital. Is there any chance that you could meet us?"

"Not one. Not unless Rob's meeting is cut short."

"No problem. I'll check in with you later," said Ramouter, and he ended the call.

"You, madam, have really messed up my day," Henley said as she watched Emma play with a puzzle, dressed in her Spider-Man pajamas and a pink glittery tutu.

"Phone," Emma shouted out as her cell beeped with a text alert.

"I know, I know," Henley said. She read the text from Pellacia. "You have got to be fucking joking."

"Mummy, that's a bad word."

"I am so sorry, angel."

Annan Press Conference. 4:30. Lewisham PS. No excuses. Be there!!!

22

Henley watched as the reporters' credentials were checked, their bodies searched, and they finally took their seats in the briefing room. Callum O'Brien, the reporter who had a penchant for possessing information that he shouldn't have, had taken up his seat in the front row. The cameras and microphones were poised at the table. A civilian officer brought in another chair to join the three empty ones at the table.

"You don't look too impressed, guv." Eastwood joined her in the small corridor.

"I'm not," Henley replied without bothering to hide her annoyance as she closed the door to the briefing room.

"How's your little girl? She must have been really ill for you not to be in."

"She was for most of the morning but now she's bouncing around pretending to be Spider-Man. Anyway, what are you doing here? You hate these things."

"I do, but I wanted to see why the boss was making us all jump through hoops to make Serena Annan happy."

Henley didn't get an opportunity to respond as the security doors swung open and Pellacia walked in with Serena Annan and a woman that Henley didn't recognize. He ushered them into a waiting room.

"Detective Superintendent Pellacia," Henley said loudly as she walked toward him.

"I'll just be a minute," Pellacia told the women, and closed the door behind them. "Inspector."

"This couldn't wait until tomorrow?" Henley spat out. "You had to drag me away from my sick child for a cheap-rate publicity stunt."

Pellacia bit the inside of his cheek and looked away for a moment, and then opened the door into a small consultation room. "Get in there."

Henley hesitated for a moment before walking into the room, and the automatic lights switched on.

"Are you looking for a complaint to be made against you?" said Pellacia as he slammed the door shut.

"By whom? You?"

"Don't be ridiculous. Do you have any idea who that woman is with Serena Annan?"

Henley kept quiet as she tried to calm her temper.

"That's Laura Halifax, the local MP," said Pellacia. "She sits on the Community Policing Panel and she's paying close attention to this investigation. Sometimes it's better to be seen doing something, when—"

"I *am* doing something," Henley said firmly. "Ramouter and I are not sitting in that disgrace of an office freezing our nuts off and doing *nothing*."

"I didn't say that," Pellacia said without softening his tone. "But it's how it looks to the media and to the public. Annan was a high-profile person and—"

"High profile? He was the pastor of a church in Deptford. People only know about him now because he was found dead on his church floor."

"According to Ms. Halifax, the local community is concerned."

"Community?" said Henley sardonically. "Politicians only use the word 'community' when they're talking about black, Asian or LGBTQ people. Actually, anyone who isn't straight and white. So, is that her intention? This politician. To have me up there as her token black woman to make herself look relevant? Don't take me for a fucking idiot. I won't have it."

"No one is taking you for a mug."

Henley took a step back from Pellacia. She knew that it wasn't entirely his fault but that wasn't enough to stop the fury inside of her. She didn't regret anything that she had just said, and she would have been more than prepared to say it in front of the cameras, and Pellacia knew that. The air was so tense in the small room that Henley was beginning to get a headache. "I don't like being used. And I won't have it. Do you understand?"

"I do understand," Pellacia said as he reached out to Henley but then pulled back when he saw the look of resistance on her face.

"So, what exactly is the problem?"

Henley was asking the question, but she already knew the answer. She had known the second that she'd seen the articles in the newspapers and the press release that had been issued. Brandon Whittaker had been written in bold type and Caleb Annan had been given a small paragraph at the bottom of the page. It was a sensitive topic which sat as a burdensome weight on Henley's shoulders. She'd had to fight against the preconceptions that she, as a detective, who was a black woman, was complicit in not making crimes against people of color a priority. Henley felt that she was often fighting two battles, but she would be an idiot to ignore the fact that the media only started paying attention when people were tired of being ignored and stigmatized.

"You know exactly what everyone who doesn't look like me is going to be saying," Pellacia said eventually. "I won't have anyone accusing the SCU of not making the brutal murder of a black man a priority. We're not like that and you know that I'm not—"

"You don't have to say it," Henley interrupted. "You don't have to prove anything to me. I know you, even if the media doesn't."

"I made a commitment to Laura—"

"A commitment to *Laura?*" Henley could almost taste the bitterness in her words. "You're on first-name terms with an MP that you've just met."

"Well, I've learned a lot about her in the short time that we've spent together. She has admirable qualities, and I can't dismiss her professional opinions."

Henley let out a short sardonic burst of laughter. "Admirable qualities?"

"We can't not do this, Anjelica," Pellacia said sternly.

"I'm not saying no, but let's talk about, what would Stanford call it, the optics. Those hacks aren't really interested in who killed the pastor. That isn't the story."

Henley knew what the public would be thinking. It was the same thing that she'd been thinking from the moment she'd opened the door and seen Brandon Whittaker tied to the bed. She thought that Caleb Annan was responsible. Henley couldn't help the feeling of satisfaction as she watched the color drain from Pellacia's face with realization.

"Brandon Whittaker is the story," Henley said. "The only thing that they will be interested in is not who killed Caleb Annan, but why was a twenty-three-year-old man, with mental health issues, left for dead in a locked room in a house of God, and if Caleb Annan was the one who did it?"

"My name is Serena Annan. The wife of Pastor Caleb Annan. My two children have lost their father and our community has lost a leader."

Serena's voice cracked as the tears free-flowed from her eyes and the cameras flashed rapidly.

"Someone is responsible for my husband's murder," Serena continued. "Someone out there knows the person responsible for taking a father away from his children."

Henley held her breath as the cameras continued to click and Laura Halifax handed Serena a tissue.

"Go on," Laura whispered, gently patting Serena's arm.

"My husband was an important and well-respected member of the community," said Serena, looking straight into the camera. "He was dedicated not only to our children but to every single member of the congregation and to those who lived and worked in the area. He didn't discriminate against anyone. All he wanted to do was support and inspire people. It didn't matter if they believed in God or not."

The camera lights flashed in a disorganized sequence as Serena lowered her head. The only sounds in the room was of shutters clicking and Serena crying. Henley was impressed that, despite the stream of tears, Serena's perfect makeup was pristine.

"I'm sorry. I'm so sorry," said Serena as she finally raised her head. "You have no idea how much of a loss this is and how much it hurts. Caleb was one in a million. He loved his family, and I can't believe that he has been taken away from us. Thank you," she said as she took another tissue from Laura.

"I'm devastated," Serena continued. "I woke up this morning and waited for Caleb to bring me a cup of coffee and a bagel with cream cheese and salmon, like every morning, before the children woke up, but he didn't come. And then all I could see was the image of him lying cold and alone in a mortuary. How could someone do that? I just can't… I can't. I don't understand why."

Serena turned toward Laura and buried her head in her shoulder. Her entire body was visibly shaking.

Henley hoped that she was managing to keep a passive look on her face as she watched this Oscar-winning performance; a performance that Serena and Laura had rehearsed. There was no sign of the cold and distant woman who Henley had met on Monday night. As if on cue, Laura eased Serena off her shoulders, took hold of her hand and turned her attention to the camera.

"I've only been the parliamentary representative for Lewisham and Deptford for eighteen months, but I know firsthand how much my constituents care for each other and work hard to ensure that their small part of the world, which has been vilified for so long, has thrived. The brutal murder of Pastor Caleb Annan, a man who was devoted to this tight-knit community, as I am, has shocked us and is hurting us. We don't want Mr. Annan's horrific murder to be another statistic in the unsolved crimes' column. It shouldn't take the intervention of an MP to ensure that Mr. Annan's case receives the exposure that he rightly deserves."

It was all Henley could do not to reach over and give Laura a firm slap. She couldn't see the reaction on Pellacia's face, but she knew that he would be just as pissed off as she was. It didn't matter how well Laura Halifax dressed up her words, she had accused Henley of not doing her job. For the first time in her career, she wished that Callum O'Brien, the permanent thorn in her side, would jump up and ask a question.

"Please, all I want is for my husband's killer to come forward," said Serena, wiping away her tears. "Someone out there knows something. Our children keep asking when Daddy will come home. They don't understand what is happening and I don't understand. They miss their father. I miss my husband."

Henley counted to ten in her head. The cameras zoomed in and snapped the grieving widow of a murder victim and her supportive MP.

"We're repeating our appeal for anyone with information about the murder of Pastor Caleb Annan to come forward. Thank you," said Henley as she looked out at the sea of reporters.

"Inspector Henley. Do you have any idea about the motive

behind the murder of Pastor Annan?" asked Olivia Cooper, a journalist from ITV News.

"No, we don't. This investigation is still in the early stages, but we will be exploring all lines of inquiry."

"Inspector Henley, is the young man who was found in the church responsible for the murder of Annan?"

"No. The young man's physical condition would have made that impossible," Henley said defiantly. She felt Serena twitch next to her and Callum O'Brien stood up.

Henley wished that he'd stood up five minutes earlier.

"Has the man been formally identified yet?" Callum shouted out.

"Members of the public have come forward with information," said Henley. "I can tell you that he's twenty-three years old, but we will not be releasing his name until his identity has been verified and his family has been informed. That will be all for now."

"Is it correct that you, Inspector Henley, found this still unidentified young man in the Church of Annan the Prophet? And from the photographs that were released, it appears that he may have been in that building for some time?"

The room erupted and the reporters started throwing questions at Henley:

"Have any witnesses be identified?"

"What have you discovered so far?"

"Did Caleb Annan know the young man that was discovered by you, Inspector?"

"Is this a serial killing?"

"Is Annan a victim and a suspect?"

"The Annan family are experiencing unimaginable grief, and they would like this investigation to be treated fairly so that they can have justice and peace," said Laura Halifax.

It was the worst thing that Laura Halifax could have said. Even though Henley was sitting at least twelve feet away from Callum, she could see the mischievous glint in his eye.

"And what about justice and peace for the man who was found in Caleb Annan's church? Surely his family will want to know if Caleb Annan was responsible?"

"This is a very complex investigation," Henley said as she pulled the bank of microphones away from Laura and Serena. "We appreciate the support of the public and ask for their patience and understanding. You can direct any further questions to the press office. Thank you very much."

Henley swiftly stood up and Pellacia ushered Serena and Laura toward the exit. She watched him from the doorway at the end of the corridor while he led Serena into a small consultation room, whilst Laura Halifax remained outside. Henley couldn't hear what was being said, but she could have sworn that Pellacia was apologizing. It was the way that Laura looked up at Pellacia and put a hand to her face, as though she was the one in distress. Pellacia put his arm around Laura and she leaned, just for a second, against his shoulder.

"I warned you," Henley said to Pellacia as she picked up her coat from the back of the door. The reporters had left the building, the camera lights were dead, and Laura had driven away with a furious Serena Annan, who had apparently forgotten her role of grieving widow as she shot Henley dirty looks from the backseat.

"Do you think that any of the papers are going to give even an inch of column space or a slot in the six o'clock news to finding Annan's killer?" said Henley.

"I think that you're exaggerating, and you're pissed off that I pulled rank and called you out," Pellacia said as he followed Henley out to the car park.

"Of course, I'm fucking pissed off," Henley said furiously. "That bloody woman Laura just sat there and insinuated that the SCU was both incompetent and biased."

"I don't think that's exactly what she was saying. That wasn't easy for her."

"Are you serious? The woman sits in the House of Commons every week with a bunch of braying buffoons; why the fuck are you defending her?"

"I'm not defending her," Pellacia said. He looked down at the ground.

"You can't stand there and tell me that you're OK with that?"

"Of course I'm not OK with that, but the fact is that we needed to hold that press conference. It was the right thing to do," Pellacia replied unconvincingly as they stopped at Henley's car.

"It needed to be done, but not like this," Henley said, rummaging in her bag for her keys. "Now you've made Annan the story but in the wrong way. All everyone is going to be talking about is 'Did Annan try to kill a twenty-three-year-old boy?' and I was put in a catch-22 situation where I couldn't give the right answer to Callum's question."

"Well, maybe if you were actually here to do your—"

"Don't you dare, Stephen." Henley stepped back to stop herself from hitting him. "I had to run around like an absolute idiot to find someone to look after Emma because you decided to throw your fucking weight around."

"Stop making this about you. It's about the investigation," Pellacia said softly. Henley knew that this was the closest that she was going to get to an apology from Pellacia, but she wasn't prepared to let him get away with how he'd behaved.

"No, you're right," said Henley. Four mounted police officers and their horses trotted into the car park. The south London symphony of sirens and traffic filled the air. "This isn't about me, Stephen. It's about you and your bruised ego. Get over it. Get over us and let me do my job."

23

"I'm so sorry," Henley said as she let out a long yawn and wondered if she'd picked up a decaf coffee by mistake. She and Ramouter were walking along the frozen Ealing street toward the Trinity Secondary School. The early morning fog hadn't lifted and still hung heavily in the air. There'd been no answer when Henley and Ramouter had knocked on the front door of Marcia and Patrick Whittaker's home. Henley had briefly considered the possibility that Amy Whittaker had told her parents that she and Ramouter were coming, but she quickly dismissed it.

"Emma keep you up?" Ramouter asked, ramming the last of his Danish into his mouth.

"I shouldn't say this, but she was an absolute pain last night," said Henley. She rubbed the spot where Emma had kicked her whilst she slept in their bed. "And then she had the cheek to wake up at 5 a.m. to tell me and her dad that she'd had a great night's sleep and that she wanted to tell us about her dream."

"Sometimes you want to give them away," Ramouter laughed.

"How's your little boy doing?" Henley asked.

"According to his teacher, Ethan's discovered that he's very good at talking back."

"Wonder where he gets that from."

"I'll have you know that I was an angel at school," Ramouter said as they approached the school entrance.

"I wasn't," said Henley. "Apparently, I talked too much and I walked around as if I owned the place. I'm now in my late thirties and I still have no idea how an eight-year-old can walk around like they own the place."

"I hated school," Ramouter said with a shiver. "Smart Asian kid, wearing a turban, who had a bit of a mouth on him was not a good combination. I think that I had a fight every second week."

"You?" Henley said, as if she was seeing him for the first time. "You don't seem the type."

"You quickly turn into the type when some spotty kid is trying to rip the turban off your head every five minutes, and my school, being as progressive as they were, sided with the bullies and threatened to kick me out."

"Is that why you stopped wearing your turban?"

"Aye. My dad was not pleased, but then my older brother stopped wearing his because he wanted to get more girls. Idiot," Ramouter said with affection.

"I didn't know that you had an older brother."

"Two of them."

"So, you're the baby of the family," said Henley as she opened the side gate that led into the school's main entrance.

"What about you? Is it just you and Simon?"

"Yep, just me and him. Even though, according to my mum, he asked if he could sell me to the next-door neighbor when I was one and he was four because he was fed up with me," Henley laughed.

"I think older brothers are all the same."

"Yeah, but I wouldn't swap him. By the way, how's Michelle?"

Ramouter sighed and rubbed the back of his neck. "She's doing OK, which is weird because a few months ago she was more...not forgetful, but distracted. I would be talking to her, and it was as if I was boring her, but the last few weeks she's been more like herself. I forgot that there was even anything wrong with her. They say early onset dementia can be like that, but it's hard when she's normal because I don't know how long that will last for."

"Maybe it would be easier if you were closer? And I'm not saying this to get rid of you because I actually…well, you're a good partner."

"Wow." Ramouter beamed. "You like me. That's the first time that you've said that to me."

"And it will probably be your last if your head gets any bigger. I'm just saying that maybe it would be better if you and her were together. Would she come to London?"

Ramouter was silent for a few seconds. "I love my job," he finally said. "And I actually like being here, but I miss my wife and kid. I want them to be happy, but I also know that Michelle wanted me to be here."

"It's not as if we don't have decent doctors down here," said Henley. "But I suppose that you wouldn't want to disrupt Michelle or Ethan."

"It's something to think about, I suppose," said Ramouter.

Henley could see the sadness on Ramouter's face and decided not to push it.

"I forgot to ask you yesterday. Have you verified that Amy is who she says she is?" Henley asked as she felt her pocket vibrate. "Hold on a sec." She pulled out her phone and checked the message from her brother, Simon:

Just left Dad's. Apparently, your husband has organized a family trip to the cemetery!!! PISSED! Call me later. x

"Her driving license was legit, she hasn't got a criminal record and she works for GCHQ," said Ramouter.

Henley put her phone away, but she couldn't ignore the pangs of anxiety in her chest as she tried to refocus on Ramouter. She loved talking to her brother, but not if it was going to be a conversation about Saturday morning.

"She would have gone through an enhanced identity and criminal record check in order to work for GCHQ."

"Exactly. She's given me her line manager's details, if you want to check for your own peace of mind, and on top of that, we've had another four people call into the SCU and say that the man you found was Brandon Whittaker."

"Who were they?"

"Top of my head: his maternal uncle, his best friend, a community psychiatric boss and an old boss. Their details are back at the SCU."

"Hold on," said Henley. "None of the people who called were his parents?"

"Nope. It could be that they haven't seen the appeal," Ramouter replied.

"That appeal has been live for twenty-four hours and their son has been missing for God only knows how long. They've seen the appeal."

"You seem pretty sure about that."

"I am. The question is why would they *not* call the police? You said that the maternal uncle had called in?"

"Yes, he did."

"You would think that calling his sister, Brandon's mum, would be the next, or even the first thing he would do, and tell her that he's seen his nephew's photo in the paper."

"The parents should have called," said Ramouter.

"Yes, they should have," Henley agreed. "You can't ignore your instincts. How was Amy when she saw her brother?"

"She held it together quite well, for about a minute, and then she was in bits," Ramouter answered. He drained the last of his coffee.

"Were you with her when she tried to call her parents?"

"No. I must have stepped out of the room, or she called when I went back to the SCU. Why? What are you thinking?"

"I'm just covering all bases. Exploring every strange possibility. Were you convinced that she was in the dark about her brother being missing?"

Ramouter pondered the question as they stepped into the reception area of Trinity Secondary School. "She put up a bloody good act if she did know," he finally answered.

Marcia Whittaker kept her head down as she pulled at the loose thread on the hem of her cardigan.

"Did you hear what I said?" Ramouter asked. He cocked his head slightly and tried to catch Marcia's eye.

Marcia had gasped when she'd reached the reception desk of Trinity Secondary School to find detectives wanting to see her. But after leading them into an empty classroom, she sat motionless as she received the news that the man in the hospital had been identified as her son. Marcia looked older than her fifty years, and Henley instinctively knew that it was from more than just tiredness. Her eyes were red and bloodshot, but Henley also wasn't convinced that this was the result of crying over her son. Marcia's heavy foundation had settled into every crease and wrinkle in her face. The makeup on her forehead had begun to flake and Henley could see small beads of sweat. Marcia's entire body was tense, but her hands were shaking.

"Your son, Brandon Whittaker, was found three days ago in a locked room in a church in Deptford. It looks like he had been kept there for over a month," Ramouter continued.

"But he's not dead?" Marcia finally said as the thread finally pulled away from the polyester-wool blend of her cardigan and the hem came apart.

"No, he's not dead but he's barely alive," Henley answered from the teacher's desk. "Your daughter Amy is with him, though. She came as soon as she saw the newspaper article asking for his family and friends to contact the police and to give him a name, which is more than—" Henley bit her tongue to stop herself.

"Amy is with Brandon? She's—" Marcia clamped her mouth shut and bowed her head, sinking into her chair. Her knuckles whitened as she tightened her fists.

Ramouter's eyes widened while Henley struggled to remain calm and resolute. Marcia jumped as the school bell signaled the change of lessons. There was the sound of overexcitable teenagers making their way down the corridor.

"Amy told us that your son Brandon had returned home after university last summer."

Marcia tried to focus on Henley, and then across at Ramouter, as though she was attempting to gauge just how much they knew.

"That's right," said Marcia. "He was home and got a job, just bar work, and then he got ill. It was the exhaustion."

"Exhaustion?" said Ramouter. "Your daughter Amy said that Brandon had been diagnosed with schizophrenia, psychotic—"

"No, no," Marcia said firmly. "It was just exhaustion and some depression. It was the pressure of university. He became ill and we took him to a clinic for a rest. He was there for about six weeks; he was discharged and then he went traveling."

Henley had lost her patience with this woman. "You're telling us that your son went traveling after he left the hospital?"

"Yes. Just after Christmas, he went traveling around Europe. Spain, Italy and France. He loves to cycle," Marcia rambled. "His bike cost him nearly £2000, a ridiculous amount of money to spend on a bike, but once Brandon gets an idea into his head...well, you can't shake him."

Marcia nodded to herself as though she was satisfied with the story. "We didn't know that he was even back in the country."

"That doesn't fit with what your daughter Amy says," said Henley.

"What did Amy say?"

"She said that she hadn't spoken to Brandon since Christmas and that you told her that you and your husband had taken Brandon to a clinic in St Albans," said Ramouter.

"My daughter has made a mistake," said Marcia. "She must have been confused with the dates because that's not what I said."

"At no point did Amy say that Brandon had gone on a cycling holiday," Henley interrupted. At this point, Henley didn't want Ramouter mentioning Amy's belief that her parents thought Brandon was possessed.

"Amy doesn't know what she's talking about," said Marcia. "She's... There's no understanding. You can't believe what she says."

"You're telling me that your daughter lied?" asked Henley.

Marcia was silent for a second. "I...but...you can't trust her," she finally said as she turned away from Henley. "Brandon went away. Cycling. Alone. As I said...we, my husband and I. We didn't know."

Henley looked across at Ramouter, who simply shook his head. "Well, now that you know about your son's condition, would you like to see him?" she asked. "We can take you now. I'm sure that the school would understand."

"No. I'll wait for my husband. He's away on business. In Sweden. He'll be back tomorrow night."

"Your son may not last until Friday evening. Look at him, Marcia."

Henley pulled out her phone and opened the photograph of Brandon that hadn't been in the newspapers. She knew that what she was about to do was cruel, but she needed to see the woman's reaction. Henley pushed the phone in front of Marcia's face and waited for her to react.

"This is your son bound to a bed. If you look closely, you can see a dead rat on the floor. And someone burnt your son's feet."

Marcia looked down at her cardigan as if suddenly aware of the damage that she had caused to the frayed edges, and folded it up.

"I have a class to teach," she said. She stood up without looking at the photograph. "You know how children can get when they're left unattended."

"And what about your child?"

Marcia looked at Henley with a clarity to her eyes that hadn't been there earlier.

"Only God can judge me." The school bell rang again. "And God will hold him."

Forty minutes later, and when they were on the right side of the river, Ramouter felt that Henley had calmed down enough so that it was safe for him to open his mouth. As Henley pulled up at the traffic lights on Newington Causeway, he asked, "So, what are we going to do about her? Marcia Whittaker."

"I would like to knock some sense into her. That's what I would like to do about her," Henley replied. She turned on the windshield wipers as the slushy rain started to fall. "Throw her off a bloody bridge," she muttered under her breath.

"Oh, she will be fine if you chucked her off a bridge. God will hold her," Ramouter chuckled.

"I haven't got an issue with God holding her. It's the lying to my face that I can't deal with."

"You mean the rubbish about him traveling?"

"Exactly."

"His passport? Amy had it and it had expired months ago." Ramouter grabbed onto the door handle as Henley hit the brakes sharply to avoid a bus that swerved in front of her. "She would have been better off saying that that they were estranged or that he'd run away. There are times when I really don't understand people."

"There's something not right about her," said Henley, pulling up to the large gates of the Southwark police station and waiting for the gates to open. "And I don't mean the 'I've got no intention of recognizing my son' bit."

"What do you think is wrong with her? Mental health issues can sometimes be hereditary."

Henley was silent for a second as she thought about her dad's own battle with depression and how she was still struggling with her PTSD.

"Her hands were shaking, and her eyes were puffy, blood-shot and unfocused," said Henley. "It's not as if I could smell it on her but, but I just thought…"

"Do you think that she's a drinker? An alcoholic?"

"Maybe, or it could just have been the stress of having to deal with us turning up out of the blue."

"I don't think that us turning up was that much of a surprise," said Ramouter. "It all sounded rehearsed. Brandon suffering from exhaustion, the brief clinic stay and then the traveling. She must have known where he really was."

"Not necessarily," Henley reluctantly concluded. "She may not have known where he was, but I'm a hundred percent sure that she knew what was being done to him."

"What? Why would she know that?"

"Haven't you worked it out yet, Ramouter?" Henley asked as she stepped out of the car and pulled the collar of her coat farther around her neck. Above the noise of the passing traffic and ambulance sirens in the distance, the one thought that had been echoing through her head was that voiced by Amy Whittaker. "They were trying to exorcise his demons."

24

"I've had another job offer," Anthony said as he held the door open for Henley and Ramouter. He looked smaller without the billowing white material of his protective suit. "Actually, it's the same job offer but with more money."

"It's always the same job, and one of these days one of those private firms is going to tempt you away," said Henley. They followed him into the open-plan office, which was unusually empty. Even on their busiest days there were a few members of Anthony's team lurking about as they picked up their job sheets or completed their reports. "Can I be selfish and say that I don't want you to go?"

"Of course you can. It gives me a warm glow inside. Anyway, you're not here for my career woes. Your dead pastor."

Anthony pushed through another door which led to the CSI laboratory. On a large table was everything that had been taken from the crime scene: clothing, shoes, bloodstained Bible, altar cloth and candlesticks.

"As you can see, these are the exhibits taken from the church area," said Anthony as he pulled on a pair of gloves. "So, here is the clothing that Annan was wearing."

Anthony pointed to the bloodstained shirt, jumper and trousers. The once white shirt was now stained a dull burgundy color. The black briefs and socks had hardened. Anthony picked up the jumper and turned it over. "Can you see that?"

Both Henley and Ramouter leaned forward as Anthony traced the bloody swirls on the jumper.

"That is a clear footprint. We also recovered footprints on the carpet. Our footprint expert has confirmed that whoever stamped on our man's back was wearing size seven Gucci running shoes."

"So, we're looking for someone who wears a size seven. Great," said Ramouter. "Narrows it down."

"He's a bit snarky this afternoon, isn't he, Henley?" said Anthony.

"Ignore him. I think he needs feeding. So, size seven. I'm putting my money on it being a woman's shoe."

"Bingo," Anthony replied. He turned to the computer monitor on another table. "So, one footprint recovered from the jumper. Take a look at these photographs." On the monitor were images of the bloody footprints that had been taken off the navy church carpet. Even to her untrained eye, she could see that she was looking at two different sets of footprints.

"And if you take a look at these photos..." Anthony tapped the mouse and the screen switched to an enlarged image of a desk covered with loose papers, a lamp—it was the pastor's office.

"Is that blood?" Ramouter pointed at the four dark specks on the back of the computer monitor.

"Yep, that's the pastor's blood," Anthony confirmed. "We found blood spatter on the computer, the desk and the office carpet on the ground floor. No footprints in there, but we did find two different sets of prints by the pastor's body."

"We've got two people downstairs in the church when Annan was killed?" Henley asked. Ramouter appeared to have brightened up at this news.

"Definitely. Your second person stepped in the blood and left a perfect footprint behind. Our footprint expert says that they're a size eleven. Men's shoes. Posh ones. Prada. If you take a closer look, you'll be able to make out the D and the A on the heel. I asked my son how much a pair would set you back. He said that he could get them for £150, but down in Selfridges, £460. Waste of bloody money if you ask me, but there you go."

"Gucci, Prada? Whoever they are, they've got expensive tastes."

"Shit," said Henley. She sat down on the stool in front of the table and slowly absorbed the significance of this.

"So, the first set of Prada footprints appear about 71.12 centimeters from the pastor's body, and the Gucci footprints are 30.48 centimeters from the body," Anthony explained. "The footprint on the pastor's back is the right foot. The Prada prints then join the Gucci prints, but if you look at the next photo…"

Anthony clicked to where the Gucci prints were smeared and were then followed by long bloodstained streaks.

"It looks like whoever was wearing the Prada trainers dragged the person wearing the Gucci trainers," said Henley.

"Exactly," said Anthony. "You then follow both sets of footprints toward the entrance. The Prada prints fade out first, which suggests that whoever was wearing the Gucci trainers was standing in the pastor's blood for quite a bit of time."

"Two killers?" Ramouter asked. "A man and a woman, but it looks as though it was a woman who put the knife in the pastor's back."

"Something still doesn't make sense to me," said Henley as she took Anthony's place at the computer monitor and clicked through the photographs. "We found the pastor by the altar. If he was stabbed in the office, why wouldn't he run straight out of the front door? He would have been in the middle of Deptford Broadway and could've flagged down help. Or why didn't he just run down the corridor and out the back? Why did Annan run deeper into the church?"

"The front door was deadlocked," said Anthony. "You could only open that door from the outside."

"So, it's possible that the killer, or killers, locked him in," said Ramouter. "There must be CCTV on Deptford Broadway. Or maybe Prada man stopped the pastor from heading to the back door and he had no choice but to go into the church."

"Where the woman was waiting and stabbed the pastor to death, stood on him and pulled a knife out of his back," Henley concluded.

"South London's answer to Bonnie and Clyde," said Anthony as he picked up a pair of men's black briefs. "Well, there's more. Ramouter, can you do me the honor of turning off the lights, please?"

Ramouter obeyed while Anthony picked up a UV wand. On the front of the briefs, streaks of dried fluid glowed against the material.

"Do I even have to ask what we're looking at?" said Henley as she screwed up her face.

"Is that semen?" asked Ramouter.

"And vaginal fluid overlapping each other," Anthony answered. "DNA results confirmed that the semen belongs to Annan, but the vaginal fluid..."

"I have a strong feeling that you're going to tell me that it's not his wife's," said Henley. "It wouldn't be the first. A woman named Raina Davison accused him of rape, but he said that it was consensual. Is it her?"

Anthony smirked and shook his head. "As per usual we took DNA samples and prints to see if we could eliminate certain people, including the cleaner who found him."

"You have her samples?" Henley asked. She recalled how reluctant Uliana had been to provide her DNA and her fingerprints.

"Yeah, she called yesterday afternoon," said Anthony. "I sent Samuel to her flat to get her samples straightaway."

"Are you about to tell me that her DNA is on Annan's boxers?" asked Henley.

"No way," said Ramouter as he switched the lights back on.

Anthony shook his head. "Semen can be detected for up to a year, so I can't tell you when Annan had sex with the cleaner, but—"

"Uliana. Her name is Uliana Piontek," said Henley.

"We also found his semen and her vaginal fluid on the sofa in the pastor's office. It's definitely Ms. Piontek's DNA. A full profile, and you know that you can't get much better than that."

"Well, that explains why she was so reluctant. She didn't want us to find out that she'd been sleeping with Annan."

"Then why did she bother to give us her samples?" asked Ramouter.

"People are strange," said Anthony. "Maybe she thought that you wouldn't be looking for signs of sexual activity because you were investigating a murder. There is one other thing. We're still going through the room where Brandon Whittaker was found. We've recovered three sets of prints. One matches the pastor but the other two are unknown."

"Where were the prints recovered from?" asked Ramouter.

"The bucket, light switch, Bible... Everywhere, really, including Whittaker's body, but that's not the interesting thing." Anthony turned back to the computer monitor and switched to an image of Whittaker's face.

"Samuel took this photograph before Linh realized that Whittaker was still alive," Anthony explained. "Take a look at his forehead."

"It just looks like black smudges," said Ramouter.

"Are you sure? Take a closer look."

Anthony picked up a pen and traced it along the markings. Henley mouthed along silently as she followed Anthony's pen.

"What on earth..." Henley said. Her phone began to ring. It was DC Stanford calling.

"Are those letters?" Ramouter asked as he leaned in closer, and Henley stepped away to answer the phone.

"There are a couple missing but it looks like L, E, don't know what that is, then maybe a V and that's just a smudge," said Anthony. "If you ask me—"

"It looks like someone was writing 'leave' on his head," said Ramouter. "Why would—"

Henley held a finger up to her lips as she mouthed *"wait"* to Ramouter before walking to the other side of the room.

"Hey, Stanford, what's up?" Henley asked. "No, we're in Borough with Anthony." A pause. "Are you sure? When was it called in? OK. We're leaving now."

"What is it?" Ramouter asked as Henley ended the call and picked up her coat from the back of the chair.

"The council sent pest control to one of their flats in Tanner's Hill. When they got there, the door was open. They thought that the tenant had just left the door on the latch. Long story short, they went in and found a woman. Bible, holy water, same paraphernalia that was found next to Brandon Whittaker."

"Is she still alive?" Ramouter asked.

"No. This one is very dead."

25

"Nice area."

Henley wasn't sure if Ramouter was being genuine or had been working on his sarcasm as she turned into the Tanner's Hill Estate. His mood had darkened significantly since they'd received the call from Stanford. Their victim was in Florence House, a gray and dirty white brick block of flats that looked as though it had been dumped into the middle of a council estate and then forgotten about by the owners.

The gathering of police cars had resulted in the inevitable thin crowd of curious onlookers: teenagers returning home from school and the occasional resident brave enough to withstand the dropping temperatures, all under the pretense of having to dispose of rubbish in the communal bins or suddenly feeling the need to walk their dogs.

"Are you ready?" Henley asked Ramouter as she parked next to Stanford's car and switched off the engine.

"Aye," Ramouter said with forced enthusiasm. "I doubt that it can be worse than anything else we've seen so far."

The council may have given up hope, but the residents of the estate obviously cared. There were plant containers of overflowing ivy and pruned rosebushes next to the broken communal doors. The glass-covered noticeboard next to the lifts was covered with posters for a new yoga, English as second language classes and a polite request for the delivery drivers not to dump parcels when no one was in, as there was no "safe place" on the estate.

"What floor is our victim on?" Ramouter asked as they paused at the sign confirming that the lift was out of order.

"Eighth," Henley sighed.

Fifteen minutes later, he and Henley reached the landing of the eighth floor. "Christ," Ramouter spluttered.

"I think I'm going to die," Henley gasped.

"I thought you were a runner?" Ramouter said. He leaned against the wall and Henley joined him.

"Me? Run? I hate running," Henley said when she finally caught her breath. It took another minute before she and Ramouter were able to complete the final steps to the crime scene.

The air was colder on the eighth floor and whistled like a warning through the corridor as the broken fire door slammed and the sound of voices and police radios grew louder. Number 62 was the second to last flat on the landing. A middle-aged Chinese woman poked her head out nearby and shot a disapproving look at Henley and Ramouter before clasping the top of her pastel blue cardigan and closing the door again.

There were two uniformed officers standing outside the partially closed door of number 62. Stanford stood outside, leaning over the balcony that overlooked the car park. The color of his face fluctuated between winter-red rawness and the paleness of nausea. The faces of the two other police officers didn't look much better as they acknowledged the presence of Henley and Ramouter.

"I'm telling you now that it's not pretty in there," said Stanford. He handed Henley and Ramouter overshoes, a mask and plastic gloves. "If I were you, I would zip your suits all the way up, wrap your scarf around your face, and if either of you have got any Vicks, stick that up your nose too."

"Is it that bad?" Ramouter asked as he bent down and slipped on the blue plastic overshoes.

"I'd rather freeze my bollocks off out here than go back in. It's just... I'm going to get a cup of tea."

"Is the CSI team here?" Henley asked, stepping into her over-suit.

"They'll be about another fifteen minutes. The team from Bromley are coming," said Stanford.

"Who's our pathologist? Linh?"

"Nope. She's at a murder in Beckenham. Husband killed his wife's boyfriend and himself. Late Valentine's present. We've got her boss Joel instead. A barrel of laughs, as always," Stanford said with a shrug as more vehicles entered the estate.

"Oh great," Henley said, and Ramouter let out a groan of regret.

"Joel makes everything so painful," said Ramouter as he zipped up his oversuit. "He treats everyone like an inconvenience."

"I think that you'll find that it's only you that he treats like that," chuckled Stanford.

"Stop pissing about, Stanford," said Henley.

"I'm just trying to lighten the mood," Stanford protested. "You're going to need it."

Henley pushed open the door of number 62 and looked down. The white and brown carcasses of maggots, dead flies and cockroaches had been squashed into the carpet. The swirled pattern on the old carpet had been worn down and was caked in dirt. Henley swatted a fly away as she looked down at the pile of unopened letters, takeaway menus and free weekly magazines from the council that had been pushed up against the wall.

"Take a look at the lock," Henley said to Ramouter as she held the door open. There were deep scratches in the black paint near the keyhole and toward the edge of the door. The wood had splintered, and a screw was missing from the handle.

"Someone clearly tampered with it," said Ramouter as he followed Henley into the flat.

"Joel!" Henley shouted. She placed a gloved hand to her mouth in a futile effort to stop the fumes of decomposition from coating her throat. Ramouter coughed involuntarily behind her as they both walked along the narrow corridor. Henley preferred the metallic, warm, almost welcoming smell of fresh blood in comparison to that of abandoned flesh.

"The bedroom is on your right," Joel called. Henley paused at the kitchen and stepped inside. A radio was on low and flies were circling around the light. A new fridge hummed quietly in the corner. On the counter were four tea-stained mugs. A half-empty bottle of milk that had expired three weeks ago sat next to a crumpled up takeaway bag. Mold had started to grow on the scrapes of leftover mayonnaise on the empty sandwich boxes that sat amongst mouse droppings and the dried shells of dead cockroaches. Henley felt the skin on the back of her neck prickle.

Henley heard Ramouter gasp as they reached the doorway of the second bedroom on the right.

"Yeah, this one is dead." Joel stood statuesque on the other side of the door and scribbled something down on his notepad. He didn't look up at Henley as she walked past him. Linh had told her once that Joel didn't like dealing with people. Dead or alive.

"How long?" Henley asked, walking farther into the bedroom. She could hear Ramouter dry heaving behind her. "The milk in the kitchen expired almost three weeks ago."

"She could have been dead for as long as that, but I'm not happy giving an estimate right now. There's a lot of decomposition but it looks to have slowed down. It's as if someone remembered to turn the heating off, otherwise your victim would have been a liquefied mess," Joel replied. He pulled a tissue out and wiped his nose.

The dying sun streamed through the unlined curtains and onto the body of a black woman on a small double bed. Her once blue knickers were lost in an already obese body that had become more engorged with death. Maggots moved like a cult around a false idol in the split blackened and green skin of her stomach, which had become too taut from the gases in her body.

"Christ," Ramouter said, taking a step back from the body.

"Yeah, I think that he may have had something to do with it," Joel muttered.

Henley moved closer to the bed. A small spider crawled along the upper lip of the woman's open mouth as the white engorged tail of a maggot wriggled out of her ear. Henley couldn't tell if she was looking at bruising or the discoloration of the skin that came with death, but she could make out long cuts amongst the rat-bitten flesh on the woman's cheeks. Her matted afro was splayed out on the mattress like a black halo. The sunlight bounced off the specks of dust and dirt like cheap glitter. The teal flowered bedsheet was stained with dried blood, the yellowing marks of urine and the decaying juices of organs which had leaked out of her orifices. Her arms were raised above her head and tied to the wooden slats of the headboard. The red twine of what looked like a washing line had become almost lost in the folds of her wrists. Henley leaned in closer to the headboard, resisting the urge to run her fingers along the crosses that had been marked in candle wax on the slats.

"This is worse than... I wasn't expecting this," said Ramouter. He moved to the foot of the bed where the woman's feet had been bound together. The mice and rats had gnawed away at her toes and had started on her calves.

Henley knew what Ramouter meant. It was worse seeing this woman, stripped, tortured and abandoned in her own home. All of the signs were there, that whoever had left her in this state was also likely responsible for Brandon. A bucket next to a brand-new IKEA wardrobe. A bottle of Florida water cologne, an open Bible and the ashes of incense sticks covered a dressing table alongside cheap makeup and even cheaper perfume.

"This would have been Brandon if you hadn't found him," said Ramouter.

"There's no point asking you about cause of death?" Henley asked Joel, finally pulling herself away from the body.

"Not until we get her on the table. It's impossible to say before we open her up. I'll be outside if you need me," Joel said as the sound of several footsteps made their way toward the bedroom.

"This is quite a sight. You have been careful, haven't you, Inspector?"

Henley recognized the stern voice of Katherine Simmons, the senior forensics investigator based at Bromley police station.

"Very careful, Katherine. We haven't touched a thing," said Henley. Relieved, Ramouter nodded at Katherine and followed Joel out of the room with a gloved hand covering his mouth.

"Honestly, you would think he started this job yesterday." Katherine moved deeper into the room, completely unfazed by the scene.

Henley was sure that Katherine had seen worse but, in this moment, she wasn't sure what "worse" could possibly be. Henley stood back as another CSI investigator entered the room and Katherine began to clarify with him how they would be proceeding with the task of recording and recovering the evidence. Evidence. This woman was no more than that, a piece of evidence to be photographed. Her position would be noted in a sketchbook, her body recovered and placed in a black body bag that wouldn't look out of place amongst the thousands of black bin bags thrown into the council's landfill.

Henley left the room as more CSI investigators filled the small flat. From the open front door, Henley could see Ramouter leaning against the balcony talking to Stanford, who had returned with tea and coffee for the uniformed officers, but with a pained expression on his face.

"You said that pest control called it in, but I've checked the front door and there are signs that someone clearly tampered with it," Henley said as she joined Ramouter and Stanford on the landing. She pulled down the hood of her oversuit, ripped off her mask and breathed in the cold fresh air. Police tape covered the faulty fire door like a game of cat's cradle.

"Pest control wouldn't break into someone's flat."

"You're right, pest control made the 999 call," Stanford replied. Henley peeled off her gloves and took the last cup of tea from the cardboard cup holder. "As I told you on the phone, Barry—that's the guy who made the call—said that he thought that the door had been left on the latch for them by the tenant. He didn't think anything of it because he says that it happens a lot with tenants who live in blocks of flats. I reckon that someone must have broken in, maybe the local crackhead, saw the body and did a runner. Pest control turned up after a neighbor complained about the mice and the maggots falling from his ceiling."

"Do we have the name of the neighbor?"

"Frank Nicolls. No one was in when we knocked earlier."

"What about the next-door neighbor?" Henley asked as the door of number 63 opened slightly and the head of the small Chinese woman poked out once more.

"Not yet. She refused to open the door, but that hasn't stopped her from being a nosy cow," said Stanford.

Henley squeezed past Stanford and made her way to the door. She put her foot in the crack in the door like a determined double-glazing salesman as the woman tried to close it again.

"Good afternoon." Henley pushed her warrant card toward the gap in the door.

The woman cowered back slightly and said, "I haven't got my glasses on."

"My name is Detective Inspector Henley. I want to ask you about—"

"I don't know anything about her."

"What do you mean, 'you don't know anything about her'? You're neighbors."

"Is she dead?"

"Didn't you even know her name?"

The woman stared back at Henley as though she was questioning the audacity of her question. "She didn't know my name either. She didn't talk to me."

"OK, so when was the last time that you saw her? Or even heard her telly through the walls or bumped into her on the landing?"

"I don't know. A few weeks ago."

"A few weeks ago? Do you think that you could be more specific?"

"I'm not sure, maybe the beginning of January."

"That's more than a few weeks ago, Mrs...."

"Zhang. I'm not sure how long ago it was, but I remember that I picked up a parcel from her and that was around my husband's birthday."

"And when was your husband's birthday?" Henley asked, growing more impatient.

"January the third."

"Did you talk to her when you last saw her?" asked Henley, quickly trying to work out the timings.

"I can't remember," Mrs. Zhang said, folding her arms.

"So, I just want to make sure that I've got this straight," said Henley as Mrs. Zhang looked at her as though she'd grown a second head. "You last had contact with your neighbor just over six weeks ago."

"Yes. I don't know. Maybe a month ago."

"And you haven't seen or heard from her since?"

"No."

"Not even the sound of the TV or radio? Or seen the steam from the boiler flue?" Henley pointed at the boiler flue above Mrs. Zhang's own kitchen window.

"I already told you no. I thought that maybe she'd gone away, or the council had moved her after she'd had the baby."

"Excuse me? What baby?" Henley racked her brain to remember if she'd seen any hint that a baby had been living in the flat next door.

"She has a baby. I don't know if it's a boy or a girl, but come to think of it, I haven't heard the baby crying for a while either."

Henley looked around the small kitchen while Ramouter stood in the doorway. No empty bottles or tins of baby formula cluttered the counters. There were no empty packets of baby wipes or used diapers in the bin. Henley opened the fridge and was greeted with the pathetic sight of wilted vegetables, hardened cheese, a few slices of bread that had escaped from the bag with an inch of white fur and green mold growing on top.

"Maybe the neighbor made a mistake," Ramouter said. "Or someone cleaned up really well."

"You can't hide signs of a baby," Henley replied. Her eye caught the edges of a blue patterned plate and the broken black handle of a saucepan poking out of the sink. Henley rolled up her sleeve and pushed her right hand into the gray stagnant water. Dead flies and cockroaches swirled around the top as she fished around the small sink. She grimaced as cold, slimy water seeped into her glove.

"Ramouter," Henley said softly as her fingers curled around hard plastic that felt familiar. She pulled out a baby's bottle and placed it on the draining board, along with a stained bottle teat.

"Shit," Ramouter said.

26

"Where's the baby?"

Pellacia had pulled up a chair next to Stanford's desk. He was physically closer to Ramouter than he was to Henley and that hadn't escaped her attention.

"Go ahead, Ramouter," Henley said.

"We only found one baby bottle and a stand for a Moses basket that had been pushed under the living room sofa, but that was it. If our victim did have a baby, then whoever took him or her cleaned that flat out of everything to do with it," said Ramouter.

"It's possible that there is no baby," said Pellacia.

"No," said Henley, "Mrs. Zhang who lives at number sixty-three is convinced that the crying stopped almost three weeks ago, and the family at sixty-one also confirmed that there was a baby. I spoke to Terry Rutherford, who lives at number sixty-one, and he said that he helped the victim carry the pram up the stairs because the elevator had broken down, and that was more than a month ago. I asked him how she was, and he said she was upset, but that might have had something to do with having to walk up eight flights of stairs with a pram."

"So, who is she? Your victim," Pellacia asked.

"*'She,'* according to the expired staff ID card that forensics found, is Alyssa Hadlow, and she was thirty-four years old." Henley felt herself shiver, not from the cold draft sweeping across the back of her neck, but from the realization that she'd been only a couple of years older than the victim when she'd given birth to Emma. "Her DNA came back with a match on the database, and she has previous convictions."

"How serious?"

"She's got seven, but it's all petty. Shoplifting, threatening words and behavior, and a common assault; but her offending only started three years ago."

"Something must have happened to her," said Ramouter. "You don't just start shoplifting at the age of thirty unless something's happened in your life."

"No, you don't," Henley agreed. "Her tenancy is with Hexagon Housing Association, and they had no issues with her until four months ago."

"What happened four months ago?" Pellacia asked.

"They have no idea. She was a model tenant, paid her rent regularly and then all of a sudden, she stopped. They wrote and tried to call her after she fell into arrears, but she never responded."

"What about family, friends?" Pellacia asked.

"We've only just started investigating," Henley replied tetchily. She checked the clock on the wall. "We left her flat two hours ago. So far, we've got a name and her last place of work." She couldn't think of anything worse than for a poor family member to look at the decomposing face of a dead relative, and for that to be their last memory. There wasn't a single day when Henley didn't regret seeing her mother looking like a poorly made-up wax mannequin in her coffin.

"And before you ask," said Henley directly to Pellacia, "we've checked with the General Register Office and there's no record of Alyssa Hadlow or any variation of that name, with the birth of a child within the past month."

"You've got forty-two days to register a baby's birth," said Ramouter. "I think that I registered Ethan's birth when he was about four days old."

"I didn't even go. Rob was down at the registry office when Emma was two days old," Henley said.

"Is she linked to the Brandon Whittaker case?" Pellacia asked. Henley had seen him grimace at the mention of Rob's name. "From the way you described the condition of her body, it looks like she is."

"The main difference is that Brandon is still alive and she's dead, and no one appears to have missed her," said Henley. "Her neighbor has been living next door to her for nearly five years and she didn't even know her name. The only reason anyone called the police was because the maggots crawling out of her body had made their way through the floorboards and fell out of the light sockets in the flat downstairs. On top of that, it looks like someone broke into her flat, saw her dead and didn't even bother to call the police. The officers came because her rotting body had become a nuisance."

There was a silence in the room. Henley took a deep breath and turned her attention toward the window. She wasn't surprised at the depth of her anger. She could never understand abandonment. How somebody could just walk away from someone and deny them their basic dignity. It was a level of disrespect that she couldn't tolerate.

"Any idea when the pathologist and the CSI team will be done?" asked Pellacia.

"You know as well as I do that they'll call as soon as the body is ready to be moved. You're literally asking me how long a piece of string is," Henley said, growing more agitated.

"You said that her staff card expired?" asked Eastwood through a mouthful of crisps.

"Nearly two years ago," Ramouter answered. "I checked

online. She was an Economics lecturer at the University of Greenwich."

"Are you serious? Your victim is an Economics lecturer."

"She's not appearing on their staff list now, but I found a couple of old posts about her on their website."

"Did you find anything else about her online?" asked Stanford.

It was obvious to Henley what Stanford and Eastwood were doing; buddying up to insulate her from Pellacia's sharp jabs.

"This is what we're going to do," said Henley. "Stanford, Eastwood. I need you to find Uliana Piontek. The only direct evidence that we've got is her DNA on Caleb's body and in the office, and right now I don't trust her to attend a police interview voluntarily. She was hesitant about providing her DNA, and now we know why."

"So, you want us to arrest her?" Eastwood confirmed. "For what offense?"

"Let's go all-in and arrest her for murder," said Henley.

"And what are you going to be doing while these two are carrying out your arrest?" asked Pellacia.

"My job," Henley volleyed back as she picked up her coat. She needed to get out of the office, to do something useful and to escape the toxic vibes emanating from Pellacia. "Come on, Ramouter. Grab your coat. We're taking a walk."

The frost-covered grass crunched under Henley's and Ramouter's feet as they walked. There was an eeriness in the air as the hostile and darkening winter sky swept seamlessly into the leaden waters of the river and back onto land. The icy air that blew in from the River Thames felt like the sharpened point of a surgeon's scalpel as it stung Henley's cheeks. She hated this time of year, which felt just as oppressive and intrusive as the hopelessness that she'd been feeling since she'd left Alyssa Hadlow's flat.

"I just keep asking myself what happened to Alyssa Hadlow

in the past few years for her to end up...well, in the state that we found her," said Ramouter.

"People's lives can change unexpectedly," said Henley. "They say that half of working people who rent privately are one and half paychecks away from being homeless. There are families out there who have to make the choice between buying food for their kids or paying the rent. There are so many out there struggling."

"I just don't understand how someone could have just left her like that. If she was struggling and needed help... Sometimes I think that I'm too gullible."

"No, you just want to see the best in people," said Henley. "And there's nothing wrong with that."

"Well, I'm struggling to see the best in the boss right now," said Ramouter.

The atmosphere had been so toxic in the office that it would be impossible for Ramouter not to be questioning why.

"Ramouter, I want to tell you something," Henley said as they stopped a short distance away from the university building.

"What is it? Have I done something wrong?"

"No, not at all." Henley took a breath. "It's about me...and Pellacia."

Ramouter's face remained impassive, but there was a glint of curiosity in his eyes.

"You know that Pellacia and I have known each other for years and that we were at police college together?"

"Aye."

"Well, we were also in a relationship together. It was before I got married," Henley said quickly as the icy wind bit into her face.

"I had no idea. No one said anything," said Ramouter.

"They wouldn't," Henley said confidently.

"Does everyone know? Including Jo... Actually, forget that I said that. Joanna knows everything."

"Yes, she does. I know things are a bit...tense at the moment, and it's just because sometimes overfamiliarity can get in the way. It's not that I don't respect his authority…"

"I get it," said Ramouter. "Sometimes the lines get blurred."

"Yes, they do," Henley said softly.

27

The University of Greenwich occupied the Old Royal Naval College which had once been a hospital for navy seamen, and before that, the favorite palace of Henry VIII. Henley had learned by rote the story of the historical site when she was eight years old and had been dragged with the rest of her class around the college, the museum and the Royal Observatory. Henley shook away the innocent memory as she and Ramouter walked past large white tents that had been erected on lawns, which were usually packed with tourists and sunbathing students in the summer. The high vis yellow jackets of the security guards were the only hint of color as they ushered a group of students away from a film set.

Henley couldn't get rid of one recurring thought as she and Ramouter headed toward the imposing colonnade of Tuscan columns. What had happened to Alyssa Hadlow that had taken her away from the grand historical halls of higher learning to a decomposing state in the bedroom of a neglected council flat?

"I can't believe it. Are you sure?" Giana Courtney, the faculty operating officer for the university, pulled a tissue from her pocket and dabbed her eyes.

"We're sure," said Henley as she and Ramouter took a seat in the spare chairs in Giana's office.

Giana sat down on the other side of the desk and pushed an empty crisp packet and coffee cup to one side. "Can you tell me what happened to Alyssa?" she asked.

Henley sat back. She liked this woman. Her pragmatism and the fact that she was someone who had once cared about this victim. *So, what had happened to Alyssa?* The question burnt like a stigma on Henley's chest.

"Her body was found this morning in her flat. We're not sure how she died but the circumstances are suspicious," Henley explained.

"Someone killed her?" Giana asked. Her eyes widened and filled with tears.

"I won't be able to say until we get the results from the post-mortem. How well did you know her?"

"She worked here for about four years. She got on well with the staff, and the students were always complimentary of her."

"Were you two friends?"

"I suppose that, yes, we were friends to an extent. We both started here at the same time and there were the usual outings for someone's birthday, leaving drinks, and she used to come to a barre class that I taught at a Pilates studio in Chalk Farm, near where I live."

"When was the last time that you saw her?" asked Ramouter.

Giana let out a breath. "I'm not too sure. Maybe eighteen months or even two years ago. Alyssa and I weren't close, like best friends. We didn't tell each other our deepest and darkest secrets, but I knew that she'd had a miscarriage and she kind of just crumbled. She stopped coming to my barre classes and then she was signed off sick for about two months."

"What was wrong with her?"

"She never said, but I suspect that it was some kind of break-down after the miscarriage. I put two and two together. Alyssa didn't drink. She told me once that alcohol affected her medication and we talked about depression, but it was superficial talk. She didn't say that she was depressed or anything like that."

"Did she come back after she was sick?"

"For a few weeks, but she was struggling. She'd put on weight, and she was late for a couple of classes, and then she disappeared for a week. And then there was the fight about three years ago."

"Fight? Do you know who the fight was with?" Henley asked, thinking back to the first entry on Alyssa Hadlow's criminal record. A conviction for common assault.

"I have no idea. She tried to deny the conviction at first, but it was right there in black-and-white," said Giana. "The only reason that we found out about it was because we had to update our personnel records and carried out a standard DBS check on all staff members."

"Don't you need consent for a DBS check?" Ramouter asked.

"Yes, you do. Alyssa had completed the consent form about a month before she was signed off sick, but we fell behind with the checks. She came back to work and about a week later we discovered the conviction. She didn't disclose it, which was a breach of her contract with us; so, she was suspended, and she never came back."

"And that was almost two years ago."

Giana nodded and turned her head toward the window. "I didn't abandon her," she said in an almost whisper.

"Why would you say that?" Ramouter asked. He heard Amy Whittaker's words repeating in his head; *I let him down.* "We didn't say that you'd abandoned her."

"I just feel as though you're thinking that I should have done more."

"We're not saying that," Henley said gently. "Sometimes friendships just break down."

"I tried to reach out to her," Giana said as tears streamed down her face, "but she wouldn't answer my calls or reply to my text messages. I even went to her house a couple of times but there was no answer. I tried and then…what more could I do?"

"You said house," said Henley. "She was found in a flat in the Tanner's Hill Estate. Where did you visit her?"

"In Tufnell Park. She lived there with her husband."

"Alyssa is married?"

"Sorry, I meant her ex-husband. They broke up shortly after she found out that she was pregnant." There was no mistaking the dark look that crossed over Giana's face as she shook her head. "I still can't believe that he did that to her."

"What do you mean? What did her ex-husband do?" asked Henley.

"Leave her. End their marriage. After she'd…"

Giana paused and moved her attention to the windows. After a few seconds she turned back with a look in her eyes that Henley recognized. It was a look of someone who'd recently had a loss.

"I miscarried my first baby at five months," said Giana. "I know what it's like and I know how important it is to have people around you. Alyssa didn't have anyone. He walked away."

"Could you tell us her husband's name?" Henley asked. She tried not to jump to conclusions as to why Alyssa's relationship with her husband broke down, and instead tried to focus on compartmentalizing her own feelings, but it was a struggle. Henley could clearly remember how it had felt when Emma had been moving around in her womb when she was five months pregnant.

"Dr. Bryan Ekubu. He's one of our visiting lecturers in International Business. He's extremely clever but he's also an absolute idiot."

"Would you be prepared to give us his contact details?" Henley asked.

"Oh, I can do better than that. I can take you to him. He's in the middle of a lecture right now."

28

Dr. Bryan Ekubu looked annoyed as Henley and Ramouter walked in five minutes before his class was due to end.

Dr. Ekubu looked to be in his early fifties and there was almost a sheen to him, from the top of his clean-shaven head to his shoes. He wasn't as tall as Henley, but there was something about the way that he carried himself that made him seem taller. Henley glanced down at the thick gold band on his wedding finger as he tapped away on his laptop.

"Can I help you?" Dr. Ekubu asked after the last student slammed the door shut. It was less of an invitation and more of a statement as he closed his laptop and rose from his seat.

"I'm Detective Inspector Henley and this is DC Ramouter— we're from the Serial Crime Unit. I need to talk to you about Alyssa Hadlow."

"Alyssa." Dr. Ekubu said the name as though he was trying to place an old student. There was no sense of concern or of a discarded love affair. Henley looked for any signs of recognition in his eyes or any other indication that he may be curious as to why two police officers were standing in front of him asking about his ex-wife.

"Alyssa," he said again. "That's a name that I haven't heard in a while."

"It wasn't that long ago," said Ramouter.

"How is she?" Dr. Ekubu asked the question as though it was the polite thing and not because he actually cared.

"Dead," Ramouter said loudly.

Henley noticed the subtle disturbance in Dr. Ekubu's demeanor. He turned his head toward Henley and back to Ramouter as though he was just seeing him for the first time. "What are you talking about? She can't be dead."

"Her body was found this—"

Henley and Ramouter both reached out and grabbed Dr. Ekubu's arm as his legs gave way. All of his efforts of maintaining a stoic figure had disappeared as quickly as the afternoon winter sky giving way to the cold emptiness of night. Henley could feel the tremors in his arm muscles.

"I'm fine," Dr. Ekubu said fiercely. He pulled his arm away, clearly disgusted at the thought that he had allowed himself to break down in public. He grabbed the arms of the chair behind him. "I'm fine. I'm fine," he said again.

"When did you last see Alyssa?" Henley asked as she positioned herself next to the desk.

"What happened to her? How did she die?" Dr. Ekubu asked, ignoring Henley's question; unable to see that the tables had turned and that it wasn't his place to ask the questions. "And you said that you were from the Serial Crime Unit? Don't you investigate serial killers? Why are you here?"

"When did you last have contact with your ex-wife?" Henley asked again.

The words "ex-wife" seemed to pull Dr. Ekubu back to reality as he leaned forward and massaged his temples. "I haven't had any contact with her since the divorce. We split up three years ago."

"You separated when she was pregnant?"

"The baby wasn't mine. I wish that it had been mine, but it wasn't."

"Who was the father?"

"No idea. She never told me."

"Was that the reason why you broke up, because Alyssa had an affair?"

"No, no. I would have stayed, but our marriage ended."

Henley was desperate to know why Dr. Ekubu hadn't answered the question. She could easily ask him again to tell her *why*, but if the man was prepared to stay and raise another man's child then perhaps the answer was simple. Alyssa didn't want to be with him.

"But you still worked here together at the university after you split?" Ramouter asked.

"I'm a visiting lecturer. It was easy for me not to see her. You still haven't told me what happened to her?" Dr. Ekubu said in a clear effort to regain some control of the situation.

"We don't know," Henley admitted. "She was found dead in her flat and all I can say is that the circumstances are suspicious. So, tell us about Alyssa. You've explained that the baby wasn't yours."

"And as I said, that's not why we broke up."

"So why did you?"

Dr. Ekubu's face momentarily relaxed. "She was exciting," he said. "She was everything. Funny. Smart, spontaneous. But then she became more manic."

"Alyssa was bipolar?" asked Ramouter.

"I didn't know about it when we first got involved with each other. She didn't tell me and there was nothing going on to make me think that she wasn't well."

"What exactly happened?" asked Henley. "We understand that Alyssa had a miscarriage. Did that bring on a depressive episode?"

Dr. Ekubu nodded. "But it started before that. I only found out about her condition when I discovered the medication box in the back of the car when I was cleaning. It must have dropped out of her bag."

"She hid it from you?"

"Yes. She was on lithium. It's a mood stabilizer. She told me that she'd been on it since she was seventeen."

"What do you think happened to Alyssa? Because you said that it happened before her miscarriage?"

"I think that she must have had a manic episode. I was traveling a lot at the time, but I never cheated on her. Never."

"But Alyssa cheated on you?" asked Henley.

"Yes, but she didn't know what she was doing," Dr. Ekubu said defensively. "I don't know whether she'd stopped taking her medication or if her GP had changed her dosage but by the time I got home, she was in full mania."

"How did you cope? You didn't know about her condition. It must have been a steep learning curve for you."

"It was," Dr. Ekubu said sadly. "The mania lasted for about ten days, she disappeared for two of those days, and then she fell into a depressive episode and then the mania was back. We went on like that for about three months. We found out about the pregnancy when we got her blood test results back. She had no idea who the father was, and it definitely wasn't mine. She was about four months gone when she miscarried. She woke me up at 3 a.m. The sheets were covered in blood."

Henley looked across at Ramouter who seemed just as exhausted as she was with the weight of the conversation and Dr. Ekubu's distress.

"So, what happened after the miscarriage?" Ramouter asked, taking the baton from Henley.

"She fell into another depression," said Dr. Ekubu. "That lasted for a few months and then she started getting manic. It was little things at first, but then it got worse. Started making all sorts of accusations. Accusing me of having affairs, which I wasn't. She harmed herself and started to attack me."

"Didn't you try and get her some help?" asked Henley.

"She didn't want the help."

"Even though she was clearly in need of it?"

"Have you had to deal with someone who has severe mental health issues?" Dr. Ekubu raised his voice. "Do you think that it's easy trying to convince someone that you're trying to do what's best for them only for them to physically and verbally attack you?"

Henley took a mental step back. Everything about Dr. Ekubu was a facade. Behind the sharp suit, the stern gaze, there was a lot of hurt.

"Did the university know about Alyssa's mental health?" Henley finally asked.

"No," Dr. Ekubu answered. "No, Alyssa was worried about the stigma that having a mental illness held. She was good at her job, when she was well. She was smart. It's one of the things that I love…sorry, loved about her. Her doctor signed her off with stress."

"What happened in the end?" Henley asked gently. The last thing that she wanted was her words to bite. It was crystal clear that Dr. Ekubu was still in love with Alyssa.

"I really tried, but, I eventually had her sectioned," said Dr. Ekubu removing his glasses and wiping the tears from his eyes. "I thought that it was for the best. She spent two months in Templey Mental Health Hospital in Stamford Hill. She refused to come home when they discharged her and then she filed for divorce. I didn't want it. I did try and get her the help but when someone is continuously fighting you…well, what are you supposed to do?"

"When was the last time that you saw Alyssa?" asked Ramouter.

"The night that the police came to my house, and she was sectioned."

"You didn't go to the hospital?"

"She refused to see me. I should have tried harder. I should have done something to hold onto her, but she didn't want me."

"Did Alyssa have any family?"

"No. Her parents are both dead. There's a half sister floating about somewhere, but it was just me really. I was all she had."

Henley looked across at Ramouter. For the first time, she felt unsure about her next move as Dr. Ekubu sat back in his chair looking despondent and guilty.

"I did try, you know," Dr. Ekubu said as he finally stood up, moved to the desk and started to shut his laptop down. "I didn't abandon her."

"That's funny. Giana said the same thing," said Ramouter.

Dr. Ekubu straightened himself and pursed his lips. "She was supposed to be her friend."

"How would you describe your relationship with Giana?" Ramouter asked. "You're both working at the university and Giana insinuated that it was you who left Alyssa. She didn't mention anything about Alyssa being sectioned."

Dr. Ekubu leaned forward and put his head in his hands as the tears finally began to fall. "I wanted to protect Alyssa," he said. "I can take it, but Alyssa was vulnerable. It was easier to let people think that I'd walked out on her."

Henley indicated to Ramouter that it was time to call it a day. It was obvious that Dr. Ekubu had done everything he could to care for his wife.

"I want to go home," Dr. Ekubu said, finally raising his head.

"Of course," Henley said. She reached into her pocket, pulled out her business card and handed it to Dr. Ekubu. "I know that you hadn't seen Alyssa for a while and that this has been a lot to process, but call me if you think of anything that could help."

"Will you let me know when her... I was her family and I want to say goodbye to her properly," Dr. Ekubu said as he took the card and put it in his laptop case.

"Of course I will," said Henley. "As soon as she's ready, I will let you know."

"There is one more thing," said Ramouter.

"Yes?" Dr. Ekubu asked.

"I was just wondering if Alyssa was a member of a church?"

"Church?" He vigorously shook his head. "Alyssa would never set foot into a church. She just about believed in marriage. We got married in a register office. Alyssa is an atheist. She didn't believe in anything."

29

"Dad," Henley called out as she walked through her childhood home, following the deep rhythmic bass of Gregory Isaacs as it pulsated through the house. Henley smiled as she reached the living room and watched her dad dancing with his grand-daughter, both of them singing loudly and out of tune.

Music playing was a good thing. The sound of Henley's dad singing badly was a positive sign. Henley pushed aside the flutter of griefs as an image of her mother singing perfectly as she seasoned meat in the kitchen forced itself into her mind.

"Hey, my beautiful star," Elijah said breathlessly, when the music stopped and he saw Henley.

It was such a change from six months ago when her dad had sat broken and trapped in the arms of a deep depression. Henley and her brother Simon had taken it in turns to gently cajole him out of his house and into the spare room of Simon's, and then to see his GP. The change in the antidepressants prescribed by the doctor and his attendance at the hospital outpatient clinic had been enough to put her dad back on the road to recovery.

"Again. Play it again," Emma said, running around her gran-dad's legs, ignoring her mum.

"Again? I've already played it three times," Elijah laughed as Henley walked over and hugged him. She breathed him in. He smelled like her dad, a combination of the same aftershave that he had been wearing for as long as she could remember, talcum powder and the faint scent of sawdust.

"So, she's been good for you today," Henley asked as she bent down and kissed Emma's sweaty forehead. Henley wasn't offended when Emma wriggled away from her and threw herself onto the sofa and asked for her grandad to turn on the television. Last summer she never would have imagined her dad looking after her daughter, even for the afternoon, but Rob had called to say that his train from Manchester had been canceled and that he wouldn't make it back in time to pick up Emma from nursery.

"Yes, she's been fine. We've had a good afternoon. She helped me to paint a cabinet," Elijah said affectionately as he walked into the kitchen and switched on the kettle.

"I'm glad that you're working," Henley said as she followed her dad. Through the kitchen window she could see the large shed that had long ago been extended and converted into a workshop, where her dad had worked as a carpenter making bespoke pieces of furniture.

"Ah, it's nothing. Just a one-off commission. She wanted it painted shabby chic. Stupidness." Elijah rolled his eyes and pulled out two cups from the cupboard.

"None for me, Dad. I'm not staying. I'm just dropping off Em's pj's and her clothes for tomorrow, and then I have to go back to the station. It's better that she spends the night with her granddad. I have no idea how long this interview is going to be, and Rob won't be home until late."

"You can at least have a cup of tea. I can't have you dropping with exhaustion," said Elijah.

"Fine." Henley knew that there was no point arguing. "You sit down and I'll make it."

"Only one sugar. I'm cutting down," said Elijah as he took a seat at the kitchen table.

"Yeah, right," Henley replied when she spotted the open biscuit tin in front of her dad.

"I saw you on the telly yesterday. So did the pastor try and kill that boy in the church?"

"Is that the only thing that you got from the press conference?"

"People always remember the first thing you said and the last thing. And the last thing that I remember is one of them reporters asking if the pastor was responsible."

"Thanks for that, Dad," Henley replied as she made the tea.

"Don't get vex with me. It just makes the story juicier."

"It's not a story, it's a murder investigation."

"If you ask me," Elijah said as he pulled out a handful of Jammie Dodgers from the biscuit tin and handed one to Emma who had left the sofa and walked into the kitchen, "I think that the pastor did it."

"You've been watching too much of that true crime channel."

"You must have a suspect. For a man like that. There must be loads."

"Why do you think that there must be loads?" Henley asked with genuine curiosity.

"Because I googled him. And there was a video of his church service on YouTube, and he looked like a charlatan. He wanted the congregation to worship him," said Elijah. "You should watch them. I'll send you the link."

"Make sure that you do, and to answer your question, no, we haven't got any suspects yet, which is frustrating. But between me and you—and I mean me and you, don't go shouting off to your mates down the pub."

"As if I would ever do such a thing," Elijah said with mock horror.

"I think that you might be on the right lines, with wanting people to worship him. He wasn't exactly practicing what he was preaching, especially when it came to, well, other women."

"That's why I wasn't keen on church," said Elijah as Henley handed him his tea at the table and Emma climbed onto her granddad's lap. "People like to use religion to justify their ill behavior. Why don't you deal with cases that are straightforward?"

"Why should my life be easy? I should be so lucky."

"Stop being so hard on yourself. You deserve a happy and peaceful life," said Elijah. "You don't have to be strong all the time, angel."

"I'm not unhappy. I'm just..." Henley's voice trailed off. It was the one thing that she couldn't do. Lie to her dad.

"You're just what?"

"I'm tired. I'm tired of second-guessing myself. I'm tired of going to bed with ghosts. Maybe it would be easier if I just got another job."

"That's not the answer," Elijah snorted. "The only person that you'd make happy is Rob. You'd be miserable and so would Stephen."

"Don't start," Henley said as she drank her tea. For some strange reason, when her dad had threatened to chase her boyfriends out of the house, Pellacia was the only one who he'd actually liked. Henley's mum had said more than once her dad was more upset about Henley breaking off her relationship with Pellacia than Henley had been.

"I'm not saying anything," Elijah protested. "So, is Stephen coming to your mum's memorial on Saturday?"

"I don't know," Henley said when she remembered the text that she'd sent Pellacia telling him not to come. He still hadn't replied.

"Hopefully, he comes," said Elijah. "Your mum liked him, and she would like to know that he's here celebrating her."

"How do you do it, Dad?" Henley asked as she took their empty teacups to the sink. "I miss her so much, but I can't... it hurts too much."

"I let myself cry when I want to cry, laugh when I want to laugh, and I don't beat myself up when I forget that she's not here, and I make a cup of tea for me and a cup of coffee for her first thing in the morning. I let myself miss her, Anjelica," Elijah said.

"I don't want to miss her," Henley admitted as she rejoined her dad at the table. "If I miss her, then I'll have to accept that she's gone."

"You can't keep fighting it," Elijah said. He pushed the biscuit tin away from Emma.

"I know, I know. I suppose that it would feel better if I was more in control."

"What do you mean *more* in control?" Elijah said as he began to laugh. "You're too much in control."

"What are you talking about?"

"I saw your face at the press conference when that pastor's wife was talking. She was too much. I don't know how you managed to keep a straight face or not drag her off the table."

"Honestly, Dad, I could have—"

Henley stopped as her phone began to ring. She turned around and took it out from the depths of her bag hanging off the back of her chair. "Sorry, it's Stanford," she told him, and answered the call. "Hey, you. Is she all booked in?"

"Yeah, she is," Stanford replied. "There was no room at Lewisham, so we had to take her to Plumstead. She started to bawl her eyes out when Eastwood told her that she was under arrest for murder."

"Did she say anything?"

"Only that she didn't do it, but she ain't that stupid. She asked for a lawyer the minute we walked into the custody suite."

30

The custody suite at Plumstead lacked the modernity of Lewisham police station. A distinct smell of chicken and mushroom pot noodles mixed with the overmarinated stench of a detainee who hadn't bathed in a week filled the place.

"Do you think that she'll talk?" Ramouter asked as he followed Henley to the interview room. "Uliana's savvy enough to ask for a solicitor, even if she does look about twelve."

"I think that she might do, but I don't think that she'll talk to me," said Henley. "I think that she'll talk to you."

"You do?" Ramouter asked with surprise.

"Positive. I'm the one who threatened to arrest her and stick her in a cold cell. She'll already have her back up when she sees me. You take the lead. She'll definitely talk if it's you."

Uliana Piontek sat red-faced and puffy-eyed on the hard plastic bench with a small pile of damp and crumbled tissues in front of her. Her solicitor, Aaron Lodge, to his credit, sat stone-faced as he straightened up his papers and smoothed out the disclosure statement that Ramouter had handed him an hour ago.

"I didn't do anything," Uliana burst out before Henley and Ramouter had taken their seats.

"Wait," Aaron said firmly.

"But—"

"Uliana. I explained how this works. Just wait," said Aaron as he picked up his pen and made a note.

"Right, let's start, shall we?" Henley said. She pressed record on the monitor, then sat back and watched Uliana as Ramouter went through the caution. Uliana looked even worse than when she'd met her at her flat. The gravity of the situation had stripped her of any confidence that she may have had.

"I haven't done anything wrong," said Uliana the second that Ramouter had finished the caution. "I didn't kill him."

"You said the exact same thing when you were arrested," said Ramouter. "And according to the custody record, you said it again when you were booked in."

"I'm telling you the truth. I didn't kill him."

"You keep saying that, Uliana, but there are two facts staring at me which make me question whether you are telling me the truth," Ramouter said calmly.

"I wouldn't lie."

"But you have lied, Uliana."

"About what?"

Henley was constantly amazed by a person's ability to convince themselves that they would never get caught, that the tangled strings of their lies would never be unraveled. She pulled a single sheet of paper and placed it in front of Uliana.

"What is this?" Uliana asked, picking up the sheet of paper with trembling fingers. "I don't understand."

"That is a streamlined forensic report which gives a breakdown on the forensic evidence that was found on Caleb Annan's body," Ramouter explained.

"I didn't touch his body. I saw him on the floor, and I ran."

"That report tells us that your vaginal fluid was found on

Caleb Annan's boxer shorts, his penis and groin area. Your vaginal fluid was also found on the sofa in his office."

"That information wasn't disclosed to us," said Aaron as he took the report from Uliana's hand. "I'm stating for the record that I specifically asked you about the form of the DNA and you failed to disclose that to me."

Henley could hear the slight quiver in Aaron's voice as he spoke.

"You had sufficient disclosure," said Henley. "The disclosure statement which you read and signed, Mr. Lodge, clearly stated that DNA belonging to Uliana Piontek was found on Annan's body and on the crime scene."

There was a brief moment as Aaron read the statement. To her credit, Uliana kept a poker face until Aaron leaned over and whispered in her ear. Her face paled.

"Carry on," said Aaron.

"That vaginal fluid is a 99.9 percent DNA match for you," said Ramouter.

"I... There must be a mistake."

"There's no mistake."

"Maybe someone put it there."

Henley caught Aaron's eye as his pen paused on the page.

"Someone put it there?" asked Ramouter without a sense of mockery. "Your DNA?"

"It could happen."

"We're not dealing with hypotheticals here," said Ramouter. "No one planted your DNA on Caleb Annan."

"No one is trying to set you up," said Henley. "If there's an explanation for your DNA being found on Caleb Annan's body then you need to tell us. He's dead and you're not. Right now, you're in the unenviable position of being the one and only person accused of murdering him," said Henley.

Uliana wiped the tears from her face with her sleeve.

"You're only..." Henley pulled the custody record sheet toward her. "You're twenty-one in June. A sentence for murder isn't really a full life sentence. Best case scenario, the judge might set a tariff of maybe twenty-five, thirty years."

"Tariff. What does that mean?" Uliana asked as she looked across at Aaron for reassurance.

"It means that you will be fifty years old before you're eligible for parole," Ramouter said.

Henley didn't think that it was possible for Uliana's face to get any paler.

"Fifty," Uliana whispered.

"If you're lucky," said Henley.

"We know that you had sex with Caleb Annan," said Ramouter. "Which means that you were with him just before he was murdered, or you were the one who murdered him. So, which is it?"

"It wasn't...it wasn't me who... I didn't do anything." Uliana leaned back against the wall and took a deep breath. It was well over a minute before she spoke again. "I was there. The Monday night."

"I know that this sounds a bit pedantic, but I need you to be clear as to where exactly you were," said Ramouter.

"In the church." Uliana bent forward and cradled her head in her hands.

"Why were you there?"

"Caleb called and said that he wanted to see me."

"Why did he want to see you? The cleaner."

Uliana sat up, leaned toward Aaron and whispered. "It's fine. Tell them."

Henley couldn't help but feel a pang of sympathy when she saw the fear and anxiety on Uliana's face.

"He wanted to see me. We...were involved," Uliana said quietly.

"In what way were you involved?" asked Ramouter.

"We were sleeping together."

"You were in a relationship."

"No, no. Not a relationship. We were just seeing each other."

"And how long had you been seeing him?"

"About four months. It wasn't long after I started working there. He told me that he liked me and that I was special. He had a way of convincing me that it was a good thing."

"So, you were sleeping with him for four months."

Uliana nodded.

"You're going to have to answer; for the tape," said Aaron.

"Sorry, yes," said Uliana.

"And where would you have sex?"

Uliana took a breath. "The first time was at the church, in his office, but I would usually meet him at a hotel. We did go to a flat in Wapping once."

"Uliana," Ramouter said gently, "Caleb Annan was a married man with two children."

"He told me that his marriage was over and that he was only staying because of the kids."

"Did you ever suspect that Caleb may have been involved with other women?"

There was a flash of confusion in Uliana's eyes. "What are you talking about? What did Nicole tell you?"

"Nicole?" Ramouter asked as he looked across at Henley. "Your friend who used to clean for Caleb?"

Uliana nodded slowly.

"We haven't spoken to Nicole yet."

"You haven't?" Uliana asked quietly. There was no mistaking the look on her face. She had realized that she had begun to dig a hole for herself.

"No, we haven't," said Henley. "What do you think Nicole would have told us?"

Uliana bit her lip.

"Uliana, when we first spoke to you, in your flat, you said that we didn't need to talk to Nicole," said Henley.

"I don't remember saying that."

Henley pulled out her notebook from the file on the table and flicked through the pages until she stopped at the one with the top left corner turned down. "Here we go. 'She will know nothing.' That's the note that I made. Why didn't you want us to speak to Nicole?"

"It's nothing."

"I don't think that's true," said Henley. "I'm going to ask you again. Why didn't you want us to speak to Nicole?"

Henley could hear the gentle whirring of the air-conditioning system as she waited for Uliana to answer.

"He was sleeping with Nicole," Uliana said eventually. She lowered her head. Her voice was barely audible.

"Uliana, you're going to have to speak up," Henley said firmly. "And it's not going to help you if you keep things to yourself because, one way or another, we're going to find out."

"When did you find out that Caleb was sleeping with Nicole?" Ramouter asked.

"I started cleaning the church in September," said Uliana. "Nicole had stopped working there in August, I think. Caleb and me...we started seeing each other in October. It was about a week after I started back at uni."

"How did it start? You and Caleb, I mean," asked Ramouter.

"He told me to come in early one morning." Uliana's voice dropped as she kept her gaze focused on the recording monitor. "I was waiting for him to open the church."

"He didn't give you a set of keys?"

"Not straightaway."

"OK, so he told you to come in early?"

"Yes, it was just me and him. He was nice and was asking me about my course, my family and then, when I was cleaning his office, he closed the door and he kissed me. He told me that I was special and that he liked me."

"And what did you do, when he kissed you?"

"I told him no at first, but then..." Uliana leaned back against the hard bench and looked straight at Ramouter. "I kissed him back and I let him touch me."

"Was that it?"

"Yes, we didn't have sex because he suddenly stopped and told me that it was wrong and that he was sorry. He then gave me some money to apologize."

"He gave you money?" Ramouter asked. "How much did he give you?"

"A hundred pounds. He knew that I was struggling with money."

"When did you start sleeping with Caleb?"

"Maybe a week or two later. It was just me and him in the church, and we had sex in one of the meeting rooms upstairs."

"But you said that you never went into the meeting rooms. I asked you specifically if you'd ever gone into those rooms and you said no," said Ramouter. "Why did you lie?"

"I… I don't… I'm sorry," Uliana said. She began to pull at the few strands of her hair.

"How often were you sleeping with Caleb?"

"Every week. He gave me a set of keys after about three weeks."

"Did you always have sex in the church?"

"No. That only happened once and we had sex in his car a few times but he would usually call or text me at night and give me the address of a hotel."

"Did Caleb give you any more money or gifts?"

"I'm sorry… I'm sorry," Uliana said. She turned her face toward the wall and began to cry.

"Maybe we should have a short break," said Aaron as he gave Ramouter a resentful look. "You can see that she's upset."

"No, no, it's fine. I'm OK." Uliana sniffed as she pushed herself farther into the corner, somehow making herself look even smaller and more vulnerable.

"Did Caleb pay you each time that you had sex?" Henley asked.

"I'm not a prostitute," Uliana shouted out.

"Inspector Henley is not suggesting that," Ramouter said gently. "But you do understand that she has to ask?"

"I don't care," Uliana said. "She's trying to make me look like a…but I'm not. I didn't do anything wrong."

"OK, let me ask you another question. Let's go back to Nicole," said Ramouter. "When did you find out that Caleb had been sleeping with your friend?"

"It was just before Christmas," Uliana said. "Caleb wanted to see me before I went back home to Lithuania for Christmas. He said that he had a present for me. He told me to meet him at a hotel on Tower Bridge Road and… Nicole was already there."

"What was Nicole doing when you arrived?" Ramouter asked.

"She was in bed," Uliana said. Her voice broke and she began to cry. "He threatened to fire me if I left and that he would tell the police that I'd stolen money from him. Which wasn't true."

"What happened after Caleb threatened you?" asked Ramouter.

"I joined them. I did it, but it only happened once."

"Did Caleb ever hurt you or force you to have sex with him?" Henley asked gently.

"He didn't force me, but he did…he hurt me."

"I'm sorry," said Henley. "But I'm going to have to ask you how Caleb hurt you?"

"Sometimes he was just…rough, and he would squeeze my neck. Once, he left a bruise, but it wasn't every time," Uliana said hurriedly. "I don't think that he meant to hurt me."

Henley wasn't surprised. It wasn't the first time that she'd seen a victim of sexual assault almost apologize for their abuser's behavior. Being so disempowered could lead to undeserved thoughts of self-blame.

"You didn't do anything wrong, Uliana," said Henley. "He took advantage of you."

"I kept thinking that maybe I said the wrong thing or sent mixed messages."

"No, you didn't," Henley said firmly. "Move on," she whispered to Ramouter.

"So, tell us what happened on Sunday night. What time did you arrive at the church?" asked Ramouter.

"Caleb texted me about 8:30 p.m. and told me to come."

"Was that usual? For him to text you on a Sunday night like that? It didn't ring any alarm bells for you?"

"Not really. He said that he was sending an Uber for me. I think that I arrived at the church at about 9:15 p.m."

"And how long were you with him?"

"Maybe forty-five minutes. I left just after ten in another Uber."

"Did you leave through the back or the front of the church?"

"The back, but the car was waiting for me on the main road, on Deptford Broadway."

"Did you notice anything when you left?"

"Not when I left, but I had to go back. I realized that I'd left my phone. So, I asked the driver to turn around. When I went back there was a car parked next to Caleb's."

"Can you describe the car?"

"It was silver. A small one. I can't remember the make. The back door was already open, and I went to Caleb's office."

"Can you remember what time this was?" asked Henley.

"I'm not too sure," said Uliana. "Maybe ten past ten. I re-membered that my sister called me when I was getting back into the cab."

"Did your sister call you on the same phone that the custody sergeant took from you when you were booked in?"

"Yes."

"Same number? You haven't changed the sim card?" asked Henley as she pushed a pen and notepad toward Uliana.

"No. It's the same. No changes."

"Do we have permission to go through your phone to check that what you're telling us about the phone calls is true?"

"Yes," Uliana replied as she released an exhausted sigh.

"Good," said Henley. "Write the pin number down."

"What did you see when you went back?" Ramouter asked once Uliana had completed her small task.

"I heard Caleb arguing with a woman in his office. I went to leave but the door opened, and Caleb came out."

"How was he?"

"Angry. He shouted at me. I told him that I had forgotten my phone. And then she came out."

"Who came out?"

"His wife. Serena Annan."

Henley looked across at Ramouter as Uliana started to cry again. She asked, "Are you sure that it was Serena Annan?"

Uliana nodded.

"I need a yes or no from you," Henley said softly.

"Yes. It was her."

"Did she say anything to you?"

"Leave. She gave me my phone and told me to leave."

31

The nightmare was a sequence of disjointed images. Ramouter was on the floor covered in Dominic Pine's bloody guts and then Olivier was on top of her, licking her face, his tongue warm and wet. She could feel him pressing down on her, pushing his knees between her legs, trying to separate them, but it was the image of Pellacia's naked body hanging from a beam that had woken her up. In the nightmare, Olivier had pushed her face into the bleeding wounds on Pellacia's chest.

"Stephen!"

Henley wasn't sure if she'd said Pellacia's name out loud or whether it had just been part of her nightmare. The bedroom was freezing. The nauseous sweat that covered Henley's chest and forehead had left her shivering.

"What's wrong?" Rob's voice was muffled and weighted down with sleep.

Henley tried to focus her eyes in the darkness. The clock read 4:28 a.m. Henley could feel the Chinese takeaway that she'd eaten the night before making an unwelcome return up her throat and her tongue was coated with soured bile.

"Anj?" Rob said as Henley threw back the covers, jumped out of bed and ran into the bathroom.

Henley's stomach was swirling like a ship on unstable waters. She felt her stomach muscles painfully contract as she breathed in the fumes from the bleach in the toilet water, but nothing happened. There was no release. She sat on the cold bathroom floor with her back against the toilet.

"You can't stay on the floor, Anjelica. It's freezing," Rob said at the bathroom door, rubbing his eyes. Henley's legs felt weak, as Rob took hold of her arm and pulled her to her feet.

"You're not OK," Rob said. He walked Henley back into the bedroom and took out a clean T-shirt from the chest of drawers. "I'll get you some water, unless you want a cup of tea?"

"No, water will be fine," said Henley, taking off her clammy pajama top. She could hear her own heart beating as she sat in the darkness. Rob left the room.

"It's not fair," she whispered to herself as she wiped away a tear. She wanted it to be over. To leave her pain, mistakes and Olivier in the past, but they kept creeping into her present.

"Here you go," Rob said as he returned and handed Henley a hot mug.

"I said that I just wanted water." Henley hoped that she sounded strong but there was no fight in her.

"You might as well have tea, as I know that you're not going to go back to sleep. I thought that the nightmares had stopped?"

"They come and go."

"I was thinking," Rob said, getting back into bed with Henley and letting out a yawn. "Maybe I should come to therapy with you. To get a better understanding about what's going on."

"Rob, this isn't about you," said Henley.

"But it is about him, though."

Henley was glad that Rob hadn't turned on the lights, as she wouldn't have been able to explain away the guilt on her face.

"You called out for him," said Rob. "That's what woke me up. You called out his name. Twice."

"I don't remember doing that," Henley said as she sipped her tea. "And even if I did—"

"No ifs. You did."

"It's just my mind messing up about with me."

"Anj, don't take me for an idiot," Rob said. He switched on the lamp, turned around and faced Henley.

"Rob, I've got to be at work in a few hours and I can't have this conversation replaying in my head."

"Something has got to give," Rob said. "If you're going to get over... If you want this marriage to continue, then something has to give."

32

"Morning, sunshine."

Henley looked up to see Stanford walking toward her carrying a greasy paper bag and a cardboard tray with two large coffee cups.

"What are you doing here so early? It's just gone eight," asked Henley.

"Gene's mum is staying with us, and I'd rather not spend my precious mornings listening to her right-wing rantings while I'm trying to eat my cornflakes."

"You hate cornflakes."

"That's not the point," said Stanford as he placed the coffees on Henley's desk, looking closely at Henley. "No offense, but you look like shit. You haven't slept."

"I don't know what's wrong with me," Henley admitted.

"I know exactly what's wrong with you," said Stanford. "You're probably not doing what you should be doing in those therapy sessions."

"And what should I be doing?"

"Talking and letting things that you can't control, control you. What do you want—sausage and egg or bacon and egg bagel?"

"Is that what you came here to tell me? Give me the sausage," said Henley.

"Actually, yes, it was, and I knew that you would need breakfast."

"Thank you, Paul," said Henley, unwrapping her bagel. "I do miss you being my partner."

"I miss you too," Stanford said as he handed Henley packets of brown sauce. "Working with Eastie is all right, but you know all my secrets. Speaking of which, I've got news."

"Make it good news. I need good news."

"Gene and I finally got approved by the adoption agency," Stanford said as he bit into his sandwich.

"What!" Henley said, putting down her bagel. "But that's fantastic."

"I know," Stanford mumbled through a full mouth.

"And you're just sitting there stuffing your face," Henley laughed. She knew that Stanford was over the moon despite his laid-back demeanor. "You'll be a great dad."

"Ta. And Emma can finally have another cousin to play with."

"How's Gene taking the news?"

"How do you think? He's been bouncing around the house since we got confirmation last night. He'll be trying to get the poor kid into every football academy that he can think of, including Palace."

"Oh, behave yourself," said Henley. "I make a bet that he or she will be a Palace signing before the Arsenal manager has even rolled out of bed."

"Don't joke," Stanford said. "I feel like I'm in a toxic relationship with Arsenal."

"Speaking of relationships," said Henley. "I told Ramouter about Pellacia and me."

"Was that a good idea?" Stanford asked with a raised eyebrow.

"I trust him, and I owed him some kind of explanation for the way that Pellacia has been behaving."

"I'm more than happy to have a word with Pellacia," said Stanford. "He's been behaving like a prize dick."

"I appreciate that," Henley said. "No, I'll be fine, but what you can do is head back to the SCU and chase Joel for his post-mortem report on Hadlow. And remind Ramouter to check for the forensic results. We need to know as soon as possible the official cause of death and if Caleb Annan had anything to do with it."

"Update me," Henley asked as Ramouter joined her in the kitchen and switched the kettle on.

"We've got the initial post-mortem results for Hadlow," said Ramouter.

"What do you mean, initial? They've had the body since yesterday."

"According to Joel, there's a queue, and that's all I got before he put the phone down on me. Anyway, the initial toxicology results showed signs of sepsis and that could also have resulted in heart failure."

"Hadlow could have got a bacterial infection from the burns on her feet," said Henley.

"Or the cuts on her wrists. You saw how tightly they were bound," said Ramouter.

"God, that woman must have suffered."

"But that's not all. Katherine from Bromley CSI called, and they retrieved four sets of prints in Hadlow's flat. One set obviously belongs to Hadlow."

"And the other three?"

"An exact match for the three that were recovered from the room where Brandon Whittaker was held. One set belongs to Caleb Annan and the other two sets match the unidentified prints."

"Shit," said Henley as she put down her fork.

"Aye, it's not good," said Ramouter.

"Things are speeding up," said Henley. "And there aren't

enough of us. We need to speak to Serena Annan, now that Uliana has placed her at the scene at the time of Caleb's death."

"But we also need to speak to Nicole Fleming. Caleb Annan was clearly a sexual predator. Do you think that his wife knew?"

"I would be surprised if she didn't have some inkling," said Henley. "And if Serena knew, then what better motive would there be for murder."

"The only problem is that Serena's prints are all over that church, which is understandable because it's her church, but we didn't find her DNA on Caleb's body and she has an alibi," said Ramouter. "I spoke to her housekeeper, Dalisay, yesterday, and she has confirmed that Serena never left the house on Sunday night. Serena had also been drinking a lot that evening and Dalisay helped her to bed."

"So, who's telling the truth?" Henley said. She opened the box of pains au chocolat and croissants that Stanford had also brought in.

"Couldn't he have bought you at least one of your five a day?" Ramouter asked as Henley handed him a pastry.

"Stanford's allergic to fruit and veg," Henley said. "Right, this is what we'll do. We're going to speak to Nicole Fleming, and there's also Raina Davison."

"The woman who accused Caleb of rape?"

"Yes, let's get everyone's story down and then we'll deal with Serena. The more evidence that we have about Caleb, then the stronger the motive will be for Serena to commit murder."

33

"Are you sure that this is the right address?" Ramouter leaned against the car door.

"Galena Court. That's the address that Uliana gave us," Henley said. She threw her battered leather-bound blue logbook onto the dashboard, which had very slim odds of warding off a traffic warden intent on meeting their monthly quota for parking tickets. The temperature had dropped even more since she had left the house earlier that morning. She wrapped her scarf around her neck as she looked up. Ramouter was well within his rights to question whether or not the address was correct. The stark gray unstable concrete of the Hammersmith Flyover loomed overhead on Henley's right. The black exhaust fumes hung in almost frozen suspension as the traffic stalled and snaked along the Talgarth Road. Galena Court was a glass-fronted new-build apartment block and stood gleaming and out of place. It was positioned between the long-abandoned magistrates' court that was still awaiting its own transformation into another boutique hotel, and a row of listed brown-brick Victorian artists' studios, which had been converted into multimillion-pound houses whose price tags didn't act as a barrier to the layers of the pollution that coated everything along the A4.

"You saw Uliana's home," Ramouter said as he followed Henley's stride toward the building. "It wasn't exactly high living. Typical student digs, but this place, there's an underground car park and a concierge." They stopped as the large gate on the side of the building lifted up and a brand-new Porsche Cayenne rolled out. "I'm starting to think that this is a wild goose chase."

"It better not be, otherwise I'm charging Uliana with wasting police time," said Henley.

"That would be a bit harsh considering what she's been through. It's bad enough that she's on bail for murder."

"Stop trying to make me look bad," said Henley. They reached the main doors to the building, and she pressed the trade button.

"We could just buzz and ask her to let us up. I should have brought my gloves," Ramouter said, pushing his hands farther into his coat pockets.

"No, I don't want to give Nicole the opportunity to run." Henley rapped loudly on the door to get the attention of the concierge, who was doing his best to ignore the buzzing trade button.

"That's assuming that Uliana didn't warn her," said Ramouter as Henley banged on the door for a second time.

The concierge, who looked to be no older than twenty-five, got up and lazily made his way to the door, but he didn't open it. "What do you want?" he asked.

"For fuck's sake," Henley said. She fished out her warrant card from her pocket and pushed it up against the glass. "Open the door," she shouted out.

The concierge's face whitened as he glanced down at the card. It took less than a second for him to reach to his right and press a button.

"Sorry about that. We get a lot of homeless people trying to come in because of the cold," he said.

"Do we look homeless to you?" said Henley as she and Ramouter walked into the lobby.

"No, that's not what I meant, sorry, I just… We also had someone come in and attack one of the tenants last week, so management has told us to…" His voice trailed off as Henley stared down at him.

"Can you tell us what floor Flat 53G is on?" she asked.

"53G? That will be on the Calla floor."

"Excuse me, what?" asked Ramouter.

"Sorry, the eighth floor. All of the floors are named after flowers. It's a bit stupid if you ask me, but yeah… Do you want me to let them know that you're on your way up?"

"No. Don't say a word," said Henley as she and Ramouter made their way toward the lift.

"Nicole Fleming?" Henley asked, pulling out her warrant card. Henley watched Nicole as her eyes scanned the card and then darted up at her. There was a mixture of fear and curiosity in her green eyes.

"Yes," Nicole said, her voice soft but cautious as she pulled her long brown hair over her left shoulder.

"I'm Detective Inspector Anjelica Henley and this is Detective Constable Ramouter. We need to talk to you about Caleb Annan."

If Nicole was shocked about hearing the name of her old boss, then she wasn't showing it. Her face remained impassive, but Henley saw her fingers whiten as she tightened her grip on the edge of the door.

"Why do you need to talk to me about him?" Nicole asked. Henley heard the brittleness creep into her voice. At that moment, she was sure that Nicole had something to hide.

"Because he was murdered on Sunday night," Henley said bluntly.

The door slammed shut.

"Not the reaction that I was expecting," Ramouter said as he knocked again. Half a minute later, the door reopened.

"Sorry," said Nicole as she reopened the door. "I wasn't dressed properly."

Nicole was shaking as though she had been thrown into an ice bath. She had pushed aside the cup of tea that Ramouter had made her and asked for a large glass of wine.

"How long have you been living here?" Henley asked.

"Five months," Nicole answered as she took the wineglass from Ramouter's hand.

"And you live here alone?"

"Yes, just me."

Henley kept her gaze on Nicole's heavily made-up face. Underneath the layers of foundation and concealer, Henley could see the swelling under Nicole's left eye, a small cut on her bottom lip and three deep scratches on the side of her neck.

"Caleb was... I didn't know."

The wine in the glass spilled over the edge as Nicole's hands shook.

"His body was found on Monday afternoon. It's been all over the news. You had no idea?"

"No, no."

"You haven't spoken to Uliana? I mean, you're friends and you used to work for Caleb as his cleaner," Henley said pointedly.

"I haven't spoken to Uliana in a while. I've been busy with uni and... I didn't know."

The glass fell from Nicole's hands and white wine spilled onto the plush rug.

"I've got it," Ramouter said. He grabbed a tea towel from the counter and cleaned up the spillage.

"Do you want to tell me what happened between you and Uliana?" Henley asked once Ramouter had returned to the kitchen area.

Nicole's hands began to tremble as she put the glass down

onto the coffee table. She curled her legs up under her and sank back into the armchair as if she wanted to disappear.

"OK. Well, let's talk about you and Caleb Annan. You worked for him as a cleaner?" Henley tried a different tack.

"Erm…yes." Nicole sniffed, still refusing to look at Henley as she held on tightly to a cushion. "I worked there for about seven months."

"Did you get another job?" Henley asked gently.

"No. This is my last year at uni. I wanted to focus on my course. I had to…" Nicole stopped and spun her head around at the sound of glasses falling against the metal draining board.

"Sorry," said Remoter as he held up a tall glass. "I just wanted to get a glass of water. Is that OK?"

"Yes. It's fine," Nicole replied hesitantly. "Just…just be careful."

"So, you're not working, and it's just you staying here in this flat?" Henley asked, wondering what exactly Ramouter was doing in the kitchen. "No flatmates."

Nicole raised her head but looked away. "I've had friends stay overnight," she said.

"Boyfriend?"

"No."

"Never had a boyfriend or he'd never stayed over?"

"No; he was…my ex," Nicole said quickly as she fidgeted in her chair. "He stayed over a few times but we broke up."

"Are your parents helping to pay the rent?" Henley asked, not quite believing Nicole's answer about an ex-boyfriend. "Student loan?"

"Everyone has a student loan."

Henley leaned forward in her chair and softened her voice. "When was the last time that you spoke to Mr. Annan?"

"I don't know. It was a while ago."

"Nicole. You do understand that we're investigating his death? His murder."

"I do, but it's nothing to do with me. Whatever happened to him, I mean."

"Which means that we will be investigating everything and everyone who was in his life; including those who left. We're checking his phone and emails. Do you understand what I'm saying? This isn't a game."

Nicole nodded slowly, with understanding. "I did text him last week but that was only because a friend of mine was looking for work and I thought that he might have a job cleaning the church."

"Even though Uliana is working there."

"I didn't know that Uliana was still there."

"You didn't know?"

Henley saw the hesitancy in Nicole's eyes as she tried to make up a lie. "It was stupid. We had an argument when we went out for drinks one night. I can't even remember what it was about."

"Weren't you and Uliana good friends?"

"Yes, we were."

"How long had you been friends for?"

"A couple of years. We met at uni."

"So why did you fall out?"

"I honestly don't remember...we're just not friends."

"OK. Well, let me ask you about your time at the church," said Henley. "Did you ever notice anything suspicious?"

"No, nothing. There was never any trouble. I mean, it's church. How much trouble can you get into at church?"

"What were your working hours?"

"I was only there in the morning. I didn't see that many people except Caleb...sorry, Mr. Annan, when I worked."

"Not even his wife?"

Nicole curled up tighter in her chair and put a hand protectively to her neck.

"No, not his wife."

"And did you ever go to Caleb Annan's home?" Henley asked. She reached into her jacket pocket and pulled out her last business card. She didn't expect to get a truthful answer from Nicole. Everything was telling Henley that Nicole's relationship with Caleb Annan had not ended when she'd stopped working for him.

Nicole shook her head. "Never. I don't even know where they lived."

Henley stood up and handed over her business card. "Call me if there's anything that comes to mind." She indicated for Ramouter that it was time to leave.

Nicole got up from the chair and stood up. She looked small, young and completely unsure of herself.

"Don't worry, we'll show ourselves out. I'm sure that you've got a lot of uni work to be getting on with; it's been years, but I know what it's like, that last year, trying to get your dissertation done," Henley said with a warm smile. "I forgot to ask. Sunday night. Where were you?"

"I was here."

"You didn't leave."

"No. I was working on my dissertation. You can check with the concierge. They've got cameras everywhere. I didn't leave. I swear."

"We'll do that. Thank you," said Henley. "Oh, do you mind if I use your bathroom? Who knows how long we'll be sitting in traffic on our way back to south London."

"Of course. It's the first door on the right."

The sound of Ramouter making small talk as she made her way along the corridor faded as Henley found the bathroom and locked the door. The room was bathed in bright LED light that bounced off the chrome bathroom fittings. Henley was impressed and would have killed for a bathroom that wasn't covered in bath toys, mix-matched towel sets and cheap shower gel because Emma was determined to empty an entire bottle into her bath.

God, you look like shit, thought Henley, catching sight of her reflection and her allergy-stricken eyes in the mirror as she washed her hands.

"Oh, Nicole," Henley said as she spotted two toothbrushes in a white ceramic toothbrush holder. She opened the bathroom cabinet to find a hard bristled brush, the same hair oil that Rob used, a half empty can of men's deodorant, aftershave and a man's razor with a scattering of black hair on the blade. Henley was convinced that if she seized the razor and sent it to forensics that Caleb Annan's DNA would be all over it.

"Thank you," Henley said, rejoining Ramouter and Nicole in the hallway.

"Do you think… Do you know who did it?" Nicole asked as she quickly unlocked the front door.

"Not yet, but as we said, we're looking into everything. And a word of advice, if I'm looking then that means that reporters will be looking too. So, if you do remember anything, make sure that you call me," Henley warned.

"I haven't done anything wrong," Nicole said quietly.

"No one is saying that you have. We're here to help. Nothing more."

"I need to show you something," Ramouter said as the lift doors closed and began to descend. He pulled his phone out of his pocket, enlarged the photograph on his screen and handed the phone to Henley.

"God, I need to be training you better. I wondered what you were doing back there in the kitchen. Oh shit," said Henley.

"I know," Ramouter said.

Henley zoomed in and shook her head. On the screen were photographs of envelopes that had been left on the counter next to the microwave. Of the five of them, only one—a letter postmarked Westminster University—was addressed to Nicole; the other four letters were addressed to Caleb Annan.

"Milton Greco." Ramouter pointed to the blue logo on the

top left-hand corner of the envelope. "They're an estate agent but one of those high-end, exclusive ones."

"There were men toiletries in the bathroom," Henley said as the lift came to a stop on the ground floor. "And there was also this."

She reached into her pocket and took out a small evidence bag.

"Is that a man's razor?" Ramouter asked. "From Nicole's... I thought that you said that you need to be teaching me better."

"I know that I've broken every single rule," said Henley. "But she's not going to miss it and she's definitely not going to be calling anyone up and say that we, sorry I, took it. There's no harm in checking if the DNA matches Caleb's."

"We won't be able to use it as evidence if it comes back as a match," Ramouter warned.

"I know," Henley sighed. "But I wouldn't have done it if I believed that Nicole Fleming was a possible suspect."

"Ah, well, she may not have been lying when she said that she was the only one in the flat if she thought that you meant literally 'living' with her."

"She's what, twenty, twenty-one years old and Annan was forty-three," said Henley as they walked out toward the lobby. "He cheated on his wife with Uliana, was sexually violent with Raina, and he set up a love nest with Nicole."

"The rent is just over two grand a month," Ramouter said. He showed his phone screen again to Henley with an identical property to rent on the Milton Greco website. "Are we going to go back up there and confront her?"

"No, I doubt that she will be going anywhere for at least a month, if Caleb was paying her rent. But let's check with the concierge about her alibi," Henley said as she arrived at the empty concierge desk. "Did you notice the scratches on Nicole's neck?" She searched and found the bell on the desk.

"No, I didn't. She has a lot of hair."

"I think that's what she was doing when she slammed the

door in our face. Covering up her scratches." Henley rang the bell again.

A door slammed and the concierge strolled out with a packet of crisps and hot tea.

"You told us that one of the tenants had been attacked last week," Henley asked.

The concierge put his cup onto the desk and ripped open the packet of crisps. "Yeah, that's what Duncan, my boss, told me when I took over from him last Friday."

"What exactly did your boss tell you?" Henley asked, knowing that she would need more than just hearsay at some point if her suspicions were correct.

"All he said was that he was taking some parcels from a courier when the tenant ran into the lobby from outside and another woman came in, grabbed her and slapped her around the face and was calling her a bitch. Duncan and the courier had to pull the woman off, and the tenant ran upstairs."

"Did Duncan describe the woman?"

"He only said that she was a black woman. He was going to call the police, but the tenant told him not to."

"But you've got cameras?" Ramouter said, pointing up to the black domes concealing the security cameras in the ceiling.

"Yeah, but I wouldn't know how to get the footage. I've only been here a couple of weeks. You would have to talk to my boss about that."

"And do you know who the tenant was?"

The concierge leaned back and fished around in his bag of crisps as he looked bemusedly across from Ramouter and Henley.

"I thought that's why you were here. It was the girl who lives in 53G."

34

Ramouter had everything in place to make his flat a home: family photos on the shelf above the gutted-out fireplace, Ethan's paintings framed on the wall and a collection of unread books on the floor. But six months in and it didn't feel like home. Home was where his wife, son and the annoying budgie were.

"Oh, well, this is pitiful," Ramouter said as he stared at the mediocre pickings in his fridge. He grabbed the bottle of beer on the shelf, picked up the last bag of crisps from the counter and went back into the living room. It was almost 9 p.m. when he picked up the phone and called Michelle.

"Daddy," Ethan shouted with excitement as his face filled the screen.

"Hey, little man," said Ramouter. A large smile spread across his face at the sight of his five-year-old son. "I wasn't expecting you to be up. It's past your bedtime."

"No," said Ethan with a giggle. "Uncle Alex said that we can stay up and watch the Spider-Man cartoon."

"Oh, you mean that Uncle Alex is using you and your cousin to cover up that he's really five years old and wants to stay up and watch cartoons."

"Uncle Alex isn't five. Are you coming home?"

Ramouter let out a deep sigh but hoped that his face didn't reflect the heaviness in his chest. "Not this weekend, little man. Daddy has an important job to finish with Inspector Henley. Do you remember the lady that you met, when you came to see me?"

"Yeah, she was nice."

"Aye, she is. Ethan, where's Mummy?"

"Upstairs. I'll give her the phone."

Ramouter waited as Ethan ran up the stairs and gave him a view of the banister until he handed the phone over to his mum.

"Miche, hey, sweetheart," said Ramouter.

"Hi," Michelle replied.

"Is everything OK?" Ramouter asked. He sat up straighter in his chair when he heard the detachment in his wife's voice. "I called you this morning and left you a couple of messages."

"I know. I left the phone in Pamela's car and then... I just forgot. It was a normal forgot, not anything for you to worry about forgot."

"That's all right. It happens. So how did the appointment go this morning? I wanted to speak to you before you went. Are you feeling OK?"

"Salim, slow down," Michelle said flatly. "It gives me a headache when you ask so many questions. I'm sorry. I'm sorry. I just... I can't help it."

"I know that you can't. You just sound so... I don't know. Just really down."

"I'm just tired," said Michelle. "They made me do a load of tests yesterday and it pissed me off. They showed me a picture of a fork and I couldn't remember what it was called. I knew what it was, but I couldn't remember the name for it. A fork, for crying out loud."

"Don't get upset," said Ramouter.

"You can't tell me not to get upset."

Ramouter winced. "I'm sorry. I just meant—"

"No, no, it's not your fault," Michelle said. "It's just frustrating because yesterday I was fine. Absolutely fine. I took Ethan to school; I went into town, and I even went to bloody yoga class and had drinks with Pamela's 'I'll faint at the sight of bread' friends."

Ramouter laughed as he saw the light return in Michelle's eyes as she continued to slag off her sister's friends and tried to ignore the fact that she may have forgotten what she had for dinner the following day.

"How's your therapy going?" Michelle asked.

"Good. It doesn't feel like therapy. Dr. Ryan, he's good. He doesn't make you feel as though you're sitting there whining."

"Maybe I should see him. Maybe I should be with you. Me and Ethan."

"You want me to come back to Bradford?"

"God no. I don't want that for you. You're happy with your job. I was just thinking that maybe we could do what we originally planned; before the diagnosis."

"You want to move to London, all of us?" said Ramouter. "Is that what you want?"

"I don't know. It was just a thought."

Ramouter knew his wife well enough to know that it was more than just a fleeting thought.

"Let's talk about it later," he said as Stanford's phone number began to flash at the top of the screen.

"OK. I better get Ethan ready for bed. I love you, Sal."

"I love you too," said Ramouter as Michelle blew him a kiss and ended the call. Ramouter took a moment before answering Stanford. The last thing he needed right now was to be told that they'd found another body.

"Hi, Stanford? Has something— Where are you?" Ramouter could hear the distinct sound of a Friday night drinking crowd.

"We're at a pub, not far from you," said Stanford. "Me, Ezra and Eastie. We're off for a Chinese and I sincerely doubt that you have plans tonight."

"Did Henley tell you to call me?"

"How dare you insinuate that I'm incapable of thinking for myself," Stanford replied with mock shock.

"So that's a yes then," Ramouter laughed as he finished off his beer.

"Of course she did," Stanford said. "Anyone would think that she actually liked you."

35

Three Months Earlier...

"Don't you want me to save you?"

He stayed on his knees looking down at the naked man in front of him. It had been four hours since Charlie had made a sound. Four hours since Charlie had cowered in the corner and clawed at the moss-covered bricks with his broken fingernails. Now he lay still.

"Charlie."

The candlelight flickered as drops of ice-cold water fell from the ceiling and nestled on Charlie's eyes; eyes that had been sealed shut with candlewax. He placed a hand onto Charlie's bare chest. His fingers pushed against the bony grooves and ridges left behind by flesh deprived of nutrition.

"This is what you need," he said as he laid his head on Charlie's chest. He breathed in the soured stench of his body as he listened.

"Is he still with us?"

The woman's voice was calm as she held the sticks of incense above bare legs. The lavender-scented smoke wafted across the room as hot ash fell from the incense and onto Charlie's dry skin. The man pressed his ear closer against Charlie's chest and listened. The breathing was labored. His heartbeat was faint and irregular. The man fell back as Charlie's body began to violently convulse. His torso contorted and his arms strained against the restraints on his wrists. The woman helped the man up as the cheap frame of the metal bed shifted across the floor.

"God will hold him," said the man as the wax cracked on Charlie's eyes.

"God will hold him," the man said again as Charlie's eyes rolled back. Tears streamed down his face and mixed with the foaming saliva that flowed through his mouth.

"God will hold him," the man said as he lifted up the black bucket that was by his feet and held it above Charlie's head.

The sound of Charlie choking as he swallowed his tongue was lost as water flowed down his nose and into the back of his throat. The 10:42 p.m. train to Liverpool Street rumbled overhead.

36

"It's bloody freezing," said Simon as he grabbed the collar of his coat and pulled it tighter around his neck. "I'm blaming your husband for this."

Henley didn't say anything as she stood on the narrow road in Hither Green Cemetery, clutching the plastic wrapping that had been around the flowers that she'd placed on her mother's grave. Their dad was there now telling her his secrets, his fears and how much he missed her.

"And he's not even here," said Simon. "It's the least he could have done after convincing Dad to come. Sis, are you even listening to me?"

"You know that Dad bought a plot for two?" said Henley. She turned away from the biting wind and faced her brother. "There's even space on the gravestone to put his name."

"Yeah," Simon replied. "You know what he's like. Practical. Either that or it was a buy one, get one free."

"Simon!"

"Sorry. I would just rather be anywhere else than here. I'm glad that we decided not to bring the kids."

"Me too. You're right though. Rob should have been here, but they wanted him at the BBC studios this morning."

"Who would have thought that being a freelance finance journalist would bring you fame," Simon said sarcastically. "Anyway, I'm just glad that Dad has made it through. I can't be going through that again. What a fucking year."

"Don't swear. Mum would tell you to watch your mouth," Henley said as she began to shiver.

"I still can't believe that she's gone. I've still got her messages on my voice mail."

"Do you listen to them?"

"I tried to but the first thing that I wanted to do was call her straight back," Simon said sadly, watching Elijah start to make his way toward them.

Henley tried to will herself not to cry, but she could feel the dam cracking. Twelve months of holding back and swallowing every pain-filled emotion that threatened to make its way up her throat and come out in an unstoppable wail.

"I want Mum here with me," she said, her eyes filling with tears. "I need my mum."

The plastic wrapping that she was holding fell to the ground as she tried to grab hold of an invisible pain and began to cry uncontrollably.

"Dad!" Simon called out, grabbing hold of Henley. "Dad, get over here."

"Come on, baby girl," Elijah said as he put his arms round Henley and pulled her toward him. "You don't have to be strong, angel."

Henley breathed in her dad's scent as she buried herself in his chest and allowed the months of grief to leave her.

Henley watched everyone celebrating her mother's life. It felt like a party. Simon had insisted there were to be no signs of misery or grief. Family and friends were scattered around the house, paying no attention to the children who were running around having the time of their lives.

"I'm topping you up," Linh said as she appeared at Henley's side with a bottle of wine. "How are you doing? Simon filled me in about what happened at the cemetery."

"Of course he clued you in," Henley said, rolling her eyes. "Any excuse to talk to you."

"I am bloody good company, thank you very much. Isn't that right, Mia?" Linh asked Simon's wife who had just walked into the kitchen with Stanford's husband, Gene.

"Yes, you are," said Mia as she handed trays of food to Gene. "Feel free to take him off my hands and convince him to come up with better baby names than Crystal Palace's first team."

"Do not let him do that," said Gene as he followed Mia out of the kitchen. "I'm still convinced that Stanford only agreed to marry me because he found out that my middle name is Arsene. That's what happens when your mum is French."

"You're lucky that she likes you," said Henley.

"I keep telling you that everyone likes me, including dead people," said Linh.

"You really do need help," Henley said as she began to laugh.

"Don't we all. Anyway, it's worth it just to see a smile on your face. So, you're feeling better?"

"A lot," said Henley as she sipped her wine. "I spent an hour crying in the back of Simon's car and then I got home and cried some more. I was absolutely knackered when I was done."

"Well, you needed to get it out. They say grief is a sign of how much you loved someone, but grief can be like an anchor, dragging you out to sea to meet the kraken."

"Linh, you are so melodramatic," Henley said. The doorbell rang.

"You wouldn't have me any other way."

"No, I wouldn't, which is why I know that you wouldn't mind if I asked you something. It's a work thing."

"Work. Really? Fine," Linh said. She saw the earnest look

on Henley's face and picked up a bottle of wine. "At least let me fill up my wineglass. What is it?"

"OK, so this is probably a stupid question, but would you be able to tell if my victim had recently given birth?"

"How recent is recent?"

"I dunno. About six weeks, maybe?"

Linh let out a deep sigh. "Six weeks? It all depends on if she was breastfeeding or not. If she wasn't then there's no way of knowing unless she had a Caesarean; but there could be various reasons for a scar in that area, Anj. What do you think happened to the baby?"

"I'm praying that there isn't a baby," Henley replied as Rob walked into the kitchen with a stern look on his face. Something had pissed him off.

"What's wrong?" Henley asked as Linh disappeared out of the kitchen with stealth-like precision.

"You could have told me," Rob said.

"Told you what?"

"You're out of order. Bang out of order."

Henley heard him before she saw him. His voice sent a ripple across the back of her neck. She heard her brother laughing in a way that he never did when he was talking to Rob.

"Hi, Anjelica."

Henley turned around to see Pellacia standing in the kitchen door.

"He brought Mum's favorite," Simon shouted out from the hallway as he held up a bottle of Rémy Martin and left to join the others.

"Afternoon, Rob," said Pellacia as he held out his hand.

"What are you doing here?" Rob asked, ignoring Pellacia's hand. "This is a day for family and friends only."

"Elijah called and invited me. I couldn't say no to him," Pellacia replied.

"I'm going to check on our daughter," said Rob, brushing past Pellacia.

"I can't believe that you did this," Henley said, walking out into the hallway. "I asked you not to."

"And what was I supposed to do?" asked Pellacia. "Tell your dad, no? Just because you can't deal with what happened last—"

"Shut up," Henley hissed. "What is wrong with you?"

"I didn't come here to make a scene. I came out of respect, and you would have done the same thing if it was the other way round."

"That's not the point," Henley said as she stepped back from him. "It's as if you're rubbing his face in it."

"Does he know?" Pellacia asked, a look of worry crossing his face.

"No, he doesn't, and I've got no intention of telling him either."

"I don't want to upset you," Pellacia said softly as Stanford walked into the hallway and gave him a look that would have put Medusa out of business.

"Just checking," Stanford said before turning around and leaving.

"I'm surprised that he didn't offer to take me out for a fight," said Pellacia.

"That's because he's hungover, but that doesn't mean that he won't ask Gene to knock you out," said Henley. She laughed in spite of the conflict of emotions that she was feeling.

Then, "I'm tired, Stephen," she admitted as she leaned against the wall.

"Just let me be there for you. Even if it's just for the afternoon," Pellacia said as he stepped forward and kissed Henley on her cheek, dangerously close to her lips. "I'm not asking for more than that."

Henley didn't say anything as Pellacia made his way into the living room. Instead she was too busy replaying one question in her head. Could she leave her husband?

37

"I should be so sorry, but I'm not."

It was Monday. Raina Davison closed the glass door of the florist that now occupied one of the converted railway arches of London Bridge station. The woman who had made the allegation of rape against Caleb Annan was not what Henley was expecting. She didn't appear broken or diminished by what Caleb had done to her. She seemed resilient, fortified by her anger. The hardness in her face made her seem older than her twenty-eight years, but she had a look of caution that was familiar to Henley. The look of someone who was on high alert. Someone who had been through a trauma and operated from a point of hypervigilance. At that moment, Henley knew that she'd made the right decision to leave Ramouter at the SCU. There were guidelines for interviewing sexual assault victims and one of them was to communicate empathy, a willingness to understand the situation from Raina's perspective but to also gather the evidence fairly and in an unbiased way. The more that they discovered about Caleb Annan, the less faith Henley had in Ramouter's ability to remain impartial and remember that Caleb was still a murder victim.

"Are you all right?" Raina asked as Henley sneezed three times in a row and her eyes began to stream.

"Sorry," Henley said. She sneezed again and searched her pockets for tissues.

"Oh crap," Raina said as she looked around the buckets of flowers in the shop. "What are you allergic to?"

"Lilies. Is there anywhere else where we could…"

"Upstairs. Come on."

Henley followed Raina up the narrow spiral staircase, along the small landing and into an office.

"Thank you," Henley sniffled as Raina opened the window and handed her a bottle of water from the small fridge in the corner. "Anything else I can handle, but not lilies. You said downstairs that you weren't sorry about Caleb's death."

"Can you blame me?" Raina replied as her eyes narrowed. "Did you read my statement?"

"Yes, I did, but I wanted to see and hear from you myself."

"I didn't lie."

"I didn't say that you lied, but someone murdered Caleb Annan and I'm trying to find out why someone would want to do that."

"Well, I didn't kill him. I've done a lot of things that I'm not proud of in my life, but I couldn't kill someone."

"Where were you last Sunday night and Monday morning?"

"I was home on Sunday as that's my only day off. I share a flat with my best friend. She was with me on Sunday and then I called in sick on Monday."

"What was wrong with you?"

"Well, I told my business partner that I had a migraine, but the truth is that I was hungover, and I just couldn't face it. The past few months have been hard," said Raina.

"I understand," said Henley. "But I am going to ask you if you can prove that you were home on Sunday night and early Monday morning?"

"You want me to give you an alibi?"

"Yes."

"Well, Katie, that's my friend and flatmate, was with me, as I said. We literally binged Netflix, ordered pizza and drank. I just needed to not feel 'me' for a while. Does that make sense?" Raina said, fiddling with the strings on her apron.

"Yes, it does," Henley replied. "But what about Monday?"

"Katie went to work, and I woke up at 8 a.m. to text Debbie, that's my business partner, that I wouldn't be coming in and then I went back to bed," said Raina. "I think that I woke up again at 11 a.m. and I didn't leave the flat, but I can only give you my word that I was home."

"I'll take your word for it," said Henley. "So let me ask you about Caleb. How did you get involved in the church?"

"My old flatmate, Morgan. She asked me to go with her one Sunday. She kept telling me that it was different and that I would like it and that it didn't feel like church."

"Was she right?"

"Yeah, it was different. Morgan was one of those people who never stick to anything; she stopped going after about a month, but I carried on going."

"Why did you continue?"

"I really enjoyed it and they made you feel like a family. I don't really get on with my own family, but the church made me *feel* as though I was part of theirs. Caleb made me feel heard, and sometimes when he was preaching it felt as though he was speaking directly to me."

Henley tried to remain passive and hoped that her face wasn't revealing her recognition of these traits in Caleb's predatory behavior and his ability to manipulate the most vulnerable women.

"So how did you get involved with Caleb?" Henley eventually asked.

"He came here to the shop first. He knew that I was a florist and first he ordered flowers for his wife, and then it was his mother-in-law's birthday, and then he put in a really big order for the church, and he praised me in his church service."

"Sounds to me as though he was grooming you."

"I suppose that he did," Raina said as she brushed away a tear. "I was flattered, and he confided in me. He told me the mistakes that he'd made in the past and that he'd been to prison. He said that the prison had put him on the path to redemption. I told you that he had a way of making you feel special, and I was in a bit of a vulnerable place; I'd broken up with my boyfriend which was how I'd ended up sharing with Katie for a while."

"Raina, last year, you gave a witness statement to Detective Sergeant Rickman where you went into detail about the rape allegation that you made against Caleb Annan and you—"

"I didn't lie," Raina said urgently. "Everything that I said was true."

"Raina, I'm not accusing you of lying. I just want to clarify something that you mentioned in your statement. You said that you'd had sex on two previous occasions and that was consensual."

"He came here when I was closing up. He said that he was just passing."

"Did you believe him?"

"I had no reason not to and why would a pastor lie?" Raina said resentfully. "We ended up going for a drink at the pub around the corner. We stayed until closing. Nothing happened that night; it was just talking. I don't even remember him really flirting with me. He just seemed interested in me." Raina shivered even though the office was warm. "He told me that his marriage wasn't how it appeared to be and that he'd wished that he'd met me first."

"He told you that?"

"He spun me all the lines." Raina shook her head as though she still couldn't believe what had happened. "And I fell for every single one. He just made me feel…desirable. He came back the next night and we went for drinks and dinner and then we came back to the shop, and we had…well, it happened here. I just told myself that there was nothing wrong because he told me that the marriage was breaking up."

"He manipulated you," said Henley.

"I thought that I was stronger than that. I'm not some naive teenager. I never would have imagined that I would have gone off with a married man. I'm not that sort of person." Raina began to cry. "Sorry."

"You don't have to apologize. We've all…sometimes we just ignore what our heads are telling us."

An image of Pellacia kissing her on the cheek at her brother's house replayed in Henley's mind. She knew exactly what would have happened if they'd been alone. It was as if common sense left her body when it came to her relationship with Pellacia.

"I thought that I was in love with him and then I found out that I wasn't the only one."

"How did you find out that there were others?"

"His wife told me. She called me up, canceled an order from the church and told me that I wasn't the only one and that Caleb would get rid of me once he got bored."

"You didn't mention that you spoke to his wife in your statement."

"I didn't think that it was relevant. She wasn't the one who raped me."

"I'm going to ask you what you might think is a stupid question, but are you sure that it was Serena who called you?"

"It was definitely Serena," said Raina. "She tricked me though because she used his phone. I thought it was Caleb calling me. I actually said, 'Hi, baby' when I answered. Such an idiot."

"Did you tell Caleb what happened? That Serena had called you?"

Raina nodded. "The way that she spoke to me… I was scared. I told Caleb that we were over. I didn't hear from him for a week and then he turned up at my flat when Katie was away for the weekend. I told him to stop, but..."

"I know this is hard. And I know this is the last thing that you want to do, but you need to tell me what exactly happened," said Henley gently. "I'm not here to judge you, I just need to know."

Raina raised her head and took a deep breath and then another before the tears started to fall again. "He was fine at first," she said. "He apologized for Serena. He apologized for himself. He said that he was weak and asked me to forgive him. I said that I forgave him and then he said that he didn't want to lose me."

"What did you say to that?" Henley asked.

"I was... I was flattered. I can't lie. He's good with words," said Raina. "Have you heard him preach?"

"I saw some of his recordings on YouTube. He did have a way with words," Henley reluctantly agreed.

"I should have told him to leave but I didn't and then he kissed me, and I let him... I blamed myself for so long."

"Raina, whatever happens, it wasn't your fault."

"I know, I know, but I felt that it was. I kissed him back and I let him touch me but no, you're right. It wasn't my fault," Raina said defiantly. "I told him to stop but he didn't. He pushed me onto the ground, pulled down my leggings and he forced himself into me. I kept telling him to stop but he kept saying, 'That's the way you like it.'"

Henley took hold of Raina's hand and simply held it.

"I didn't like it," said Raina as she cried. "I didn't want it. I told him to stop but he didn't. He only stopped once he'd... excuse me."

Henley stood up and worked the crick out of her neck as Raina left the room. She hated seeing the path of destruction that Caleb had left behind. Women who he'd manipulated and emotionally and physically abused. As much as Henley hated that a man's life had been viciously ripped from him, she couldn't help herself from thinking that Caleb Annan deserved every single one of his forty-eight stab wounds.

"I'm sorry about that," Raina said as she returned to the office and sat back in her chair, clutching a wad of toilet paper in her hands. Her mascara was now dark brown smudges under her eyes. Her cheeks flushed red.

"I should have said something sooner," she continued. "I should have called the police as soon as he left."

"The most important thing is that you did call the police. Did you tell anyone else what Caleb had done to you? Friends. Family."

"No, no," Raina replied. She absently picked up a strand of long brown hair and started to pick away at the ends. "I couldn't say it to them, not yet, but I did…" Raina leaned forward and covered her face with her hands. "I shouldn't have done it," she said, her voice muffled and strained. "I don't know why I did. I just remembered being so angry."

"Shouldn't have done what?" Henley asked even though she had a good idea of what Raina did.

"I called her," Raina said. She sat up, her face pale and her eyes pained. "I called Caleb's wife and told her what he'd done to me."

38

"So, Caleb Annan really is a shit," Ramouter said to Henley as he stared at the whiteboard with an empty suspect list and a growing number of victims. The photograph of Caleb Annan had been placed on the far left but with a blood-red line that connected his image to the photograph of Brandon Whittaker. "When are we going to add his name to the suspect list? His prints were all over Hadlow's flat. He even ate there. Remember the takeaway boxes in the kitchen? His prints were on the box and on the straw. We've also got his prints in the room where Brandon was held, and this all took place in his church. Whether he actually hurt Brandon or was just standing watch, he was in up to his neck."

"I don't disagree," Henley said. She picked up a black marker and walked up to the board. She wrote Annan's name next to suspect number one under Whittaker's photo and placed a question mark under the numbers two and three. "But we need more than just a location and prints."

"Did Raina have anything to say about Whittaker or Hadlow?" Ramouter asked as they walked toward Eastwood's desk.

"No. I asked her about them but she didn't recognize them,

and she stopped attending the church four months ago once Serena Annan warned her off her husband. How are you getting on, Eastie?" Henley stared down at the contents of the plastic bag that Eastwood had scattered in no particular order on her desk.

"This is all the paperwork that CSI recovered from Hadlow's flat," Eastwood answered, looking equally unimpressed at the contents. "There's no passport, no driver's license, even though she's registered on the DVLA database, no NHS medical cards, no bank statements, no doctors' letters. She was a university lecturer but other than the staff ID that we found, there is nothing to show what she achieved in life. All we've got in here is a load of junk mail, some Christmas cards, bill reminders. No birth certificate. There is nothing here to document her life."

"There must be something," Henley said. She sat down and started to shift through the feeble amount of paperwork. "Everyone has a box or a drawer filled with their crap that they've been promising to throw out, but they never do."

"I found the microchip documentation for my cat the other day," said Eastwood.

Henley looked up with confusion. "You don't have a cat."

"Exactly. Monty disappeared about five years ago and I'm still finding his shit. I still think that my old neighbor nicked him but anyway, the point is, looking at the stuff that was found..."

"It's as if someone cleaned the place out," Henley answered. She pulled out a brown envelope that hadn't been opened yet. She recognized the logo of a credit card company that offered build-your-credit-back accounts for extortionate interest rates. "But why would someone do that? I could understand if you've killed someone, and you attempt to wipe out any trace that *you've* been in the property, but why would you clear out any evidence of who the victim was but then still leave the body?"

"It doesn't make any sense," said Eastwood. "Why wouldn't they want anyone to know who she is? I mean, it's not as if we wouldn't have found out eventually. Her DNA is on the database."

"Maybe it's not about finding about who she is," Henley said as she opened the envelope. Her heart caught in her chest as she unfolded the sheet of paper and scanned the page. "Shit."

"What is it?" Eastwood asked.

"This isn't junk mail. It's a credit card statement for last month," said Henley. "The first transaction is dated 26 December. She spent £759 at John Lewis online, £180 in Tesco's and £585 at Zaida & Pia."

"What's Zaida & Pia when they're at home?"

"It's like a posh Mothercare in Dulwich. My sister-in-law Mia loves the place."

"Our victim was shopping for a baby. Her baby."

"The DWP check confirmed that she was on universal credit," said Ramouter. "How much was her credit card limit?"

"Two grand," Henley read out.

"Are you saying that she took out the card just to buy baby stuff? And how did she get a card if she's on benefit?"

"It's a high interest card—39.9 percent. I doubt that they even checked," said Henley bitterly.

Eastwood took the bill from Henley. "Whoever killed Alyssa, took that baby."

"Playing devil's advocate," said Ramouter, "we still don't know if Alyssa actually had a child. Her ex-husband told us that she had mental health issues; what if she just imagined that she had a baby?"

"Where is the nearly two grands' worth of baby stuff if all Alyssa had was a phantom pregnancy?" Eastwood asked. "Someone is looking after that baby. I mean, if something had happened to the child, then there would be no need to take the pram or any of the clothes."

"She could have been having a manic episode," said Ramouter. "Her husband, sorry ex-husband, explained that she was bipolar—what if she was having a manic episode and was just buying… I don't know, stuff."

"Then we would have found the 'stuff,' Ramouter," said Henley. "Hadlow's flat was not only cleared out of paperwork but other stuff too. There was no TV, clothes or even shoes. There was nothing in that flat that was new."

Caleb had seen some kind of vulnerability in Uliana, Nicole and Raina. Caleb had also had contact with Alyssa Hadlow, whose child had been taken away from her. Henley couldn't ignore the two questions that were itching away at her like an infected mosquito bite. Did Caleb sexually assault Hadlow, and was he responsible for taking away her child? Henley took a breath and pushed aside her personal feelings, trying to ignore the voice in her head telling her to walk away from a murder investigation. She supposed that it was the question that people asked lawyers. *How could you represent a guilty person?* Now she was asking herself how she could be committed to investigating the murder of a man who had sinned and hurt women.

"The killers weren't trying to hide who Alyssa was," said Henley. "They wanted to stop anyone discovering and finding that child."

"I think we may be getting somewhere," said Ramouter as he put the phone down. "According to the Hospital Episode Statistics, there is no record of Alyssa Hadlow, or any variation of that name, being admitted to the maternity wards of any hospital in the United Kingdom, but there are two out-patient appointments for her at King's College Hospital about three months apart, an admission to Oxleas eighteen months ago and the admission to Temperly Hospital when her husband had her sectioned. What's Oxleas?"

"It's the mental health hospital in Woolwich," Henley explained. "Did you get any information about her GP?"

"The Rosefinch Health Centre on New Cross Road," Ramouter confirmed. "I sent off the application to request her medical records on Friday morning. I've chased them but they still haven't responded."

"Chase them again and threaten to escalate it," said Henley. "Throw in Laura Halifax's name if you have to. You might as well use her for something. We can't be working on the basis that there *might* be a missing baby, we need to treat this investigation as though there *is* a missing baby out there. There can be no waiting for them to call us."

Henley sat back in her chair as she checked her emails. There had been no change in the status of Brandon Whittaker, which on one hand was a good thing, because it meant that she wasn't investigating another murder, but no change also meant that the chances of Brandon waking up and being able to provide her with any information was slowly slipping away.

"Even though Whittaker's mother denied it, both Hadlow and Whittaker have mental health issues," Henley pondered out loud. "They both were found in similar circumstances, and then we have the fact that Whittaker's sister said that her parents thought that her brother was possessed."

"Are you seriously trying to tell me that in this day and age there are people who believe in demonic possession and think that *The Exorcist* was a documentary and not a film? It's just ridiculous," said Ramouter.

"I don't disagree with you, but we can't dismiss what we saw at the Whittaker and Hadlow crime scenes." Henley reasoned.

"But what actual evidence do we have of Caleb and the anonymous two performing exorcisms? I think that we need more than just the Bible that was found in Alyssa's flat. There wasn't anything that suggested that she belonged to Caleb Annan's church, or any church."

"It's been a week since Caleb Annan was found and we've only managed to speak to two church board members. No one else on the church board has returned our calls."

"I have tried," Ramouter said with a clear hint of annoyance. "It's like they closed ranks. They must have something to hide if they've got the barricades up."

"That's why I want you back out there knocking on their doors. And remember, they may let you cross their threshold but that doesn't mean that they will be open with you."

"You make them sound like a cult," Ramouter answered as he tapped away on his keyboard.

"Well, I'm hoping that they're not, but before we start with the church let's deal with the girls. The concierge of Nicole's building has now confirmed that she didn't leave her building on Sunday night. We also know that Caleb Annan was sleeping with Uliana and that he raped Raina. Right now, the only direct evidence that we have implicates Uliana."

"Boss," Ramouter pushed back his chair and pulled a face, "don't you think that we should take no further action against her? I really don't think that she did it."

"Don't look at me like that," said Henley. "What else are we supposed to do? She's the one who found him and, as I said, DNA. Everywhere."

"But she's so…well, you saw her. She's tiny."

"When has size ever mattered when it comes to murder?"

"It just doesn't feel right," Ramouter replied stubbornly.

"This entire investigation doesn't feel right," Henley said with a long sigh.

39

"Alyssa Hadlow was a member of the Church of Annan the Prophet," Stanford shouted across the room.

"Are you sure?" Henley asked. She made her way over toward Stanford. His desk was covered with paperwork and she looked in vain for a space to put down the cup of tea that she'd made him.

"A hundred percent," Stanford said as he opened a folder. "We started going through the papers from the Annans' office in the church. Ezra is still going through the computer, but this is a list of all of the current members of the congregation and their monthly donations. It's odd because it's like they're paying a membership to the church."

"How many members are there?"

"Currently, 387," Stanford answered, "but that doesn't include the number of paying members of the Deptford branch. Do churches have branches?"

Henley shrugged.

"Well, whatever you want to call it, they have another branch of the Church of Annan the Prophet in Plaistow and one in East Acton."

"There are just shy of a thousand members, and they all seem to be paying a membership fee of £595 per month," said Stanford. "That's just shy of sixty grand a year before anyone has stood up and said, 'Open your hymn books to page forty-eight.'"

"A membership fee. For a church," Henley said disbelievingly. "But's that just—"

"Extortion. A rip-off. A cult," Ramouter interjected as he pulled a chair up and sat down in front of Stanford's desk. "I bet they're still taking their money at every service."

"It's called a *collection*," Stanford said. "Anyway, Alyssa Hadlow has been a member of the Deptford branch since December 2018."

"But the university suspended her back in March 2018 and she didn't go back to work and wasn't on benefits. How on earth would she have been able to give the church nearly £600 a month?" asked Henley.

"Maybe she had savings?" said Stanford. "I mean, she was a lecturer in economics of all things. She of all people should know how to handle money, or the church made an exception for her. Faith, hope and charity. Isn't that what church is supposed to be about?"

"It doesn't even make any sense, the membership," said Henley.

"Other than it being straight-up exploitation, why not?" asked Ramouter.

"Because I've never heard of a church, any church, requiring that its members pay a monthly fee. I would understand a tithe."

"What's a tithe?"

"Jesus Christ," said Stanford as he rolled his eyes. "There are times where I'm really surprised that you passed your detective exams. Let me explain it to you, Ramouter. A tithe is a contribution that you make to the church. Ten percent of your earnings. It's supposed to go toward the upkeep of the church. If you can give more then you give more, but the priest isn't going to be knocking down your front door and threatening to take out your kneecaps if you don't pay up."

"But what about Brandon Whittaker?" asked Henley as she continued to scan the list of names, wondering how many of these people had been able to happily hand over their money. How many others were struggling and had put Caleb's church in front of making sure their cupboards were filled with food?

Stanford shook his head. "Brandon's not, but his parents have been members of the East Acton branch since 2014."

Henley scanned the sheet of paper where the names of Patrick and Marcia Whittaker had been highlighted. "The Whittakers live in Isleworth; it would make sense for them to be attending the East Acton branch, but how the hell did Brandon end up in a back room in Deptford? Someone brought him there for a specific reason. It can't be because his parents fancied a change of scenery."

"Yeah, well, this might shed some light on the situation," Stanford said grimly as he turned his computer screen toward Henley. "I got tired of looking through the papers and went online to see if there was anything derogatory about the Church of Annan the Prophet, any complaints, that sort of thing."

"What did you find?"

"The first is that your husband wrote an article about the church and their financial issues."

"Rob?" Henley said, stunned.

"How many husbands do you have? Unless something changed after Mr. Misery turned up on Saturday."

"Shut up, Stanford," said Henley as she started to read through the article on the screen.

"It was a report about the Charity Commission, and he interviewed David Onyeka which we know is one of three aliases used by Annan," said Stanford.

"Are you sure?"

Henley wondered why Rob hadn't mentioned it as she skim-read the first page of the report and saw the photograph of Onyeka aka Annan. At the moment, she and Rob were barely speaking, but it'd been a full week since Caleb's body was found and it had been all over the news.

Stanford raised an eyebrow. "I don't know any other financial journalists called Robert Campbell. Anyway, while you work out how to bring it up over dinner tonight, there's this also. It's a blog."

"It's over a year old," Henley said.

"It doesn't matter how old it is; just read the entry called 'My mental health is not your demon.'"

Henley felt as though a rock was sinking through the bile in her stomach as she read the third paragraph:

I knew that I was unwell. Everyone knew that I was unwell, but they refused to call it by its name. Bipolar Disorder. My family was insistent that there was no such thing as bipolar, schizophrenia, psychosis or anti-personality disorders. When I had decided to study psychology at university, they thought that it was because I wanted to become a therapist and listen to people talk about their failed marriages. That wasn't the reason why. I wanted to learn about the part of me that took over my body and my senses and made me behave uncontrollably, and then make me sink into the darkest of graves. I called this side of me 'Bippy.'

My family refused to believe that Bippy was a mental illness because as far as they were concerned, mental health illness has been created to cover up the fact that our souls are exposed to demonic forces. I always thought that my family was eccentric but not crazier than me. They wanted to pray the devil away. I got more and more ill but somewhere deep inside I knew that I needed help. One morning my mum woke me up and told me that she'd found someone who would help me. My aunt Gretta was in the kitchen with my mum and a man called Keith; to this day, I'm still not sure how Keith is related to us; he could be a third cousin or the plumber. They called it an intervention and that they were going to take me to a church meeting for support; not help. I was entering a manic stage and Bippy made me agree to it. When they said church, I was expecting a cathedral and ceilings painted with celestial art. Instead, we turned off the main road and into a dark industrial estate. I could see the headlights of the trains overhead and I remember thinking that I wouldn't like to go that way. They said it was a church and when I got inside, it smelled like a church. To be honest, the church itself wasn't bad. I quite liked the singing but at the end they took me upstairs.

They were determined to pray away Bippy. My aunt stood in the corner of the room reading the psalms. My mum removed my clothes. Keith pushed me onto a bed and tied my hands. I remember chanting, the heat of the flames and hands being pushed hard onto my chest. I screamed. Bippy screamed. A hand pushed my head against the pillow which smelled of old oil and the pastor. The pastor with the nice singing voice told the devil to leave.

"Do we have any idea who wrote this?" Ramouter asked, his voice piercing the dead silence.

"The blog is anonymous," Stanford replied. "I've asked Ezra to do, well, whatever it is that he does, to find out who wrote this."

"I don't like this at all," said Henley as she handed copies of Rob's article and the blog to Ramouter. "The blog could be fake. The names in that blog could be fake."

"It could be," said Ramouter. "But we'll never know for sure until we track down the author. This person could be the missing link in this case. This could be our biggest lead unless Brandon Whittaker wakes up and is able to tell us who were the two other people in the room with Caleb Annan."

"That's if he wakes up," said Stanford. "How long has he been in a coma for?"

"A week now," said Henley. "And his parents still haven't made an attempt to visit him yet or even get in contact with us."

"There is something very wrong there," said Stanford, frowning. "Right, any of you lot fancy a quick drink?"

"I thought that you weren't drinking again," said Eastwood who had just walked in.

"Yeah, well, I think that we need it. This case is stressing me out," said Stanford. "What do you reckon, Henley?"

Henley let out a sigh. She was in no real hurry to go home and deal with Rob, but she was trying to make more of an effort to spend more time with her daughter.

"We're not having a late one," she warned. "Give me an hour and I'll get the first round in."

"I really don't like this case," said Eastwood as Henley carefully placed the tray of drinks on the table.

"I would be surprised if you did *like* anything about this case," said Henley before she finally sat down and picked up her vodka and tonic.

"I've got no sympathy for Annan; absolutely none. He's a nasty piece of shit. I know that we're supposed to care about the victim but how can you when he's been mistreating women and people who are mentally ill? I just can't deal with it."

Henley looked around the table at her team. All four of them had had their "Far too close to home" experiences with mental health, both in their personal and professional lives.

"Forget the other two, because we don't have a clue who they are; but people like Caleb are supposed to be helping people with mental health issues," Ramouter said bitterly as he twisted his wedding ring.

"Are you all right, mate?" Stanford asked with concern.

"Yeah, I'm fine," said Ramouter. "It's just that I keep thinking, what if Michelle didn't have the support of her family and she put her trust in someone else like a priest or even a counselor? It's the worst kind of betrayal."

"I suppose that we have to be grateful that people's attitudes to mental health are different now," said Henley. "Do you know how long my dad has been battling depression? Over forty years. Since he was twenty-one years old."

"That long?" said Stanford as he drank his beer. "I didn't re-alize."

"No one realized, because we didn't talk about it. No one talked about it because of the shame attached," said Henley.

"So, what did you think was happening to your dad when you were a kid?" asked Ramouter.

Henley shrugged. "They didn't tell us anything. Only that he wasn't well. That he had the flu or a migraine. It's a good thing that he worked for himself because I can't imagine any employer accepting my dad being off work for two months be-cause he was depressed."

"They would now though," said Eastwood. "Look at you, Henley. No offense, but you had support."

"But that's because I had Rhimes," Henley explained. "I knew that whatever happened, Rhimes would have my back. I don't know if I would have felt that confident if I was working in another unit. It's bad enough that I've had to deal with rac-ism and sexism in this job, but can you imagine adding men-tal health issues to the list? That's what I mean about stigma. I shouldn't have to worry about people talking behind my back and saying that I couldn't handle it."

"We've always got your back," said Stanford as he put his arm around Henley.

"I wish that Rhimes knew that we'd had his," Eastwood said sadly.

"He must have known," said Stanford.

"How can you say that?" asked Eastwood. "He recruited us, and he was the one who held us together, but he didn't confide in any of us and tell us that he wasn't coping."

"I don't know." Stanford shrugged. "Maybe he thought that we would be able to cope and keep the SCU going even if he wasn't around."

"That's not a good enough reason for him to top himself," Ezra said angrily. "That would have been all right if he'd cashed in his pension and retired to Majorca, but he gassed himself in his garage."

"Ez," Henley said in an attempt to reach out. "I understand that—"

"Do you *really* understand?" asked Ezra. "Because I don't. I will never get it. Why didn't he talk to any of you lot if he was going through shit? He could even have talked to me. I stayed over at his house more than once and I even made dinner with Mrs. Rhimes. It's just shit."

They all knew how close Ezra and Rhimes had been, even Rhimes's own son had joked that Ezra had been the son he'd always wanted. There was an uneasy atmosphere at the table as they all thought about their personal struggles and how Rhimes hadn't shared his.

"I'm still pissed off with him," said Ezra quietly. "It was selfish."

"It was, mate," said Stanford. "Well, this has turned into a barrel of laughs."

"Bloody hell. This feels like a wake," said Henley, trying to lighten the mood. "I'd rather talk about work."

"I'll tell you one thing," said Eastwood as she indicated for Ramouter to drink up. "What I don't understand is how Annan and his mates would have convinced Whittaker and Hadlow to take part… I refuse to call it an exorcism."

"They were ill, Eastie," said Henley. "And I can only assume that when you're mentally ill you have no awareness of your boundaries and you want whatever pain you're in to stop."

"Wanting the pain to stop is one thing, but what Caleb and his friends were doing was just evil. It was about power," said Eastwood, downing her drink. "And it all boils down to Caleb Annan being a narcissist, a bully and picking on people who couldn't fight back."

40

Henley stood in the middle of the living room and watched her husband. Rob had fallen asleep in front of *Terminator 2*. There were empty beer bottles and a half-eaten pizza on the coffee table. Henley picked up the cushion that he had kicked to the ground and threw it at his head.

"Ow! What the—" Rob exclaimed as he sat up, slightly dazed. "Did you just throw a cushion at me?"

"Why didn't you tell me?" said Henley.

"Tell you… What time is it?"

"Almost eleven."

"And you've just got in?"

"Rob! Caleb Annan."

"Who?"

"Oh my God," Henley said as she sat down on the sofa next to Rob. "The murder investigation that I'm on."

"We agreed that you wouldn't bring your work home and talk about your cases around the dinner table; that is, if you ever made it home in time for dinner."

"Don't do that." Henley bristled at Rob's sharp dig. "This isn't about you and me right now. This is about Caleb Annan.

The pastor that was murdered last week. Didn't you see the press conference?"

"I make a point of not watching your press conferences, especially if that dickhead Pellacia is—"

"You've met the victim," Henley said, raising her voice to stop Rob from launching into a full-on rant about Pellacia.

"What do you mean I've met him?" Rob asked suspiciously. "How would I have? I'd never heard of him until you mentioned him."

"You interviewed him for a piece you did for the *Guardian* about five years ago," said Henley.

"Five years? Anj, I can hardly remember stuff that I did five minutes ago," Rob replied as he shook the sleep out of his head.

"It was a piece on the Charity Commission," said Henley. She picked up Rob's laptop from the floor and opened it up.

"You know my password?" Rob asked as he shifted along the sofa, away from Henley.

"Of course I do."

"Do you know my email as well?" Rob asked suspiciously.

"You need to be more imaginative," Henley replied. She found the article and pointed to a photograph. "That is Caleb Annan."

"Oh, I know him," said Rob.

"What do you mean you 'know him'? I've never heard you mention his name before?" Henley muted the television.

"Why would I have mentioned it. It's not as if I *knew* him, knew him. He's not a mate or anything. I interviewed him a few years ago, as well as a bunch of other people, and that is an old photograph."

"What was he like?"

"You could smell the dodginess off him. He could sell ice to a snowman. So, is this your dead pastor?"

"Yes. To be fair on you, he's put on a bit of weight since you last saw him."

"And he wasn't calling himself Caleb Annan when I interviewed him," said Rob as he scanned through his article. "His name was David Onyeka. Look, it says it in my article."

"That was one of his aliases that he used."

"Well, that explains why the name Caleb Annan didn't ring any bells with me."

"Tell me about him and how you found him."

Rob leaned back against the sofa and squinted his eyes.

"So, about five years ago, the Charity Commission launched loads of investigations into some of these megachurches. You know that charities don't have to register with HMRC; they don't pay taxes on their income as long as they can show that they're using the money for charitable purposes."

"So, if our church down the road can legitimately show that they're using our 50p donation to actually repair the church roof, then they're good."

Rob didn't laugh. "Exactly, but there were a lot of allegations flying about that a lot of these megachurches that were sprouting up out of nowhere were showing all sorts of irregularities which caused the charity commission to launch an inquiry. I interviewed loads of people from different churches and children's charities. Your dead pastor wasn't calling himself 'The Prophet' or Caleb Annan back then, but his name had popped up in the Charity Commission's 168-page report. It triggered my interest, so I got in touch with him."

"What was he like?"

Rob leaned back into the sofa and closed his eyes, as though he was trying to retrieve a recording in his brain.

"He was open. Which immediately made me more inquisitive. No one is ever that open when a journalist comes knocking on their door asking questions about allegations of procedural and financial irregularities. I'm more likely to get a door slammed in my face."

"But he welcomed you with open arms?"

"Invited me to his church and to his trustees' meetings. He did all he could to show me that everything was aboveboard."

"And did you believe him?"

"You can dress it up as much as you like, stand in front of a pulpit with a Bible in your hand and tell the world that you've been saved; but dodgy is still dodgy."

"Why did you think that he was dodgy?" asked Henley.

"Instinct. He also had an answer for everything and was wearing a very expensive watch, even though he was saying that the church was struggling financially. When I checked with the Charity Commission, his church had filed annual returns showing an income of six million pounds."

"Six million quid!" Henley exclaimed.

"Yeah, but when I dug deeper, well, the figures didn't add up. Most of that income should have been spent on charitable activities, but I couldn't find any evidence of that, and I couldn't get access to the full accounts."

"So, you didn't know that Annan, or Onyeka, had done time inside for fraud?"

"Really? No, didn't have a clue. I should have done a follow-up," Rob mused. "Maybe I could still do a follow-up."

"Not until this investigation is over," Henley said firmly. "I don't want anyone accusing me of giving you inside information."

"Don't worry about it. I'll wait. Right, I'm going to bed," Rob said, standing up and yawning.

"Are you coming back to our bed?" Henley asked as she put Rob's laptop to the side. "You can't sleep in the spare room forever."

"Can't I?"

"Rob, please." Henley hoped that she sounded genuine. "We need to talk about what happened on Saturday at Mum's memorial."

"There's nothing to talk about," Rob replied. "Your ex turned up when you knew how—"

"Keep your voice down. You're going to wake Emma. And before you go on, I told him not to come, but Dad—"

"Don't bring your dad into this. Pellacia came because of you. I told you before that I'm not an idiot. I see how he looks at you."

"You're seeing things that aren't there."

"I don't think that I am, Anj. I think that I'm seeing things very clearly, and do you know what pisses me off the most?"

"Rob, nothing has—"

"I've been trying. I've been making the compromises. Trying to see things from your point of view. Supporting you—but you're not even prepared to meet me halfway."

Henley searched Rob's face for any signs that he was hurt, but he just looked angrier than he was on Saturday night when they'd driven home from Simon's house without saying one single word to each other.

"Rob, you act as though I'm not trying," said Henley. "I am doing my best, but it doesn't help when you make me feel as though you're judging me."

"I'm not judging you. I just want you to remember that you're my wife, but you keep pushing that fucker between us."

"Nothing, and I mean nothing, is going on between Pellacia and me," Henley said slowly. Her phone began to beep with a text alert.

"Why don't you get that? It's probably him."

"For fuck's sake, Rob," Henley said as she picked up her phone from the sofa.

"I don't want him around my family," said Rob. "Keep it at work."

"Rob, please. It's Linh," Henley said.

"I'm going to bed. In the spare room," Rob replied as he walked out.

"You absolute prick," Henley said to herself before she opened the text message. "Oh no."

Finished Hadlow. Signs of pregnancy! Where's the baby?

41

Alyssa Hadlow's lungs had been removed, dissected and were lying in a metal bowl. Her heart was in a second container. The rest of her body was on the examination table, her hollowed-out chest exposed. Ramouter had taken up his usual spot between the door and the cabinet, arms folded defensively, face partially obscured by his mask.

"I hope that Henley has promised to treat you to a nice breakfast," Linh mused as she swiveled on her chair, her eyes twinkling with amusement. "I quite fancy a full English myself. Crispy bacon, fried tomatoes, black pudding, lots of—"

"What is wrong with you?" said Henley. "And why are you so cheerful this early in the morning?"

"His name is Jake. He was very good. I was upside down at one point. I probably won't see him again. Too needy. Wanted to cuddle."

"Linh! I didn't—"

"Sorry, sorry," said Linh as she jumped off her chair and Ramouter chuckled away in the corner. "Right. So, I checked her lungs and there is evidence of lactation." Linh picked up Hadlow's lungs from the bowl and placed them on another examination table. Henley wasn't exactly sure what she was looking at as Linh angled the black speckled section of lung in her direction.

"Because of the lactation of the lungs, I can say with about 95 percent certainty that Hadlow was pregnant at some point and had been regularly breastfeeding," said Linh.

"Can you say how long she was breastfeeding for?" Ramouter asked.

"It could have been four days or four years," Linh answered. "There's no actual way of knowing, but if you take a look here"—Linh moved over and folded back the skin over Hadlow's chest and lifted up the flaccid breasts—"the bruising goes down into the adipose tissue of both breasts. Either the suction setting on the breast pump was too high or it was a very cheap pump. There's also signs of infection in her nipples."

"The toxicology report showed signs of sepsis. Wouldn't that have affected her breast milk?" asked Henley.

"It doesn't happen every time, but breast milk can transmit serious viral and bacterial infections."

"And how serious is it for a newborn if the milk is infected?" asked Ramouter. All signs of joviality were gone.

"Best case, the baby just has a fever and jaundice," said Linh. "Worst case, the poor thing has respiratory problems, hypertension, abdominal distention, seizures and dies."

"Christ," said Ramouter.

Henley leaned in and saw the purple circular bruising that surrounded the darkened skin of areola. She subconsciously moved her hand to her own chest as she remembered the anguish and the feeling of failure when Emma refused to latch onto her breast. "Can you date the bruising?" she asked.

"I can only conclude that it's recent. A few weeks, maybe."

"So how exactly did she die?" Ramouter asked. "Because this is all seeming a bit *Handmaid's Tale* to me."

Henley didn't bother to chastise him because she was starting to think the same thing.

"Heart attack, but there's also damage to her kidneys. Her body couldn't cope with the extreme pressure that she was being subjected to. Take a look at her ribs." Linh folded back the skin on Hadlow's chest again and shone the light onto her rib cage.

"Ramouter, get over here." Henley walked around the table and Ramouter reluctantly followed.

"Her ribs are broken in half," Ramouter said as he leaned in.

"Not just broken, but actually snapped in half. Three ribs on the left and four on the right," said Linh.

"How much force would you have to use to crack a rib in two?" asked Ramouter.

"A lot," said Linh. "I would expect to see this sort of damage if she'd been hit by a car, but there's nothing to suggest that."

"Brandon Whittaker had bruising consistent with sustained pressure on his chest," said Henley.

"Someone has either pushed down or even kneeled on her chest," said Linh. "Also, her collarbone is broken. These fractures are consistent with a lot of pressure being placed as if she was held down. If you look at her wrists…"

Linh lifted up Alyssa's left arm and gently turned it around. "She was found tied but there are significant rope burns. I pulled out numerous fibers on both her wrists and ankles. I sent them to Anthony, and he confirmed that they match the fibers from the rope that was used to tie Brandon Whittaker to the bed."

"Bloody hell," Ramouter said.

"There's bruising to her kidney and across her back," Linh continued. "She was either pushed or fell against something with a sharp edge. She also has a small fracture to the back of the skull. I've extracted skin from underneath her fingernails, which I sent off to the lab on Saturday morning. Hopefully, we can match it to the skin extracts taken from under Brandon Whittaker's nails."

"Thanks, Linh," Henley said gratefully. "I can treat you to a late breakfast if you like."

"It would be brunch now," said Ramouter.

"Brunch is not a thing, Ramouter. It's just an excuse to get pissed on cheap Prosecco whilst you're eating bacon, eggs and pancakes," said Linh as she covered up Hadlow's body with the green protective plastic sheet. "But I will take you up on your offer."

"Did you find any water in her lungs?" Ramouter asked as he stepped back from the body. "They found water in Brandon Whittaker's lungs consistent with waterboarding."

"Her lungs were slightly elevated in weight," said Linh. "And there was some water in her stomach which would suggest an intake. As odd as it sounds, Hadlow was also suffering from dehydration. The sodium and creatinine levels were high, which would have impaired her kidney function. We can last for up to three weeks without food, but water is another thing. We can only last three to four days. Your victim had been physically abused, her kidneys damaged from both dehydration and blunt trauma. Her heart couldn't cope."

"And they took her baby and left her to die," Henley said, unable to contain the anger that had been bubbling away in her stomach.

"Are we seriously suggesting that…" said Ramouter as he sat down on Linh's chair and rubbed his temples, "that they tortured Hadlow, pumped her breasts for milk, left her for dead and took the baby?"

"It doesn't make sense," said Henley. "It would have been impossible for Hadlow to produce milk if she was dehydrated and not eating food. They must have taken the baby away at least a couple of weeks before they decided to—"

"Do what?" asked Linh. "What were they doing to her?"

"An exorcism," Henley replied wearily.

42

Later that morning Henley found herself staring quizzically at the murder board. She turned around and faced her small team. Pellacia was sitting to Henley's right. Henley was aware of his every movement as he impatiently cleared his throat and folded his arms.

"We still don't have definitive proof that there is a baby," said Pellacia.

"Other than a lactating corpse in the freezer up the road," said Henley pointedly.

Pellacia opened his mouth to reply, but clearly thought better of it as he moved his chair away from her. Stanford leaned forward in his chair and dunked a custard cream into his tea, but his attention was on Pellacia. Outside, a thick snow fell.

"I've already put together an urgent press release appealing for information about the Hadlow baby," said Henley.

"And as I said, we still don't have definitive proof of the existence of this baby," said Pellacia. "You haven't got a birth certificate, hospital confirmation or any photographic evidence."

"Well, I'm sorry that Hadlow's baby doesn't have their own Instagram page to prove it to you, but I would rather take the

risk of putting out an appeal instead of doing nothing and finding a dead baby in a couple of weeks," Henley snapped back.

"So, we've got two murders, one attempted murder and a
missing baby," said Eastwood as she tapped her teaspoon against
her mug. "Great."

"Linh has confirmed that Hadlow was breastfeeding, but
we've got nothing else to confirm *when* she had the baby, *where*
she had the baby and, right now, we have no clue as to *what*
happened to that baby," said Henley.

"What about the ex-husband?" asked Pellacia. "Could he
be the baby's dad?"

"He said that he's had no contact with Hadlow for three
years. The court records state that Hadlow was the petitioner
for divorce and that she cited irreconcilable differences."

"Do we believe him though?" asked Stanford.

"Unless there is evidence to prove otherwise, then yes
we're—*I'm* accepting what he said."

"Babies don't just disappear," said Stanford.

"We suspect that the person or persons responsible for Hadlow's death took the baby. If we identify these people, then
we will find this baby. I'm sure that you wouldn't want Laura
Halifax MP accusing us of causing infanticide as well as a race
war in Deptford," Henley said to Pellacia.

"Is Hadlow linked to Whittaker in any way?" Pellacia asked.
He looked anywhere but at Henley. There was no warmth to
his voice. It sounded almost as if he expected Henley to fail.

"We haven't found any evidence that Whittaker and Hadlow
knew each other, and technically Whittaker wasn't a member
of the church, but they both suffered from mental illnesses, the
same rope was used to bind them and we've got the three sets
of fingerprints that were recovered from both crime scenes."

"Is that confirmed or just speculation? The mental health
issues."

"I doubt very much that the boss is making it up," Stanford

said loudly and with a sharp warning tone to his voice as Henley focused on the spot just above Pellacia's head.

"We've got Whittaker's medical records," Henley replied firmly.

"And we've just had our application request for Hadlow's GP records accepted," said Ramouter, just as defensively. "We should be getting them later this afternoon."

Pellacia's face was frozen in visible annoyance, but he didn't acknowledge either Ramouter or Stanford. His entire demeanor was dropping the temperature in the room.

"Whittaker's condition still remains critical, but he is stable." Henley slightly widened her stance in order to anchor herself and clasped her hands behind her back. She didn't want Pellacia to see how tightly she was gripping the marker pen. Pellacia's phone started to ring. He stood up and marched toward his office.

"Moody fucker," Stanford muttered.

"Someone needs to have a word with him," said Eastwood. "Not that I'm volunteering."

"Don't look at me," said Stanford. "This case is messy enough as it is. We don't need—"

"Let's all just stop with the slagging off session for a minute," said Henley. She couldn't let Pellacia's attitude derail them. "Stanford, I want you to go through HOLMES and see if there are any open or cold murder investigations where the victim's injuries or the circumstances of their deaths are similar to that of Hadlow and Whittaker."

"Are we marking this as a serial crime?" asked Eastwood.

"It's impossible not to," said Henley. "The MO is the same for Whittaker and Hadlow. The only difference is the location of Hadlow's body, and that she's dead."

"What about Caleb Annan?" Pellacia said as he returned to the room. "He's the reason that you're on this investigation in the first place. It looks like you're stalling."

Henley raised her eyes to the ceiling. Pellacia was deliberately testing her this morning. If the murder weapon had been found or if the search of Uliana's flat had produced more than just dust, and if she'd been able to verify Raina Davison's alibi, then maybe Henley wouldn't be so stuck. She wanted to shout out that she was doing her best, but she was acutely aware that doing so could be perceived as a sign of weakness. Silence descended as Henley waited for Pellacia to ask the question that she knew was on the tip of his tongue.

"So why haven't you arrested Serena Annan?" asked Pellacia. "We know that she was at the church, and I'm pretty sure that she must have known that her husband was screwing anything that had a pulse."

Henley kept her eyes on Pellacia, searching for any hint of the empathy that he'd shown her on Saturday. "I've got no CCTV, her housekeeper verifies her alibi, her DNA isn't on Caleb's body. What exactly would I be arresting her for?"

"This case is dragging. Annan's body was found nearly a week ago and you've got Whittaker and Hadlow tagging along like a bad smell. Do better."

Henley took a step back and turned her back as the door to the office swung open and Joanna walked in, stern-faced, with Laura Halifax behind her.

"What is she doing here?" Henley asked Pellacia.

Joanna led Laura into Pellacia's office and closed his door. "I'm not your bloody butler," Joanna said to Pellacia as she walked back to her desk.

"I'm attending the community policing meeting this morning," said Pellacia.

"Another one. You never go to those things, and now you've gone to two in a week."

"This isn't a normal case, Henley, as you keep on reminding me. This entire investigation is heading down a road that I don't like, and anything that can be perceived as slowing it down or taking attention away from it is going to be a problem. So yes, I will be going to another meeting."

"That still doesn't explain why she's here at the SCU," said Henley angrily. Pellacia stood up with force and sent his chair to the floor as the phone on Henley's desk began to ring out with an internal ringtone. She didn't need caller ID to know that Ezra was on the other end of the line.

"Ramouter, can you get that for me?" Henley asked as she picked up the chair that Pellacia had forced to the ground.

"What the fuck is wrong with him?" Stanford said after Pellacia had entered his office and firmly closed the door behind him.

"God knows. He's been a right moody bastard for the past week. She's very attractive though," said Eastwood as the sound of laughter rang out from Pellacia's office. Less than a minute later, Pellacia had his coat and was leading Laura out of his office. Henley watched as he placed his hand on the small of Laura's back and ushered her out of the room.

"Cozy," said Stanford.

"What does Ezra want?" Henley asked Ramouter. She began to rub away a knot in her neck. Her body was reacting to a stress that had nothing to do with the investigation.

"Ezra requires your presence downstairs," said Ramouter. "He also said that he's going to need therapy."

43

"I thought that I might be doing some fun stuff when I agreed to work here," said Ezra as he lowered the volume on his speakers. "But here I am freezing my boll—Well, it's a bit cold in here and—"

"Ezra, if you've called me down here just to have a moan about the lack of fun in your job, I'm telling you now that I'm not in the mood," said Henley.

"I'll save the moaning for my appraisal."

"You've never had an appraisal."

"Exactly. Anyway, I am very distressed about what I have seen."

"What are you talking about?" Henley asked. She sat down in the chair and took a long sip from her bottle of water. She felt overwhelmed with exhaustion; not the physical kind that weighed you down as it penetrated the marrow in your bones, but mental exhaustion that came from defending yourself against someone else's anger while trying to settle your own demons.

"I went through the camera that you found in the church and there was nothing on it."

"So why are we here?"

"I've been going through the external hard drives and… well, he's nasty."

"How nasty?"

"It's just as bad as that case we took from the Sapphire Unit last year. That level of nasty."

"Oh God," Henley said.

"What case was that?" Ramouter asked.

"The case of Backshaw. We charged him with multiple rapes, about a month before you joined us," said Henley. "He was a physiotherapist who specialized in sports injuries. He filmed his victims and attempted to blackmail a couple of them."

"I hate sex cases. Your dead pastor had a personal laptop but he's used up all the memory," Ezra explained as he turned on the large monitor in front of Henley and Ramouter. "So, he has been saving stuff onto an external hard drive."

The screen mirrored what Ezra was viewing on his own monitor. On the white screen were nine blue folders.

"The first folder is full of porn that he's downloaded," said Ezra. He clicked on the folder and a list of thumbnails appeared. "Do you want to see them, because I'm happy to leave the room?"

"Not particularly," said Henley.

"Well, you're going to have to look at these ones," said Ezra grimly. "They were recorded on the pastor's phone. Some were made at home, in some kind of recording studio."

"Caleb had a recording studio at the church, but we haven't recovered his phone," said Ramouter.

"Yeah, well, there's this thing called *the Cloud* which I checked but that was empty too… Anyhoo," Ezra said and pointed at the monitor. Henley and Ramouter leaned closer as Ezra opened another folder which contained six subfolders. The folders were titled only with initials: *CH, UP, PD, KF, NF, TT, AH.*

Henley knew what she was going to see before Ezra pressed play on the first video. She sat back and squinted at the screen as the pastor's office came into view. The camera turned toward the navy sofa. A woman that Henley didn't recognize and was definitely not Serena Annan was sitting naked in the corner of the sofa. The clock on the wall showed that it was almost eleven o'clock but there was no way of telling if it was day or night. Henley watched as Caleb came into view wearing a shirt but no trousers.

"Are you sure that we're alone?"

"I've told you that it's just us. Now come over here. On your knees…"

"OK, OK, pause it," said Henley. "I'm getting the picture. The next video."

"That's Uliana," said Ramouter as the video opened with Uliana sitting on the edge of the bed in her underwear.

"We haven't got much time. They'll be back by five."

"Well, they're definitely not in Uliana's flat," said Henley as she indicated for Ezra to move to the next video. "That could be the Annans' house," she continued, trying to keep the anger out of her voice. It was one thing knowing that Caleb had taken sexual advantage of these women, but it was another thing seeing it. Henley wondered when she would reach the point of not recognizing Caleb Annan as a murder victim.

"Which meant that she lied about being there. I don't think that these women knew they were being filmed," said Ramouter as Ezra moved on through the videos and Nicole Fleming was in view, straddling Caleb. "Not one of them has looked down the lens or played to the camera."

Ramouter moved back against the wall. The air in the room was still and cold.

"We need to trace all of the women who've appeared in these videos."

"Do you think that they're members of the church?" asked Ramouter.

"I wouldn't be surprised," said Henley as she stood up and stretched her legs.

"Don't go yet," said Ezra. "There's more."

Disgust kept Henley rooted to her spot as Ezra played the video that was simply named *A★ Fear*. She recognized the dressing table, the curtains scattered with purple flowers. A streak of light fell against the white wooden slats of the headboard. The early beginnings of black mold sprouted from the walls.

"That's Alyssa Hadlow's bedroom," said Ramouter.

"I'm going to save you."

Caleb Annan's voice was barely audible, but he was on the screen, naked and standing over Alyssa Hadlow, and then he lay on top of her. Henley wanted to reach in and pull his heavy and sweaty bulk off her.

"You promised. Make them stop."

"Make them stop?" Ramouter asked, looking down at the space between his feet. "What did she mean by 'make them stop'?"

"She could be talking about the other people who were working with Caleb, or she could have been hearing voices. I don't know," said Henley.

"She needed help and he did that. Bastard."

"Turn it off," Henley said as she put a hand over her stomach. She felt nauseous. "Do you have a date for those videos?"

"Yeah, easy. Let me just open the properties. That last one was filmed last year on the second of April. All of the videos I've shown you are just for this year."

"April. That's just over ten months ago," said Ramouter. "Caleb Annan could be the father of Hadlow's baby?"

"Boss, he definitely didn't look like he was being careful," said Ezra. "And I'm not watching any more to find out. That's not in my job description."

"Serena Annan must have known what was going on," said Ramouter.

"I would be very surprised if she didn't. She attacked Nicole Fleming and threatened Raina Davison. Serena Annan knew exactly what her husband was doing," said Henley. "Ezra, do me a favor. I want you to download, extract, or whatever you want to call it, all of the videos and photos that you can find and send it all to Eastwood to go through. I'm hoping that there aren't any more women that he's been secretly filming. That is in your job description."

"Boss, there are two more external hard drives and the desktop to go through. He's a dog, there's probably loads." Ezra pulled a disgusted face. "He's probably filled them with those videos."

"How long will it take you to go through it all?"

"Not long. There's not many people out there who encrypt their hard drives. Eastwood will have it way before lunchtime."

"Thanks, Ez, I know that this is a horrible case, but seriously, thank you for your hard work. It's definitely a breakthrough," said Henley.

"I mean, I would rather be doing some *Mission Impossible* stuff but, you know…" Ezra said, a look of embarrassment crossing his face.

"I'll order you a pizza for lunch."

"Don't be stingy. I want buffalo chicken wings too."

"So, what next?" asked Ramouter as he and Henley stepped out into the cold corridor and made their way back to the incident room.

"We're going to talk to Serena Annan."

44

"So, what exactly are you doing here?" asked Serena as she stood defensively in front of her desk. "I would have thought that you would have far more important things to do, like finding my husband's killer."

Ramouter silently took the seat next to Henley and pulled out his notebook. He was more than happy to sit back and watch Henley take the lead, which was for the best. Ramouter didn't trust himself not to tell Serena Annan how much he despised her husband.

"That's exactly why we're here, Mrs. Annan. The identification and arrest of the person or people involved in your husband's murder is always the highest of priorities, which means that I have to pursue all reasonable lines of inquiry; regardless of where they may lead," said Henley. She sat down on the armchair that was more expensive than the entire sofa suite in her front room. Serena's office was on the first floor of a Victorian terrace overlooking Blackheath Village. Henley had said nothing when she had parked in the car park that faced the heath where Olivier had stabbed her. She had thought it would've triggered her, but she remained numb.

"I'm not happy with how things are progressing," said Serena.

"And what exactly are you unhappy with?" Henley asked as calmly as though she was requesting a window seat.

"His blood is still on the carpets of the church floor," said Serena. "The entire building is in disarray because of your forensics people. When will the police be cleaning my church?"

"That's not our job. We don't clean up crime scenes. We investigate."

Serena shook her head with disgust. "Is that how you treat all of your victims or is this just how you've decided to treat me?"

"Bethany, your family liaison officer, will be able to provide you with details of a private cleaning service who specialize in crime scenes, but we don't pay for it," said Henley. "Now, back to your husband's case."

"Has there been progress?" Serena asked. "I need to start making arrangements for my husband's funeral. The church needs closure."

"The church?" Henley asked. "What about closure for you and your family?"

"It's all the same thing," Serena answered as she sat down beside her desk.

"We need to ask you some questions about your relationship with your husband." Henley inwardly cringed at the forced empathy in her voice.

"I don't see what our relationship has to do with catching my husband's killer."

"It might have everything to do with it," Henley countered. "How long were you together?"

"Fifteen years, married for thirteen."

"And you have just the two children?"

"I don't want to talk about my children."

"Well, then let's talk about the other women in your husband's life."

The words hung unanswered in the air. Serena stared at Henley with fury in her eyes.

"We have evidence that Caleb was with another woman on the night he died. The night that he texted you to say that he was going to be late home," said Henley.

"You're talking nonsense," Serena said.

"And it wasn't the first time that he's cheated on you," said Ramouter.

"Is there actual evidence or is this just something that you've made up?"

"We don't make things up," said Henley.

"Please," Serena snorted. "As if the police play by the rules."

"You didn't answer the question."

"This wouldn't be the first time that some dirty—"

Henley caught Serena's quick inhale of breath as she composed herself.

"Some woman has said that she's sleeping with my husband," Serena concluded.

"'Some woman'? So, you have firsthand knowledge of the women who have slept with your husband?"

"I didn't say that it was true. They were just baseless accusations of women who were jealous of me."

"We have DNA evidence and videos of your husband with other women."

"Videos?" Serena bit her lower lip, smudging her lipstick. She cleared her throat as she adjusted the bow of her silk blouse. "I don't believe you."

"We've recovered footage from your husband's laptop and external hard drives. Fifty videos, to be exact."

Serena stood up and walked over to the window. She placed her hands on the windowsill. Henley watched her shoulders rise and then drop as she took deep breaths.

"Serena," Henley pleaded, hoping the extension of familiarity would break through the invisible barricade that surrounded her.

"I don't accept that," Serena said as she continued to face the window. Her words were flat and emotionless. "Caleb was a man of God. He wouldn't."

"DC Ramouter can show you some screenshots from the videos. You can take a look for yourself and confirm whether the man in those videos is your husband or not," said Henley.

"There's no need," said Serena as she turned around. There were no tears on her face. No signs of distress over her husband's betrayal. "I was pregnant with our son the first time that he cheated on me. I mean, there are…were, always women trying to get his attention, wanting to take my place. You would think a wedding ring on his finger would stop them. You would think that Caleb being a man of God would stop them."

"Have you ever confronted these women, or any woman that your husband was—"

"What do you take me for?" Serena said frostily. "I wouldn't lower myself to talk to them. They were disgusting."

"So, you never spoke to these women in person about your husband's behavior?" asked Henley.

"No."

"What about on the phone?"

"Absolutely not."

"But you knew who they were?"

"Not all of them but I had to look at some while they sat in the front row in the church on Sundays."

"But you never confronted them?" Henley checked, knowing full well that Serena would lie to her again.

"I told you no."

"What about their husbands or partners?" Ramouter asked. "Did they ever confront your husband?"

"Not as far as I know, and if they did then I'm sure that it was dealt with," said Serena.

"How would it have been dealt with?" asked Ramouter.

"You would have to ask the board. They deal with all of the church issues."

Henley pondered how the church could have any say in a

marriage. The only way was if the women who Caleb had assaulted had complained to the church board.

"This wasn't a church issue," said Henley. "This was your marriage."

Serena shrugged. "It's one and the same thing."

"Did you confront your husband about the affairs?" said Henley. "Were there arguments?"

"Of course. He cheated and embarrassed me."

"Embarrassed you. Well, that must mean that other people knew about Caleb's behavior."

"You're twisting my words."

"Were those arguments ever physical?"

"No." Serena shook her head. "No," she said again. "He never laid a hand on me. I would never stand for that."

"Did you ever hit him?" asked Ramouter.

There was a dead pause in the air as Serena looked at Henley and then at Ramouter, as though she was silently deciding whether to tell the truth or not.

Serena sat back down without answering or acknowledging the question.

"One of the women that your husband took advantage of sexually has been identified as Alyssa Hadlow," said Henley. She pulled out her mobile phone and opened up the photograph of an alive Alyssa Hadlow. "We're also investigating the circumstances of her death...her murder."

"Her murder?" Serena asked. She kept her hands clasped tightly in front of her and her eyes focused on Henley, refusing to look at the phone.

"She was also a member of your church and, in fact, didn't live too far from it."

"I don't know her."

"Whoever is responsible for her death left her to rot. She wasn't found for three weeks. The people involved, and I'm telling you as a matter of courtesy, the people involved includes your husband."

For the first time since Henley had opened her mouth, Serena looked shocked. She shook her head. "Is this how low you will go? To accuse my husband? My children's father of being a murderer?" Serena's voice cracked.

"As I told you," said Henley, "we're following the evidence."

"I don't know why you're telling me this," said Serena. "I didn't know the woman and I didn't know that she was sleeping with my husband, and Caleb didn't kill her."

"I didn't say that Caleb Annan was sleeping with her," said Henley. "I said that he took advantage of her sexually in the same way that he took advantage of Raina Davison."

"Raina!" Serena released a bitter laugh. "Please, is that what she said, that Caleb took advantage of her?"

"Raina also said that you called her, told her to leave Caleb alone and that you threatened her."

"I did no such thing," Serena said firmly.

"So, you're denying that you called her?"

"How many times do I have to tell you? I did not call her. She's a lying bitch."

Henley had the strange feeling that Serena's sudden anger was a result of knowing the truth about what her husband had done to Raina. Henley glanced over at Ramouter's notebook and saw that he'd written:

SA losing it re Raina? Why? She knows.

"OK," Henley said calmly as Serena became more agitated. "Can you explain where you were on the Friday before Caleb was murdered? What was the exact date, Ramouter?"

"The fourteenth of February," said Ramouter.

"Ah, Valentine's Day," said Henley. "You should remember what you were doing on that day, around 7 p.m.?"

"I was home with my children. Dalisay was also there."

"You didn't leave your home?"

"No. I cooked a Valentine's dinner for Caleb."

"So, not in the Hammersmith area?" Henley asked as Serena stared at her with absolute fury.

"I don't have to answer your questions," said Serena defiantly.

"Did you ever go back to the church on the evening that Caleb was murdered?"

"I've already told you no, and Dalisay has already told you that I was home with the children. Is this really how you choose to conduct an investigation?" said Serena. "Repeating the same ridiculous questions."

"These aren't ridiculous questions," said Henley, finally losing her patience. "Your husband has been accused of rape and there's evidence of him—"

"No, no," Serena said as she stood up and walked to the door. "You need to leave. You have the audacity to come here and slander my husband. You're just trying to cover up for the fact that you haven't given his case the same due care and attention that you've given to that boy and this...this woman. You need to leave. Now!"

Henley bit her tongue and stood up. "Mrs. Annan."

"I will be speaking to Laura Halifax about this and maybe the press about your biased and irresponsible approach to my husband's case."

"Go ahead," said Henley. "If you think that your baseless allegations will make the evidence against your husband go away, then you go ahead and call everybody."

45

"I'm starting to think that she did it," said Ramouter, pulling on his gloves. "The only thing that she seems concerned about is her reputation. But, regardless, she blatantly lied."

Henley stared at the heath, clutching her car keys. She could see herself running after Olivier. She needed to stop him. With every breath she relived the moment. She winced and put a hand to her stomach. In that brief moment it felt as though Olivier was stabbing her again.

"Boss," Ramouter called out. "Are you all right?"

"Sorry, sorry," Henley replied. She refocused her mind and faced Ramouter, away from the ghosts.

"It must be hard, not thinking about what happened to you here?" Ramouter said as he looked out onto the heath.

"It's weird. Sometimes I can drive past and it won't even bother me, but other days, it's as if I can see it playing out in front of my eyes and it feels like it's happening all over again. Do you understand what I mean?"

"Aye," said Ramouter. "I was looking for somewhere to park when I had to go to Camberwell Green Magistrates' Court for warrant. I parked on Hanover Street, two doors away from Pine's house and it was like it was happening all over again."

"It will get easier," said Henley. "It has to. Anyway, you were saying. Serena Annan."

"Aye, Uliana says that Serena was at the church that evening but we've got nothing to back that up, unless the council recovers the CCTV."

"Serena's prints are all over the church but that doesn't mean anything; she's always at the church," Henley said as she opened the car door. "We know that there were two people at the church that night, but again, the only other DNA on Annan's body belongs to Uliana."

"What do you want to do? What should we do?" Ramouter asked. He slumped back in his seat and Henley started the engine. She looked into the rearview mirror, hoping that her reflection might give her answers as she put the car into reverse. The truth was that she didn't know what to do.

"I'm conflicted," Henley admitted. "I want to arrest her and put her arse in a cold cell but all we've got is the word of Uliana who places her at the church. And at the moment her alibi seems rock solid with the housekeeper backing her up."

"Do you think that she'll go to the press?"

"Nah, she can slag me off until the cows come home, but that won't stop the press from asking 'Did your husband kill Brandon Whittaker and Alyssa Hadlow?' And imagine how much worse it will be now that the appeal for Hadlow's missing baby is out there."

Henley's ringing phone interrupted the Chelsea v West Bromwich Albion game. She didn't hesitate to answer the call when "ANTHONY THOMAS CALLING" appeared on the screen.

"I'm in the car with Ramouter," said Henley as she headed toward the South Circular.

"Good," said Anthony. "I've got two sets of results for you.

First, we recovered a set of fingerprints from the front door, and we got a match on the database. A fourteen-year-old kid and, no surprise, the little shit was just sentenced to a twelve-month youth rehabilitation order for burglary."

"I'm going to stick my neck out and say that I doubt that this kid was involved in what happened to Hadlow, but I'll get Eastwood to have a word with him," said Henley. "What about the second set of results?"

"I found strands of Whittaker's hair on Hadlow's body."

"What does that mean?" asked Ramouter. "That Whittaker and Hadlow were in the same room together?"

"Possibly," said Anthony. "Either they were in the same room together at the same time or at different times, or it's an issue of cross contamination. But that's not all. The DNA that we extracted from the fingernails of both Hadlow and Whittaker are an identical match for three people," said Anthony.

"Please tell me that Caleb Annan is one of the three?" asked Henley.

"Bingo. One identical match for Annan."

"Just to be clear," said Henley. "You found DNA markers for three separate people." said Henley. "One that belongs to Caleb Annan, but the other two?"

"Yeah, and that's where your luck runs out. No match on the database for those two," said Anthony. "But although they're unknown, I can confirm the gender of both. You're looking for another man and a woman."

A baby had been screaming in Henley's dream. She could hear the baby and she could see the baby wrapped in a black blanket in the middle of the snow-covered grass of Blackheath. Henley ran toward the distressed cries, but Olivier was quicker, he pushed Henley to the ground, stamped on her chest and grabbed the baby.

The scream was stuck in Henley's throat as she woke up with a start. She could feel the hot sweat clinging to her scalp and running down the back of her neck. Her pillowcase was damp against her face. Henley put a hand to her chest to calm the erratic beating of her heart as her phone vibrated and beeped on her bedside table. She closed her eyes and the phone beeped again. It would have been a call if there had been a dead body waiting for Henley.

Henley raised her head from the pillow and reached for the phone; grateful that Rob was still sleeping in the spare room. Henley knew that it was Pellacia messaging. She squinted, as the screen had illuminated her face at 1:48 a.m. There were three deleted WhatsApp messages on Henley's phone. She had never understood the point of deleting a message when you knew full well that the receiver would see that you had been on their mind in the middle of the night.

Henley rolled over onto her back and raised her phone. Pellacia was online. She wondered if he was waiting for her to ask, *What do you want?* or *What did you delete? Online* switched to *typing…*

"Oh, for God's sake," Henley whispered as *typing* disappeared but there was no message in its place.

Rob had never asked her directly if anything had happened between her and Pellacia. There had been the indirect comments, the silent looks from the other side of the sofa when Pellacia called her phone, but never a direct accusation. Henley leaned back on the pillow and closed her eyes. She could hear the naked branches of the magnolia tree banging against the window. The phone beeped again and vibrated in her hand.

I'm sorry.

46

She sat on the floor and put a hand to the back of her head. She could feel the warm heat from the blood that had started to seep from the cut there. Strands of her hair clung to the blood as she pulled her hand away. The ringing in her right ear grew louder as the pain radiated across her scalp.

"Make him shut up," she shouted as the man's voice screamed out.

"I'm fucking trying. You don't think that I'm trying? I can't do this on my own."

The light in the room was dim but she could make out her husband straddling the man on the bed, trying to pin him down.

"We need Caleb," she said. Caleb had been stronger, and he'd had a way of soothing them when they began to fight. She wished that she knew what Caleb had whispered into their ears when they'd screamed that they wanted to die.

"Will you get over here? I need you. Get the rope."

She fell onto her knees and reached out and grabbed the edge of the small antique table. She grimaced through the pain as she eased herself up. It felt as though her brain was rolling around in her skull.

"Come on," she said through gritted teeth as she brought herself to her feet. She felt a pain in the left side of her stomach. The flesh was already bruised and tender from where he'd kicked her.

"This one is a fighter." She picked up the red rope that was on the table.

"Hurry up and tie his legs."

Her husband shifted down and sat firmly on the man's thighs as she wrapped the rope around the man's ankles and then secured the rope to the bed frame.

"I need to release you," she said. She picked up a candle and held the dancing flame to his feet. His screams bounced off the walls as she moved the flame from left to right. The smell of burning flesh didn't bother her anymore.

His screaming became muffled as her husband leaned forward and pushed both hands against the man's mouth. She stood up and limped toward the top of the bed. The ringing in her head had stopped by the time she'd put the candle down and picked up the bucket. Her husband released his hands from the man's mouth. The man was crying now. Big choking sobs that rattled his chest.

"All we're doing is trying to save you," she said. Her husband got up off the man and picked up a black piece of cloth which he tied around the man's mouth. The man's chest rose and fell at a quicker pace as he tried to bring oxygen into his lungs. She raised the bucket above her head and let the water fall.

"Leave him," her husband said. He picked up a small red Bible and began to read. The man tried in vain to breathe against the torrent of water that ran down his nose, the back of his throat and entered his lungs.

"Be alert and of sober mind. Your enemy, the devil, prowls around like a roaring lion looking for someone to devour. Resist him, standing firm in faith," she said as she placed the empty bucket down. She felt proud that she'd remembered the words that Caleb had spoken just before he'd cast out the demon. She watched the man as his body contorted and the skin on his chest strained as he tried to release himself from the restraints.

Kneeling down, she placed her palm against his hot forehead and whispered, "Leave him. Leave."

"Stop," said her husband. "Can you hear that?"

She stood up and listened, putting a hand to her chest to calm down her heart that was pulsating with excitement. His crying never failed to bring her joy. She knew that all she had to do was to hold him close to her.

"You just changed him," said her husband as he checked his watch, and the crying grew a little louder.

"I think that it's time for his feed. Hopefully he'll take a bit more of the bottle this time. I'll get him," she said. She couldn't stop smiling when she thought about the baby that God had chosen to place in her care. "You pray for him," she said, "and I'll take care of the baby."

47

Henley was debating whether or not to walk out of the coffee shop.

"I've got you a latte and a blueberry muffin," said Pellacia, pushing the steaming cup of coffee and the plate toward the empty chair opposite.

"I don't want a bloody muffin." The seating area of the café was only a quarter full as the early starters grabbed their teas and coffees to go. The sun was still being held hostage by the darkened winter sky. She had barely slept and had given up at 4 a.m. and dragged herself exhaustedly out of bed to her kitchen table with the Annan, Whittaker and Hadlow investigation file, watching the snowflakes fall like fairy lights as they caught the orange glow of the streetlights.

"Please, Anj," Pellacia pleaded. "I said that I was sorry."

"It's not me that you need to apologize to," Henley said. She relented and unwrapped her thick scarf from around her neck then wriggled out of her coat and sat down, facing Pellacia. "It's the team."

"I know." Pellacia pushed the bowl containing the sachets of sugar toward Henley. "I'll make it up to them."

"No sugar for me," Henley said as she picked up her spoon and stirred the white foam in her cup.

"Since when?"

"We have to give up the things that are not any good for us."

"Is that a dig?" said Pellacia, pulling apart his ham and cheese toastie and placing half on Henley's plate.

"Of course it's a dig. I'm pissed off with you, Stephen. You woke me at stupid o'clock with your messages."

"I deleted them."

"As if that makes a difference. You know full well that I would see them."

"I didn't get much sleep either, you know."

"Guilt will do that to you," Henley said. She picked up her half of the toastie and began to eat. She kept her eyes firmly locked on Pellacia's. He had spent so much time avoiding her gaze or even looking straight past her over the last few months that she'd forgotten how intense they were.

"Well, if you talked to me then I wouldn't have anything to feel guilty about."

"There's nothing for us to talk about." Henley did her best to keep her voice level and calm. They could have had this conversation in one of the abandoned rooms at the SCU but there was danger in being alone, in any capacity, with Pellacia. The truth was that she didn't trust herself with him.

"You keep saying that." Pellacia looked around to make sure that there was no one within earshot. "But you and I both know that that's rubbish. You can't keep brushing *us* under the carpet."

"I'm not brushing us under the carpet. You have no idea how much worse you made things between me and Rob when you turned up on Saturday."

"You know why I was there. Rob needs to get over himself."

"That's not the point and you know it. Look, I'm not going to sit here and act as though you and I didn't happen, but I can't give you hope that we can continue to happen." Henley looked down at her wedding ring, the overhead spotlight il-

luminating the platinum band as though the universe was trying to make a point.

"You make me sound like some desperate saddo," said Pellacia as he sipped at his coffee cup. Henley tried to keep herself contained. "This situation isn't easy for me, you know."

"Stephen, I don't mean to be cold, but we're not in a situation."

"No, you're right. It's not a situation. It's a mess."

"I thought about leaving again," said Henley.

"Too much wishful thinking that you're talking about Rob?"

Henley pushed a piece of the still warm sponge into her
mouth and admitted to Pellacia the thing that only Dr. Isabelle Collins knew.

"It's not wishful thinking," she said softly. "After last year
with Olivier...my mum. I wanted to run."

"From Rob?"

"From everyone and everything. Including the job...and you.
I know that I hurt you, and Olivier, he hurt you because of me."

Pellacia's face had darkened at the sound of Olivier's name.
Henley wondered if the scars that had been left behind from
the symbols that Olivier had carved on Pellacia's chest had
begun to fade, or if they glowed as red and fierce as the night
the knife had been pushed into his skin. At least she'd had Rob
to call when she'd crumbled into pieces onto the wet concrete,
and to be there when the nightmares left her in a cold sweat.
Henley had no idea who Pellacia called when the nightmares
woke him up at night.

"I'm always checking the CADs from the river police," Pellacia said as he pushed his empty cup away.

"What about the coast guard?" Henley asked with a wry
smile.

"Them too."

"I don't like the idea of Olivier being out there. Drifting. It
means that he could always come back, even though—"

"He is dead," Pellacia said definitively.

"Don't you want to see his body?" Henley asked.

"No. I don't need to see his rotting corpse," Pellacia said. His phone began to ring on the table.

Henley glanced down to see Laura Halifax's name flash across the screen.

"It's not what you think." Pellacia silenced the phone and put it in his pocket.

"I didn't say a word," Henley said as she wondered what Pellacia was keeping from her. Her own phone began to ring from the depths of her bag. "We need to be better. No more late-night texting."

"It won't happen again," Pellacia said as he twisted around and took his coat off the back of the chair.

Henley pulled her phone out and Stanford's name flashed large across the screen. "What's happened?" She stood up and picked up her coat and the rest of her muffin. "It's not even 8 a.m."

"Well, nothing has *just* happened, but something did happen about three months ago," Stanford said cryptically. "I think we've got another victim to add to our exorcism gone wrong list."

48

"His name is Charlie Jensen and it's an open murder investigation," said Stanford. He opened the brown paper bag that Pellacia had dumped in front of him and picked up the grease-wrapped roll, holding it suspiciously to his nose. "Is this real bacon and not that stuff that pretends to be bacon?"

"Just eat it," said Pellacia. He prized his second cup of the coffee for the morning out of the cardboard tray. Stanford winked at Henley.

"So, you were saying," asked Henley as she pulled up a chair and sat next to Stanford. "Charlie Jensen? Who is he?"

"He's a sixty-two-year-old white male and three months ago, his body was found wrapped in a sleeping bag outside a garage in Plaistow. A man named Nathanial Freer had the shock of his life when he found Mr. Jensen."

"Plaistow. East London. That's the wrong side of the river for us," said Henley.

"The garage is less than a mile away from the east London branch of the Church of Annan the Prophet." Stanford took a bite of his bacon roll and closed his eyes in satisfaction. He chewed away for a minute before setting his roll back down on the paper bag.

"Do you feel better now?" Henley asked, shaking her head.

"Makes coming in here at the crack of dawn almost worth it," said Stanford. "Anyway, the church also owns a house less than a quarter of mile from where this Jensen was found."

"What about the garage where he was found?"

"The garage is a converted railway arch. It's owned by Newham Council but it's currently rented out to David Onyeka."

"David Onyeka. Why does that name seem familiar?" asked Pellacia.

"David Onyeka is one of the aliases used by our very own Caleb Annan."

"And it's also the name that he was using when Rob interviewed five years ago," said Henley.

"Shit," said Pellacia. "I've never had a murder investigation like this."

"First time for everything," said Stanford.

"What do we know about this Charlie Jensen?"

"Jensen was reported missing from his supported accommodation six weeks before he was found dead outside the garage."

"Why was he in supported accommodation?" asked Henley. "Actually, I'm going to take a wild guess and say mental health issues."

"Bull's-eye. Jensen had been diagnosed with paranoid schizophrenia in his thirties. In and out of hospital, a couple of stints in prison and then he ended up in supported accommodation."

"How did he die?" asked Pellacia as Ramouter and Eastwood entered the room.

"No idea. I couldn't get access to the full post-mortem report. I kept getting an error message, but there is an in-situ photo."

Stanford turned the monitor toward Henley where there were two photographs. The first showed the crime scene. Late November, when the weather had been unseasonably warm for a week. Jensen's body had been wrapped in a dark green sleep-

ing bag, marked with patches where his decomposing waste
had leaked through. A wheelie bin had been placed on its side
and dried leaves pushed around the bag in a poor effort to conceal it. Henley could see a thin arm escaping from the seams
of the makeshift burial shroud. The skin had taken on a whit-
ish-blue hue.

"He was found outside the garage that Annan rented," said
Henley. "I don't understand why the killer would dump their
victim outside on their own property. It doesn't make sense."

"Maybe Annan wasn't the one who killed him," said Ramouter. "Remember what Anthony said. What if it was the
other two who worked with Annan?"

Henley clicked on the arrow and moved onto the next photograph. She felt the latte and the blueberry muffin that she'd
eaten earlier threatening to make a reappearance. It didn't matter how many times she saw a dead body, there was something
unsettling about seeing death captured in a photograph like an
exhibit in a Victorian museum. Charlie Jensen's face was skeletal. His sharp cheekbones jutted out through his sunken skin.
His mouth was open as though death had captured him in an
extreme moment of pain. His cheeks were covered in deep,
blackened scratches and the skin under his eyes was bruised.
Jensen's hair was gray but patchy. The dry skin of his scalp was
pinpricked with dried blood spots.

"Is there a forensic report on HOLMES?" asked Henley as
she zoomed in on Jensen's forehead looking for any signs of ash
or the word 'leave'. There were black markings, but she wasn't
sure if she was looking at bruising or smudges of charcoal.

"Could be. But as I said. Error message," Stanford answered.

"What about suspects?" Henley moved out of the way to
make room for Ramouter and Eastwood.

"Not that I could see," said Stanford as he finished the rest
of his bacon roll and started on a ham and cheese croissant.
"To be honest, this isn't the best CRIS report that I've seen.

It could have been some newbie trying to put the info in and screwing it up."

Henley remembered the first time that she'd tried to update the Criminal Reporting Information System. It had taken her three months to get the hang of it.

"All of the SIO's inquiries seem to have hit a dead end," said Stanford. "The last update was on the fourteenth of January. It could be something or it could be nothing, but the circumstances match Hadlow and Whittaker."

"Who's the SIO?" asked Henley.

"DI Ben Clarke at Forest Gate."

"Clarke? That can't be our Clarke, can it? I thought he'd retired." Henley thought back to when she and Stanford had spent six months working in the CID as newly qualified detective constables.

"It has to be," Stanford said as he rocked back nostalgically. "God, he was a miserable git, and a lazy one, which would explain why the CRIS report entries are so crap."

"I'll give him a bell and ask him if he's OK with us taking a look at the Jensen investigation. If it is our Clarke, he'll be happy to reduce his workload."

"And remember to play nice if it isn't him," said Stanford. He happily screwed up the empty paper bag and threw it into the bin. "The last thing you want is another headache like DS Lancaster last year and be accused of stealing cases."

"I will be an absolute delight," said Henley as she indicated to Ramouter to follow her. "Oh, and Stanford. Good work."

Stanford grinned as he turned back toward his computer screen. "You can buy me lunch later as a reward. I heard on the grapevine that was your thing now."

"What can I do for you, boss?" Ramouter asked, perching himself on the edge of Henley's desk. He stood up again when he saw the look on Henley's face.

"Are the remaining church board members still playing hide-and-seek?" Henley asked.

"Yes and no. I've got statements from two more; Solomon Ndya and Josiah Rosa and they're both basically saying the same thing. They have no idea why anyone would kill Annan, all deny knowledge of Whittaker and Hadlow and the…the exorcisms, and they both have verified alibis and have supplied DNA samples, but there are two board members, a Lincoln Okafor and a Derrick Sullivan, who haven't replied to my emails or voice mails."

"Go and see them."

"What, now?"

"Yes now. There's got to be a reason why those two are so resistant to talking to us. Look, the Hadlow and Whittaker investigation is gathering pace and I don't want us to be accused of neglecting the Annan murder even if he is up to his neck in it with these… I can't believe that I'm saying it, with these exorcisms."

"I've been going through the board minutes for the church meetings and there seems to have been a lot of disagreements between them. I was thinking about what Serena Annan said about the church being involved in their marriage. That could be a course of disagreement."

"Someone will talk," said Henley. "There's got to be someone in that church with a conscience." She leaned back in her chair and tapped her pen thoughtfully against her lips. "I'm going to stay here and chase up this Jensen case," she said. "I would be very surprised if someone on that board, someone close to Caleb, didn't know what he'd been up to with all of those women."

49

If Lincoln Okafor was surprised to see DC Ramouter standing on his doorstep, he was doing a good job of hiding it.

"You haven't returned any of my phone calls or replied to my emails. DC Ramouter," he introduced himself as he held out his warrant card.

"It's been a very busy time." Lincoln Okafor stood by his front door with sweat dripping from his forehead and a towel around his neck. He zipped up his hoodie and folded his arms to protect himself against the cold.

"I called you when I was on my way over." Ramouter tapped the side of his left ear. "You sent me straight to voice mail." Lincoln pulled the AirPods out of his ear and managed to feign a look of surprise as though he'd forgotten they were there.

"Yeah, these things. They're always playing up."

"Aye," Ramouter replied as he turned his head around at the sound of the gate being dragged across gravel and a postman made his way up the path. "Look, it's freezing out here and I don't think that you want the local postman to hear us talking about a murder investigation on your doorstep. If he's anything like my postman he'll be telling all of your business to all your neighbors. But if you're happier standing out here," Ramouter continued, "then I can ask you about the investi—"

"Come in," Lincoln said quickly. He moved to the side and allowed Ramouter to step into the house.

Ramouter sat on an uncomfortable stool with a steaming cup of tea in his hand. He pressed his ring finger against the ceramic cup. He still wasn't used to the fact that he couldn't feel anything in that finger. The doctor had diagnosed a peripheral nerve injury. Another reminder of the damage that Olivier had caused when Olivier had stabbed Ramouter's arm. Lincoln's house wasn't as big as the Annans', but it was equally impressive. And unlike the pastor's house, it looked like a home. Cereal-crusted bowls filled the kitchen sink, and the table still contained a young hurried family's breakfast crumbs. Ramouter felt a pang of sadness. He didn't expect dirty cereal bowls to remind him what he'd been missing.

"To be honest, I'm surprised to find you at home," said Ramouter as he took a sip of weak tea.

"I don't usually work from home, but I've got the gasman coming around at some point today," Lincoln replied as he stirred sugar into his own cup. "Sorry about the mess. I had the school run and the cleaner's called in sick. So, you wanted to talk about Caleb."

"I've been trying to talk to you about Caleb for over a week."

"Well, it's been a lot for us to deal with. Caleb was an important part of the church and for him to be taken from us like that..." Lincoln put his hands to his face and squeezed his eyes shut. "I still can't believe it."

"You're the finance director for the church?" Ramouter asked.

"Yes, that's what I do."

"And you've been the director from the very beginning?" Ramouter asked the question, though he already knew the answer.

"Yes, I can't remember when exactly Caleb asked me to be

the finance director, but it was about two months after the church started."

"How long did you know Caleb for?"

"Over twenty years. We met at university."

"Did you know that Caleb had previously been investigated by the Charity Commission and sent to prison for fraud?"

Lincoln's face grew ashen and the cup of tea that he was drinking was suspended in midair. "What are you talking about?" he finally said. "I didn't know about that."

"You just told me that you'd known Caleb for over twenty years; he managed to keep from you that he'd been inside? He got a three-year sentence, so he would have had to have spent at least eighteen months in prison."

"There was a time that he was away, but he told me that he was in Ghana, and that was just after his granddad died so that's where I probably thought he was. In Ghana. Not prison."

"If Caleb had disclosed his criminal convictions, would he have been allowed on the church board?" asked Ramouter.

"No. No," said Lincoln. "He would have been automatically disqualified. We all could have been in trouble for allowing him on the board. But we didn't know."

"You never said what your day job is?" Ramouter asked as he pulled out his notebook.

"I'm a financial advisor," Lincoln said quietly. "That's why it made sense when Caleb offered me the finance director role."

"Right. So, if the Charity Commission was to launch an investigation into the church, they would be looking at where the money was going, and also looking at you."

"I never did anything wrong. I would never do anything... I have a family." Lincoln's face crumbled as he put down his cup.

"So why were you avoiding us?"

"You wouldn't understand."

"How close were you and Caleb Annan? Would you call him a close friend?"

"He wasn't the godfather of my children if that's what you're asking, but I…respected him and what he did for us, the church and the community."

"Respect," said Ramouter caustically. "Were you aware that Caleb was accused of rape?"

Lincoln, still standing, gripped the back of his chair.

"I didn't know about that. No, no, it must be a mistake."

"It's not a mistake. What about the young man who was found in the church? Brandon Whittaker?"

"I don't know him. The first I knew about him was when I saw the news."

"You'd never seen him before?"

"Never."

"What about Alyssa Hadlow?" Ramouter asked as Lincoln grew more agitated.

"I've never heard of her. You have to understand. We're not a little village church on the green. We have a large congregation. It's impossible to know everybody."

"She was found dead in her flat and she was a member of the church, and we know that she was in physical contact with Caleb Annan."

"Why are you doing this to us? Why are you trying to tarnish us?"

Lincoln looked distressed as though he was personally being attacked. Ramouter could clearly see the panic in his eyes and the spotlights in the ceiling made the beads of sweat on his forehead glisten.

"We're not," said Ramouter. "All we want to do is find out who killed Caleb Annan and who in your church is responsible for nearly killing Brandon Whittaker and leaving Alyssa Hadlow dead in her flat."

Lincoln said nothing. The only sound came from the ticking of the kitchen clock and the motor of the tumble dryer.

"When was the last time that you saw Mr. Annan?" Ramouter asked.

"Erm… Sunday afternoon. We had the church service, and we had a short meeting afterward."

"How short is short?"

"Maybe twenty to thirty minutes." Lincoln looked around the kitchen as though he expected the walls to be collapsing around him. "I didn't kill him… I wouldn't…couldn't break a commandment like that."

"I didn't say that you did," said Ramouter. "What was the meeting about?"

"About expanding and opening another church in Balham."

"How did the meeting go?"

"Not well," Lincoln said. He picked up a tea towel and wiped away the sweat from his brow. "We had an argument about money that had been taken from the church accounts. Everything must be recorded for all of the churches, but Caleb had a habit of making large withdrawals. There were some things that I missed because I was looking after the accounts for three churches."

"Was there a lot of money going into a different church?"

"It was more a case that there was a lot of money coming out of all the churches that I couldn't account for. We'd had a letter informing us that the Charity Commission would be performing an audit. Audits are fine if you can account for the money coming in and out, but I couldn't."

"How much money did Caleb withdraw?"

"It wasn't a lump sum, but, all together, just over £300,000."

"What was Caleb doing with the money that he was withdrawing?"

For the first time, Lincoln looked away.

"Lincoln, I'm going to ask you again. What was the money for?"

Lincoln let out a long sigh and finally sat down. "Some female members of the church had made some complaints about Caleb's behavior. I don't know the full details but I know that they were alleging that he'd been sexually inappropriate, so I think that you should be asking *who* the money was for."

"Caleb paid the women off?"

"I don't know for sure, but that would be my guess, because the complaints stopped as soon as the money went out."

"OK," Ramouter said. He scratched his head, unsure as to how he was going to phrase his next question. "Right, I'm just going to ask you. What do you know about Caleb performing exorcisms at any of his churches?"

Lincoln stared at Ramouter as though he was speaking a foreign language.

"Exorcisms? Is that what you just said?"

"Yeah, it is."

"Like the film. Spinning heads and priests turning up out the blue? I mean, I won't lie; I've heard of other churches who mess around with things like that, but not us. I mean...no. We didn't do anything like that."

"Are you sure that you didn't ever hear Caleb talking about exorcisms?" asked Ramouter.

"I suppose that he talked about them in his sermons but that was just normal Bible, fighting temptation, not listening to the devil on your shoulder stuff. Not people actually being possessed and healed. He used to say that if you believe in God then you have to believe in the devil, but that's just common sense."

"The man that was found in your church, Brandon Whittaker, he'd been tied to a bed and basically tortured," said Ramouter.

"No. I can't believe that Caleb was involved in anything like that. I just... I can't imagine Caleb being so cruel," said Lincoln. "I can't have people thinking that I was involved in something like that. Is that why you're here? Do you think that I was involved?"

"Well, I'm going to need a sample of your DNA in order to prove that you weren't," Ramouter said.

"I promise you that I had nothing to do with it, but whatever you want me to do, I'll do it."

Even without his DNA sample, Ramouter believed every word that Lincoln had said. "Did you trust Caleb?"

Lincoln looked up at him with crystal clarity in his eyes. "You always look for the best in people, but did I trust him? No. No, I didn't."

50

Henley braced herself against the wind as she watched the cars driving past. It was almost 2:30 p.m. when she'd realized that she'd worked straight through lunch. The delivery driver from the local Indian takeaway had called twice to say that he couldn't find the place.

Henley stopped silently cursing to herself as she caught sight of a figure making its way up the snow-covered ramp toward the boarded up front doors of Greenwich police station. At the same time, the sound of screeching brakes pierced the air and a blue Ford Focus pulled up to the barriers.

"Sorry, sorry," the driver said as he jumped out of the car and ran up to Henley with two red carrier bags in his hands. "I thought that you were closed."

"You've been here before," Henley said. The driver thrust the bags into her hands and ran back to the car. She chuckled to herself as he slipped in the snow and fell onto his arse, but she stopped laughing when she turned around. The person that she'd seen earlier was still standing on the ramp, waiting. The logical part of Henley's brain told her that she was being irrational, that there was nothing to fear, but that didn't stop a small voice in her head, telling her to run.

"Detective Inspector Henley."

The voice was muffled and unrecognizable.

"Yes?" Henley replied as she used her free hand to check her pockets for anything that she could use as weapon. She relaxed as the person pulled the scarf away from their face.

"Dalisay. What are you doing here?" Henley asked.

Dalisay looked nervously around her as she pushed back the hood from her head. She looked up at Henley with fearful eyes.

"I'm sorry. I couldn't call. I didn't know... I shouldn't have come."

"What's happened? Who did that to you?" Henley asked. She took a step forward and saw Dalisay's swollen lip and the small cut on her forehead.

"Oh this...it's nothing. Mrs. Annan," Dalisay said softly, her voice almost carried away by the lunchtime traffic as she quickly pulled up her hood again and lowered her head.

"Did she do this to you?"

"No, no and that's not why I'm here," Dalisay replied as she shivered in the cold. "Mrs. Annan. She lied to you. She wasn't home the night that Mr. Annan was killed. She didn't come home that night."

Henley sat down on the chair and tried to catch her breath after running up four flights of stairs. She had dumped the steaming takeaway bags unceremoniously on Stanford's desk with no explanation, grabbed her notebook and pen and run back downstairs. Dalisay was sitting in the same spot where Amy Whittaker had sat earlier in the week. Dalisay kept her coat on as though it was armor and held her bag in front of her like a protective shield.

"Are you sure that you don't want anything? Tea or coffee?" Henley asked.

"No. No thank you," Dalisay replied, looking anxiously toward the door. "I don't know if I'm doing the right thing."

"The fact that you came here means that you've done the

right thing," said Henley as she bent down and turned on the fan heater under her seat, grateful that it hadn't chosen that moment to sound like a jet engine. Henley made sure that the voice memo app was open on her phone and placed it in the middle of the coffee table.

"How did you know where to find me?" she asked, knowing full well that the location of the SCU wasn't information that would casually be released by whoever picked up the phone in the 101 call-center.

"Mrs. Annan threw your card in the bin after you left last week," Dalisay replied, pulling out a tea-stained and creased business card from her pocket. "I wanted to call but I was scared. Things haven't been the same since Mr. Annan died." Dalisay pulled out her phone from her bag and tapped the screen of her phone. "I haven't got long. Mrs. Annan will be calling the house soon to make sure that I'm home. She doesn't know that I have a mobile phone."

"How long have you been working for the Annans?" Henley asked.

"Two years. I came from the Philippines to work for another family but when I arrived, they told me that they didn't need me anymore. I had nowhere to stay and if the Home Office found out that I didn't have a job they would have taken away my work visa and sent me home, and I couldn't go back home."

"How did you find Mrs. Annan?"

"I was staying in a hostel and one of the women told me about the church that she went to and how they sometimes gave food to the congregation. I went because I was hungry. Then, my friend, she introduced me to Mr. Annan and told him that I didn't have work. He told me to go to Mrs. Annan's agency in Surrey Quays shopping center."

"An agency?" Henley asked, confused.

"Mrs. Annan has a recruitment agency as well as her interior design business," Dalisay explained. "The Annans have many businesses."

"So, you went to her agency, and you ended up working for her?"

"Her last housekeeper walked out. I was desperate and she offered me the job. She said that they would pay for my Tier 2 sponsorship."

Henley knew that a Tier 2 sponsorship was a work visa that would allow Dalisay to work in the UK for up to five years, but it wasn't cheap.

"Do you have your visa?"

"No. I asked for it many times, but Mrs. Annan kept saying it was being processed and then I stopped asking."

"You said outside that Mrs. Annan lied about being home on Sunday night."

"Yes." Dalisay's voice cracked but she stood up a little bit straighter. "Mr. and Mrs. Annan came home from church about three o'clock. I had dinner ready for the family."

"Doesn't Mrs. Annan cook?" Henley didn't consider herself to be winning any *MasterChef* prizes any time soon, but she always cooked Sunday dinner in her skewed way of making up for how much Rob did for the family during the other six days of the week.

"That's my job. Everything is my job."

"So, they came home after dinner."

"Yes, but before they ate, I could hear them arguing in the bedroom. I was helping Zyon, that's their youngest, change out of his church clothes."

"Do you know what they were arguing about?"

"I could only hear pieces. Something about Mr. Annan embarrassing her again and that she wouldn't stand for it. That's all I heard because Zyon was getting upset."

"Mrs. Annan said that Caleb left at 6:30 p.m."

"That's correct. He left at 6:30 p.m. He had another argument with Mrs. Annan when they were in kitchen, and he stormed out."

"What did Mrs. Annan do after Caleb left?"

"She went into the second reception room, and I got the children ready for bed."

"Do you know what she was doing?"

Dalisay looked away.

"It's OK," Henley said gently. "You've already done the hard thing and come here to see me."

Dalisay smiled and her eyes brimmed with tears. "Drinking. She drinks a lot. Every time Mr. Annan doesn't come home. She drinks. It's the only time that she ever takes any rubbish out; so that she can hide the bottles."

"Did Mr. Annan come back home again that evening?"

"No," Dalisay said as she began to cry.

"So, when did Mrs. Annan leave?"

"It must have been just after 9:30 p.m., I was cleaning the dining room when I saw Mrs. Annan in the hallway. I thought that she was going upstairs but then I heard the front door slam shut. I heard the car on the driveway. I opened the front door and Mrs. Annan's car was gone."

"Are you sure that she definitely left?" Henley asked.

"Yes. I went to the window, and I saw her car leaving."

"Dalisay. Are you telling me the truth?"

"What do you mean?"

"Last week you told DC Ramouter that Mrs. Annan never left the house on the night Caleb was killed and now you're telling me that she did?"

"I'm sorry," Dalisay said as the tears fell faster from her eyes. "I shouldn't have lied. I was scared."

"Scared of what?"

"You don't know what it was like. What she is like."

"Mrs. Annan?" Henley asked.

Dalisay nodded slowly as she pulled out a tissue out her bag and wiped her eyes.

"When did you see her again?"

Dalisay took a breath and began to fidget, turning the mobile phone over in hand. "Not until the morning. I was up at six and Mrs. Annan wasn't home, and neither was Mr. Annan."

"When did she come back?"

"I don't know, but she was home when I came back from taking the children to school."

Dalisay jumped as Henley's phone began to ring.

"I'm sorry about that," said Henley. "I should have put it on silent. Hey, what's wrong?" Henley asked as Dalisay, visibly pale, stood up and started to make her way to the door.

"I'm sorry. I should go. Mrs. Annan can't find out that I was out."

"How would she find out?"

"If she knew that I was here. Will you tell her that I was here?"

"Of course not," said Henley. "But I will be talking to her, and I'm going to be putting what you told me in an official statement."

"A statement! No. I don't want to be involved. I can't have my name—"

"Dalisay, it's nothing to panic about. I'm not going to do anything right now. OK?"

"Are you sure?"

"I'm sure. Just go home and act normal. You know where I am if you need me, or if something happens."

Henley knew it would be a waste of time trying to convince Dalisay to stay for a little while longer. It was obvious that she was scared shitless of Serena Annan.

"That cut on your forehead looks painful," Henley said as she opened the interview room door. "You didn't say how you got it. Did someone hurt you? You can talk to me."

Dalisay touched her forehead and winced as though she had forgotten that the bruise was there. "Oh, it was… Zyon. An accident. He's always playing football in the house."

"Kids being kids, right. My little girl treats our house like an adventure playground," said Henley, hoping that her jovial tone covered up the fact that she probably had *you're talking rubbish* written all over her face.

"I have to go," Dalisay said again.

"Is there anything else that you want to tell me before you go? Did Mrs. Annan say anything to you in the morning when she got home?" Henley asked as she led Dalisay down the maze of abandoned corridors and back toward the outside world. "It doesn't matter how small any detail is."

"She didn't speak to me, but that's not unusual. She can go for days without talking to me. She leaves instructions on Post-it notes stuck to the fridge." Dalisay paused as they reached the staircase. "But she wasn't wearing the same clothes when I saw her. She was wearing…she calls it loungewear. It's cashmere. I always have to dry-clean it, but when she came home she was wearing jeans and a jumper, and Mrs. Annan never wears jeans. Never."

"Did you take her loungewear to the dry cleaners?"

"No. I haven't seen it and I wash everyone's clothes."

Henley thought back to the night that she and Ramouter had driven into the driveway of the Annan house. There had been two cars, a Mercedes and an Audi Q5, both displaying personalized number plates. SER 1AN and SER 2AN.

"Which car did Mrs. Annan take?" Henley asked.

"The Mercedes," Dalisay answered as Henley opened the door that led her outside the building. Snow had started to fall heavily in the thirty minutes that she and Dalisay had been sitting in the interview room. The wind blew a flurry of snowflakes into Henley's face.

"Be careful out there," she said as her stomach rumbled again. "And you know that there are people who can help you if you need it. I can help you."

Dalisay turned her back. "I know where you are," she said. She stepped out gingerly onto the snowy pavement. Henley watched as Dalisay held onto the white guardrail and began to walk down the path.

51

Henley was multitasking while on hold, waiting for DI Clarke to come to the phone. She had it on speaker while she ate her reheated lamb biryani and sent another email to Lewisham Council urgently requesting their CCTV footage of Deptford Broadway from the night Caleb Annan was killed.

"DI Clarke speaking."

Henley dropped her fork and smiled for the first time that day. She recognized the deep voice of the man who always sounded as though he had just woken up.

"Bloody hell, it is you. Hello, stranger. It's Henley."

"Henley," said Clarke. "Hello, stranger, yourself. The idiot who picked up my phone never said who it was, just that it was another DI."

"What are you even doing at Forest Gate CID? Stanford and I came to your retirement party."

Henley could imagine Clarke sitting at his desk, rubbing a hand over his bald head searching for his long-gone hair and wearing a shirt that hadn't been ironed properly.

"I got bored," Clarke said. "And I was getting on my missus's nerves. It was either come back part-time or get a divorce. So, what can I do for you and the Serial Crime Unit?"

"The Jensen murder investigation. HOLMES has you down as the SIO."

Clarke let out a very loud groan of despair. "Yeah, I am. Which is a bit ridiculous considering that I'm in only three days a week. Why are you interested in it?"

"We think that it may be linked to a murder investigation that we're working. We've got two victims, one alive, one dead. Their injuries are almost identical to Jensen. Both victims had mental health issues and have been linked to the Church of Annan the Prophet in Deptford. The church also has a branch in Plaistow. Not too far from where your victim was found."

"I see," said Clarke thoughtfully. "I don't recall his family saying that Jensen was particularly religious."

"But they didn't report him missing?"

"No, his supported-living manager did. But that's not where he disappeared from."

"So where did he disappear from?"

"Jensen was last seen on Kingsland High Street in Dalston two hours after he'd left the Cooper Group Therapy Clinic in Forest Hill. We got a statement from…oh bollocks, give me a sec. Ah, found it. Dr. Gregory Jones."

"What was Jensen doing at this clinic?" said Henley as she tried to speed Clarke along.

"It's a private mental health clinic, a bit like that posh one that all the celebs go to," said Clarke. "Every couple of months they take on some charity cases as outpatients, I think that it's a tax write-off thing, and Jensen was one of those cases. Anyway, the day that Jensen disappeared, he'd had an appointment at the clinic, but he got into a fight with one of the resident patients. Jensen storms off and that's the last that anyone sees of him."

"Did you speak to this patient?"

"Yep, but he didn't leave the clinic that day or any other day until Christmas. He suffers from agoraphobia. We also interviewed a geezer called Samuel Barnes. He was seen fighting with Jensen outside a pub about three days before Jensen went missing, and police were called to Jensen's flat about a week before that."

"Why were they called?"

"Jensen apparently kicked off. Samuel turned up at his flat, Jensen accused him of stealing from him and then smashed Samuel on the head with a toaster. Jensen, he locked himself in the bathroom, said that the PCs were secret agents and that he was on a mission for the president and that everyone was mad."

"So, he was off his meds?"

"Definitely. The post-mortem showed that there were no drugs, illegal or prescription, in his body."

"The same PM report that's not on the system?"

"Don't start. Three days a week, remember. They're lucky that I even log on."

"So, what about forensics?"

"We've actually got good forensics. We just can't match it to anyone. DNA from two individuals, and fingerprints. A thumbprint was on his forehead, left behind from some kind of carbon substance."

"But no matches?" Henley said as she pushed her plate away.

"Not when they were retrieved and checked against the samples on the database three weeks ago," said Clarke. "The pathologist said that it looks like Jensen was tortured. Someone had literally put his feet to the flames, and you won't be able to tell from the in-situ photos, but when we took Jensen's body out of the sleeping bag, his hands had been tied together with red rope and there were fragments of the same rope around his ankles."

"And you've got no leads on where Jensen had been in the six weeks before his body turned up?" Henley asked. She opened a file and pulled out the photographs that had been taken of both Whittaker's and Hadlow's bodies. The red rope was visible on both of their wrists. Henley didn't believe that the rope had been used just because it was available or the nearest thing to hand.

She was convinced that there was a deeper meaning behind that specific rope being used to restrain the victims.

"None, and to be honest, with the amount of murder investigations that we've got going on, this case isn't exactly being treated as a priority."

"So, you won't say no to me taking the Jensen case off your hands?"

"Be my guest," said Clarke, clearing his throat. "I'll clear it with the guvnor, not that he knows his arse from his elbow, but as far as I'm concerned you can have it."

52

Ramouter was convinced that he hadn't seen daylight. He had gone to work when the sun was struggling to peek through the winter clouds, and the sky had already darkened again. The snow was falling heavier as he drove slowly along Crystal Palace Parade, the red light from the transmitter in the park hazy in the distance. There was one person left on his list of people to visit. He double-checked that he had entered the correct address in Beckenham.

"This can't be right," Ramouter said as he turned off the car engine. In comparison to the homes of Annan and Okafor, the house that belonged to Derrick Sullivan was modest. A Georgian terraced house with a concreted-over front garden. Damp cardboard boxes and the collapsed base of a king-size divan had been propped up against a small wall. Ramouter could see the flashing glow of a television against the curtains as he pressed the doorbell and waited.

"Oh hello," he said as the door opened and he found himself looking down at a young girl, dressed in her school uniform and holding on to a chocolate brown cockapoo puppy. "Is your dad home? My name is Detec—"

"DAD! There's someone at the door for you," the girl screamed out before running up the stairs.

"Sara, what have I said about just running up and opening the front door? I'm fed up of telling you."

There was a tea towel over Derrick Sullivan's shoulder and a spoon in his hand. Ramouter stayed on the doorstep, holding out his warrant card.

"I'm DC Salim Ramouter from the Serial Crime Unit. You're Mr. Derrick Sullivan and you haven't returned any of my calls."

"This isn't really a good time. I'm just getting the kids' dinner ready."

"I would have come at a time that was convenient for you but as I said, you didn't return any of my messages."

Derrick had the good grace to look embarrassed. "Can we really not do this another time?"

"We're in the middle of a murder investigation so I'm sorry, but no," Ramouter said firmly.

"Fine. Do you mind taking off your shoes when you come in?"

"Of course," Ramouter replied as he stepped inside the house. He took in the surroundings as he sat on the bottom step and untied his boots. There was an array of unopened parcels behind Ramouter and a pile of neatly folded clothes on the stairs, and a cascade of family photographs on the wall in front of him.

"Would you like a cup of tea or coffee? You look frozen," said Derrick.

"Coffee would be great," said Ramouter, following Derrick into the kitchen. He could feel the heat from the underfloor heating through his socks.

"It costs a fortune to run," Derrick said as he watched Ramouter wriggling his toes. "My missus, Tameka, went to our neighbor's house for drinks and turns out that she had underfloor heating and the next thing I know, Tameka is getting the quotes in."

"It feels nice though," said Ramouter as he took a seat at the table.

"Are you fussy about the coffee? We've got a selection to rival Starbucks."

"Not fussed. I'll just have it black with sugar."

"Americano it is then," said Derrick. "I still can't believe that Caleb is dead."

"It must have been a shock for you," said Ramouter as Derrick handed him his coffee.

"A big shock. He was such a big part of the church; actually, you could say that he *was* the church."

"But you left the church. You and your wife."

Derrick didn't reply; instead he turned around and busied himself with taking some bowls out of the cupboard.

"I left the church four months ago," he finally said as he spooned spaghetti Bolognese into two bowls and then placed slices of garlic bread onto a plate. "Sorry, let me just give these to the kids. We don't usually let them eat their dinner in front of the telly. They're going to think that they've won the lottery. I'll be back in a sec."

Ramouter pushed aside a football magazine and a stack of Match Attax playing cards and settled himself at the kitchen table. He took some comfort in Derrick Sullivan's seemingly normal family life. The washing machine whirled in the corner as it completed its cycle, and the fridge was covered with children's drawings.

"How old are your kids?" Ramouter asked, when Derrick returned.

"Sara's ten going on thirty," said Derrick as he lifted up a basket of clothes from the chair and moved it onto the floor, "and Haylie is eight and forgets that she's the younger sister."

"Two girls," Ramouter remarked.

"And another baby on the way in four months."

"Another girl?"

"No idea," Derrick said with a smile. "My wife wants to be surprised."

"Where is your wife?"

"Work. She's a dentist. Have you got any kids?"

"One. A boy," Ramouter replied. He swallowed down the feeling of sadness as Ethan flashed in his mind. "You said that you left the church four months ago, but you and your wife are still listed as being trustees on the Charity Commission directory page."

Derrick sank back in the chair with slight irritation. "We asked Caleb and the rest of the board to remove us ages ago and they still haven't done it," he said.

"Why did you want to leave?" Ramouter asked as he opened up his notebook and took out a pen.

"We should have left a long time ago. Tameka, that's my wife, hadn't been happy with certain things that were happening and the direction of the church."

"What things were they?"

Derrick looked down at the table. "You have to understand that even though I was on the board, I didn't actually have control of anything; well, not the things that mattered."

"So, what was your role?"

"Glorified admin, really. I would produce the service programs, maintain the website, complete the applications for government grants, that sort of thing. It took up a lot of time and to be honest it was getting to be too much with my day job."

"What do you do?"

"I'm a graphic designer. I'm one of the partners in a design agency in Old Street."

"That would keep you busy. How did you manage that with being on the church board of trustees?"

Derrick shook his head. "Name only. It made the church look good and proper. I mean, I know how to run a business but there were really only two people in charge, and that was Caleb and Serena."

Ramouter leaned back and folded his arms. "That still doesn't explain why you and your wife left."

Derrick took a deep breath. "There had been problems with his behavior toward women in the congregation."

"I don't want to put words in your mouth, but I need you to clarify what you mean by problems with his behavior."

"He forgot about the bit in the Bible that said 'a man shall cleave unto his wife: and they shall be one flesh.'"

"You're saying that Caleb was unfaithful?"

"I didn't see him with anybody, but there was talk. Rumors. I didn't believe it at first until he tried it on with Tameka."

"Tameka? Your wife."

Derrick grimaced as though he was reliving the moment. "She didn't tell me at first. She said she thought that she could handle it."

"What did he do?" Ramouter had to wait for the answer as Derrick's daughters burst into the room with their empty bowls, talking loudly.

"Sorry," Derrick said. "Look, can you two go back in the living room and watch TV quietly?"

"But I need a drink and ice cream and my cards," said Haylie as she made her way to the freezer.

"Fine. Here, take these," Derrick said. He picked the football cards up from the table and went to the freezer, took out two mini tubs of ice cream and handed them to the girls. "Do not tell your mum. Just eat your ice cream. I won't be much longer." Derrick waited for the girls to leave before he returned to the table. "Just stick with the one kid," he said to Ramouter.

"So, your wife?" Ramouter continued. "I'm sorry if it makes you uncomfortable."

"I know that it sounds a bit nineteen fiftyish, traditional roles and all that, but I'm supposed to be her protector. I'm her husband but Caleb..." Derrick's voice became icy. "He liked the power, and people, well, they listen to him. I mean, I listened to him. You're not supposed to be mistrustful of the man who stands up every Sunday and speaks the word of God, but when your wife tells you that the pastor has been making lewd comments to her and then she tells you that he locked her in his office and...and..."

Derrick took a couple of breaths and looked up at the ceiling.

Ramouter tried to imagine how he would have reacted if someone he'd trusted and looked up to to be leader and the symbolism of virtue had taken advantage of his wife. He would want to kill him.

"I'm sorry," Derrick said as he took another breath. "Caleb pushed her against the wall and tried to kiss her and put his hand up her skirt."

"When did this happen?"

"Sometime in November. Around Guy Fawkes Night. She was only about two months gone at the time. He didn't know that Tameka was pregnant. We hadn't told anyone yet. Anyway, that happened and the next thing I knew Serena was accusing Tameka of coming on to her husband, she did a great big sermon about 'Faithfulness and Commitment' on the Sunday. Tameka said that Serena sounded like she was giving a warning to every woman in the church. Hands off my man, that sort of thing."

"Did you confront Caleb?"

"No," Derrick said quietly. "There wasn't any point. Serena caught them and blamed it all on Tameka. They would have damaged us if we'd made a lot of noise. We've got our kids and our business. It was better just to walk away."

"Did they threaten you?"

"Not directly, but it wasn't worth the risk."

"You know that I'm going to ask you where you were the night that Caleb Annan was killed? From 9:30 p.m.?" Ramouter asked.

"The Sunday night? Airport run to Heathrow. My brother

flew out to Dubai that night. I should have his flight details on my phone, but I picked him up from his house in Wanstead at about six o'clock. I can't remember exactly what time I got home. Maybe about quarter to ten, something like that."

"Your wife can probably confirm when you got back?"

Derrick started fiddling with an abandoned sachet of salt on the table. "She wasn't home. She and the girls spent the weekend with her parents in Southampton. It was an inset day, so they didn't come back until Monday lunchtime."

Ramouter scribbled down the information in his notebook. "I'll need to double-check with your brother. Is he back from Dubai?"

"No, he's still out there for another month but it's hard to get hold of him. He's really busy with work. You don't really need to talk to him do you?"

Ramouter caught the nervous twitch in Derrick's voice. "Do you have a problem with me talking to your brother?" he asked.

"No, no. Its just...maybe I could talk to him first."

"There's no need for that. The last thing you want is to be arrested for perverting the course of justice," Ramouter warned.

"No of course not. I just thought," Derrick lowered his head slightly in dejection. "I'll give you his number and email," he conceded.

"That's great. How many other people knew about Caleb's behavior?"

"I wouldn't be surprised if everyone on that board knew what Caleb was up to."

"What about the exorcisms?"

"Exorcisms? What are you talking about?" Derrick replied quickly, his tone slightly high pitched.

"We understand that Pastor Caleb and other members of the church were performing exorcisms," said Ramouter. He placed the photograph of a once-alive Alyssa Hadlow and a half-dead Brandon Whittaker on the kitchen table. "This is Brandon

Whittaker; the man that was found in a concealed room upstairs in the church."

"I honestly don't know anything about a concealed room, and I definitely don't know anyone called Brandon Whittaker. I maintained the member list and I never saw his name on it, unless he joined after I left. I was shocked when I found out about that poor man. Tameka and I would have left a long time ago if we'd known that sort of thing was going on."

"So, you'd never heard Caleb discussing exorcisms with anyone in the church?"

"Never."

"What about anyone coming to the church for help because they were told that they were possessed when in fact they were mentally ill?"

"Look, people seek help for all sorts of reasons and it's our job as spiritual leaders to help them, but there are limits. You don't mess about with people's mental health."

"What about Alyssa Hadlow?" Ramouter asked as he pushed the photograph toward Derrick.

"I don't know. She looks familiar but I can't be a hundred percent sure if I ever saw her. Caleb has…sorry had, three branches of the church, but I do remember seeing her name on the members' list."

"About the membership. As I understand it, the fees are nearly six hundred pounds."

"Yeah," Derrick replied as he looked away with embarrassment. "I thought that it was too expensive, but people paid."

"What about people who were on benefits, like Alyssa?"

"The church had a charity we asked members to contribute to to cover fees for those who couldn't afford it. That's how Alyssa's fees would have been covered, and it also covered the church when we had to account for charitable expenditure."

"How usual is it for church members to make home visits?" Ramouter asked as he took the photographs back.

"Not unusual," Derrick said with a shrug. Ramouter could see the tension leave his body as the subject changed. "It would be no different to calling out a doctor. Spiritual healing is no different to physical healing."

"So, you wouldn't have been surprised if Caleb had visited the home of Alyssa Hadlow?"

"No, I wouldn't... Hold on," Derrick said as the penny obviously dropped. "Did something happen between Caleb and this woman, Alyssa Hadlow?"

"We had evidence that Caleb was in her flat. That's all I can say for now."

"Shit, that man. I shouldn't speak ill of the dead but what the hell was wrong with him?"

"Do you have any idea of who would want to hurt Caleb?"

"Take your pick," Derrick said angrily. "From what you're telling me, it could be anyone. I'm glad we left. I couldn't have my daughters growing up around that."

"No, you couldn't," Ramouter agreed. He pushed back his chair and stood up. "Well, I'm going to leave you to get on with the rest of your evening with your girls."

"Thank you. Is it hard?" Derrick asked as he walked Ramouter back to the front door. "Investigating the murder of a man who wasn't...well, not very nice?"

"It doesn't matter whether he was nice or not," said Ramouter. "At the end of the day, someone took his life, and that can never be justified."

The door slammed behind Ramouter as he walked toward his snow-covered car. He took out his phone.

"Shit," he said. Six missed calls from his sister-in-law Pamela. The panic rose in his chest as he called her back.

"Where the hell have you been? I've been calling and calling," screamed Pamela.

"I'm sorry, my phone was—"

"I don't really give a shit. It's obvious that your work is more important to you than your own wife."

Ramouter stopped in his tracks. "What's happened?"

"Michelle is gone."

53

"We need money," said Henley as she planted herself on the spare chair in Pellacia's office.

"What for?"

"To pay Mark." Henley checked her watch. It was 5:40 p.m. and she still hadn't heard from Ramouter since he'd left to interview Lincoln Okafor and Derrick Sullivan. "I need him to run a profile on the sort of person who would, well, believe in exorcism and kill two people. I've got forensics that are leading to dead ends and my only witness is in a coma."

"Hold on, you said two murder victims," said Pellacia.

Henley ran through the Charlie Jensen investigation while Pellacia buried his head in his hands and let out a low groan.

"I know that it's the last thing that you want to hear but if Jensen is victim number three, then that means that there is a strong possibility that someone else may be at risk. For all we know someone could be falsely imprisoned right now while some nutjobs try to exorcise their demons. I can only prove one thing, and that is that Caleb Annan was involved."

"But the fact that Caleb Annan is involved in these murders

doesn't mean that you can neglect his own murder investigation," Pellacia said.

"I would never do that," Henley said firmly. "And you know that. My personal feelings have got nothing to do with this case."

"Good, because I'm meeting Laura Halifax in an hour."

Henley pulled herself up in the chair and took a closer look at Pellacia who was looking surprisingly fresh faced at quarter to six on a Wednesday afternoon.

"And what exactly are you meeting her for?"

"Damage control," Pellacia said. He started to straighten the papers on his desk.

"And does damage control include having a shave in the men's toilet and drowning yourself in aftershave?"

"No, it means doing what I can to stop the complaints that Laura has received about how we're conducting this investigation and letting the press persecute Annan."

"It's a murder investigation. What do they want me to do? Send them an online survey and a fifty pound Amazon voucher?"

"Don't be snarky, just do your job. Speaking of which, did Eastwood track down the kid who broke into Hadlow's flat?"

"Yes, she did," Henley confirmed. "He actually admitted that he broke in, but that he never went in because of the smell. He said he threw up on the stairs because the smell was that bad."

"What about the Annan investigation? We need a viable suspect, and you and I both know that Uliana Piontek doesn't belong on that list."

"I know that she doesn't, but tactically it may be better to keep her on bail."

"Why would it be better?"

"Because it will give the real killer a false sense of security, which means that they might slip up."

"So, enlighten me. Who is the real killer?"

"All roads seem to be pointing to Serena. Her housekeeper

Dalisay has changed her story and is now saying Serena wasn't home on the night Caleb was murdered."

"Is she telling the truth?"

"Well, I didn't wire her up to a lie detector," Henley said sarcastically.

"It's a simple question."

"You should have seen the state of her. She's having to put up with a lot in that house and it took a lot for her to come and see me."

"But is she telling the truth?" Pellacia asked again.

"I can't see any reason for Dalisay to lie," said Henley. "Serena's alibi is shit and Uliana has placed her at the crime scene."

Pellacia let out a wry laugh. "I'm sure that you're enjoying this."

"Enjoying what? I'm doing what you told me to do," said Henley as she stood up. "I'm doing my job. So, tell your 'friend' Lorraine—"

"Her name is Laura Halifax."

"Whatever," Henley replied, fully aware of how petulant she sounded. "Tell your friend the MP that it might be in her best interest to distance herself from Serena, as I will be doing my job and arresting Serena for murder, and I'll probably do it in front of her church mates."

She stood up, grateful that Pellacia's phone had chosen that opportunity to ring. "I'm going to call Mark. Tell him to get started on the profiles."

"It's Ezra," Pellacia said as he picked up the phone.

Henley listened as Pellacia mouthed *don't move.*

"Yeah, she's here," Pellacia said. "What's wrong?"

"What is it?" Henley asked as she felt a familiar sense of anxiety prickling her skin.

"Are you sure?" asked Pellacia. "No, we're not coming to you. You can come to us." He put the phone down.

"What is it?" Henley asked. She wasn't sure if it was relief or distress that was causing Pellacia to loosen his tie and throw it onto his desk.

"I don't know if it's a good thing or a bad thing," said Pellacia.

"All I know is that from the look on your face, my job is about to get a bit more difficult."

A photograph of a newborn baby filled the SmartScreen on the wall. The baby's eyes were barely open and the gray and white striped hat, which barely fitted the baby's head, had pushed the flurry of black curls against the baby's forehead.

"Where did you find these?" Henley asked Ezra, who was sitting on the spare desk next to the SmartScreen.

"Annan," Ezra answered. "I had to access his cloud drive. He'd deleted it but..."

"We know," said Eastwood. "Nothing is ever deleted."

"Exactly. There's two more baby photos, which he received and deleted on the same day."

Henley felt as though a stone had been dropped in her stomach as Ezra clicked on the second image of a baby asleep in a Moses basket and the third image of Alyssa Hadlow holding onto her child.

"Ezra, can you put all three photos up on the board?" Henley asked as she walked up to the SmartScreen.

"Not a problem."

"Is it a boy or a girl?" Eastwood asked.

"I'm not too sure," Henley replied. "The first photo is definitely a newborn. Ezra, are you able to determine when these photos were taken?"

"That's what I was about to tell you," said Ezra. "The first photo and the one with Hadlow was taken five weeks ago, but the photo of the baby in the basket was taken two weeks ago."

"Two weeks? Are you sure?" Henley asked, her voice rising.

"A hundred percent. I just haven't worked out who sent them though," Ezra said with a trace of disappointment.

"Are you sure that you can't pin down a location or a sender?" Pellacia said from his favored position by the window.

"Boss, I just found the pics when you ordered me to come

down here, but I will let you know as soon as I find something," said Ezra.

"Thanks, Ez," Henley said as Ezra picked up his laptop and left the room.

"I wasn't having a go at Ezra," Pellacia said with genuine concern. "He's done really good work."

"Well, make sure that you tell him that before you go off and meet Laura," Henley said and turned her back on Pellacia. "And tell him to go home."

"Fucking hell. I was really hoping that there wasn't a baby," said Pellacia.

"We need to put those baby photos out there and organize a press conference. I'll do it outside the SCU in the bloody snow if I have to," said Henley.

"Do what you need to do. And I'll sort the money for Mark," said Pellacia as he went back to his office.

"Whoever sent that photo to Caleb has the Hadlow baby," said Eastwood. "It has to be one of the two unidentified people who were with Caleb and in the room with Brandon."

"And who also killed Charlie Jensen and Hadlow," said Henley.

"That baby was taken, what, three or four weeks ago. That puts us at a significant disadvantage for a missing baby case. Anything could have happened; they could have left the country or done something to that child."

"No," said Henley, looking back through the images on the SmartScreen. "Look at the most recent photos. That baby is being cared for."

"Do you think that whoever has the baby, knew that Caleb could be the father?" asked Eastwood.

"No idea. They could have just sent him the photo because they were all involved, but you're right, Eastie. Time isn't on our side, and who knows how Caleb's murder may have affected their decision making."

"I'll go and tell him now. I'm also going to call the press

people. We need to put out an urgent appeal, now that we've got the photos."

"Well, look on the bright side," Eastwood said. "At least we know that there is a baby, and someone is looking after him or her, even if that person is probably responsible for killing their mother."

"I've sent the updated information to the press office, and I've confirmed the press conference arrangements. You two might as well call it a day," Pellacia said as he left his office. "It's been a long enough one."

Henley checked the clock. It was nearly six thirty, and she would have been well within her rights to pack her things and go home, but the image of Brandon Whittaker in his hospital bed played in her mind.

"I'm going to go and see Brandon's parents," she said as she picked up her coat. "I can't just go home and do nothing. Brandon Whittaker is the key to all of this. He didn't get to that church on his own. His parents know a lot more. Ramouter's not back, but there's no reason why I can't see them on my own."

"You could arrest them for obstructing the course of justice," said Pellacia. "You've given them enough time."

"I can come with you," Eastwood said. "The only thing I had planned was a takeaway."

"Are you sure?"

"Of course. I doubt that I would be able to eat anyway, thinking about that poor baby. Also, I want to see what these Whittakers are all about."

54

Henley checked her phone. Ramouter's last message to her had been sent at 3:46 p.m. to tell her that he was on his way to see Derrick Sullivan. Her WhatsApp messages had been left on two gray ticks and he hadn't responded to her voice mail messages.

"So how are we handling this?" Eastwood asked as Henley knocked on the door. "Good cops, or drag them out by their heels kicking and screaming? I've already decided that I don't like them so I'm happy to drag them out."

"How about we just play by ear and see what they have to say for themselves, and if they start talking shit, then we'll drag them out." Henley watched a distorted figure appear in the yellow light of the frosted glass. Eastwood busied herself with adjusting the lanyard around her neck and wiping crisp crumbs off her face as the front door opened.

A middle-aged man appeared on the doorstep, so tall that Henley had to look up to meet his eyes. He had the appearance of someone who had lost a lot of weight in a short space of time. The collar of his jumper gaped at the neck, exposing puckered and loose skin.

"Are you Patrick Whittaker?" Henley asked as she held out

her warrant card. She didn't have the patience to engage in pleasantries.

"I am. What do you want?"

"Detective Inspector Henley from the Serial Crime Unit. We need to talk to you about your son, Brandon."

"Inspector Henley," he said. "I thought that you would have called first."

Henley bit her tongue, for a brief moment slightly thrown off by the abruptness of Patrick Whittaker's tone.

"Did your wife tell you that we came to see her?"

"Yes, she did, with a DC Ramouter, but you are?" Patrick looked down on Eastwood as though she was something that he'd cleared from his throat.

"I'm DC Eastwood. Perhaps you would like to let us in. It's cold."

Patrick wordlessly stepped aside. A small suitcase rested in the hallway and the harsh smell of burnt vegetables lingered in the air. Marcia Whittaker stood nervously on the bottom of the stairs; her hands clinging to the banister. Her eyes were red and swollen and her face was makeup free; a complete contrast to how she looked when Henley first met her.

"Please, this way," Patrick said, showing Henley and Eastwood into the living room. They took a seat on a leather sofa that had long ago lost its buoyancy. There were no signs that this was the home of religious zealots. The bookcase was overflowing with books and DVDs, and Henley could pick up the scent of stagnant water from the vase of a decaying mixed bouquet on the side table. Patrick took a seat in an armchair as Marcia stood hesitantly in the doorway. Eastwood elbowed Henley as Patrick raised his hand, clicked his fingers and Marcia entered the room and sat down next to him. Henley forced herself not to say anything about what she'd just seen.

"Your daughter Amy and your wife said that you were away last week," said Henley. "Where were you?"

"Sweden."

"And when did you get back?"

"On Friday, but I really don't see what me being away on business has to do with my son."

"Would either of you like a cup of tea or coffee?" Marcia spoke so quietly that Henley could barely hear her.

"No thank you," Henley said with a smile. "But thanks for the offer."

"So, you're here about Brandon," said Patrick, directing Henley's attention back to himself.

"Brandon is your youngest, isn't he?" asked Henley.

"Yes, he is."

"Parents are usually more overprotective with the youngest. It must have been a shock to you when you found out about your son?"

"Of course it was," said Patrick.

There was no sense of warmth, appreciation or anything that resembled love on Marcia's face as Patrick went through the motions of taking hold of her hand.

"When was the last time that you saw your son?" asked Henley.

"It was the day before he went on his cycling holiday."

"Can you remember the exact day that he left?"

"No, I can't," Patrick said firmly.

"Well, was it in the morning or the evening that you last saw Brandon?"

Henley caught the look that Patrick gave Marcia, who quickly looked down at the ground. It was a look that said, *What the hell did you tell them? This wasn't the plan.*

"It must have been the evening," said Patrick. "I can't remember."

"Did Brandon call you when he was away? Just to let you know that he was safe," asked Henley.

"There were a few calls to his mother. Isn't that right, Marcia?"

"Yes, yes, that's right," said Marcia with a sense of urgency.

"So, you never spoke to him, Mr. Whittaker?" Henley asked pointedly.

"What can I say? Mothers and their sons," Patrick said with a smile that was more like a grimace.

"I can't imagine the shock when you found out about Brandon's condition and that he was in hospital?"

"Of course I was shocked. I thought that my son was away doing what he loved."

"But you didn't cut your own trip short once you found out that Brandon had nearly died and was in Lewisham Hospital?"

"Look, Inspector," Patrick said as he leaned forward, put his hands in a steeple and propped up his chin. "My son is twenty-three years old. A grown man. Our relationship was strained. We didn't keep a tight rein on him, and his mother..." Patrick looked across at Marcia with a look that could only be described as disgust. "His mother was a bit blinkered to Brandon's issues."

"Issues?" Henley replied. "You mean your son's mental health issues."

"He didn't have mental issues. He had confidence issues, bouts of anxiety, he was spoiled and he lacked discipline, but he wasn't mentally unwell."

"Marcia, have you seen your son yet?" asked Eastwood.

"No, we haven't," said Patrick. "We're going to see him tomorrow. He's all the way in south London and, with restrictive visiting hours, well, there's not much point in us racing down there now. But I understand that he's being well cared for by the hospital staff."

"Amy has been to the hospital every day since she saw her brother's face in the newspaper," said Eastwood. "She's very committed."

"Every day," said Marcia, tears running down her face.

"Marcia," Patrick said sharply.

Patrick was still holding onto Marcia's hand and Henley could have sworn that she saw her wince.

"Have either of you spoken to your daughter?" asked Henley.

"No, we haven't spoken to her," said Patrick. "Amy's lifestyle is in direct conflict with our beliefs. She has a complete lack of respect for us."

"Marcia, Amy said that she left you some messages," said Henley. "Did you read them?"

Marcia shook her head, but Henley knew she was lying. There was no way that a mother would ignore her hurting child.

"Your son was found locked in a room in the Church of Annan the Prophet in Deptford, and you and your wife are both paying members of that church," Henley said harshly.

"Yes, we are," said Patrick. "But our church is in East Acton. We weren't even aware that there was a branch in...where did you say it was?"

"Deptford," Henley said, growing more agitated.

"I don't know what Brandon would be doing down there, but as I said, our relationship was strained, and he didn't always tell us the truth. It's not the first time that he disappeared on us."

Henley tried not to retaliate. At least Marcia had shown some emotion, but Patrick was treating his son's situation like an inconvenience. Rob would have been raising hell if anyone had harmed their daughter, and Henley would have been right there beside him. She hated moments like these that made her question if, by staying in her job, she was harming Emma.

"You and your wife believed that Brandon had gone off on a cycling trip around Italy."

"That's correct," said Patrick. "He's gone off without telling us many times."

"But he did tell you," said Henley. "You told me that you said goodbye to him."

"I meant change his plans without telling us," Patrick said confidently. "I can show you his room and you can see his obsession."

"Let's do that," Henley said as she stood up. "It would be good to get a sense of who your son is."

"Don't worry, Mrs. Whittaker," Eastwood said as Henley caught the wary look on Marcia's face. "You're in safe hands with me."

★ ★ ★

"Are you OK?" Eastwood asked Marcia, who was rooted to her seat as if she was afraid to move.

"I do love my son," Marcia whispered.

"No one has said that you don't."

"All you want to do is protect your children. You want them to flourish. Not suffer."

"Did you know that Brandon was suffering?" Eastwood asked.

"No, no. If I knew then I—" Marcia stopped talking as though she'd just realized that Eastwood was in the room. "Have you seen him? My son?"

"Not in the hospital, but Inspector Henley has. You do know that she's the one who found him? He would have died if she hadn't."

Marcia pulled out a makeup-stained tissue from her pocket and blew her nose.

"Will you thank her for me?"

"Of course."

Eastwood let Marcia cry as she looked around the room. She didn't see a single photograph of Amy or Brandon.

Henley stepped into a large bedroom. The bed had been stripped bare and the curtains were closed. A bike missing its wheels sat in the corner next to a cabinet filled with cycling equipment.

"What did Brandon study at university?" Henley asked as she scanned the titles of the books on the desk.

"Digital media design and development," Patrick answered. "He got a first and he'd just started a master's degree."

Henley picked up the pride in Patrick's voice as she walked around the room. "So why did Brandon decide to go off cycling if he'd just started his master's?"

"I think that you've seen enough. There are more of his bikes and other stuff in the shed," said Patrick. He moved out into the hallway and turned off the bedroom light.

"Someone hurt your child," said Henley as she joined Patrick in the hallway. "Someone brought him to that church, tied him to a bed, beat him, poured so much water down his throat that he nearly drowned and burnt his feet."

"I didn't… I didn't know that," said Patrick. He backed away from Henley. "And I don't know why anyone would do it."

"What didn't you know? That someone beat Brandon, tried to drown him or burn him? Which is it?"

Henley could clearly see the distress flash on Patrick's face. It was the distress of a father who has only just realized the harm his child had been subjected to. Patrick took off his glasses and rubbed away at his eyes.

"Didn't Marcia tell you how badly hurt Brandon was? Didn't your wife tell you that you son was in a coma, fighting for his life?"

"Stop," Patrick said softly but with a clear tone of warning.

"I will not stop. Brandon nearly died. He could still die," Henley said without bothering to hide her anger. "Your son was mentally unwell, and he needed help."

"Stop," Patrick said, holding up his hand. Henley stepped back; her fists balled at her sides. "Amy probably told you that we believed that Brandon was possessed by demons," Patrick added, drily.

"She did, actually."

"I'm not surprised. Did she tell you that we were estranged and that she stole from us? I thought not." Patrick walked down the stairs, leaving Henley with no choice but to follow him. "Is there anything else?"

"When will you be going to see your son? We might meet you there." Eastwood rolled her eyes at her as she followed Marcia into the hallway.

"We'll see our son tomorrow," Patrick said as he indicated for Marcia to open the front door.

"Good, I'll have a forensic examiner waiting for you. We're going to need your DNA and fingerprints."

"What on earth for?"

Henley didn't bother to reply as she followed Eastwood outside and Marcia closed the door behind her.

"What an absolute twat," Eastwood said as she stormed onto the driveway. "Did you see that shit that—"

"Shh," Henley whispered. She put her fingers to her lips and stepped to the side of the front door.

"What is it?" Eastwood mouthed. She joined Henley's side and listened. Henley didn't say a word as they listened to Marcia's hysterical voice.

"She knows, Patrick," Marcia said. "That inspector knows."

As they walked away from the door and through the snow back toward the car, Eastwood asked Henley, "What do you think that she meant when she said 'She knows'?"

"That I know that they're lying about everything," said Henley. "That I know that Patrick and Marcia knew exactly where their son was being held. Caleb and whoever he was working with had the Whittakers' consent."

"Well, we already know that Caleb was involved. Do you think that Marcia and Patrick know who the other two are?"

Henley remembered the look on Patrick's face when she'd asked him about the burns on his son's feet: hurt, surprise and a look of failure.

"If they knew… Actually, scratch that, Marcia is just following her husband's lead," said Henley. "I think that Patrick Whittaker would have said so, if he'd known."

"You really believe that?" Eastwood asked.

"Yes, I do," Henley replied as she brushed the falling snow out of her eyes. "Patrick Whittaker doesn't strike me as the sort of man who'd take responsibility for anything. If he can find someone to blame, then he will. He sat in front of us and tried to blame his son for his own disappearance."

"You've got a point. He's more interested in covering his own back."

"Yes, he is. We need Brandon to wake up. He's the only one who can tell us about the man and woman who were with Caleb."

55

Ramouter rested his head against the steering wheel as the car engine died down. His heart was beating fast, and he could feel the lactic acid building up in his legs. He'd thought through every possible scenario on the four-hour journey. Maybe Michelle had lost her phone or perhaps she'd got on the wrong bus. Every time his phone had rung, he'd prayed that it was her. He'd almost crashed into another car twice when images of Michelle's dead body floating in the icy waters of Bradford Beck had flashed in his mind.

"Come on. Pull it together." He opened a bottle of water and splashed his face. He fought back the tears as he recalled how loud Ethan's crying had been when he'd called to check in. They hadn't told Ethan that his mum was slowly forgetting things and that there may be a time when she wouldn't remember him. All Ethan knew was that his mum hadn't picked him up from school and that she hadn't come home.

"She gave us her maiden name," said Sergeant Boulton as he led Ramouter through the familiar corridors of Manningham police station.

"Didn't she have any identification on her?" Ramouter asked

as they stopped at the custody suite door. He automatically pressed his warrant card against the security pad and the light flashed red. "I wasn't thinking," he said as Boulton pressed his own card against the security pad and opened the door.

"Old habits die hard. Don't worry about it. But in answer to your question, no. She had no ID, no bag, no phone. Nothing on her, except the clothes on her back."

"The PC I spoke to said that she broke into the house."

"Slight exaggeration. She used a key, apparently she had a spare," said Boulton as they entered the custody suite, which was unusually quiet at 11:35 on a Tuesday night. A sole custody sergeant sat at the desk eating fish and chips while TalkSPORT radio played in the background.

"Oh shit. We used to hide a spare underneath one of the plant pots in the garden. I don't know how she remembered that."

"The brain is a funny thing," said Boulton. "So, by their account, she used the spare key and they found her in the kitchen, complaining that things were in the wrong place."

"Where is she?" Ramouter asked as he looked up at the bank of CCTV monitors that showed the three empty cells that were usually reserved for women.

"I moved her into one of the consultation rooms. She was obviously very upset about being arrested and she refused to be interviewed. You're lucky that I came on duty."

"She's not well," Ramouter said sadly.

"The best that I can do for now is to release her under investigation and ask the arresting officers to have a word with the new owners. You know what it's like, sometimes these RUIs disappear—just give me five minutes to start booking her out."

Ramouter looked through the peephole of the consultation room. Michelle was sitting nervously with a half-eaten cheese and tomato sandwich on the table. She looked as though she'd lost weight since he'd last seen her. Ramouter tried to swallow down the pain in his chest. He wasn't used to seeing his wife so anxious and so small. Even when Michelle had first been diagnosed with early onset dementia, she approached it with quiet acceptance, rationalizing that perhaps she'd saved their son from the disease.

"Miche," Ramouter said. He opened the door and stepped into the small, overheated room.

"Oh, Salim. I'm so sorry. I'm so sorry," Michelle said, sliding along the bench toward him.

"What are you apologizing for?" Ramouter said as he helped Michelle up and pulled her toward him. "It's not your fault, baby."

"Of course it's my fault. I thought that I was getting better, that maybe I was OK but… How could I forget him? How could I forget my baby?"

"You didn't do it on purpose," said Ramouter as he held Michelle. "It was just…not every day will be like this."

"But one day, every day will be like this." She began to cry even harder. "I don't understand what happened. I really don't. I just want to go home. Please can I go home?"

Which home? That was the question that Ramouter wanted to ask. Back to Pamela's house, back to their old house in Bradford, or back to London?

"Come on, Miche. Let's go," Ramouter said, his tone filled with false confidence. "You'll feel better once you've had a shower and a good night's sleep."

"But I won't be *better* in the morning," said Michelle. Her voice was strained and weighed down with grief. "I'm never going to get better."

Ramouter was lost for words as he helped Michelle to her feet. Their lives should have been straightforward. They'd done everything in the right order. They'd met, fallen in love, married and had a child. They'd been making normal plans. A decision about where to live as a family should have been an easy one to make, but Ramouter felt that anything he decided now would be the wrong choice. He couldn't tell Michelle that he didn't know what the right choice was, that he didn't know what to do and he felt like a failure.

56

I'm never going to get better.

Ramouter had woken up with Michelle's words ringing in his ears. The fact that her illness would get worse was an unavoidable truth. His pillow had been cold and damp when he'd opened his eyes, in an unfamiliar room, and Ramouter wondered if it was possible to cry in your sleep. He sat wearily on his bed and his mobile phone began to beep again with a text alert. He didn't need to look to see that it was Henley replying to his earlier message that he had a stomach bug and wouldn't be coming into work.

Really. How old are you? 12. CALL ME!

Ramouter left Henley's message unanswered and put his phone down amid the crumpled material of the duvet as his wife stood in the doorway of the spare bedroom. He understood why Pamela had treated him like the enemy, as though he was responsible for Michelle's disappearance when she'd ushered him into the spare room at 1 a.m. He could see the accusation in her eyes. That none of this would have happened if he hadn't abandoned his wife. Ramouter had tried to convince himself that Michelle would have been lost no matter where they'd been living.

"I'm sorry. Sal, I'm so sorry," said Michelle as she took a tentative step toward the bed.

"I keep telling you that you've got nothing to be sorry for," Ramouter said. "This isn't your fault."

"Of course it is. I thought that I was OK. That things were returning to normal and perhaps the doctors had made a mistake."

"Michelle, don't do this to yourself." Ramouter took hold of his wife and held her. Everything about Michelle was so familiar, but he could feel the anxiety in his wife's body as her shoulders hunched up around her ears. "Come on, sit down."

"Pamela said that you took Ethan to school?" Michelle said as she looked down at her hands.

"She didn't have much of a choice. He's my son," Ramouter replied. He failed to keep the toxicity toward his sister-in-law out of his voice.

"You've probably made his day."

"I promised that we would pick him up later."

"I don't think that would be a good idea. Can you imagine what the other parents must be saying about me? Look at her, the loon who abandoned her son in the playground in the middle of winter."

"No one will be saying that," Ramouter said even though he wasn't entirely sure of that when he'd arrived with Ethan at the school gates and had caught the stares of a few of the parents. "Miche, I'll be with you. Nothing is going to happen."

Michelle shook her head as she began to cry. "You don't know that. Look at what happened yesterday. I ended up in a police station."

Ramouter let out a deep sigh. He didn't want to say that it could have been worse, that she could have ended up freezing to death in a field after she'd got lost.

"They shouldn't have arrested you. They should have seen that something wasn't right, that you weren't..."

"You can say it," Michelle said. "I'm not well, Salim. I'm going to get worse."

"But that might not be for years yet, and if I'm honest, I don't think that you being here in the middle of nowhere with your sister is helping."

"Don't be angry with her. She's doing her best. She's looking after me and Ethan."

"That's not her job. I'm the one who's supposed to be looking after you and our son. It's bad enough that your family thinks I abandoned you to swan off to London."

"No one is saying that."

"Of course they are," Ramouter said solemnly. "I should have just packed it all in after—"

"You wouldn't have been happy if you had walked away," said Michelle, reading his mind.

"That's not the point. I've got my priorities wrong, and I've let other people take charge."

"You mean my sister. She means well."

"Meaning well isn't enough. Look at us."

"I don't know what to do," Michelle said. "It's not as if I've broken my leg and it's going to get better. The best that we can hope for is that the medication delays it a bit, but at some point, I'm going to lose myself."

"What do you want, Miche?" Ramouter asked. He had the sudden realization that decisions had been made around her and for her, but no one had ever asked his wife what she herself wanted. "I'll do whatever you think is best. This isn't about me anymore. It should never have been about me."

"We don't know how long it's going to take before this thing completely takes over," said Michelle. "We should be spending as much time as we can together, but not here."

"What do you mean?" Ramouter asked. His phone rang out

in his hand and Henley's name flashed on the screen. "Do you want to come back to London with me?"

"Maybe—I'm not sure. I just know that you and Ethan are my home, but I don't know. Will it make things worse?"

Ramouter tried to think of the right answer as his phone rang for a second time.

"You can't keep avoiding her," Michelle said as Ramouter declined the call. "And you can't stay here forever."

57

"Boss, I've got something," Eastwood shouted out.

"What is it?" Henley asked as she gave up waiting for Ramouter to reply to her message. His explanation for not being at his desk or shlepping around the streets of southeast London looking for a murderer was a load of rubbish. She thought that they'd reached a point in their partnership where they almost shared the same scars, where trust would have been automatic. Henley was more than prepared to keep whatever secret Ramouter was holding. She owed him that. Now she felt as though Ramouter had pushed her ten steps backward.

"Footage of Brandon Whittaker and Alyssa Hadlow," said Eastwood, rubbing away at her eyes. "Caleb Annan definitely had a thing for the camera. The sound quality isn't great. It breaks up and is a bit choppy and muffled."

"Christ," Henley exclaimed as Eastwood pressed play. The light was poor, but they could clearly see Alyssa Hadlow running to a locked door. She was crying hysterically as a man entered the shot and grabbed her arms.

"Hold her down, hold her down."

Henley said nothing as she watched Alyssa's pregnant belly

strain against her jumper while she was forced down onto the ground.

"This isn't her flat," said Eastwood. "From the crime scene pictures it looks like—"

"That's the same room where I found Brandon Whittaker."

"Be careful. The baby."

A woman's voice. Distorted. Concerned. Scared.

"Whatever dwells within the body of Alyssa, you cannot hold her. I told you to hold her down."

"That's Caleb Annan's voice," said Henley. She put her hand to her stomach. Nausea was swimming through her.

"Get off me. Get off me. It hurts."

Henley could feel the anger swelling inside her as she heard Alyssa Hadlow's tormented and scared voice. Tormented and scared.

A man wearing a deep burgundy gown came into view. He kept his back to the camera. He was slender and raised a bowl above his head. Caleb appeared at his side and kneeled down by Alyssa. Henley could see the red rope in his hand which he began to tie around her feet.

"Pray therefore the God of Peace to crush Satan beneath our feet, that he may no longer retain men captive."

"No. No. No."

Alyssa kicked out. Her foot landed against Caleb's face, and he fell backward onto the floor. A pair of arms appeared. The rest of the woman was just out of shot. The sleeves of her shirt had been pulled up, revealing white forearms. A gold-colored watch on her right wrist.

"Christ." Eastwood shook her head as the man in deep burgundy upturned the bowl in his hands and water spilled onto Alyssa's face.

"We drive you from us, whoever you may be, unclean spirits, all satanic powers, all infernal invaders."

The man picked up another bowl and poured it over Alyssa as she coughed and spluttered.

"How long does this carry on for?" Henley asked wearily.

"Another ten minutes, and before you ask, Alyssa Hadlow and Caleb Annan are the only ones who can be identified, but there's definitely two other people involved in this...thing."

"Is there a date on this video?"

"Not that I can see. I'm sure that Ezra can find that out for us, but from the look of her, Alyssa Hadlow is heavily pregnant."

"I wouldn't have been surprised if she gave birth shortly after this. The stress on her body..."

"So, what did they do? Take Alyssa home and bring Brandon Whittaker in? And who are the other two?"

"Another man and what could be a white woman or just someone with a lighter complexion, but there was definitely a woman's voice in that video. Are there any more?"

Eastwood nodded as she opened another video. "There are others. Not the so-called..." She paused.

"You can say it. Exorcism."

"I refuse to say it. They're taking advantage of people who are mentally ill, but anyway, these are interviews not exorcisms. Caleb Annan is clearly in them but there's someone else there. I'm pretty sure that it's the same man who was in the room with Alyssa."

Henley leaned in as an image of Brandon Whittaker slumped on a chair filled the screen. His lips were moving, but they made no sound. There was no sound, as though he was talking only to himself.

"Don't touch me."

"He's always like this. He's unwilling to let us help him."

Caleb walked into view and kneeled in front of Brandon. He placed a small Bible on Brandon's lap.

"Will you let me talk to Brandon?"

"Don't touch me."

Brandon threw the Bible across the room. He stood up and the camera followed him as he walked up the aisle and returned to his seat.

"*Do you have the medication that he was prescribed?*"

"*I have all of the medication here. His parents are still picking up his prescription from the chemist just to keep up appearances, but we've made sure that Brandon hasn't taken anything. Even when he's asked.*"

"*Remember it's not Brandon who's asking. It's the voice of those that are within him.*"

"Who is this guy?" Eastwood asked.

"*Brandon. Please come and sit down.*"

Brandon moved his chair to the aisle and sat down again.

"*Pastor Annan. I've got something to tell you. I have a very important job to do and something to tell you.*"

Caleb Annan walked over to Brandon and pulled a chair from the row next to him. The camera zoomed in as Brandon leaned forward and said in a conspiratorial whisper:

"*At night, I look at my arms and I can see spiders walking under my skin.*"

"*The devil can manifest himself in many ways. That's why you're here with us. So that we can help you.*"

"*The devil? Really?*"

Caleb Annan sat back as Brandon began to laugh.

"*And you think that I'm the one who's mad? You're the one who's mad.*"

"Well, he isn't wrong," said Eastwood as she stopped the video. "I'm starting to think that the only sane person in that room was Brandon Whittaker."

"I don't disagree at all," said Henley. She tried to make sense of the complex wave of emotions that she was feeling. She had done the thing that she was not supposed to do. She'd become emotionally attached to the case. She felt anger for the way in which Brandon Whittaker, Alyssa Hadlow and Charlie Jensen had been abused, and the way in which their mental health has been used as a target for people who were misguided in their beliefs. Henley tried to rationalize the behavior of Caleb and the others, but it was hard to when all she could do was think about her dad and Rhimes, who had both suffered and battled with their own mental health.

"So, all we need to do is identify that man and woman. The odds are in our favor that we've got their DNA, but we just don't know who they are," said Henley.

"We get one step closer and then it's as if the rug is taken out from underneath us," said Eastwood. "I was doing some research last night and there were eight cases in England and Wales last year where the defendants were found guilty of everything from murder to false imprisonment because they were carrying out exorcisms on family members."

"Eight," repeated Stanford. "Can you imagine how many haven't been caught? I still can't believe that people are actually doing this shit to people that they're supposed to care about."

"It's a messed-up power trip," said Eastwood. "One of the defendants, in their trial, said that he'd been given the authority to drive the demon out."

"By beating someone to death?" said Henley. "It makes no sense. I just want to stop them before they kill someone else."

"Do you know what sickens me?" said Stanford as he swiveled in his chair in front of his computer. "It's the way that they just dumped our victims."

"They literally dumped Jensen like rubbish on the street and left Hadlow to rot," Henley said bitterly. "They're a bunch of hypocrites. They talk about saving people, but they have no respect for human life."

"Well, I've got some good news for you," said Stanford. "Lewisham Council has finally sent over the CCTV of Deptford Broadway and of Vanguard Street."

"Took them long enough," said Henley. She picked up her coat and bag from her desk. "Are you good to go through it?"

"Not a problem. Where are you off to?"

"Ezra managed to track down our mysterious blogger."

"Oh shit," said Stanford. "The person who wrote that post

that I found about being an exorcism victim. They're actually real?"

"Yes, and her name is Rebecca Keeler. She works in a women's refuge in Woolwich. Eastie, can you do me a favor and email the video over to me? I want to see if Rebecca is able to identify the voices."

"It's a big file. I'll see if I can get Ezra to just isolate the sound, but I'll get on it," said Eastwood.

"Thank you. This woman may be the only person who can tell us who these people are if Brandon doesn't wake up."

58

Henley walked toward an anonymous brown-brick building in Woolwich that was nestled between a gym and a car wash. There was no sign that this was a hostel for women. She pressed the buzzer.

"Can I help you?" said the disembodied voice from the intercom.

"Yes." Henley held up her warrant card to the camera on the intercom. "I'm Detective Inspector Henley. I'm here to see Rebecca Keeler."

"One sec."

Henley stood back and watched the passing traffic and groups of schoolchildren making their way toward the bus stop across the road. It was a busy area. Henley's mum had always said that people never look in the most obvious places. Better to hide in plain sight.

The buzzer sounded and Henley pushed the door open. She stepped into the corridor with the requisite health and safety posters on the wall, and found herself standing within a small space with another security door in front of her. It reminded her of the entrances into the cells at the local magistrates' court.

Henley wondered how many men had come here looking for their wives and had made it into the building before the extra security had been added.

A woman with brightly dyed red hair appeared at the window and waved a set of keys in her hand. Henley stepped back as the door opened.

"I'm so sorry. We've been having problems with this door. I think there's something wrong with the electrics. Please follow me. Sorry, I didn't even introduce myself. I'm Rebecca."

"Oh," said Henley. She took in the flawless skin on Rebecca's face that made it impossible to guess her actual age. Her bright green eyes were emphasized by a streak of black winged eyeliner. "Sorry, that was rude of me."

"Am I not what you were expecting?" Rebecca said with a smile. "I think that most people expect someone older and more wizened with age to be working here."

"I should know better than to judge by appearance," said Henley as she followed Rebecca along the corridor. The building was a hive of activity, with the sounds of women talking over the television, a washing machine on a spin cycle and someone running up the stairs and a door slamming.

"I'm not going to take up a lot of your time," Henley said as Rebecca showed her into a small office. "As I said on the phone, we identified you as the owner of a blog that you wrote several years ago."

"And as I told you on the phone, it's all true," said Rebecca. "I didn't make it up." Henley picked up the defensive tone in Rebecca's voice.

"Did you tell anyone about what happened to you?"

"No, if I'm honest, that period of my life is very hazy. I was struggling with my medication, and I'd moved back home with my mum, which wasn't the best decision that I made."

"Why was that?"

"My family has a history of mental illness, but they also have this history of not talking about it and not accepting it. My dad was better at dealing with my illness, but he died of cancer when I was twenty-four and I didn't handle it very well."

"I'm sorry about your dad. That must have been hard for you; losing him."

"It was," Rebecca said sadly. "I'm not sure if your dad is supposed to be your best friend but he was. We liked the same things, laughed at the same silly jokes and he heard me when I said that I didn't feel right. I couldn't put it into words, but he understood me."

"You fell into a depression?" asked Henley.

"That's an understatement. Life just became…hard. It was like being in a permanent fog, but it was inside of me." Rebecca picked up a purple crystal on her desk and started to roll it in her hand. "Long story short, I made the very bad decision of going back to my mum. The strange thing is that she was good at first, she looked after me, but when I think about it now, she was using me as an excuse not to deal with her own grief. She was helping me physically but not really helping me emotionally, does that make sense?"

"Yes, it does."

"Mum made sure that I was taking my medication, but I think she was struggling with me. I don't think that I was easy to deal with, and she started looking at different therapies."

"What sort of therapies?"

"A more holistic approach, she called it. I'm not saying that there isn't a place for natural remedies but that wasn't what I needed."

"So, what happened?" asked Henley.

Rebecca started to fiddle with the stack of papers that were on her desk. "Would you like a cup of tea?" she suddenly asked. "We've definitely got milk, as we've just had a food delivery."

Henley wanted to reach out and hug her. She knew firsthand how difficult it was to talk about the dark moments in your past. "I really admire you for being brave enough to talk about this," she said. "It's not easy."

"Thank you," said Rebecca. "I guess that's why I wanted to work here, with vulnerable women. I just wanted to stop them being hurt. To protect them. I think that my mum was doing the right thing but then she made the mistake of listening to my crazy—sorry, I shouldn't be calling anyone crazy."

"How about eccentric?"

"Yeah, that will have to do," said Rebecca with a small smile. "My eccentric aunt convinced her to take me to this church."

"The Church of Annan the Prophet."

"I honestly don't know what it was called or where it was; as I said, that time was a bit of a blur, but I do remember what they did to me in that room."

"How long ago was this?" Henley asked as she shifted her chair forward.

"It must have been about two and a half years ago," said Rebecca.

Shit, Henley said to herself. There was a possibility that Charlie Jensen wasn't the first of Caleb's victims and that there were more bodies waiting to be found. Henley shivered, even though the office was warm.

There was silence as Rebecca wiped away a tear. "No one should have to go through that. I needed help, actual medical help, but all they did was hurt me."

"Rebecca, I know that this is very hard and that it probably feels as though you're reliving it, but anything you tell me can help," said Henley. "Can you remember what they did to you?"

"I relive it every day." Rebecca pushed up her shirtsleeve, revealing the three scars on her left forearm. "They said that they had to beat the demon out of me," she said, pulling down her sleeve again. "Can you imagine such a thing? It sounds crazy to even say it."

"Was that all that they did?" asked Henley.

"No. They threw water on me and they tied me to a bed. I remember thinking that I was drowning."

"How long were you kept in the room for?"

"I don't know. It could have been a day, could have been two, it could have been a week. That time is all a bit of blur; all I know is that I somehow managed to get out. Maybe I had a moment of lucidity, but they left me alone and I got out."

"And you still don't know where you were?"

"The only thing that I can tell you is that there must have been a train station nearby, because I can remember hearing the sound of a train, but that's it."

"Where did you go afterward? After you got out?"

"I don't remember it, but the doctors said that someone found me and called an ambulance. I woke up in Guy's Hospital and apparently, I was a hysterical mess. I was there for about a week and then they discharged me."

"Did you go back to your mum?"

"Are you mad? I'm so sorry," Rebecca said as she put her hand to her mouth. "That was so rude of me."

"It's OK. I just have to ask."

"I know, but that was so rude of me. I actually ended up here in the refuge. I was here for about three weeks before I got moved to a hostel, and then I got my own place in Tulse Hill."

"Didn't you get any help, I mean, counseling or referral to the mental health team?" Henley asked with surprise. "You'd been through so much; I can't imagine that you would just be left alone."

Rebecca looked away with embarrassment. "I was sectioned for twenty-eight days," she finally admitted. "I shouldn't be ashamed but, no one ever made me feel that it was OK to talk about being in a mental health hospital."

"Did your mum try and visit you when you were in hospital?"

"She tried but I didn't want to see her."

"What about your aunt?"

"She didn't even bother. It felt as though she'd washed her hands of me," Rebecca said caustically.

"Did you report any of this to the police? You were basically kidnapped and assaulted."

"I remember a couple of police officers came to see me before I was discharged from the hospital, but I think that's the reason why I ended up being sectioned. I must have told them that whoever had me thought that I was possessed."

"So, nothing happened?"

"They probably just thought that I was mad as a box of frogs and got into a fight with someone, and just handed me over to someone else to deal with."

Henley sat back and looked at Rebecca. If it hadn't been for the scars, she would have difficulty believing that she had suffered physically, mentally and emotionally.

"How are you doing now?" Henley asked. "I'm sure that you still have your battles."

"I'm good," Rebecca replied. "I'm not miraculously healed or anything, but I take my medication, I've got a really good psychiatric nurse, my boyfriend is really supportive, and I've also got a little boy, so I need to make sure that I'm on top of things for him."

"Kids are a good motivator," Henley said as she thought about her own daughter. "I know that you said that that time is a bit of a blur, but would you mind listening to this recording? I'm warning you now that you might find it a bit distressing."

"That's fine. I'm good."

Henley pulled out her phone and pressed play on the recording that Eastwood had sent her. "Just let me know if any of those voices sound familiar."

"Whatever dwells within the body of..."

"No, I don't recognize that voice," said Rebecca as Caleb Annan's words played out through the speakers.

"OK, how about this one?" Henley fast-forwarded to the second voice. "Sorry, the audio isn't the best."

"Be careful. The baby."

Rebecca screwed up her face in concentration. "Sorry, it's sounding a bit like a Dalek. It doesn't sound familiar."

"It was probably a bit of a long shot," said Henley. "Here's the last one."

"I have all of the medication here. His parents are still picking up his prescription from the chemist…"

"I know that voice." Rebecca's eyes widened in recognition. "I know that voice," she said again.

"Are you sure?" Henley asked.

"A hundred percent. That's the man who was with my aunt, the one who tried to… Keith."

"Are you sure?"

"Absolutely." Rebecca nodded her head determinedly. "Except his name isn't Keith, that's just what I called him, but that's the same guy."

"Can you remember what he looked like?"

"Oh God," Rebecca said as she closed her eyes. "All I can tell you is that he was white, maybe in his late forties. He had brown hair and he wore glasses. That's it. That's the best that I could do."

"Don't worry about it. What about your aunt and your mum? Maybe they could help. I know you said that your aunt washed her hands of you, but do you have any contact details for them?"

"Well, my aunt died, and my mum moved to New Zealand with my stepdad, but I'll give you her number," Rebecca said. She scribbled the number down on a Post-it note and handed it to Henley.

"So, you and your mum are on speaking terms?"

"Well, I've got my own family now and I didn't want my little boy not knowing his nan, but we don't really talk like mothers and daughters should."

"How are you getting along with everything now?" asked Henley. She knew how easy it was to believe that asking for help was a sign of weakness and to pretend that you had moved on from a tortured past. Henley didn't want to leave without knowing that Rebecca was on track to living a fulfilling life again, despite her trauma.

"There was a time when I didn't want to be here," said Rebecca. "I wasn't thinking straight. So much had happened and I just wanted to forget, but my counselor, he encouraged me to report it to the police, what had happened to me. I think that it was just another step that I had to take in my therapy."

"And did you report it?"

"Yes, I did. To Brixton police station. I've still got the crime reference, give me a sec." Rebecca pulled open a desk drawer.

"Sorry, I'm a bit of a hoarder," she said as she rifled through the drawer. "There you go."

"Thank you." Henley wrote the number on the same Post-it note that Rebecca had handed her a few moments ago, and then she stood up. "Thank you for everything."

"I'm just sorry that I couldn't be of more help," said Rebecca. "I hope that you find them. It could have been me that was left for dead in that place."

It was 6:15 a.m. in New Zealand. Henley would be pissed off if a person called her at that time. She would be convinced that someone was dead. She ran into the coffee shop across the road, which was thankfully empty, and dialed Rebecca's mum number. She picked up after the fifth ring.

"Hello?"

"Is that Mrs. Keeler?" Henley asked.

"Speaking. Who is this?"

"My name is Detective Inspector Henley, from the Serial Crime Unit in London."

"Oh my God." Henley pulled the phone away from her ear as Mrs. Keeler's screech battered her eardrum. "Has something happened to my Becky? What is it?"

"Mrs. Keeler," Henley said repeatedly as she tried to get a word in. "Rebecca is fine."

"She is? Thank God."

"I just have a few questions to ask you about when she wasn't, OK?"

"What are you talking about?"

"After your husband died, Rebecca became very unwell, and she told me that her aunt took her to a church."

There was no response.

"Mrs. Keeler, are you still there?" Henley asked.

"I'm here. I don't want to talk about it."

"Mrs. Keeler. You're not in any trouble. I've got a case that involves a missing baby, and whoever is involved has already killed this baby's mother. I just need some information," Henley almost pleaded whilst praying that Mrs. Keeler didn't put the phone down.

"That's...oh my. That's awful, but I really don't know how I can help you."

"Do you remember what the church was called?"

"No, I don't. I never went there. Gretta, that's her aunt, she took her. She knew how much I was struggling with Becky, how desperate I was, and she wanted to help."

"How did she want to help, exactly?"

"By bringing her to the church. She and her friend described it as counseling."

"A friend?"

"Yes, he came to the house with Gretta. His name was something like Neil or Niall. I can't remember exactly, but he was very nice, and Becky was actually a bit calmer after he spoke to her. So, I let them... I let them take her."

Henley wanted to reach down the phone and comfort Mrs. Keeler as she began to cry.

"He said that he wanted to help her," said Mrs. Keeler. "He said that he wanted to rid her of her demons, but I thought that he meant her depression. I thought that he was going to fix her, not break her. I didn't want that for my baby girl. What mother would want that?"

59

Henley picked up her wineglass and took the biggest mouthful of mellow red wine as she watched Rob make his way toward the table. She'd been surprised when he'd texted to ask if she wanted to meet him for dinner. Stanford's husband, Gene, had offered to babysit Emma. Henley had quickly typed back, *Yes*. She was tired of fighting.

"You look knackered," Rob said as he sat down and began to pull apart his bread roll.

"I am," said Henley. "But I'm glad that you suggested it. Things have been shit with us, and I'm sorry about that."

"I'm sorry too. I'm trying not to let things rub me up the wrong way but it's difficult when you feel like things are being thrown in your face."

Henley took another sip of wine to stop herself from saying *"That doesn't sound like an apology."* Instead, she said, "I understand why you felt that way."

"And I was probably throwing my toys out of the pram when I moved into the spare room."

"Does that mean that you're coming back?"

"If you want me to."

"Of course I want you to. And it makes it less confusing for Emma."

It was Thursday night and the restaurant was packed. Henley could hear cheers coming from the downstairs bar. A waitress rushed over with Rob's steak and Henley's fish and chips.

"Am I allowed to ask how work is? I know that it's on your mind and it's better that we get it out of the way now while you get some food and a decent drink inside of you."

"You really know the way to a girl's heart, don't you." Henley tapped Rob's leg with her foot.

"Well, *my* girl's heart. I don't know about anyone else."

Henley looked around her, knowing full well that the first-floor restaurant overlooking the river wasn't the ideal place to discuss an ongoing investigation with her husband.

"You're allowed to ask about work, but I don't really want to talk about it here," she said as she swirled a chip around the dollop of tartar sauce on her plate. "I just want to pretend that everything is normal, even if it's just for a little while."

"That's fine, but I need you to know that I am here, if you do want to talk."

They said nothing for a few minutes as they ate, drank and listened the rhythms of the restaurant.

"I've been thinking a lot about us. I mean, the three of us." Rob refilled Henley's glass.

"No, Rob, I know what you're going to say and just no," Henley said, not bothering to hide the annoyance in her voice.

"What do you mean no? We've spoken about having another baby before."

"Rob, can't you see how inappropriate it is?" Henley said, and muttered *"Bloody men"* under her breath.

"How is it inappropriate?"

"Do you want me to spell it out for you?"

"I'm just talking about us. Our family, and that's just as important as the cases that you're working on."

She took a breath. She knew that it would be coming. The

conversation that she'd been skirting around and avoiding ever since Rob's mother had begun to state, on repeat, that it was unhealthy for Emma to be an only child.

"And you want to talk about this now? Here, in a crowded restaurant?"

"It ain't that crowded, and no one is listening to us. I just think that it's time that we talk about it. Neither of us are only children. It's not as if we can't afford another child and, as much as we all love Luna, a dog is not the same as a brother and sister."

"Take a look at my face, Rob. Do I really look like I want to talk about having another baby right now?"

"Sometimes I wonder if you really want us to make progress with our lives."

Henley sighed as she saw the crestfallen look on Rob's face. There was no good financial or humane reason why Emma should be denied a sibling except for one simple truth: Henley didn't want another child.

"I just don't think that it's the right time. I'm still working on myself. Don't you think that I need to get myself in the right head space first before we start thinking about expanding our family?"

"That doesn't make any sense though. You were already thinking of baby names when we had the scare last year."

"But that was last year and that was before Olivier did a runner and tried to kill me for a second time."

"You can't keep using him as an excuse. He's dead. Gone. I'm not. I'm here."

Henley concentrated on eating instead of telling Rob that he was right, but that had been a different time.

"Rob, I know what you're going to say, that we're not getting any younger."

"Well we're not."

"And I'm very aware of that. I'm not saying no. I'm just saying not right now. Let me just get myself straight first."

There was no mistaking the fact that Rob's face had brightened and that the only part of that sentence that he would choose to retain would be "I'm not saying no."

"I can live with that. I'm sorry if things got heated," Rob said as he cut into his steak. "So, I was talking to your brother earlier and we were thinking about an Easter getaway before their new baby arrives."

Henley sat and half listened as Rob talked about their holiday plans. Her mind drifting to the victims' names on the murder board, and the fact that Brandon Whittaker still hadn't woken up. Rebecca's mother had only been able to tell her that the man who had sat at her kitchen table and attempted to exorcise her daughter's 'demons was called Neil or Niall, but she had no other details for him.

"Earth to Anj," Rob said. "Didn't you hear what I said?"

"Sorry, what?" said Henley as she put down her knife and fork.

"I said, who is that woman who's just walked in with Stephen? On your right."

"What are you talking about?"

"Don't turn around," said Rob. He rolled his eyes as Henley did exactly that. "You never listen."

Henley watched Pellacia sit down at a table with Laura Halifax. There was a twist in her gut as she spotted Laura's hand reach under the table and squeeze Pellacia's leg.

"They look cozy," said Rob, popping another piece of steak into his mouth. "You didn't say that Stephen was seeing anyone."

"She's not just anyone," Henley said as she stood up, rattling the wineglasses on the table.

"Where are you going?" Rob hissed. "Just leave them to it."

"You don't understand, Rob," Henley said.

"Leave it, Anjelica." Rob grabbed her hand at the exact moment that Pellacia looked over and caught Henley's eye. Henley was convinced that time had stopped for a minute. He looked embarrassed, then guilty. Laura touched his face. Pellacia's mouth opened as if he wanted to say something but then he looked away. Henley reluctantly sat back down as Pellacia leaned over and said something to Laura. A second later, Laura looked at Henley triumphantly, and then leaned forward and kissed Pellacia. Henley swallowed down her fury.

"Looks like they're leaving," Rob said. Henley turned around again to see Pellacia helping Laura with her coat.

"He's a fucking idiot," Henley said as she picked up a glass of wine and looked out of the window.

"Why are you upset?" Rob asked, his voice hard. "Look at me, Anj. Why are you upset?"

"I'm not upset. I'm pissed off."

"Same difference."

"It's not what you think. He's playing with fire. That woman is far too involved with our murder investigation, and I don't like it. I don't like it one bit."

Ramouter opened the fridge, took one look at the expired milk and slammed it shut. He hadn't eaten since he and Michelle had pizza at the local Italian restaurant with Ethan after picking him up from school. He'd thought that Ethan would have been in tears when he'd told him that he was going back to London, but he'd been fine, and that scared Ramouter just as much as when Michelle had gone missing. The kids are more resilient than us, is what Michelle had said, but Ramouter had thought it was more than that. He couldn't ignore the fact that Ethan was getting used to not having his dad around.

Ramouter checked the time on his phone. It was almost 2:30 a.m. He'd left it until the last possible minute to depart Bradford after Michelle had convinced him to come back. Ramouter looked around his flat. It was a two-bedroom ground-floor flat with access to a small garden, which he and Michelle had chosen before the diagnosis. The local primary school was still holding a place for Ethan. Ramouter was just waiting for Michelle to make a decision.

He hadn't been in bed for five minutes when his phone started to ring.

"Shit," he said when he saw Pellacia's name on the screen. He was still debating answering the call when a text appeared.

PICK UP THE PHONE! NOW

"Guv," said Ramouter.

"Well, you don't sound sick," said Pellacia.

"Guv, I can explain."

"You can explain it to Henley, when you see her at the scene."

"Scene. What scene?"

"Southwark Park. It looks like we've got another victim to add to the list."

Henley woke up shivering with the cold and damp material of her pajama top clinging to her back.

"Fuck," she said as goose bumps appeared on the skin. She was sick of the nightmares and even more sick of the broken sleep. It was about time she took the prescription for sleeping tablets out of her glovebox.

Henley sat up. She wasn't sure if she'd heard her phone beeping or if it had been part of her nightmare. She looked across at her bedside table as she unbuttoned her pajama top, her skin prickling with the residual memories of her nightmare. She couldn't remember the last time she'd slept throughout the night. Rob didn't move as Henley's mobile phone began to ring.

"For God's sake," she muttered, getting out of bed and picking up the phone.

"A body has been found," Pellacia said without giving Henley a chance to even say his name or hello.

"It's almost three in the morning. Is this even one for us?" Henley whispered as she pulled her dressing gown from the hook on the door.

"You know that I wouldn't be calling you if it wasn't. Ramouter will meet you there. I'll send you the details," Pellacia replied and then put down the phone.

Henley begrudgingly headed to the bathroom and turned on the shower. She didn't want this. She didn't want to be dealing with another victim whilst also dealing with her growing hate for Caleb Annan and his unknown accomplices.

60

A man's body was hanging from the bandstand in the middle of Southwark Park. The light bounced off his ribs. His emaciated chest had been stained red with the blood that had drained from the opening in his throat. The few fingernails that were left were ragged and dirty. The remains of red rope were still tied tightly around his ankles. Henley let out a sharp breath as she shone her torch on the red rope that bound the man's wrists to the rafters.

"He's been hanging here for a while," Henley said as the light from her torch illuminated the small flecks of ice on his eyelashes. The cold had burnt away the thin membrane of skin on his lips. His cheeks were blackened with bruises. Henley pushed back his hair with a gloved finger. The word "LEAVE" had been etched in ash across his forehead.

"I don't understand," said Ramouter as he stood by the ladder. "Why here? And why display him like this?"

"This is more than just exorcising demons. Whoever is responsible is starting to enjoy themselves." Henley made her way back down the steps. This was the most that they'd said to each other since Ramouter had arrived at the park gates almost thirty minutes ago and she had told him that he looked well.

Henley peeled off her latex gloves and pulled out her own leather gloves from her pockets. The one thing that she was grateful for was that it was now past 4 a.m. and the minus degree temperatures had meant that no curious onlookers were around, but Henley wasn't sure how much longer that would last as another light turned on in a nearby flat. Anthony's CSI team, who had been on the late shift, were already securing evidence. Henley moved out of the way as Anthony's assistant started taking photographs while police taped off the area around the bandstand.

"Well, this is unusual," Linh said as she set her case down onto the ground. "He's been up there for a while. His arms have dislocated from the sockets."

"Morning to you too," said Henley as she turned around and faced the body.

"It's not morning, it's the middle of the night," Linh grumbled, pulling out her notebook. "I would rather have been in my bed or, if I had to be out, sitting in a nice warm café eating a full English breakfast instead of freezing my bollocks off in the middle of a park, but what can you do?"

"Are you able to estimate a time of death?" Henley asked as Linh walked up into the bandstand and prodded the body with her finger.

"Well, unlike Brandon Whittaker, I can confirm right now that he's dead."

Henley rolled her eyes and looked at Ramouter. Usually, he would have been sniggering away at Linh's bad jokes, but he looked drained. Henley recognized the distant look of a man who was trying to make sense of a recent trauma.

"And he was already dead when whoever it was strung him up and cut his throat," said Linh. "There's no arterial spray. All of the blood has drained out, if you look down at his calves."

Henley walked up to the bandstand and shone the torch onto

the man's calves where the skin had discolored and had taken on a purple-red hue.

"Post-mortem stain," Ramouter said flatly.

"Clever boy," Linh said as she shivered. "Someone has been doing their homework. Post-mortem stain, or livor mortis, usually starts about thirty minutes after death but it's not visible to the human eye until two hours after death."

"The 999 call was made at 2:15 a.m.," said Henley.

"Where's the witness?" Ramouter asked as the headlights from an encroaching police van illuminated them, slowly making its way across the park.

"The witness is Kenton Wallace. A couple of PCs have taken him home. He lives over there." Henley pointed at a row of gray stone terraced houses to the right of the park. "He says that he was out for a run."

"At this time of night, in this weather?"

Henley shrugged. "Maybe he had arranged to meet someone at the bandstand. But the reason why Wallace was out here doesn't matter. Right now, we need to work out how long this guy has been here and where exactly he was killed."

"Not that I'm telling you how to do your job," said Linh as she took out a scalpel, made a small incision on the right side of the man's ribs and inserted a thermometer. "But a dead body, even one that looks starved like this—"

"It's still going to be a hassle to carry him," said Ramouter. "Carrying dead weight is not easy."

"I'm rubbish at weights," said Linh. "I couldn't tell you how much he weighed, but it wouldn't be easy to hoist him up here if he was already dead or even just dying."

"How would you even get him here?" asked Ramouter. "Look at the state of Brandon Whittaker when you found him."

"We thought that Brandon was dead. This guy would have been weak, literally a burden to carry," said Henley. "Can you see anything to give an idea as to how he died?"

"It looks like there's a stab wound on the left side of his chest.

I need to open him up to see if it penetrated the heart. There's no arterial spray, so this cut to the throat, it would have been pointless. Why cut his throat if he was already dead?" Linh removed the thermometer and moved carefully away from the bandstand. "But as I said, he was already dead when he was tied up here. There's no sign of rigor mortis and your man's core body temperature has only gone down four degrees to 34.3C so, rough estimate, he's been dead for two hours."

"Our witness must have seen more than just a body hanging from the bandstand," said Henley. "It's nearly 4 a.m. and Wallace called 999 at 2:15 a.m. And as you've both pointed out, dead weight is not easy to carry and then to hang him up from the bandstand—that's a job for at least two people, and it's definitely not a ten-minute one."

"It's pitch-black out here though," said Ramouter as he looked around. "It would be impossible to hang someone up with just guesswork."

"Whoever killed him must know this area," said Henley. "It's possible that they live nearby. The gates are locked at night, and it wouldn't be worth the hassle if you didn't know how to get in."

"Why would the killer or killers cut his throat? It doesn't make any sense," said Ramouter.

"It makes perfect sense," said Henley. "Brandon, Alyssa and Jensen. They were accidents. Something went wrong with Annan's exorcisms of those three, but this one. This man. Whoever it was wanted to kill him."

61

Kenton Wallace was sitting on the edge of his sofa with his hands clasped around a cup of tea. According to the police officer who had been keeping an eye on him, he hadn't taken a sip. He lived less than a five-minute walk away from where the body had been found. His front room was cluttered with kettlebells, gym weights, exercise bands and a medicine ball.

"Mr. Wallace. I'm Detective Inspector Anjelica Henley. I just wanted to ask you a few questions about what happened a few hours ago. Do you want to tell us why you were out?"

Kenton looked down at the cup in his hand and placed it on the floor. "It's stupid, but I was out for a run."

"A run?" asked Ramouter. "At this time in the morning?"

Henley shot Ramouter a disapproving look and he stepped back.

"I have trouble sleeping," said Kenton. "I've been an insomniac for years and…but…"

Henley could tell that he was struggling with a lot more than insomnia.

"Sometimes the running helps," said Henley as she took a seat next to him, careful not to invade too much of his personal space. "It sort of calms everything down when your mind is determined to go into hyper drive when you need to be asleep."

"That's exactly it," said Kenton. "Do you run?"

"God no, I mean I used to, but I realized that I'm not eighteen anymore. So, Kenton," Henley said softly, "tell me what you saw."

"Shit, sorry," Kenton said as he stretched his leg out and knocked over his tea.

"I'll sort it," said the police officer who had been standing near the sofa. He swiftly picked up the cup and disappeared to the kitchen.

"I'd already done two laps of my usual route. It usually takes me twenty to thirty minutes. I've got an app on my phone that tracks me," Kenton said as he kept his gaze on the police officer who had returned with a cloth and was mopping up the spilled tea from the sodden carpet.

"What time did you leave to go for your run?"

"I got out of bed just after half past one and I must have been out of the house just before quarter to two. They lock the park at 7 p.m. but you can get in. I ran twice around the lake, which is the other side of the bandstand, which took me about fifteen minutes, and then I ran down toward the tennis court and headed toward the bandstand."

"What happened when you got there?"

"I slipped on something, must have been a patch of ice, but I fell over. I went to get up and then someone pushed me back down. I didn't hear him coming because I had my headphones on."

"Were you wearing this same top when you were out?" asked Henley.

Kenton turned his head and pulled at his sleeve as though he was checking that it was the same top. "Yeah, I was."

"We're going to need to take it," Henley said. She took out her car keys and handed them to Ramouter. "There are some large evidence bags in the trunk."

"I fell onto my face." Kenton indicated the red scratches on his face. "I shouted out, but he was already gone when I stood and looked up at the bandstand, and I saw—"

Kenton put his hands to his face and fell back.

"It's OK. I've got you," Henley said as she reached out, grabbed hold of Kenton's arms and eased him up. The last thing she needed was to be losing the most minuscule amount of evidence on Kenton's sofa.

"Sorry. I'm sorry."

"It's OK," Henley said as Ramouter returned to the room. "If you stand up, DC Ramouter is going to help you to remove your jumper."

"I didn't think that it was real, but then I saw the blood. I took out my phone to call 999 and then I heard something."

"What did you hear?" asked Henley.

"Breathing. I could hear someone breathing, and it definitely wasn't coming from that poor guy."

"There was someone else there? Are you sure?"

"Definitely."

"Were you on the phone to 999 when you heard them?"

"No. I took my phone out and then I heard someone shout out 'Come on' and then I... I panicked. I ran, but whoever it was ran straight into me. I heard them fall down but I was running, mate. I wasn't hanging around. I was shitting myself. I got up, ran straight home and called you lot."

"The person who you knocked over. Did they say anything? Did you get a glimpse of what they looked like?"

Kenton shook his head. "I couldn't tell you; I just ran. There is only one thing that I can tell and that is there was definitely two of them in that park."

62

"Thank you," Henley said as Ramouter placed a cup of coffee on her desk. She tried and failed to suppress a yawn.

"Why were you off? And don't give me the 'I had a stomach bug' shit," said Henley. "I'm too tired and I'm not in the mood."

Ramouter sat back sullenly in his chair. They were the only ones in the SCU, and the dawn hadn't officially broken yet.

"I don't want there to be an atmosphere between us." Henley could hear the hardness in her voice. "If we can't be honest with each other, after everything, then this partnership isn't going to work."

Ramouter remained silent.

"Salim, the SCU works, and it survives because every one of us has each other's backs."

"Even Pellacia?" he said. "He hasn't exactly been the most supportive of bosses. I saw how he was with you."

"We're not talking about him right now. I'm not defending him being an arsehole, but he has a lot on. He has to keep the SCU alive and that's not easy when the powers that be are looking at ways to cut us adrift. Anyway, I know how to manage him and if we can get a break with this case, well, that will keep the dragons at bay for a bit."

"I'm sorry about yesterday." Ramouter buried his head in his hands. "It's just..."

"I need to know what's going on with you. Ramouter, you can trust me. I'm here to support you," Henley said as she picked up the box of tissues and walked around her desk. "You're a good detective and I don't want to lose you. But I'm selfish, and I've got to learn that it's not always about me. When you're ready and only if you want to, I'm here."

"Thank you," Ramouter whispered as he reached for the tissues. "It wasn't a stomach bug."

"Yeah, I figured," said Henley. The door of the office opened and Pellacia walked in. "You could have come up with something better than that?"

"I know it was shit. It's just...can I talk to you about it later?" said Ramouter said as Pellacia approached them.

"Yeah, of course," Henley said as Ramouter stood up. "Thanks for the coffee."

"I'm going to the café to get some breakfast." Ramouter picked up his coat. "I'll get you the usual."

"Make it a sausage and egg bagel and a blueberry muffin," Henley said as she kept her eye on Pellacia hovering around Henley's desk.

"Can I have a word with you?" Pellacia asked, once Ramouter had left the room.

"If it's not about any of these investigations, then the answer is no," said Henley. She turned her back and switched on her computer.

"Please, Anjelica. I need to explain."

"I am not interested in anything that you have to say to me." It was almost 6 a.m. and Henley wasn't sure if it was the anger or the lack of sleep that was causing her to act so irrationally. As she reached for her coffee her mobile phone began to vibrate across her desk. It was a private number. She had half a mind to send the call straight to voice mail, but she picked it up.

"Detective Inspector Henley? This is Niamh Dillan."

Henley couldn't place the name. "I'm sorry, who?"

"I'm the ward nurse at Lewisham Hospital. It's about Brandon Whittaker."

Henley felt a cramping in her stomach as a door in the building slammed. "What's happened?"

She looked up at Brandon's name written in black ink on the whiteboard, picked up a red marker and walked up to the board, prepared to change his status.

"Brandon Whittaker woke up an hour ago."

"Brandon Whittaker is awake and according to the nurses, he's talking. They're carrying out tests to check his cognitive ability, but the doctors said it's going to take a little while before we can sit down and ask him questions about what happened to him," Henley told her team. She was standing in front of the investigation board that now had an A4 photograph of the murder victim that was found hanging in Southwark Park.

"Do they have any idea how long it will be before he's talking sense?" asked Stanford. "I don't mean to be funny but the sooner the better. The last thing we want is for another body to turn up."

Henley sighed. "We've got to consider his mental health. You have to remember that his medication had been taken away, but Ramouter and I will head to the hospital later this afternoon. We don't want to overburden Brandon and stress him out. We have to take it gently. The nurses and doctors who are attending are going to do their best to keep us updated on his progress throughout the morning, but I don't want his parents to go anywhere near him."

"Well, considering that they didn't even bother to turn up since we last saw them, I'm not exactly expecting them to be rushing down to the hospital first thing," said Eastwood who was perched on her desk.

"I don't get it," said Ramouter. "It doesn't matter how delusional they are, Brandon is still their son, and he isn't dead. I thought that they would have been down there in a heartbeat."

"You would think so," Henley answered. "But they haven't made much of an effort so far. The fact that he's awake and somewhat coherent may change that. He could drop them right in it, and also tell us who the people were that nearly killed him."

"Is he being protected?" Pellacia asked from his position to the left of Henley. "The last thing we want is for his life to be put in jeopardy again. He's vulnerable. Mentally and physically."

"He's got his own room and the hospital has placed a security guard outside it," Henley said, keeping her back to Pellacia. "I would love to have actual police officers protecting him."

"I've tried," said Pellacia. "But they're not giving us the money or extra manpower. We're on our own."

"Sorry, guv, but this is mad," said Stanford. "We've got four murder victims."

"Not all connected though," said Henley. "There's no evidence that the person or people who killed Annan are the same people responsible for Hadlow, Jensen and our new victim."

"And we're definitely sure that we're dealing with two murderers for both our cases?" Pellacia asked.

"No," said Henley. "We're looking at four. For Annan, there was definitely a second person present, but we don't know if their involvement was active participation or if they disturbed a crime scene. And the case is different for the body that was found in Southwark Park and also for Hadlow, Jensen, and Whittaker."

"How so?" asked Eastwood.

"I would say that Hadlow and Jensen's deaths were accidents. They both suffered organ damage, which includes heart failure, and their bodies were abandoned. The same would have happened to Whittaker if I hadn't found him. This third victim is different. His throat was cut and then he was displayed. The intention was clearly murder with the third victim."

"When is Dr. Ryan arriving?" Pellacia asked.

Stanford groaned. "Do we really need to get him in to tell us the blindingly obvious? That we're dealing with a bunch of psychopaths."

"I couldn't think of anyone better to come in and give us our monthly TED Talk on psychopaths," Ramouter mocked.

"I don't know why you lot worship him so much," said Stanford. "I can go online and find myself a course for a hundred pounds and by the end of the afternoon I'll have a certificate and a badge confirming my new job as a criminal profiler."

"He's a forensic pathologist," said Ramouter as he briefly wondered how Stanford would feel about his therapy sessions with Dr. Mark Ryan.

"If you two have quite finished. He should be here in the next half hour," said Henley.

"Psychos. We're looking for psychos," said Stanford.

"Where are we on the identification of our Southwark Park victim?" Pellacia asked.

"Nowhere," Henley said. She turned and faced Pellacia for the first time that morning. "I'm crossing my fingers for a DNA match. There was nothing found near him or on him to confirm his identity, but CSI did find his blood on the stairwell of Nightingale House in the Kirby Estate."

"When you say blood, how much are we talking?" asked Eastwood.

"Not much. There was a small pool on the steps outside that lead into the block of flats. It could be that the killers put him down briefly because it was an effort to carry him. It's possible that he was initially killed in one of the flats and then the killers dragged his body to the bandstand. We didn't find any blood on the stairs inside the block."

"He could be local, or most likely he was taken and held nearby, but whoever it was wanted him to be found," said Ramouter. "The park doesn't open until 8 a.m. There's a secondary school nearby so the chances are that he would have been found by a bunch of schoolkids."

"How far is the Kirby Estate from the bandstand?" asked Stanford.

"It's not even a five-minute walk," said Henley. "It would be longer if you're dragging a dead body behind you, but this happened in the early hours of the morning, in the middle of February when it was minus four. The only people around at that time were Wallace and our killers; I haven't got much hope for any other witnesses."

"Maybe they drove up to the park," Ramouter volunteered.

"Why would anyone drive to Southwark Park and go through all that hassle of trying to find a point of entry and then somewhere suitable to hang this man?" asked Stanford. "That doesn't sit right with me."

"Aye, you're probably right."

"Well, it looks like you've got a good handle on this," said Pellacia as he stood up. "We need a press conference, ideally as soon as this afternoon. I'm going to get in touch with our media communications manager."

"Stanford, how did you get on with the CCTV?" Henley asked as she watched Pellacia walk back into his office.

"Well, that was a joke," said Stanford. "Everything that they sent was corrupted. Me and Ezra tried but it was a waste of time. I'm heading over to the council offices to watch it myself. It's only CCTV but it's been like trying to find the lost ark."

"Great," said Henley as the sound of the intercom buzzing reverberated around the room.

"Great," repeated Stanford. "It looks like your favorite psycho doctor has just turned up."

"You've got another victim?" Mark asked as Eastwood handed him a cup of tea.

"I would say that it was the same MO, but whoever it was

left this poor guy hanging from the bandstand in Southwark Park after they cut his throat."

"Bloody hell." Mark placed his tea on Henley's desk and sat back. "So, your killers are escalating."

"That's exactly what I said," Stanford said snidely.

"Of course you did," Mark replied as though he was talking to a toddler.

"So, who are we looking for? And Stanford, if you say a pair of psychos one more time, I swear..." said Henley.

"I promise I'll be good," said Stanford, taking a seat next to Ramouter.

"You're looking for two killers who share the same belief system and I would suspect that at least one of them is experiencing a form of depressive psychosis. The fact that your third victim was placed on public display makes me surer of that."

"But how does Caleb Annan fit into this?" asked Ramouter. "We've got evidence that places him with both Whittaker and Hadlow."

"And also Jensen," said Henley. "Anthony ran the forensics through the database again and it was a match for Caleb Annan and the two unidentified DNA matches that we found on Brandon and Alyssa, and before you ask, Eastie, we checked and the Whittakers aren't a match for those two."

"That's a crying shame."

"From what you've told me, and as strange as this may sound, considering his treatment of women and his numerous affairs, Caleb Annan may have been some kind of moral barometer for your two killers," said Mark.

"Are you seriously suggesting that Caleb Annan stopped these two from killing Whittaker?" said Henley.

"If that's true, then why do we have Jensen and Hadlow on our murder board?" asked Eastwood.

"From the post-mortem reports I would say that the intention wasn't to kill," said Mark.

"That's what Henley said," said Stanford. "I really don't know why we call you."

"Stanford, I swear that I will knock you out," said Henley.

"I apologize," Stanford said begrudgingly. "Please continue, Doctor."

"Jensen wasn't just dumped in the middle of nowhere," Mark continued. "Someone wrapped his body in a sleeping bag and placed him somewhere where he would be found. That person, as bizarre as it sounds, cared about him. Hadlow, on the other hand, she was found at home; again, I suspect that Caleb intended for her to be found. But your bandstand victim is different. His throat has been slit and he's been displayed on a stage for the world to see. Annan is dead and your killer's behavior has changed."

"You're making Annan sound like a saint," said Stanford.

"Not at all," said Mark. "The man has very few redeeming qualities."

"Do you think that our two killers are involved with each other romantically?" asked Henley. "The gender markers in the DNA results confirm a man and woman."

"I can't say definitively, but I would say yes. They have the same beliefs, and they trust each other enough to work together. What makes these two dangerous is that they're mission orientated."

"They believe that they're doing society a favor?" asked Henley.

"Yeah, they think that they're doing good," said Mark.

"That's crazy," said Ramouter who was once again transfixed with Mark's explanation. "I still don't understand the exorcisms. Can't they see that they're hurting people? What part of their brain can believe that torturing them is helping them? Alyssa Hadlow clearly told them to stop. Why didn't they listen?"

"Because they thought that it was the devil talking," said Mark. "The best way to explain is that they no longer saw Hadlow, Whittaker and Jensen as people."

"What about the red rope that binds them all?" asked Eastwood. "Is there anything behind that?"

"Absolutely. Binding the victim's hands and feet has significance in the majority of religions, and also cultural significance.
For example, in Buddhism, one of the reasons for wearing the
red string bracelet is to remind the wearer to demonstrate compassion to others."

"Do me a favor," said Stanford. "I don't see much compassion being demonstrated with this bunch of loons."

"You'd be surprised," said Mark. "In your suspects' minds,
they may believe that they're showing compassion by performing the exorcisms. They're saving someone's life and their soul.
How compassionate an act is that?"

"As I said. They're loons."

"To be fair to you, Stanford, I'm not quite buying the compassion angle," said Mark. "In the majority of religions, for example, Kabbalah, Christianity and Hinduism, the red string is
worn for protection and to ward off misfortune. The red rope
that was used had a dual purpose. The most obvious intention was to restrain your victims, but the second purpose was
to prevent your victims' bodies from being inhabited by more
evil spirits."

"If our killers are such strong believers in the red rope being
a sign of protection, why wasn't Caleb wearing a red string,
or bracelet or whatever you want to call it?" asked Eastwood.
"The only item of significance on his wrist was a very expensive watch."

Mark's forehead wrinkled as he pondered the question.
"Well, going by his sexual behavior, it doesn't seem odd that
Caleb Annan was effectively not practicing what he preached.
It could be that as a pastor and a conduit for God's words, he
believed that he didn't need any material symbols of protection."

"You're telling us that on some deep but warped level, our
killers believe that they're being compassionate—but what about

the baby?" asked Henley. "That child belonged to Alyssa Hadlow; how would they perceive the child?"

"It could be that they see the baby as confirmation that they've saved a life and that looking after the baby is a reward for their devotion. Life is not one-sided, and these two people clearly believe that they're on a mission. That they're angels of mercy. So, if they believe in God and they also believe in the devil, and if they don't believe that mental illness is real, then for them, demonic possession is the natural answer."

"It's not natural," said Stanford. "All right, Doc, I like to think that you're not off-the-wall nuts, so what would you do if Eastie turned up at your door and told you that she was possessed?"

"More chance that it would be you," said Eastwood.

"Well, if she did," said Mark, "I would conclude that she was suffering from some kind of psychosis, but I would also look at the people around her. The problem is when you have family or friends who don't believe in mental health issues or because of the stigma, it's more acceptable to say that someone is possessed."

"It's like Ramouter said, why would you want to cause someone pain if you're in theory trying to save them?" said Henley. "I can't get my head around that."

"Because whoever is performing the exorcism has no idea what they're doing," said Mark. "When you investigate a crime, there is a procedure, right? An order in which you preserve the scene, retrieve the evidence?"

Ramouter nodded.

"Right, the same would apply for performing an exorcism. There's no instruction manual in the Bible, but there is an order that has developed over time. The Vatican has an entire department dedicated to this sort of thing. As I understand it, you would perform tests to establish if a demon truly had entered the body, including asking the entity that was within the body to speak. Then there are prayers, the laying on of—"

"But the laying on of hands doesn't include beating someone to death, waterboarding and cutting their throats," said Henley.

"As I said, your two killers have escalated. The important thing out of all of this would be to preserve life and if your killers were truly religious, then they would understand that taking a life is not the right of man. These two, they don't believe that anymore."

There was silence as everyone absorbed what Mark had just said.

"How do you know so much about exorcisms anyway?" Stanford asked, his voice dripping with skepticism.

"I lectured and wrote a couple of articles on it for a psychology journal," said Mark.

"Of course you did," Stanford said after a brief pause. "I still think Caleb Annan is equally responsible."

"I don't disagree," Henley said as her computer pinged with an email alert. "Ramouter, grab your coat."

"What is it?" Ramouter asked.

"Linh wants us down at the mortuary."

"Oh great," said Ramouter. "I'm sure she just loves seeing the pain on my face when I'm down there."

"Oh, she definitely enjoys seeing that," Henley replied as she completed scrolling through her email. "And it also looks like we've got an identification on our latest victim."

63

Twenty-seven-year-old Kyle Baxter was lying naked with a Y incision on Linh's examination table.

"With the exception of the stab wound to the heart and his throat being cut, the injuries are exactly the same as Alyssa Hadlow, Whittaker and, from the post-mortem report, the same as Jensen," said Linh as she let out a yawn. "Sorry, I feel like I've been up for days, but it's still Friday. Anyway, Jensen is still in the freezer in East Ham mortuary. The report seems pretty thorough, though, so there's no need for me to take a look at him."

"So, what killed Kyle Baxter? The stab wound to the heart or was it something else?"

"One stab wound to the heart with, unsurprisingly, not a very large knife," said Linh as she sat back in her chair and spun left and right. "Wound itself is only seventeen millimeters long. I've sent the photographs off to a knife expert because, as you know, I don't have a clue about knives. When I've seen wounds that small, they've usually been caused by something like a Stanley knife, a folding knife or a paring knife. Ramouter, why don't you go over and take a look at his hands?"

Ramouter didn't bother to argue as he dragged his feet over toward the body.

"I've never known a detective less inclined to go near a dead body," Linh said with an amused tone in her voice.

"I don't have a problem seeing corpses in situ, but there's just something about seeing them in here," Ramouter said. He picked up Baxter's left hand and turned it over. He ran his finger over the two deep cuts on his palm, placed it down gently onto the cold metal table and walked over to the right side and picked up the other hand. "He's got defensive wounds… on both hands. He fought back."

"Bingo," said Linh.

"Whittaker, Hadlow and Jensen. They didn't have any defensive wounds on their hands."

"There were cuts and scratches, but they were old. At some point, most likely when they were first taken, they had fought back, but by the time they died, they were too weak to do anything. But this dude…"

"He was alert enough to know what was going on and tried to defend himself," said Ramouter.

"There was also dried blood and other nasty bits under his fingernails. Samples have been retrieved and they're with Anthony. Hopefully, the DNA of your killer is there."

Henley struggled to feel relief. Even if there was a match to the unidentified DNA on Whittaker, Hadlow and Jensen, they were still no closer to confirming who they were, and no closer to finding the baby. Henley needed a name.

Kyle Baxter's dad, Nathan, sat at the dining room table. Three blue helium-filled balloons emblazoned with the number 50 floated in the corner.

"Mr. Baxter, we are really sorry for your loss," said Henley.

"You can call me Nathan," he said. He looked up at Henley with red-rimmed eyes. "I was only twenty-two when we had him. I was planning on traveling for a year when…" His voice trailed off as his gaze moved to the photographs on the bookcase.

"I know that this is hard, and if I could avoid doing this then I would, as the last thing that I want to do is cause you any more pain," said Henley. Ramouter was sitting on the opposite side of the table.

"When the policewoman turned up on my doorstep this morning... I knew. I think that I knew before that... I just felt that he was gone," said Nathan. "But I still need to see him... for myself."

"We'll make arrangements for that to happen," said Henley. She took out her slim blue notebook, which always felt less impersonal than pulling an iPad from her bag. "You reported Kyle missing six weeks ago?"

"Nathan! Did you hear me?" asked Henley as she called out his name for a second time, but he continued to stare off into the distance. "Nathan."

"Sorry. Sorry," said Nathan, sitting up straighter and rubbing at his eyes. "You were asking about..."

"Reporting Kyle missing," Henley said gently.

"I did. He... Kyle had a few problems. Mental health problems. It started when he was about twelve years old. He was diagnosed with bipolar disorder and schizophrenia. It was hard, really hard, but..." Nathan paused as he looked away. "We'd learned how to manage it. Therapy, medication, diet. Making sure that he was physically fit, all of that is important to keep on top of it. And then about five months ago...well, Kyle wasn't on top of it."

"What happened five months ago?"

Tears welled in Nathan's eyes. "He'd been managing really well," he said. "It's important that you have a good support system, and he did: me, my parents, my sister, his stepmum."

Henley hadn't failed to notice that there had been no mention of Kyle's mother. She looked again at the photographs. One with Kyle sitting on the sofa with two children, a boy and girl.

There were obligatory school photographs of the children. Kyle hugging an elderly woman. Nathan standing with a flower in his lapel, kissing the cheek of a beaming black woman. Where was Kyle's mother?

"What happened five months ago?" Henley asked again.

Nathan took a deep breath as he brushed away the tears from his face. "There was a lot going on for Ky. He broke up with his girlfriend and he was having problems with his new line manager. He worked as a management consultant for a bank in the city. The pressure was getting too much for him, he hit a depression and then...she got in touch."

"Who's 'she'?" asked Ramouter as he leaned forward.

A dark shadow crept over Nathan's face and his eyes hardened as he picked up a purple envelope and began to open it, eyes focused downward. "Kyle's mum... Stella." He pulled out the birthday card and stood it up on the table. "Stella came back."

"Came back from where?" asked Ramouter.

"Prison. She's been in and out of Kyle's life, but he must have reached out or something. I don't know. Perfect storm, really."

"What was the problem with Stella?"

Nathan shook his head as though he didn't want to go through the torture of reliving the obvious pain that Stella had inflicted on his life.

"We should never have got married. There was no way that her parents and mine were going to accept us, living in sin and bringing Ky into the world."

"Were they very religious?" Henley asked.

"That's an understatement. Very, very Catholic. Don't get me wrong, I love my parents to death but with some things, they were...anyway, we got married and things were fine for a while, but then the marriage just wasn't working. I tried but, it's marriage, and then Kyle got sick."

"That must have been hard."

Nathan nodded as tears dripped down his face. "We'd stopped going to church regularly. I still believe, but you know...life," he said. "But Stella. She changed. Even before Ky got ill. It was like she was searching for something. She couldn't find it in me, but she found it in religion. She joined a new church."

"Can you remember the church?" asked Ramouter.

Nathan shook his head as he began to cry. "She went to loads of different churches...we should have been enough. Looking after Ky should have been enough. God, I don't know how I'm going to tell the kids about their brother. They thought that we were having a birthday dinner tonight."

"What happened with Stella?" Henley asked firmly. She knew that Nathan probably felt that he was having questions fired at him, but she had to pull him out of the rabbit hole of grief, even if it was only for a little while.

Nathan gulped back tears. "She tried to kill him. She tried to kill our son."

64

"Fourteen years ago, Stella Baxter pleaded guilty to attempted murder, theft of a motor vehicle and kidnapping," said Ramouter as he handed Henley the printout of the investigation report. "It's only a summary. It looks like there may have been a codefendant too. Someone called Niall Graff."

"Niall. That's the same name of the man who was introduced to the blog writer, Rebecca Keeler, and who was working with Rebecca's aunt. Her mum confirmed it."

"It can't be just a coincidence. It has to be the same person," said Ramouter. "I've made a request for the full investigation file. She got seven years in prison."

"Seven years," Henley exclaimed. "And an IPP. Shit." Henley shook her head at the judge's decision to impose a sentence of Imprisonment for Public Protection, which meant that she would have had to serve a minimum term before she was eligible for parole. "Wow, she ended up serving eleven years in prison. Eight years in Holloway before she was moved to Laleham. IPP was such a fucker. She served almost double her sentence."

"It looks like she appealed her sentence and that was the reason for her release. No parole," said Ramouter. "If they weren't even considering her for parole once she'd done her seven years, that would mean that she wasn't repentant. That she hadn't changed."

Nathan and Stella Baxter had been separated for almost eighteen months. Nathan won custody. Stella was granted weekly contact, but visited only sporadically. Kyle developed mental illness and had been calling for his mother. Nathan had agreed that Stella could stay overnight and that they would take Kyle to the hospital in the morning. But when he woke up, Stella, Kyle and his car were gone. A neighbor of Stella's had called the police after hearing a child screaming continuously throughout the night. The police arrived at the scene and found Kyle tied to a bed.

"He had six broken ribs, burns to his feet, cuts, bruises and the word leave written in ash on his forehead," Henley spoke out loud.

"Fuck," Ramouter said. "She thought that he was possessed. She was trying to save him. The only good thing is that she didn't kill him."

"Not back then, but he's dead now," said Henley. "We need to find her."

"Nathan was no help. He doesn't have an address for her. Best we can do for now is put out an alert for her as wanted... but for what, exactly? Other than the same MO, we haven't got any physical evidence. Her DNA has been on the database for nearly fifteen years—we would have had a match if it was her."

"You're right," Henley said. "So, we need to find her and this Niall Graff. You said that he was a codefendant."

"He was arrested but he was never charged with anything, and before you ask, I can't find any sign of a criminal record, DNA samples or fingerprints on the system."

"Well, that's shit," said Henley, just as Stanford walked into the room waving a disc in his hand. "What is that?"

"This is the result of me spending the entire morning in a dingy little office in Catford watching CCTV."

"Tell me it produced something?" Henley pleaded.

"At 9:14 p.m., the CCTV camera on Harton Street, which faces the church car park, captures Uliana entering the church via the back door. At 10:02 p.m. Uliana leaves the church."

"That fits with what Uliana told us in her interview. She said that she was with Caleb for about forty-five minutes."

"But a little bit earlier, at 9:58 p.m., Serena Annan's car is first spotted at the Greenwich South Street and Lewisham Road junction heading south toward Deptford Broadway and is then seen pulling into the church's car park at 10:03 p.m. She parks up and enters the church through the back door."

"So, Uliana just misses Serena by a minute?" Henley clarified.

"Not that it matters," said Stanford. "Because Uliana then comes back at ten past ten and runs out of the church at 10:13 p.m. The CCTV cameras on Deptford Broadway capture Uliana getting into a Toyota Prius at 10:16 p.m. which heads south toward New Cross."

"What about Serena? Where's she?" Henley asked.

"That's the interesting bit," Stanford replied. "The thing is that she leaves the church after twenty minutes at 10:22 p.m. and her car is on Blackheath Road heading north at 10:25 p.m."

"So at 10:25 p.m. Serena is on her way home."

"Yeah, but an hour later, at 11:22 p.m., her car is seen again, heading south, on Deptford Broadway, I'm assuming back toward the church."

"Do we see her enter the church again?" asked Henley.

"No, there's some kind of malfunction with the camera," said Stanford. "But forty-one minutes after that, at 12:03 a.m., the camera on Vanguard Street picks up someone running west, away from the church, and at 12:07 a.m. Annan's car is on CCTV speeding north along the Broadway."

"Who's the person running along Vanguard Street? It can't be Serena because she's presumably getting into her car," said Henley.

"No idea," Stanford answered. "But what I can tell you is that Serena Annan was very busy that night."

"That's got to be enough to arrest her for murder," said Ramouter. "We just have to work out who was that person running away from the church. Which reminds me, the owner of the design studio next door to the church has been in touch so I'm going to pay him a visit and take another look around the place."

"Good. Have you had any further baby Hadlow updates?" asked Henley.

"Other than the usual nut—sorry," said Stanford when he saw the disapproving look on Henley's face. "Irresponsible members of the public calling in with the usual bollocks, there haven't been any leads."

"Great," Henley said. She leaned over her desk and let out a yawn.

"You've had a long day," said Stanford as he looked up at the clock on the wall. "It's almost 6 p.m. You've been working for sixteen hours."

Henley looked over at Ramouter who was collapsed in his seat and looked shattered. "I don't feel right just stopping."

"You and Ramouter are both dead on your feet," Stanford said. He picked up Henley's coat and threw it at her. "Go home. I doubt that anything is going to happen tonight. We'll all just come in tomorrow, even if it will be a Saturday."

"Fine," Henley said as she sat up and switched off her computer, and Stanford left the office.

"He's very protective of you," said Ramouter as he yawned and sat up.

"I know. I'm the sister he never had," Henley said affectionately. "Do you want to tell me what happened? Where you were yesterday?"

Ramouter looked up, and Henley couldn't tell if he was overtired or about to cry.

"Michelle went missing," Ramouter said. "I'd just left Derrick Sullivan's house and I had all these missed calls from Pamela—that's her sister."

"You went straight to Bradford?"

"Aye. By the time I got there they'd found her. She went back to our old house. I had to pick her up from the station."

Henley rolled her chair forward and put her arms around him. "I am so sorry. I feel terrible."

"Don't. I should have said something."

"It's fine. I told you that we're a team here. I've got you. We're all here for you. Have you got that?"

"It's been a shit year," said Ramouter.

"Yeah, it hasn't been the best," Henley agreed.

"I just want things to be normal."

"Me too. How's Michelle now?"

"Still upset but it's hard to say—every day is different. I just want to be there for her."

"No one would blame you for going back to Bradford," said Henley.

"Oh aye, but… I don't know. One thing at a time. I'm going to go. If I'm lucky, I'll catch Ethan before I go to bed. I'll catch you tomorrow morning."

"Meet me in the café. I'll get the breakfast in," said Henley as she put on her coat. She gave it a few minutes after Ramouter had left and walked up to the whiteboard where photos of their five victims, including Caleb Annan, had been stuck. She still had four murderers to identify and a missing baby to find. As Henley walked out of the SCU she wondered if this might be Ramouter's last case.

65

Henley had flashbacks as she walked along the hospital corridors. Her mum had been dead for eight minutes when Henley had finally made it to her side. She pushed aside the painful memory as she entered Brandon Whittaker's ward. There was no way that Henley could have gone home to her family without checking on Brandon first.

"I wasn't expecting to see you tonight," said Niamh, the nurse who had called Henley earlier that morning.

"I wasn't expecting to see you either. Hasn't your shift finished?" asked Henley.

"Don't even get me started," said Niamh. "Give it a couple of years and the government will be expecting us to do this job for free."

"Has anyone been to see him?" Henley asked. "I know that I've banned his parents, but I thought that maybe they might have tried."

"Not as far as I know, but his sister has been here since 3 p.m."

"How's he doing?" Henley asked Amy as she stood in Brandon's door while the doctor finished assessing him.

"He's awake and that's the main thing," said Amy as she joined Henley. "He said my name when he saw me and then he fell asleep for an hour."

"Have the doctors said anything about his prognosis?"

"Only that it's a good sign that he's responding to requests. He knows his name; he can blink when you tell him to, but he's still confused. They call it post-traumatic amnesia, so his short-term memory may be a bit, well, shit for twenty-four hours or longer. Hopefully it's not longer."

Henley hoped that Brandon's PTA wouldn't be longer than twenty-four hours. She needed answers and to find out who was responsible for putting him in the hospital.

"Have you spoken to your parents?" Henley asked Amy.

"I spoke to my mum this morning, after I got the call from the hospital that Brandon was awake. I was surprised that she actually picked up."

"What about your dad?"

"I didn't even bother. He still hasn't read my last WhatsApp message."

"What did your mum say when you spoke to her?"

"'Thank you for letting me know,'" Amy said with an air of disbelief. "Anyone would think that I was confirming a fucking boiler checkup. I'm sorry, but she makes me so angry. They both do."

"It's all right. I understand," said Henley as the doctor finally left Brandon's room. "Come on, let's go in."

Brandon was sitting up in bed staring quizzically at the TV remote in his hand. His head was still bandaged, and he was still connected to the drips. His fluid drainage bag was thankfully clear.

"Brandon," Amy said as she sat in the chair next to his bed. "This is Detective Inspector Henley. This is the lady who found you."

"Found me," Brandon said with a confused look on his face. "Where? I'm here." His words were slightly slurred.

"Hi, Brandon," said Henley. "How are you feeling?"

"Hungry and I've got a headache."

"Well hopefully you'll get something to eat, and your head will stop hurting soon."

"What's your name?" Brandon asked.

"Inspector Henley, well, Anjelica is my first name."

"My name is Brandon."

"Nice to meet you, Brandon." Henley knew that it was pointless, but she thought that she would ask anyway. "Brandon, do you remember anything that happened to you before you went to sleep?"

Brandon looked at his sister and then at Henley as though he was just seeing her for the first time.

"It's all right if you don't remember. I'm just glad to see that you're awake." Henley turned away. "I'll come back another time."

"They hurt me," Brandon shouted.

"Who hurt you, Brandon?" Henley swung round and took a step closer to his bed.

"I told them that I didn't like it," Brandon said. He took hold of his left wrist and started to pull at the bandages.

"Don't do that, Brandon," Amy said. She took hold of her brother's hands and clasped them gently in hers.

"Can you remember what they did to your wrists?" Henley asked. The image of the day that she found Brandon, the red rope cutting into his swollen wrists, flashed in her mind.

Brandon stared emptily back at Henley.

"You said that they hurt you," said Henley. "Can you tell me who they were or what they looked like?"

"I don't know," Brandon said quietly as he began to cry. "I don't know. I want to go home. Can you take me home?"

"I'm sorry," Henley said softly. She wanted to hold him and tell him that he was safe and that he would be OK, but Brandon looked so fragile she was scared that he would physically break if she touched him.

"I'm sorry, maybe it's best that you go. Hopefully, he'll be a lot better in a couple of days," said Amy.

"Don't apologize. It's the best thing. Your brother has been through a lot," said Henley as she stepped away. "The most important thing is that you're with him."

"I hope that you find them, whoever they are," said Amy as she followed Henley out into the corridor.

"I'll speak to you again soon," Henley said, without acknowledging Amy's request. She didn't want to make a promise that she didn't know she could keep.

66

"Breakfast always tastes better when someone else has cooked it," said Eastwood as she pushed her empty plate aside. "Thank you very much, ma'am."

"Don't ma'am me," said Henley. "It makes me feel old."

"Someone get the violins out," said Stanford.

"Right, I'm going to leave you two to bicker," said Eastwood. "I'll call you as soon as I've got the warrant for Serena."

"It's a shame that Ramouter couldn't make it to breakfast," Stanford said as they walked back to the SCU.

"He needed the rest and it's not as if he's got the entire day off," said Henley. "He's got a witness to see. Which reminds me, I need to ask him if he chased up on Derrick Sullivan's brother about the airport run that he made."

"I hate this case," he said. "It's enough to make me give it all up and just hand out speeding tickets until I retire."

An hour later, Stanford waved Henley over to his desk. "I've found Stella Baxter," he said. "She was placed on license, which expired two years ago, and there was also a restraining order, but that expired halfway through her prison sentence. But here's the thing. A second restraining order was put in place on the twenty-second of December last year." Stanford handed over a copy of the restraining order to Henley.

"Non-contact directly or indirectly with Kyle Baxter. Not to go within five hundred meters of Kyle Baxter. Not to go to any address where Kyle Baxter is known to reside," said Henley. "Kyle was so concerned about his safety, that he applied for a restraining order against his mum even though she'd spent nearly half of his life in prison?"

Stanford shook his head. "Kyle wasn't the one who made the application. It was his dad."

"Kyle is an adult; the only way that his dad could have applied for a restraining order would be if he had power of attorney."

"He's had power of attorney since Kyle was twenty-one years old."

"Something serious must have happened if Nathan had to apply for a restraining order."

"Apart from the fact that she tried to kill her son," said Stanford.

"I was going to say that was a long time ago, but you have a point," said Henley as she looked in the direction of Pellacia's office.

"I haven't been able to find anything as to why Nathan originally got the order in place, but what I do know is that Stella Baxter was arrested for breaching her restraining order the week that Kyle went missing."

"You're joking," said Henley. "The fact that she had breached the order has to be linked with Kyle's disappearance, but there's a difference between harming your son and actually stabbing him in the heart. Whatever was going through her mind thirteen years ago, I don't think that it would ever include actually killing her son."

"She couldn't have done it anyway. Killed any of them, I mean," said Stanford. "She's been on remand at HMP Laleham since the eighth of January. She's due to appear at the Crown

Court next week. Her DNA has been on the database for years. Her name would have lit up like a firework if her DNA had matched any of the samples that we've recovered from the crime scenes and the victims."

"I'm going to have to go to Laleham to see her." Henley picked her coat up from the table.

"You're going right now?"

"What else am I going to do? If I'm lucky and the traffic isn't too bad, then I should get there by 1:30."

"What about Serena Annan and the warrant?"

"I'll call Ramouter and tell him to liaise with you as soon as Eastwood confirms that the judge has signed the warrant. CID at Plumstead have loaned me a couple of officers to help with the search. Hopefully, I'll make it back in time. Did he say that he was coming in?" Henley asked as she pointed at Pellacia's door.

"Yeah, he said that he would be in at lunchtime," said Stanford. "What's going on with you two? I mean, I don't think that anything *like that* is going on but there's definitely something."

"It's nothing," Henley said, yet knowing full well that Stanford was one of the few people that she couldn't lie to. "He's been seeing Laura Halifax."

"Who has? Oh." Stanford let out a low whistle. "The dirty dog. You shouldn't be getting upset though, he is free and single."

"Don't be ridiculous. I'm not jealous or upset. I just think that it's inappropriate."

"Are you sure that's all it is? She's not linked to the investigation in any way."

"But she's linked to Serena Annan, and she's been poking her nose in from day one and now Pellacia's... I don't know, going on dates with her."

"You are jealous," Stanford said with a grin.

"Shut up."

"I'll tell you what. I'll have a word with him."

"No, you're right. Just leave it. It's not as if he's screwing a suspect."

"You wouldn't like anyone that he was screwing," said Stanford.

"Shut up," Henley said again as she turned her back to Stanford. She didn't want him to see from the look on her face that he was right.

Ramouter got off the bus and walked the same path that Uliana Piontek had taken last Monday morning when she had made her way to the church, completely unaware that she would find Caleb Annan's dead body. Ramouter stopped at the opened gates and read the yellow Met Police sign appealing for any witnesses to a murder. Ramouter pressed the buzzer of Payton Studios and pondered if anyone in London actually paid any attention to the appeal signs as he noticed a boarded up window to his left.

"*Yes?*" said the disembodied voice from the intercom.

"This is DC Salim Ramouter. I'm here to see Tom Payton."

"*One sec.*"

Ramouter looked around the car park as he waited for the door to open.

"Sorry about that. Our door is busted. I'm Tom. Do you mind showing me some ID? It's just that we've had a lot of journalists over the past week."

"Not just the door," said Ramouter as he flashed his warrant card. "What happened to the window?"

"Come to my desk and I'll show you."

Ramouter walked through an open-plan office filled with headphoned workers focused on their computer screens. Even though the atmosphere in the office was slightly tense, Ramouter wondered if he would have been much happier designing games and apps instead of chasing after delusional serial killers.

"How long have you been based here?" Ramouter asked as

he took a seat on a sofa that was much more comfortable and expensive than the one he regularly fell asleep on.

"I set up on my own about twelve years ago and we moved in nearly ten years ago. It was a lot cheaper than renting a space in Shoreditch."

"So, you've been here as long as the church next door?"

"Yeah, they came after. I thought that having a church next door would be an issue, but to be fair on them, they're pretty quiet during the day and we're not usually working here on weekends unless we're really up against it on a project; which we are."

"You said in your message that you weren't in the country when Caleb Annan was killed?"

"Yeah, otherwise I would have been in touch straightaway, but I was in Germany for a video games expo. We—well, Daisy, Niko and me—went to Germany and then I was away on a ski trip. Everyone else was here. Paulo, he's not in today but he's the one who told me about what happened to Caleb."

"Did you know him well?"

"Only to say hi and bye. And we chatted a bit about the football. It's not as if he was knocking our door and trying to convert us, but after the fight, he kind of kept his distance for a little while. He was probably embarrassed or something. He gave me money to cover the repairs to the glass. I just haven't got round to sorting it out yet."

"Tell me what happened. This fight."

"As I said, it was a few weeks ago, about three or four days before I went to Germany. I came in on a Saturday afternoon just to finish things up. When I got here there was a car parked in front of the office. People are always doing that, especially on a Saturday when it's market day on the high street, they think that it's free parking. I took a photograph of the car, and I came into the office. I hadn't even put the kettle on when I heard shouting outside and then there was a bang. I went to the front and could see that the window was smashed. I opened the door and Caleb was having a fight with this man."

"It was definitely Caleb?" asked Ramouter.

"Yeah, definitely him."

"Did you recognize the other man that he was fighting?"

Tom shook his head. "I've never seen him before."

"Can you describe him? The other guy."

"Black, he was lighter skinned than Caleb, medium build. Sorry, it all happened pretty fast, maybe if I saw a photo of him...but without one, that's the best I can do."

"So, you said that they were fighting?"

"Yeah, this guy had Caleb up against the wall and said that he was going to kill him."

"This man said that he was going to kill Caleb?"

"Definitely. Clear as a bell. Caleb said that he was crazy. I came out and Milo, he works in the brewery two doors down, he came out and it took both of us to separate them."

"What happened next?"

"I asked Caleb if he wanted me to call the police. He was a mess. His eye was swollen. He had a busted lip. There was blood coming from somewhere. Anyway, Caleb told me not to call the police. Milo told the man to go."

"And did he?"

"Yeah, eventually. He went for Caleb again and he ended up punching Milo, which was a mistake as Milo ended up lamping him one and told him to fuck off. Which he did. I pulled Caleb inside and this guy jumped in his car and drove off."

"Did he say anything else before he went?" Ramouter asked. "Did Caleb call him by his name?"

Tom shook his head. "Not that I can remember. As I said, it all happened really quickly. I haven't been involved in a fight since I was in school. I ended up with a ripped jumper. I remember that the guy was bleeding from his eye. He did tell Caleb to 'stay away from her' and that he would kill him if he touched her again."

"Can you remember anything about the car? It doesn't matter how small."

"I told you. I took a photo of it. It was the same one that was parked in front of the studio. Here, I printed it off for you."

Ramouter stepped back out in the cold and took out his phone. The brewery was closed. He made a mental note to chase Milo for a statement as he waited to be connected to the traffic police operator.

"Hi. This is DC Salim Ramouter, warrant number 2873PY, attached to the Serial Crime Unit. I need to check the registration details for a silver Volkswagen Tiguan. Registration PF68 ESY."

"Just give me a minute, this computer is on a bit of a go-slow," replied the operator. "That vehicle is registered to a Tameka Sullivan, date of birth, fourth of June 1984. MOT exempt. Insurance is in the name of Tameka Sullivan and Derrick Sullivan, DOB 27 February, 1982."

67

HMP Laleham looked more like modern housing than Europe's largest women's prison. Henley's phone beeped with the arrival of another text message from Ramouter as she followed the prison officer down the corridor. Ramouter had called her when she was speeding along the M4 to tell her about Derrick Sullivan's assault on Caleb Annan, and she'd instructed him to obtain a search warrant for Sullivan's house.

"Just through here," said the prison officer, opening the door. "We had an incident in the legal visits room so that's unavailable at the moment, and you're going to have to see her in here. There are no socials today so you can take as long as you want."

Henley felt her heart sink a little as she walked into the visitors' center. A children's play area was filled with brightly colored miniature chairs and an overflowing toy chest. Henley couldn't imagine anything worse than bringing a child here to see their imprisoned mother. She wondered, if she was ever in the unfortunate position to be serving a prison sentence, if she would want Rob to bring Emma to see her.

Stella Baxter was sitting at a table wearing a blue prisoner's bib while another male and female officer stood nearby.

"Mrs. Baxter—" said Henley.

"No. It's Webb," Stella said. "I don't use Baxter anymore. What was the point after he divorced me?"

"Is it OK if I call you Stella then?" Henley asked as she pulled out a bright orange overstuffed chair.

Stella shrugged, and the prison officers left the room. Henley took in her hardened features. It was hard to imagine that she was the same age as her ex-husband Nathan. Life had ravaged her prematurely. The custody photograph taken when she was first arrested for the neglect of her child had shown a woman with thick, curly brown hair that stopped at a slender neck. Her eyes had been bright and her face almost unlined. Her hair was now gray, and the few brown strands had dulled and lost the luster of youth. Her lips were pursed tight as though she was permanently worried, while her dry skin seemed almost too big for her face. She raised her watery, reddened and haunted eyes up at Henley.

"Do you know that he didn't even have the decency to tell me that my own son was dead?" Stella said with surprising strength in her voice. "I knew that something wasn't right. A mother knows these things. You can feel your child even when they're not with you."

"How did you find out about Kyle?" Henley asked.

"The prison governor told me. I think that she actually took pleasure in telling me. They all have the devil inside of them."

All the psychiatric reports concluded that Stella didn't have a borderline personality disorder or any other form of psychosis, just a strongly held religious belief.

"I'm extremely sorry about your son," said Henley.

"They didn't tell me how he died. Do you know who killed him?"

"No, we don't," Henley admitted. "That's why I'm here to talk to you."

"Me?" Stella put a bony finger to her chest. "I don't know anything. I have no idea why anyone would want to hurt my

Kyle. All I've ever wanted to do and tried to do is help my son. To heal him."

"There is a restraining order that stops you from having contact with Kyle."

"That wasn't Kyle. That was his dad. Kyle wanted to talk to me. I'm his mother."

"Look, Stella. I'm not here about you breaching the terms of the restraining order, and in light of what's happened, I'm sure that the CPS will be reviewing the decision to continue the prosecution."

"Do you have any idea how much time I've spent in prison? They continue to punish me when all I did was look after my son. To heal him."

"Stella," Henley said, trying to bring her back on track. "When was the last time you saw Kyle?"

Stella sniffed loudly and brushed her tears off her cheeks. "I knew that something was wrong. He had been well for a long time, and he came to see me when I was in prison. He was the one who campaigned for my appeal. He thought that I had been punished enough. He's very forgiving. Not like his dad. I had no help when I was released six months ago. I didn't know what to do or where to go. Kyle found a hostel for me. A hostel for women, and I stayed there for a little while."

"Where was this hostel?" Henley asked.

"It was in Woolwich. They were very nice there."

"Stella, forgive me if this sounds a bit blunt, but why would Kyle help you after everything that happened when he was a kid?"

"Because I'm his mum," Stella said as she started to cry.

"It just seems a bit at odds with what Nathan—"

"Nathan never understood me," Stella said as her voice grew shrill. "He never understood my bond with Kyle."

"Calm down, Stella. I have to ask these questions."

"I'm being punished for loving my son," said Stella. "Kyle just wanted to help me."

"OK, so Kyle wanted to help you and he got you into the hostel. How long were you there for?"

"Two, nearly three months. They helped me sort out my benefits and eventually I was given a flat."

"Who helped you specifically with your benefits?"

"The manager, Rebecca. She was very nice. I told her all about my son and what had happened. She understood that I'd never tried to hurt him."

"Did Rebecca ever talk about herself?" Henley asked.

"Yes, she did," said Stella. "She was lovely. She was a bit like Kyle."

"In what way was she like Kyle?"

Stella sighed and looked away. "She understood that Kyle's spirit had been taken over, just like hers had been."

"You spent a lot of time together?"

"Yes," Stella said with a smile. "She took me to church with her."

"Was this the Church of Annan the Prophet?"

"Yes," Stella said slowly. "Has something happened to Rebecca?"

"No, no," Henley said, trying to keep her voice steady. "Did you know anyone else in the church? Did you meet anyone? Become friends with anyone?"

"Not friends, but I spoke to people. I spoke to the pastor. He understood how important it was to heal the spirit and not to fall for this mental illness rubbish. It wasn't the church. The church has only ever wanted to help people."

"Is that what happened with Kyle when he was twelve? Did the church help you heal Kyle?"

Stella nodded. "But they didn't hurt him. I wouldn't let them do that."

"You tried to heal him instead? With Niall Graff?"

"Yes."

"How did you try to heal Kyle?"

"We prayed for him. I bathed him with holy water. I held him when he was...when he was angry."

"What was Kyle like when he was angry?"

"He would throw things and he would hit me, but that wasn't his fault."

"What did you do when Kyle hit you?"

"I would try to talk to him, but he wouldn't listen. Niall said that we needed to be stronger because the devil was too strong in him, but I never hurt him," Stella said between tears. "I sang to him and tried to hold his hands, but I didn't hurt him; but he was too strong, and Niall told me to leave."

Henley thought that her heart was going to break as Stella crumbled in front of her and she realized what had happened.

"You didn't hurt Kyle, did you, Stella? You weren't the one who beat him?" asked Henley.

"No. Niall told me that the devil would tempt me, and he told me to leave."

"You never hurt him?"

"I could never hurt my baby. When they arrested me and told me that Kyle's bones were broken...but I didn't."

"Stella, what I don't understand is why you pleaded guilty to hurting Kyle when it wasn't you?"

"Niall said that I had to, that God wanted it that way, so I pleaded guilty, but I didn't think that they would put me in prison."

Now, Henley understood why Kyle had remained close and tried to help his mum. He knew the truth.

"So, Kyle helped you when you came out of prison. Did Nathan know that you were seeing each other?"

"No. He would have tried to stop him. He only found out when I saw that Kyle had the devil inside of him again."

"How did you know that?"

"I know the signs. He was withdrawn and he would only answer the phone after I called him three times. Then he started hearing voices."

"What did you do?"

"I was worried about him. I knew what was happening, and then he stopped taking his medication."

"How did you know that he'd stopped?" Henley asked, surprised that Stella had managed to maintain such a close relationship with her son in spite of the fact that she'd nearly killed him. Henley wondered if it was true forgiveness that had led to their reconciliation or something else.

"He told me that he didn't think that he needed the medication and he'd got himself an idiotic girlfriend who thought that he could deal with his...issues...organically."

Henley could see that it pained her not to use the word devil. "What do you mean organically?"

"Natural methods. Homeopathic remedies. CBD and...cannabis," Stella whispered. "I don't know what she gave him to smoke, but it must have been mixed with something, it wasn't all natural, and he began to spiral. His girlfriend left and he came to me in a state. I didn't know what to do, so I called Rebecca but then I made the mistake in going to see his dad."

"OK, let's take this step by step. What did Rebecca say when you called her?"

"She said that I should bring him home back to my flat and that she would help me."

"And how long ago was this?"

Stella blew out her lips and started counting on her fingers. "About ten weeks ago?" Stella answered. "It was just before Christmas."

"That's great," Henley said, though she felt anything but great as her stomach knotted. She had spent nearly an hour with a woman who Henley believed was a victim, and couldn't think of any reason to doubt that Rebecca had been emotionally and physically abused. Rebecca had been manipulated by the people that she trusted, but as the pieces clicked into place, Henley realized that Rebecca had been the one in control. She had taken the opportunity to also manipulate Henley.

"So, what happened when you went to see Nathan?" Henley asked.

Stella bent her head as tears began to stream down her face. "He went mad. Absolutely crazy. Said that I was a murderer and that he was calling the police. I told him that Kyle needed our help. I tried to convince him that I wasn't going to hurt Kyle and that I just wanted to help him, but he pushed me off the doorstep and then a week later, the court sent me a copy of the restraining order. I couldn't see my son for Christmas. How cruel is that?"

"Did you speak to Rebecca again after you got the restraining order?"

"Yes, I told her what happened, and she told me not to worry."

"You weren't arrested until three weeks after the restraining order," said Henley. "You were complying. So why did you breach it?"

Stella took a deep breath. "Kyle called me. He said that his dad wanted to have him sectioned. There are moments when he was incredibly lucid, where you wouldn't think anything was wrong with him. He said that he was worried that he might hurt his little brother and sister. I didn't want him to go through that again. So, I told him that I would take him to a clinic."

"What clinic was this? It wasn't mentioned in the missing person's report," said Henley.

Stella nodded. "It's a private clinic in Forest Hill."

Henley felt as though a stone had dropped in her stomach as more pieces slotted in place. It had to be the same clinic where Charlie Jensen had been an outpatient, but she needed Stella to say it.

"What was the name of the clinic, Stella?"

"The Cooper Group Therapy Clinic."

"How did you find out about it, and wouldn't a private clinic be expensive?" Henley rubbed away at the throbbing pain in her temple.

"Rebecca told me about the clinic and they had a...scheme to help people and Kyle had some savings. All I did was help him."

"So, what did you do?"

"I went to Nathan's house in an Uber. I knew that he would be at work and Kyle let me in. I packed some clothes for Kyle. We were just getting into the cab when Kyle's stepmum, Elise, turned up. She wasn't supposed to be home. She must have called the police."

"So, this is six weeks ago, which is when Kyle was reported missing. Did you book him into the clinic?"

"No, I went home first. Rebecca told me to meet her there."

"Hold on, I'm confused," said Henley. "Why were you meeting Rebecca?"

"She's the one who told me about the clinic, but she thought that it would be better if she took him."

"Did you hear from Kyle again once he was booked into the clinic?"

Stella shook her head and began to cry. "No. The police turned up after they left, and they arrested me. I've been here ever since. I want to see my son. I just want to see him."

Henley didn't know how to respond to Stella's grief at losing her son and knowing that she may have been responsible for his death.

"Do you know who took him from me?" Stella asked.

"Not for sure," Henley admitted. "But I might be getting a bit closer to finding out. I'm not going to keep you much longer. I've just got one more question for you?"

"Don't worry yourself. You could stay for as long as you want. I mean, what else is waiting for me?"

"What happened to Niall Graff?"

A shadow crossed Stella's face. "What about him?"

"Well, he was never charged with the attempted murder of Kyle twelve years ago. I was wondering if you have had any contact with him after you were released from prison or even while you were serving your sentence."

Stella shook her head. "He didn't stand by me at all. He disappeared once they dropped the charges against him. He made me stand trial all by myself."

"So you've had no contact with him."

"No," Stella replied. "I don't know what happened to him. He always wanted to go further. He said the devil was strong and that he had to break the vessel that contained the evil."

Henley's stomach churned. She felt sick when she thought about the harm and intense pain that Stella had inadvertently caused her son, yet he still loved her. "And what did you want to do?" she asked.

"I wanted to save him. I just wanted my boy back."

68

"I don't understand. He's done nothing wrong. Let go of me," Tameka Sullivan screamed. DC Eastwood took hold of her arms and led her away from the living room where officers began their search.

"Mrs. Sullivan, you need to calm down," said DC Eastwood as a couple of officers made their way upstairs.

"Calm down? How on earth am I supposed to calm down when you just come into my house and make these ridiculous accusations against my husband?" Tameka said, sinking back against the staircase as another police officer entered the house. She pulled out her phone. "I'm not having this. I'm calling Derrick."

"Put the phone down," said Eastwood. "I've already warned you that if you contact your husband I will have no choice but to arrest you for obstructing a police officer in the execution of their duty and I really don't want to do that, Tameka. The last thing you want is for your kids to find out that their mum and dad are sitting in a police cell."

"You're making a mistake. I don't know who's been giving you dodgy information, but this is wrong," said Tameka, but she placed her phone back into her pocket.

Eastwood sighed. They had been searching the house for twenty-five minutes while Tameka had grown increasingly incensed. She had scrutinized every line of the search warrant, but there were no loopholes and lines to read between.

"This is down to her, isn't it? Serena is trying to get us back," Tameka said almost under her breath.

Eastwood was tempted to ask what she meant by that, but she knew the rules. It was better to keep quiet and save any questions for a recorded interview. Even if Tameka was to answer, Eastwood doubted very much that she would be signing her notebook to confirm that everything she said was true.

A sharp gust of wind swept through the hallway as the front door swung open and a police officer ran into the house.

"DC Eastwood, we need you to come outside. Derrick Sullivan has just pulled up and we've found something in the garage."

"Derrick's here?" Tameka made her way toward the opened door.

"No. You're staying right there," said Eastwood firmly. "Keep an eye on her for me. Don't let her leave this house," she said to the police officer who'd just entered.

"What the hell is going on?" said Derrick as Eastwood stepped outside the house and intercepted him.

"We have a warrant to search your property as we believe that there may be material evidence in relation to the murder investigation of Caleb Annan."

"Wha-What, I don't..." Derrick stuttered. "I didn't have anything to do with it."

"Word of advice," said Eastwood. "If I was you, I wouldn't say a word."

Eastwood was convinced that it was colder inside the garage than it was outside. A large, dented fridge freezer was in the corner next to cardboard boxes, children's bikes and a broken scooter.

"Someone broke in a few days ago," said Derrick. "The lock was broken when I took the—"

"I told you not to move," Eastwood said, inching herself around the blue Mini that had been parked inside.

"Over here," said PC Firth as he pulled aside a large cardboard box in order to give Eastwood room to join him. "They were stuffed behind the suitcase in the bin bag."

Eastwood pushed aside the black plastic and pulled out a navy tracksuit that was stiff with dried blood. As she lifted up the jumper, a pair of bloodstained latex gloves fell onto the ground. She picked them up and placed them into an evidence bag.

"There's something inside the trainers," said PC Firth. Eastwood picked up the pair of black Prada trainers. She could see smooth, rounded metal pushing against the shoe tongue.

"No," Derrick said as Eastwood pulled out the knife from the shoe and handed it to Firth. There was no mistaking the dried blood that was on the blade and a clear and visible fingerprint.

There was silence for a few seconds, as though the world had briefly stopped spinning. PC Firth placed the knife into an evidence bag.

"Oi, he's running," called DC Ward by the doorway, and began to give chase.

"Fuck," Eastwood said, banging her leg against the bumper of the Mini.

Derrick was quicker than he looked. He had already run across the road and was making his way up the street. Eastwood tried to ignore the sleet as she ran past DC Ward. Derrick tripped over a slab of broken pavement and fell heavily onto the icy ground.

"That was not clever. Not clever at all," said Eastwood. She pulled out her handcuffs and dropped to her knees.

"Ow. Stop it, ow!" Derrick screamed.

"Oh shit," Eastwood said as she took Derrick's arm. It was hanging at an odd and unnatural angle.

"I think it's broken."

"It seems that way, but Derrick Sullivan, I'm arresting you for the murder of Caleb Annan—" said Eastwood as DC Ward finally appeared at her side.

"No, no. I didn't... I don't..."

"You do not have to say anything. But it may harm your defense if you do not mention when questioned something which you later rely on in court. Anything you do say may be given in evidence."

"You've made a mistake," Derrick pleaded. He winced in pain as Eastwood and Ward helped him to his feet.

"That's what they all say," Eastwood replied.

"That was Eastwood," Henley said to Ramouter as she walked down the staircase of the Annans' home and put her phone away. "She's arrested Derrick Sullivan for murder."

"Did they find something in his house?" Ramouter asked. The last police car was pulling out of the driveway.

"Knife, bloodied gloves hidden in the garage, apparently. I'm trying to get hold of Anthony and have him submit an urgent request on forensics. By the way, did you ever get in touch with Sullivan's brother?"

"Yeah, I did. With everything that's been going on, it kept slipping my mind," Ramouter said remorsefully. "His brother, Omar, said that Derrick picked him up at 4:30 p.m., which is ninety minutes earlier than what Derrick told me. Omar said that they got to Terminal 5 at Heathrow just after 6 p.m., and that Derrick dropped him off and left."

"He didn't go into the terminal with him?" asked Henley.

"No, it was a straight drop-off and he left. Let's say we give Derrick a two-hour window to get home to Croydon. He would have been home by 8 p.m."

"And would have enough time to get to the church. We know that Caleb was still alive at 10 p.m., according to Uliana."

"Is Eastwood on her way to the station with Sullivan?"

"We're out of luck there. Derrick did a runner, fell and broke his arm. Eastie is at the hospital with him now, but on the positive side it gives us time to get the forensic results."

"Shame we didn't have much luck at Caleb's house," Ramouter said as they walked back to Henley's car. The Annans' home had been searched thoroughly but had produced nothing. "I just hope that Dalisay hasn't called her boss and told her that we're coming to search her office."

"Who knows. Dalisay is scared shitless of Serena. I wouldn't be surprised if she's already on the phone to her now."

"What about this Rebecca Keeler?" Ramouter asked, waiting for Henley to open the door.

"Still no sign of her," Henley said. Henley had called Pellacia as soon as she'd left the prison and told him about Rebecca being a possible suspect. "Uniform confirmed that Rebecca hasn't been at work since I saw her. They also checked her home address and there was no sign of her. We've got an alert out. The thing that's bothering me is the connection with Niall Graff. He has to be the same man who was with Stella Baxter and was responsible for nearly killing Kyle when he was twelve, and he has to be the same Niall that Rebecca's mum mentioned when I spoke to her. The problem is that if Niall was arrested with Stella, then his DNA and prints would be on the database, but there's nothing."

"If they are the same person, do you reckon that Rebecca started with a relationship with Niall after she was released from hospital?" asked Ramouter.

"She must have, and she spun us one lie after the other."

"Maybe it was something like Stockholm syndrome and she fell in love with her kidnapper."

"It's fucked up, whatever happened. I'm just thinking that Kyle wouldn't have died if he'd found a different refuge for his mum," said Henley.

"What about the clinic that Stella Baxter mentioned?" asked Ramouter. "The Cooper Group Therapy Clinic. Surely that's the missing link. We know that Jenson had some kind of loose association with it."

"And according to Stella Baxter, Rebecca had a contact at the clinic," said Henley. "We'd be idiots not to think that the clinic wasn't involved in some capacity."

"I can't believe it," Ramouter said as he got in the car and Henley started the engine.

"Bollocks, I never asked her how old her son was," Henley said. She hit the steering wheel with frustration.

"What do you mean?"

"Rebecca said that she had a little boy, and you know what it's like, when you've got kids. You always ask how old the kids are, share war stories, but I never asked her."

"But even if you didn't ask her, she would have told you. You remember what it's like when you've had a baby. You shove photographs of your kid to anyone who utters the word 'baby.' Were there any baby photos in her office? You've got photos of Emma on your desk, Stanford has photos of her on his desk, Joanna's got all of her grandkids on hers and Ethan is my screensaver."

"I don't remember seeing anything."

"There's a reason why Rebecca didn't show you a photo of her child. And that's because she's stolen Alyssa Hadlow's kid," said Ramouter.

"You have absolutely no right to be here," said Serena Annan as she stood at the doorway to her office, oblivious that a small crowd had gathered on the high street. Stanford was standing in front of her, holding a piece of paper up.

"For the fifteenth time, Mrs. Annan, this is a warrant signed by District Judge Walston to search your properties. Including this office," said Stanford. "Step aside."

"You cannot come in," shouted Serena.

"If you're going to be like that, I'm more than happy to ar-rest you for obstructing a police officer in the execution of their duty. In case you haven't noticed, I'm the officer, and you're obstructing me."

"I see that Stanford is being his usual charming self," said Henley and Ramouter as they pushed their way through the crowd.

"Why hasn't he arrested her yet?" said Ramouter.

"I want to be the one who does it," Henley admitted.

"Mrs. Annan," Stanford said gently as he held out the warrant, "I've already told you that we have a warrant. Now the last thing that I would want, if I was you, is to be causing a scene. We've already searched your house so you're just delaying the inevitable, really."

Henley could feel the sharpness of Serena's stare. "You need to move aside right now, Mrs. Annan, because I seriously have no issue with physically removing you from the premises."

"This is unbelievable. This is harassment. I'm the bloody widow, for crying out loud," Serena shouted, but she moved away from the office. "So, what am I supposed to do? Just sit here and watch you ransack my property?"

"That's exactly what you're going to do," said Henley, pulling on her gloves. "PC Bride is going to keep an eye on you while we search your office."

"You're just wasting your time. You should be looking for whoever killed my husband instead of harassing me. I've had enough of you. I'll be putting in another complaint to your bosses."

Half an hour into the search and Henley still had Serena's voice ringing in her ears. The fact that Caleb Annan had been a somewhat minor celebrity had placed undue pressure on the investigation. Henley couldn't understand how Serena could be so desperate to preserve her late husband's reputation even as he had continued to disrespect her in every conceivable way.

"Starting to think that this may be a waste of time," Ramouter said as Henley followed him downstairs into the basement. The room was filled with archive boxes, pieces of furniture, old tins of paint.

"You never know." Henley walked to the back of the room and pulled out a large box. She and Ramouter worked silently, pushing aside boxes of stationery, expensive fake plants covered with dust and office furniture that didn't fit the current decor.

"Henley," Ramouter called out. "Henley, I've found something."

Henley felt a muscle twinge in her back as she rose from her uncomfortable position on the floor.

Ramouter held up a mobile phone. "There's dried blood on it and it looks like some hairs are stuck on it," he said, carefully placing it into an evidence bag.

"That has to be Caleb's phone," said Henley. She took the evidence bag from Ramouter, pressed the power button on the side and waited to see if the black screen would come alive. Henley turned the phone around and showed Ramouter the photo of Caleb's two children on the home screen.

"I think that pretty much confirms it," said Ramouter.

"Where did you find it?" Henley asked.

"Stuffed in the back of this cabinet. There's something else there. I need to get this drawer out."

Henley moved out of the way as Ramouter pulled out the drawer that was rigidly stuck to the rusty runners. He yanked hard, then stumbled back, pulling the drawer out with him.

"Be careful," Henley said. Shreds of blue plastic were caught in the rusty runners. Ramouter pushed his fingers against the plastic bag.

"It feels like clothing and…there's something hard," he said as he cautiously opened the bag.

"Anthony said that the women's trainer was a size seven," said Henley.

Ramouter held up the trainer. The white rubber of the sole and the green badge on the side was covered in dried blood.

"I can't see the shoe size properly," he said, pushing back the tongue of the shoe. "FR, 41. What's that in UK sizes?"

"I think that's a seven. Here, drop the shoes in here." Henley held out a second evidence bag.

"Why would she stash all the clothing in here?" Ramouter asked, gently lifting out a pair of cashmere tracksuit bottoms. "I don't understand people. Why do they hide stuff? Burn the evidence, that's what I would do."

"I've never—" Henley didn't get a chance to finish her sentence as something small and hard fell from within the clothing, bounced against the cold metal of a filing cabinet and onto the floor.

Henley knew what it was before she even removed the pen from her pocket and used it to retrieve the piece of evidence that Serena Annan had specifically asked for after she'd identified her husband's body.

A thick, bloodstained band of 24-karat gold.

69

"So, we've got both Serena Annan and Derrick Sullivan in custody," said Pellacia. Henley, sitting at her desk, ignored the look that he was giving her; the look that said she should have had Serena Annan in custody a week ago.

"No," Henley said. "Annan has been booked in, but Sullivan is still at Croydon University Hospital. Eastwood is with him. He broke his arm."

"During the arrest? Tell me that Eastwood wasn't her...let's just say, robust self when she arrested him?"

"No, this was nothing to do with Eastwood. You've got to give her a bit more credit than that. He ran and fell."

Pellacia opened his mouth as if he was to apologize, but then changed his mind.

"Sullivan has got no one to blame but himself," said Henley.

"The fact that he ran is more than evidence that he was involved in the murder of Caleb Annan," said Pellacia. "The fact that he's waiting to be discharged means that you can delay starting the custody clock for him."

"That's just going to piss Serena Annan off even more," said Henley. "She's been screaming all sorts of accusations down at the station and her lawyer has already been making a nuisance of himself. Demanding that she's interviewed immediately."

"Who's her lawyer? Any of the regulars?"

Henley shook her head. "Nope."

"Is he legit? It wouldn't be the first time that a suspect's solicitor or legal rep turns out to be dodgier than they are, or isn't even qualified."

"I'm sure that he's legit. I don't think that Serena is the type of woman who's going to put her trust in any old Tom, Dick or Harry," said Henley. "What was his name again, Ramouter?"

"Edward Basser of Marlaj Solicitors," answered Ramouter. "I checked him out while Serena was being booked in. They're a private firm based on Chancery Lane, and from the look of their website they don't have a criminal department, they just seem to specialize in high-net-worth divorces and reputation and privacy."

"And what does Basser specialize in?" Henley asked.

"Give me a sec. Let me just click on his profile," said Ramouter. "Divorce. Wow, very big ones. Bloody hell, he represented Carl Simpkins in his divorce."

"Simpkins." Pellacia's eyes lit up. "The same Simpkins who plays for Chelsea?"

"The same one," answered Ramouter.

Henley looked thoughtful. "Why has Serena instructed a high-profile divorce lawyer to represent her?"

"Maybe he's a mate, or someone from the station recommended him," said Ramouter.

Henley shook her head. "The custody sergeant would have told her that she could have the duty solicitor. What if Serena Annan was going to divorce Caleb?"

"No one could blame her," said Ramouter. "From the looks of things, he was sleeping with half of the women in the church, and he may have been the father of Alyssa Hadlow's baby."

"As a pastor, I doubt very much that Caleb would want it known that his marriage was a failure, even if he was a serial adulterer. It's all very well and good that he was breaking one of the commandments," said Henley.

"Sixth commandment in the Catholic Bible," said Ramouter. "'Thou shall not commit adultery.' I did my research."

"And thou shall not kill is the seventh," said Henley. "What if Serena was divorcing Caleb and he wasn't having it?"

"People have killed for less," said Pellacia.

"I'll be back in a minute." Henley got up and made her way toward the door. "I need to speak to Ezra."

"What for?" Ramouter asked, frowning.

"The registration of a divorce is a matter of public record," said Henley. "But the lodging of the petition isn't."

"Ezra, are you busy?" asked Henley. "I need a favor."

"Does it involve me doing mission impossible stuff?" Ezra asked as he stood up and stretched. "Because if I'm honest, I'm not emotionally ready to be looking at any more videos of you-know-what."

"No, it's nothing like that," said Henley. "I need you to get some information for me."

"From where?"

"Ministry of Justice."

"The government? You want me to hack into the government's system?"

"You don't have to put it quite like that."

"I thought that you were going to ask me to do something hard," Ezra laughed as he picked up his bag of popcorn and sat back down. "What am I looking for?"

"I need you to see if Serena or Caleb Annan have lodged a petition for divorce."

"Not a problem," replied Ezra as he started to tap away.

It was almost 9 p.m. Her message to Rob was still unread and she was still waiting for Anthony to call her with the forensic results for the items seized from Sullivan's garage and Serena Annan's office basement. Henley looked across at Stanford who had his head down diligently going through paperwork. She wondered if Gene was giving him grief about the growing number of unsociable hours that he gave to their job. She picked at the prawn crackers left over from the large Chinese takeaway that Pellacia had ordered for them. He'd even gone downstairs and handed Ezra his food personally.

"Good, you're all still here," said Eastwood as she walked into the office, pulling off her hat and unbuttoning her coat. "It's freezing out there."

"What are you doing back here?" said Henley. "You should have gone straight home. There's no need for everyone to be here."

"It's fine. Ooh, Chinese. Is there anything left?"

"I've got some beef in black bean sauce and the house special rice left over if you want it?" Stanford shouted over.

Henley pushed two containers toward Eastwood. "Kung Po pork, noodles and some spring rolls. I couldn't finish it."

"You never finish it," said Eastwood as she picked up the containers from Henley's and Stanford's desks.

"How's Sullivan?" Henley asked, following Eastwood toward the kitchen area.

"He's a pain in the arse. Started complaining about police brutality even though I didn't lay a finger on him."

"I know that you didn't," Henley replied.

"Good thing I turned my bodycam on," said Eastwood as she put her now filled plate into the microwave. "Anyway, he's booked in at Lewisham police station. He's requested the duty solicitor and he's refusing to speak to his wife even though he's fully aware that she's called the station at least six times since he was arrested."

"Is he fit to be interviewed?"

"Not yet. He's on pretty strong painkillers. The station nurse gave him his tablets after we booked him. He was spark out, half an hour after we put him in the cell."

"Aw, bless him. He's had a hard day," Henley said sardonically.

"Haven't we all," said Eastwood as the microwave pinged. "I'm going to open up the CRIS report now and get everything ready for the interview tomorrow. His custody clock is going to run out at 8:21 p.m."

"Good work, Eastie," said Henley.

"Oi, Henley, get over here," Stanford said. He was standing up from his desk and holding up a small bundle of papers. "I think I've got a lead on Alyssa Hadlow's missing baby. I've been going through the bank accounts for Alyssa."

"I thought that we did all that," said Henley, leaning on his desk. "The only thing that she had coming in was her universal credit benefit and Personal Independent Payment."

"Yeah, that's another thing. The DWP clearly haven't got the memo that Hadlow is no longer with us and have still been paying her. There have been two deposits in the past ten days: £1433.34 in Universal Credit and £902 PIP. Cash has been withdrawn on eight different occasions since Tuesday 25 February. The account currently has a balance of £3.34 and the last withdrawal of £430 was made four days ago."

"Do you know the locations of the ATMs that were used?"

"Five withdrawals were from Jamaica Road, two from Surrey Quays overground station and one from HSBC on Powis Street, which is not far from the refuge where Rebecca works."

"Five on Jamaica Road," said Henley. "That's also just down the road from where Kyle Baxter's body was found. Whoever has been making the withdrawals has to be living nearby. So, the baby?"

"Right," said Stanford, "so, the neighbor two doors down dropped these into Deptford police. Apparently, the postman delivered the bank statements to his flat by mistake and he wasn't too keen on having a dead woman's post in his house, which is how we got these latest statements. There was one payment, a large one of £1350, that sent her into her overdraft, made to Serenity Nurture."

"When was that payment made and what is Serenity Nurture?"

"It was made on the eleventh of January, five and a half weeks before Hadlow's body was found. Serenity Nurture is a doula."

"What on earth is a doula?" asked Eastwood as she popped the last dumpling into her mouth.

"Someone who will support you through pregnancy and childbirth," explained Stanford. "Gene was looking for his sister, when she was having her twins; they're not medically trained or anything."

"So, Alyssa Hadlow made a payment for a doula. If she was in the depths of a psychosis, I'm surprised that she would have been able to organize the services of a doula."

"Unless someone else arranged it for her," said Eastwood. "It seems to me that anyone who was involved in her life was just manipulating her for their own needs."

"Who runs Serenity Nurture?" asked Henley.

"Someone called Victoria Reynolds. I've been on her website. She's based in Bromley. I've emailed her and left a message on her mobile. Let's hope that she gets back to us and hopefully find that baby."

"Do you think that this can be it?" asked Eastwood. "That we could actually find Hadlow's baby?"

"I don't know." Henley stood up and rubbed away at the ache in her shoulders. "But what I don't get is why this Victoria Reynolds hasn't contacted the police, if she was involved in the birth of Hadlow's baby. We've posted those photos everywhere and it's been all over the news. I just don't get it."

"Stop," said Stanford as he got up and placed his hands on Henley's shoulders. "Let's take it step by step."

"I just don't want to be wasting time, chasing ghosts."

"You're not wasting any time and however this lead pans out, we will find Alyssa Hadlow's baby," said Stanford.

70

Henley squinted at her mobile phone. She felt as though she'd just placed her head on the pillow.

"Anthony? It's five thirty in the morning. On a Sunday," she whispered.

"And you know that I wouldn't wake you up at such an ungodly hour if it wasn't worth it," Anthony replied. "I need you to sit up and pay attention. I've got the forensic results for the evidence that was seized from Derrick Sullivan and Serena Annan. Caleb Annan's blood is all over everything that was seized. Serena Annan's DNA is inside the latex gloves that were found in Sullivan's garage and her hairs were found on the clothing."

"What about the knife that was found? There was a fingerprint."

"Fingerprint belongs to Derrick Sullivan."

"Serena's prints aren't on the knife?"

"Nope. Don't get me wrong. You can still leave fingerprint impressions through latex gloves and it's possible that Serena did leave her prints behind, but the only print I found belonged to Sullivan. I'm concluding that Sullivan smeared her prints off the handle when he took the knife from her. You saw the scene? There was a lot of blood, but a few strands of Serena's hair were stuck on the knife. Anyway, you've got the knife, the DNA match, bits of her hair and the footprints left on the scene match both pairs of shoes. You would have a full house if you had an eyewitness."

"If I can't get a full house then I need the knife expert to take a look at it. I just want to make sure that I've got all bases covered." Henley shifted as Rob turned and placed a heavy arm across her chest. She pushed it off her and got out of bed. "Where are you now?"

"I'm on my way to a murder-suicide in Kentish Town. Three bodies. I've got everything ready for you. Samuel will drop it off for you when you're ready." Anthony let out a long sigh.

"Is that it? It doesn't sound as though that's it," said Henley.

"No, it's not. I've got a match for one of the DNA samples taken from Jensen, Whittaker and Hadlow."

"I thought that you said that there was nothing on the DNA database," said Henley.

"There wasn't anything on the database and that's because, four months ago, the Home Office, in their wisdom, accidentally deleted 150,000 fingerprints, arrest records and DNA," explained Anthony. "That's why I couldn't get a match and DI Clarke didn't get a match when he opened the murder case for Jensen."

"So, what exactly are you telling me?" asked Henley.

"Ezra says nothing is ever really deleted, so I asked him to help me out and he somehow, don't ask me how, managed to retrieve the full arrest record, fingerprints and DNA for Niall Owen Graff."

Henley ended the call, went downstairs to the kitchen and picked up her bag, dumping its contents onto the table. She pulled out the contact details for the lawyers who were representing Serena Annan and Derrick Sullivan. She left the same message for both as she waited for the kettle to boil.

"We're ready to interview. Attend Lewisham police station at 9 a.m."

★ ★ ★

Henley examined the evidence bag. The knife was a large silver kitchen knife. The blade was thick and covered in dried blood and flecks of what looked to be dried skin. The sharp point of the knife was missing and had left jagged impressions on the plastic. They had gone back to Serena Annan's and had taken photographs of her kitchen, including the magnetic knife rack on the wall. Henley had done her research while she'd drunk her coffee and eaten her sausage sandwich. The set was valued at just under a grand, each knife made from high carbon stain-free steel. Lightweight for agile handling. This was the missing knife from the seven-piece set in Serena's kitchen.

"So, who are we going to interview first?" said Ramouter dropping a slim folder of witness statements and photographs onto the table.

"Tactically, I think that we should go with Sullivan first," said Henley as she put the knife back in the evidence box. "He's the runner and it looks to me that he's more likely to break."

"It looks like Sullivan asked for the duty solicitor. He's never been in trouble before," said Ramouter. "You would have thought that he'd been running the 'Why do I need a lawyer, I haven't done anything wrong' line. It just makes me think that even though he ran, he may be a little bit more clued up than we think."

"Why did he run and keep the bloodied knife in his garage if he was that clued up?" said Henley.

"Maybe he was going to use it to blackmail Serena?"

"Why would he want to do that if they were working together?"

"I dunno," said Ramouter as he raised his hands in resignation. "I also spoke to Milo at the design agency who confirmed that he broke up a fight between Derrick and Caleb. Maybe Derrick and Serena were involved? I mean romantically. Not just in some 'help me kill my husband' sort of way?"

"I honestly have no idea," said Henley. Her phone began to

ring. "It's Ezra." She answered the call, opened up her notebook and scribbled down the information that Ezra gave her before hanging up.

"We really don't pay him enough," said Henley. "He should be working for MI6 or something."

"I've learned never to ask him how he does his thing, but just to thank him with fast food and green juice," said Ramouter.

"It's the best way. So, it turns out that Serena lodged an application for divorce on the seventeenth of January this year."

"So, she definitely wanted to end the marriage. Well, it's not as if she would have to look that hard to find evidence of Caleb committing adultery."

"That's also the same date that Caleb received the photographs of baby Hadlow."

"Do you think that Serena knew about the baby?" asked Ramouter.

"Possibly, but the strange thing is that according to Ezra, the reason that she gave for the breakdown of the marriage was unreasonable behavior."

"Adultery is being unreasonable."

"Of course it is, but with adultery she would've had to name every single woman that Caleb slept with."

"I don't think that there would be enough room on the application form," said Ramouter.

"Maybe she didn't want to put the other women through the embarrassment. I mean, Caleb leaving his dirty boxer shorts on the bathroom floor or not taking the bins out could be unreasonable behavior, too. Anyway, on the thirteenth of February, Caleb served acknowledgment of service and refused to agree to the divorce, and then he's murdered a few days later."

"When was Serena notified that Caleb didn't want the divorce?"

"Almost immediately. Ezra said that the notification was emailed to Serena's lawyer and to her on the fourteenth of February."

"That was a nice Valentine's present. He really was a piece of shit. I'm not surprised that she killed him," Ramouter said, shaking his head.

"Well, let's see if we can get her to admit it."

Serena Annan and her solicitor, Edward Basser, were both sitting rigidly upright as though they were concerned that they would catch something from the hard plastic bench that they were perched on.

"This interview is going to be both audio and video recorded," said Henley as she waited for the touchscreen monitor to get over its mini breakdown before she could continue tapping in her details.

Edward Basser brushed away at something invisible under his eye. Henley didn't miss that he'd also wiped away a small amount of fake tan that hadn't had time to set.

"This is an absolute waste of my time," said Serena as she folded her arms. "I've already instructed my solicitor to put in a formal complaint of harassment against you personally."

"That's entirely up to you," Henley replied. Basser leaned toward Serena and whispered something into her ear. He then laid his hand on Serena's arm, and Henley had to wonder where he had placed his left hand, which had disappeared under the table. "DC Ramouter is going to make the introductions and repeat the caution to you."

"Do you understand?" Ramouter asked, once he'd finished his small but necessary task.

"Of course she understands," said Mr. Basser. "Let's not waste time on theatrics."

"I need to have confirmation from Mrs. Annan, not from you," said Ramouter.

"I understand," Serena said with a voice full of annoyance.

"Serena Annan, you were arrested yesterday afternoon at 4:57 p.m. for the murder of your—"

"I. Did. Not. Kill. My. Husband."

"—of your husband, Caleb Annan, on Monday seventeenth of February," Henley finished. She picked up the evidence bag containing the knife and placed it on the table. "Well, all the evidence seems to suggest that you did, and that Derrick Sullivan, the husband of Tameka Sullivan, a woman that your husband sexually assaulted, helped you."

"My husband never touched Tameka. That woman is a liar."

Henley hid her surprise. If she'd been sitting on the opposite side of the table being paid privately to represent Serena Annan, she would have advised Serena to keep her mouth firmly shut.

"We've spoken previously about your husband's affairs," Henley stated. "At the last count, your—"

"They were not affairs," Serena interrupted.

"At the last count, your husband had had sexual relationships with eleven other women."

"They were not relationships either."

"Mrs. Annan, I'm not going to sit here and argue with you about the semantics of what your husband was doing, but you were aware that he'd been sleeping with these women and that he'd allegedly raped one of them."

"I don't know anything about a rape allegation. I would never have...but I knew about the women."

"But that's not quite correct, is it?" said Henley as she pulled out a sheet of paper from her file. "This is a statement from Raina Davison where she confirms that you called her from your husband's phone and threatened her."

"That's not true."

"You warned her off your husband and threatened to destroy her business."

"Why the hell would I threaten to destroy her cheap flower shop?"

"So, you do know her?"

"Only because she supplied flowers to the church for a while, but my husband didn't rape her, and I didn't threaten her."

"Did you ever challenge your husband about these women?"

"Of course I did. Every week he would stand up in the pulpit and preach and I would sit on the side and watch those women in the congregation. They had no shame, no respect for themselves. They even had the cheek to try and shake my hand in the end."

"Did you ever confront these women?"

"No. I told you before that I wouldn't lower myself."

"But you did confront your husband?"

"Of course."

"And how did he respond?"

Serena laughed and shook her head. "The first time he denied it, but when it came to the third and fourth woman, he didn't bother to hide it. He found and reinterpreted some Old Testament scripture to justify his behavior. He said that King Solomon had seven hundred wives, princesses and three hundred concubines. I told him that he is Caleb Annan; a man from southeast London with a criminal record, and not a bloody king."

Henley could feel the vibration of Ramouter next to her as he tried not to laugh.

"You thought that he'd stopped sleeping around?" said Henley.

"Yes, he'd stopped his behavior."

"Until you discovered the sex videos on his laptop?" said Henley.

Serena's eyes widened as she turned and looked at her solicitor. She pursed her lips together and brushed her hair from her eyes.

"You discovered the videos four weeks ago," said Henley.

"How do you know that?"

"These are screenshots taken from Caleb Annan's mobile phone. The same phone that was found in the basement of your office in Blackheath." Ramouter opened his folder and laid out five sheets of paper.

"I told my solicitor that I have no idea how Caleb's phone got there," said Serena with unmistakable panic in her voice.

"These are copies of text messages that you sent to your husband the same day that you filed for divorce."

"Those messages weren't provided to me in disclosure," said Basser as Serena hungrily pulled the sheets of paper toward her.

"We provided you with written disclosure," said Ramouter. "Serena, as you can see, you sent a message to your husband telling him that you had the video of him and Nicole Fleming."

"You can't prove that I sent that message."

"We checked and can prove that all of those messages were sent from your phone to your husband. 'How dare you? You are a disgusting pig. I've seen the videos, all of them.' That's the message that you sent to Caleb. But he didn't reply."

"I don't remember."

"'This marriage is over.' He didn't reply to that message either. You then sent him a video of his laptop and of the film. How did you get into his laptop?"

"I didn't go into his laptop."

"You then sent him another message which said, 'Whose child is this?'"

Serena said nothing as Ramouter took out photographs of baby Hadlow and placed them in front of her.

"Are these the photographs that you saw on your husband's email account?" he asked.

"I've never seen those before." Serena pushed the photographs back.

"How did you feel when you saw a photograph of your husband with another woman?" Henley asked, knowing that each word stung.

"You have no idea what you're talking about."

"You then sent Caleb a message that you were seeing a lawyer and that you wanted him out of the house," said Henley. "Caleb then replied that it was his house."

Serena didn't answer.

"You were angry that your husband betrayed you, which is perfectly understandable," said Henley.

"I'm not answering any more of your questions," said Serena.

"Well, that's tough, because I'm going to keep asking you questions," said Henley. "The day after you received the acknowledgment of service that confirmed that Caleb Annan wouldn't give you the divorce that you wanted, you sent another message. 'You are a piece of shit. I will not let you do this to me. You're dead.' You kept your word, didn't you?"

Serena continued to silently stare at her.

Henley laid out a series of A4-sized color photographs of the murder scene. There was no reaction from Serena. No look of sorrow or horror or shock. Just an unnatural calmness emanating from her as she looked down at the photographs.

"Those forty-eight injuries were caused by this knife which is part of a set that you own."

"I didn't kill my husband."

"This knife has your husband's blood and strands of your hair were stuck in the blood."

"That's impossible. I don't do any of the cooking, so there is no way that my...my hair or anything else would have been on that knife."

"We recovered fingerprints," said Henley. "Prints that belong to Derrick Sullivan."

"Well that proves that I never touched that knife."

"And we also found a pair of latex gloves covered in your husband's blood and your DNA was found inside those gloves."

"Which means," said Ramouter, "that this was a premeditated murder. You planned to kill your husband and you wore the gloves because you didn't want to leave any fingerprints behind."

"I never touched that knife and I already told you that I was home with the children when Caleb was killed."

"Serena, Serena," said Henley. "This entire process would be better for you if you just told the truth about what happened on Sunday the sixteenth of February. There's absolutely no point sitting here and treating DC Ramouter and me like a couple of idiots."

"Well, you're not giving me much of a choice. I told you that I never left the house after my family and I returned home from church. Caleb left and he didn't come home that night. I didn't think anything of it because, as you already know, he was sleeping with every dog with a tail."

"And you had already filed for divorce."

"And he texted me in the morning. You saw the text on my phone."

"A text message that you obviously sent yourself as it would be physically impossible for a dead man to text his wife," said Ramouter.

"Let's talk about the lie," said Henley.

"I have never lied."

"That's not true. I've got at least ten lies right here in my notes," said Henley. "But I want to ask you about one particular lie. Uliana Piontek said that she saw you at the church on Sunday night between 10:10 p.m. and 10:14 p.m. Is it true that you handed her back her mobile phone?"

Edward Basser didn't hide his surprise when his pen stopped in midair, and he turned his head toward Serena. Not for the first time, Henley wondered what the actual point of Edward Basser was to this interview, as he certainly wasn't doing what he was being paid for.

Serena didn't reply.

"You removed the knife from your kitchen, and you left your house probably around 9:50 p.m. On a good day it's a ten minute drive from your house to the church but there were road works and diversions on Blackheath Road. At 9:58 p.m. your car stops at the traffic lights on the Greenwich South Street and Lewisham Road junction. Here's a still photograph taken from the CCTV footage."

Henley heard Serena take a sharp inhale of her breath as she placed the photograph in front of Serena.

"This is another photograph of your car entering the church car park at 10:02 p.m."

"No, that's not me. No. This is a mistake," Serena said as she pushed the photographs away.

"How can it be a mistake? You can clearly see the personalized number plates. SER 1AN. Doesn't that belong to you?"

"It does but that wasn't me. I wasn't there."

"You were in the middle of a full blown argument with your husband by the time Uliana arrived," said Henley. "You went there with the express intention of killing him."

"I did not kill him."

"Uliana saw you arguing with him, and you told Uliana to leave."

"And I left straight after and went home."

"I thought that you said that you never left the house after you came home with the children?"

There was silence as Serena looked at her lawyer in a panic.

"She's confusing me, Edward," said Serena. "Stop her. That's not what I meant."

"Maybe you should rephrase the question," Edward suggested.

"Fine," said Henley. "Serena. You left your house at 9:50 p.m. and you arrived at the church and argued with your husband, didn't you?"

"No," said Serena.

"Uliana saw you and you gave her back her phone and told her to leave."

"That didn't happen."

"You then left the church but you then came back an hour later after you'd made arrangements with Derrick Sullivan to meet you back there."

"That didn't happen."

"You then stabbed Caleb in his office. We found drops of blood on his desk and you pursued him into the church where you stabbed him another forty-seven times."

"That's not true," Serena shouted.

"And at some point Derrick Sullivan joined you."

"I had absolutely nothing to do with Derrick Sullivan. We haven't spoken since he and his wife left the church."

"That's not correct," said Henley. "Mobile phones are amazing things. People think that just because they hit delete then that's it. Or they think the other person might delete their messages also."

Ramouter pulled out more sheets of paper. "These are taken from Derrick Sullivan's phone. A series of texts that you sent him on Sunday evening, both before you arrived at the church and once you got home."

"What are you talking about? I didn't send any messages. Why would I?"

"'I'm leaving now. Meet me at the church.' That was the first message that you sent him," said Ramouter. "Then you sent another message: 'Where are you?' Then—"

"I didn't send those messages," Serena said hysterically. "Edward. They can't do this. What are they talking about? I didn't send any messages."

"And then the final message was 'Thank you,' which you sent to Derrick's phone at 12:12 a.m."

"I didn't send any messages. I would have been asleep at the time. I was on strong painkillers. I was on tramadol and codeine. I suffer from meralgia paresthetica, it's a compressed nerve in my left leg. I had a flare-up that evening. I was in immense and unbearable pain. I took codeine and I also drank a couple of glasses of red wine. I just wanted the pain to stop. I was passed out once I got ho—"

Serena put a hand to her mouth and leaned back.

"Once you got home. Is that what you were going to say, Serena?" Henley asked. "'I was passed out once I got home.'"

"I never said that," said Serena.

"What time did you get home after you'd stabbed your husband forty-eight times?"

"Are you going to let her talk to me like that?" Serena shouted at Basser. "She can't talk to me like this. She's making all of these accusations and you're doing absolutely nothing about it, Edward. What use are you?"

"You stabbed Caleb, and I'll be honest, I'm not sure if Derrick tried to help you or stop you, but either way, I'm sure that he'll happily tell us," said Henley.

"He didn't help me do anything because I wasn't there. I mean…yes, I was, but I left… I don't know what Derrick Sullivan was doing there, but I did not kill my husband."

"These are white Gucci trainers. Size seven. If you look at the red and green stripes, on the side of the trainers, you can see that they've been monogrammed with your initials, SA, and they're covered in your husband's blood," Henley said. She turned the exhibit over so that the bloodstained soles were visible. "These were found in the basement of your office, in the same bag as your husband's ring."

"I don't know how they got there, and I've only worn them twice. They're practically new."

"Well, it would be hard to wear them again when they're covered in your husband's blood, and your DNA was found on the laces, the tongue and inside the trainers," said Ramouter. "You admit that these trainers belong to you?"

"Yes, they do."

"And you wore them on the night that you killed your husband?"

"No, I did not. I wasn't wearing them that weekend. I couldn't find them. I have no idea how that blood got there and I have no idea how they got into my office. I did not kill my husband."

"The prints from these trainers match the bloody footprints that were found around Caleb's body and also on Caleb's back."

"What do you mean, on his back?"

"You know exactly what I mean, Serena," said Henley. "Why don't you tell us how it felt when you literally stabbed Caleb in the back and that moment when you placed your foot on his body and pulled the knife out."

For the first time since Henley had started the interview, Serena looked scared.

"Caleb had been embarrassing you for years," Henley said slowly. "He insulted you, made a mockery of your marriage and made you look like a hypocrite. It must have burned. To feel that Caleb, your husband, the man that you had chosen to commit to, had stabbed *you* in the back."

"You have no idea what you're talking about," said Serena. "You're sitting here clutching at straws and accusing me of committing the most heinous act. You know nothing about my marriage. You know nothing about me."

"I know that you're a murderer and that Derrick Sullivan was there when you stabbed your husband." Henley picked up the last small evidence bag and placed it on the table. "When you were at Greenwich mortuary, you specifically asked for Caleb's wedding ring, chain and watch."

There was a dull thud as the thick band of gold landed on the table.

"The watch and chain were on your husband's body," said Henley. "But we found the ring hidden in your office. I'm guessing that you thought that it would distract us from looking at you if you asked about the ring at the start of the investigation."

"Someone must have planted that ring in my office. I know nothing about it," said Serena.

"We found fragments of his skin stuck to the blood. He was most likely still alive, taking his last breath, when you ripped the ring off his finger. How did it make you feel to do that?"

Serena looked at Basser who had been impassively making notes, barely aware of the change in the atmosphere.

"I'm sacking you," Serena said to Edward.

"Excuse me?" Edward looked startled. "Serena. Why don't we briefly stop the interview and have a consultation?"

"There's nothing to discuss. They said that I had a right to legal advice, but it doesn't mean that I have to take it, especially when all you're doing is sitting here and letting this woman make these scandalous allegations against me."

"Inspector, could we stop the interview, so that I could have a further consultation?" said Edward.

"We're stopping the interview but we're not having another consultation," said Serena. "This is over. I've had enough of this."

"We'll suspend the interview and resume once you've completed your consultation with your solicitor," said Henley.

"You're not suspending anything," said Serena as she stood up and walked up to the corner of the room where the black dome of the camera that was recording the interview was located. "This interview is finished. We are done. You can put me back in my cell until you've either charged me or released me."

"Jesus Christ," Henley muttered under her breath as Ramouter collected the evidence together.

"Serena. Let's—" Edward said.

"I have nothing more to say to you," Serena said as she returned to her seat. "You're no longer representing me. I need someone who knows what they're doing."

Henley didn't say anything more. Ramouter terminated the interview and she completed the paperwork. She watched as Serena signed the written notice and handed it back to her.

"Before I return you to your cell, are you sure that you no longer want Mr. Basser to represent you?" Henley asked Serena as she stood up and opened the interview door.

"I'm done with him."

"Fine. We've got time. Your custody clock doesn't run out for ages yet and we can always ask the superintendent to extend it."

"There'll be absolutely no point," Serena replied as she followed Henley along the corridor and back to the custody area. "I've finished talking to you."

"Is it OK to return Serena Annan to cell fifteen?" Henley asked the custody sergeant as she reached the desk.

The custody sergeant raised his eyes toward the bank of monitors that showed the cells and then checked the custody board. "Yeah, it's fine. Chuck her back in there." He handed Henley the keys.

"Ramouter. Why don't you show Mr. Basser out and I'll meet you upstairs," said Henley.

"I'll see you in a bit," Ramouter said. He indicated for Basser to follow him and Henley walked away with Serena.

"Do you want anything to eat or drink?" Henley asked as she opened the cell door and Serena stepped in. "It's going to be a while."

"I don't want anything from you people," Serena answered.

Henley sighed. "I'll get someone to bring you in a cup of tea and some biscuits."

"Whatever."

Henley slammed the cell door shut and locked it. She leaned back and closed her eyes. She had to do this all over again with Derrick Sullivan. She hoped that he wouldn't be as difficult as Serena. She opened the wicket in the door and peered through the small opening.

"You're not helping yourself," said Henley.

"You can't talk to me like that," said Serena.

"This isn't an interview. This is advice. You do realize that I'm going to charge you with the murder of your husband? You're going to be taken away from your children, Serena. You should cooperate."

Henley automatically stepped back as Serena made her way to the cell door.

"Cooperate? I told you that I didn't kill my husband, but you've been determined to pin this on me since day one. What's wrong with you? Is your life so miserable that you want to destroy someone like me?"

"This isn't about destroying you."

"I don't know how you sleep at night," said Serena. "Knowing that you're doing this to another black woman. You're a fucking embarrassment to yourself and your family. You should be ashamed of yourself."

71

"I don't like the look on your faces," said Pellacia as both Henley and Ramouter wearily took a seat in his cramped office. The smell of Pellacia's takeaway lunch hit her nostrils. She had been feeling nauseous all morning. It wasn't the first time that the stresses of a demanding investigation had manifested themselves physically. She'd lost count of the number of times she'd found herself doubled over with cramps in the middle of the night as an investigation hit its peak, a leftover symptom of her PTSD.

"Derrick Sullivan gave a no-comment interview," said Henley as the wave of nausea passed. She sat up straighter in her chair. "I wasn't in the least bit surprised though; I would have kept my mouth shut too. He struck gold when he landed Miles Kelly as his duty solicitor."

"He got Miles?" Pellacia let out a low whistle.

Miles Kelly was on the opposite end of the spectrum from Edward Basser. He had been specializing in criminal law for forty years and had represented some of the most notorious criminals ever to grace the streets of England and Wales. Henley had often told herself that if she'd ever found herself in the unfortunate position of being charged with any criminal offense, she would call Miles Kelly.

"So, he didn't say a word?" asked Pellacia.

"Not one. He did look like he was going to burst into tears at any minute though," said Ramouter. "I don't think that he'll last a week in prison, but we've got enough for a charge of murder."

"What about the wife?" asked Pellacia. "Serena Annan."

"I was very surprised that she talked," said Henley. "I don't know what she and her useless solicitor were thinking. I could understand it if she'd had a defense to put forward, but she's got nothing."

"I would have at least chucked in a prepared statement and then kept my mouth shut," said Ramouter.

"She kept saying that she didn't kill her husband, but the evidence says that she killed him."

"Is everything with the CPS? I don't want their lawyers calling me and complaining that they're missing a statement."

"There's nothing missing." Henley raised her head and checked the clock. It had just gone 2 p.m. "There's six hours and fifteen minutes left on the custody clock for Sullivan, and another two for Annan. I don't want to be running down the superintendent for an extension of their detention, but I might have to if the CPS don't get a move on. I want both of them charged and in court in the morning. Are you going to tell Laura Halifax that we're charging Serena? It will probably be a shock for her."

"Serena Annan has already instructed another solicitor," Pellacia said. He ignored the question about Laura. He turned away from Henley and spun his computer monitor around. "Her lawyer has already been making noises while you've been sorting out the file for the CPS."

Henley leaned forward as she watched the news clip that showed the familiar entrance of Lewisham police station. A woman appeared on the front steps with a gaggle of reporters in front of her.

"Serena Annan's new lawyer," said Pellacia. "And she's having a whale of a time slagging off your investigation, and I quote, 'The persecution of a woman committed to the community and a victim of the coercive and manipulative behavior of her husband who will be fighting this miscarriage of justice.' It's a bit dramatic for my taste, but she's getting attention."

"Serena Annan murdered her husband," said Henley. "I think that she's looking in the wrong direction if she's talking about a miscarriage of justice."

"So that's Annan sorted, where are we with the exorcism cases?"

"Ramouter and I are heading to Lewisham hospital to speak to Brandon," said Henley. "And I've split Eastwood and Stanford up. Stanford should be on his way to meet with this doula and Eastwood is tracking down Niall Graff. We, well actually not we, Ezra did a search and Graff is a consultant at the Cooper Group Therapy Clinic."

"Isn't this the same clinic where Jensen was an outpatient?" asked Pellacia.

"And it's the same clinic where Kyle Baxter was supposed to have been admitted," Henley confirmed.

"And Rebecca Keeler?"

"Still no sign of her," said Ramouter. "If she's as unhinged as Mark suggested in his profile, then I'm worried to think what she would do about the Hadlow baby if she has him or her."

"I honestly had no idea that Alyssa had died. I've been rushed off my feet these past few weeks," said Victoria as she placed the tray containing two cups of tea carefully onto the glass table. "Sorry, I'm out of biscuits. My husband is on a no sugar thing at the moment, and I ate the last custard cream. I've got these rice cracker things but to be honest they're awful."

"Don't worry about the biscuits," Stanford said as he gratefully reached for her tea. "So, when did you last see Alyssa?"

Victoria sat down. "It must have been three days after she had the baby."

"Was it a boy or a girl?"

"A little boy," Victoria answered hesitantly. "How come you don't know this? What happened to him?"

"That's what we're trying to find out. When did she have the baby?"

"He would be almost seven weeks now. He was six pounds eight ounces when he was born. Perfectly healthy. He was a beautiful little boy. I still can't believe that Alyssa is dead. I thought that it was a mistake until I went online and saw it for myself."

"Alyssa never registered the baby's birth," said Stanford. "We've also checked the NHS database and there's no record of her admittance to an NHS, or a private, hospital, for that matter."

"She didn't have the baby in a hospital," said Victoria. "She had a home birth. I've been a midwife for twenty-eight years and if I thought for a second that Alyssa or the baby would be in any distress or that the birth was problematic, I would have made sure that she was in the hospital."

"Were you aware that Alyssa had mental health problems?"

"That was one of the reasons why she wanted me as her doula. I have a niche practice in looking after women with mental health problems. Some of my clients are repeats who have developed post-natal depression. Alyssa came to me when she was about six months pregnant. She'd just come through a depressive episode, and she was concerned."

"Did she say anything about the father?"

Victoria shook her head. "No, and I didn't ask, and she didn't say. I learned a long time ago that there are some things that you don't ask questions about, and you don't make assumptions."

"How many times did you see Alyssa?"

"We had three appointments before the birth and then I was there for the birth, of course, and then one visit three days after. I would have seen her a lot sooner but one of my clients went into labor early."

"And how was she?"

"She was fine. Obviously tired and a bit overwhelmed. She was concerned about taking her medication while she was breastfeeding and how she would manage once she got home."

"Did you know if she was taking her medication?"

"She was inconsistent—there were some days when she took it and days when she wouldn't. I suspect that she'd stopped taking her medication completely a week or two before her due date."

"Wouldn't that have been dangerous for her mentally, to stop and start like that?" asked Stanford.

"In my opinion, yes. There needs to be special care when adjusting the dosage. It can be done but ideally with the help of a doctor."

Stanford put his half-drunk cup of tea down and pulled out his notebook. "What did you mean when you said 'once she got home'? I thought that you said that Alyssa had a home birth?"

"She did, but it wasn't at *her* home."

"She didn't have the baby at her flat in Tanner's Hill in Deptford?"

"No. She had the baby at her friend's house. I went to her flat for the first two appointments but the third and the actual birth were at her friend's home."

"She didn't have the baby at her flat?" Stanford asked again, just to make sure.

"She went back after the birth as I went there for my last visit. She had everything set up for the baby. She was having trouble breastfeeding, so I taught her how to use the breast pump and that was the last time I saw her."

"Do you have a name and address for her friend?"

"Yes. Just give me a minute. They're in my office. Actually, why don't you come with me?"

Stanford finished his tea and followed Victoria into a converted utility room at the end of the kitchen.

"I call it the office. My kids call it the dungeon. But honestly, anywhere where I can get some peace is a blessing," said Victoria as she picked up a lever arch file from the shelf. Stanford looked around while Victoria flicked through the file. The large noticeboard on the wall was filled with school reminders, prenatal classes information and photographs of women with their babies. Stanford scanned the board for a photograph of Alyssa.

"Here we go," Victoria said. She unclipped the folder and took out a sheet of paper. "This is her friend's address. It's in Welling, but I would be surprised if she was still there. I remember that she'd just had an offer accepted on a flat. I'll make a copy for you."

Stanford grew angrier as he tried to sort through the confusion in his head. Except for being inconsistent with her medication, Alyssa had been doing all the right things while she was waiting for her baby to arrive, but someone—and Stanford had a good idea who that person was—had taken advantage of her when she was at her most vulnerable.

"What was her friend's name?" asked Stanford as Victoria waited for the small photocopier to warm up.

"Oh God, I can't remember. I only met her on the day of the birth. She was at work the other day, but I think it was Rachael or Rebecca, I can't quite remember."

"Can you describe this woman?"

"She was white with stunning green eyes. And her hair was bright red. I remembered thinking that she must have dyed it because it didn't look natural to me."

Rebecca Keeler, Stanford said to himself as he recalled the description of the woman that Henley had met.

"Thanks for this," he said as he took the sheet of paper. "Was there anything that concerned you about Alyssa the last time that you saw her?"

"No. The baby was only three days old, and I had no concerns about him. She knew what she had to do about sorting out the checks for him, and registration, and she was taking her medication. She was fine. I just hope that you find the baby."

"How many babies have you delivered?" asked Stanford.

"God, I've lost count. A lot more in the last four years or so. Doulas seem to be a trend at the moment. Not that I'm complaining. It pays the bills. Have you got children?"

"Not yet. Hopefully soon," said Stanford. "I've got a couple of nieces, nephews and my goddaughter, Emma. She's three. Love her like she's my own."

"They're either an absolute delight or a complete nightmare at that age. I really hope that you find him."

"Me too. Do you know what she called him? We've just been calling him baby Hadlow, and he deserves a lot more than that."

"She named him Isaac."

72

Eastwood read the brass plaque above the intercom: Cooper Group Therapy Clinic. The rest of the street was residential. One of those secret south London streets that sat quietly away from the noise and despair.

Eastwood pressed the buzzer and waited.

"Can I help you?"

"Yes. This is DC Roxanne Eastwood from the Serial Crime Unit. I spoke to Dr. Gregory Jones this morning. You're expecting me."

There was no response. Eastwood wondered if they were busy burning files or escaping out of the back window as she waited for them to buzz her through. She watched the digits on her watch roll through minutes as she stood in the cold. After four minutes, Eastwood heard a loud electrical buzz, and the latch was released. As she walked up the driveway she looked up and noticed a face watching her from the second-floor window. She wondered if the man in the window was a patient or an employee.

"I'm really sorry about making you wait out in the cold. I'm Dr. Gregory Jones. We spoke earlier this morning."

The man standing in the doorway reminded Eastwood of a

secondary school science teacher whose wardrobe seemed to consist of different variations of the color beige. At five foot eight he was only an inch taller than Eastwood, but she could see the muscles on his biceps straining against his fitted jumper.

"How long has the clinic been here?" Eastwood asked as she walked in and the door was closed behind her. The sound of someone shouting could be heard from upstairs. Eastwood felt herself get defensive as a woman appeared in the hallway, looked at her and then walked away.

"I think that the clinic was established nineteen years ago. Sorry, I'm not sure of the exact date. Before my time."

"How many patients do you have here?" asked Eastwood.

"We admitted someone last night. He's the one that you can hear upstairs, so that would take us to twelve patients who are resident here and then we have our day patients. Please, follow me through to my office."

"How long have you been working here?"

"Must be coming up to seven years now. It's both intense and rewarding," he replied. Eastwood followed him up the stairs and to a room at the front of the house. She took off her coat and looked around. A small two-seater sofa lay to her right, next to a desk with a laptop. There was a wilting plant in the corner and certificates of achievement on the wall. Framed photographs on the shelf showed Dr. Gregory Jones shaking hands with people that Eastwood didn't recognize. The room was purely functional.

"Have you always specialized in mental health?" Eastwood asked as she scanned a certificate from St. George's School of Medicine.

"Pretty much. I discovered pretty early on that I didn't really have the stomach for the bloodier intricacies of medicine. That doesn't stop anyone wanting to tell you about their latest symptoms or showing you the funny lump under their arm once they find out that you're a doctor," Gregory said with a grin. "Where are my manners? I didn't even offer you anything to drink."

"Don't worry about it. I know that you must be busy. I just want to ask you a few questions about Kyle Baxter and also one of your employees, Niall Graff."

"Well, as I explained to you on the phone, Kyle never arrived. I assessed him myself when his mother brought him here for an appointment. He was experiencing an episode, but he was able to express that he wanted to be here and that he wanted us to help him."

"Did you discuss how you would help him?"

"Yes. We have a number of therapies, all dependent on what the patient wants. If they're lacking the mental capacity to have that discussion, then we will discuss it with their next of kin. Luckily, Kyle had his mother. There are some who are abandoned because their family don't understand mental health issues."

"What about Kyle's father? Were you aware that he had power of attorney over his son? That he was responsible for all of his medical and financial affairs?"

"I had no idea. There was no indication that his father was in the picture. When Kyle came with his mother, it was clear that he needed help, but he was also a twenty-seven-year-old man who understood what was happening to him. We discussed the different options."

"What were the options?"

"To continue with the medical, chemical-based treatment and adjusting the medication that he was on, or taking a more holistic approach to his treatment, either as an outpatient or as part of a residential program."

"Which did you recommend?"

"To slightly adjust his current medication and to gradually introduce complementary and holistic therapies to his treatment but as part of a residential program."

"And what did Kyle agree to?"

"He and his mother wanted the residential program, but Kyle didn't want to start straightaway. So, we made arrangements for him to start the following week, but he never came back."

Eastwood leaned forward. "I'm just trying to understand what happened in here that led to Kyle Baxter hanging dead from a bandstand in Southwark Park. Did you know that Kyle's mother had served a prison sentence for the attempted murder of her son when he was twelve years old?"

Gregory sat back in his seat with a look of shock. "I wasn't aware of that."

"I doubt that it's information that she would volunteer," said Eastwood. "So, I can assume that you didn't know that Kyle's mother knew your employee Niall Graff."

"No. Niall is one of our consultants and he showed Kyle and his mother around the clinic. I had no idea that they knew each other. They didn't act as though there was any association and Niall didn't say anything to me."

"Did you know that Niall had been arrested for the attempted murder of Kyle Baxter when Kyle was twelve years old? He was never charged by the CPS but the arrest would have turned up an enhanced DBS check."

"Attempted murder!" Gregory exclaimed as he rose from his seat. "No, absolutely not. That doesn't make any sense."

"Did you carry out a DBS check on Niall Graff?"

"Of course we did. We have vulnerable patients here, but we may have just carried out a standard DBS check."

"I'm going to suggest that you carry out an enhanced check in the future. That will bring up details of an arrest and charge even if the case is dropped," said Eastwood as she took note of Gregory's distress.

"If I'd known about the arrest then I would never have employed him. The attempted murder of a child. There's no way that Niall would have worked here."

"When was the last time that you heard from Niall?"

"About two weeks ago. He called in sick with the flu and

then he sent us a doctor's note confirming that he had bronchitis and that he was signed off for another two weeks."

"Do you know anything about Niall's private life? Is there a wife, girlfriend, boyfriend?"

"He has a wife, her name's Rebecca."

"Rebecca?" said Eastwood, the adrenaline pulsating through her body. Rebecca and Niall had done their best to cover their tracks, but it was all now unraveling.

"I never met her," Gregory continued, "but Niall spoke about her. They'd just adopted a baby."

"Did Niall show you any photos of the baby?"

"Yes, he did. It was a little boy. Apparently, the mother abandoned him. I think that they named him Shia."

Eastwood didn't experience any joy or a sense of relief with this revelation. Instead, she felt sick and also angry that this baby's entire existence had been rewritten.

"We need to find Niall and we need to find him urgently," said Eastwood. "Do you have a current address for him?"

"I'll have to check with admin but I'm pretty sure that we sent flowers to his home to celebrate the baby's arrival."

"And what about an up-to-date photograph? I notice that your staff have photographic ID badges."

"They do. If you just give me half an hour, I'll be able to get you everything that you need."

73

"Well, that's something?" Henley said as she read the text message from Pellacia. For a brief moment she allowed herself to enjoy the feeling of closing one door in the investigation.

"What's going on?" Ramouter asked as he reached for the hand sanitizer on the nurses' station.

"The CPS have just come back with a charging decision for Annan and Sullivan," said Henley. "They've both been charged with murder, which means that we can finally put Uliana Piontek out of her misery and officially take no further action against her."

"To be fair, we should have NFA'd her ages ago."

"Don't start," Henley said as she double-checked the time on her phone. She needed to get home and salvage a part of her Sunday. She hadn't seen her family for two days. "Pellacia's going to head over to Lewisham to officially charge the pair of them. They'll be at court first thing tomorrow morning."

Ramouter let out a sigh of relief as they headed toward Brandon Whittaker's room. "I just hope that the poor kid is able to help us."

Henley's phone began to ring.

"It's Eastwood," Henley said. They stopped outside Brandon's room near a bored-looking security guard. "You go in. I'll join you in a bit. Hey, Eastie, what is it?"

"I'm just leaving the clinic where Niall Graff works," said Eastwood. "Graff hasn't been at work for almost two weeks, but Dr. Gregory Jones confirmed that Niall Graff had taken three days' annual leave at the exact same time that Kyle Baxter disappeared. Graff's boss also confirmed that Graff's wife is called Rebecca."

"Are you a hundred percent sure that's what he said?" Henley said as she leaned her forehead against the wall.

"That's exactly what Dr. Jones, that's his boss, said. He's also given me an address for Graff. It's in Welling. I just wanted to double-check what you wanted me to do next. I'm more than happy to go and—"

"No, no. Don't do that," Henley said firmly. "I want you to liaise with Stanford, arrange backup and go to the Welling address. I don't want you going there without backup, do you understand?"

"Don't worry," said Eastwood. "I'll head back to the SCU and wait for confirmation."

Henley hung up, took a deep breath and tried to shake off the heavy weight of responsibility that was resting on her shoulders. The last thing that she wanted was to make any mistake that could place any of her team in danger.

"What's wrong?" Henley asked as she suddenly became aware of the security guard a few feet away, reaching for his radio.

"You need to get someone up here. That woman is back again," the security guard said.

Henley turned around to see Marcia Whittaker making her way manically along the ward floor.

"I want to see my son," Marcia screamed. "I want to see him. You can't stop me from seeing my son! Brandon!"

"Madam, you can't be here. You are disturbing the other

patients. You need to leave," said a female nurse who had managed to stop Marcia outside the door of a small waiting area.

"Do not touch me!" Marcia screamed out again as another guard entered the ward.

"Marcia, why don't you calm down? You're not helping yourself," Henley said. She moved toward Marcia and motioned for the nurses to step aside.

"They won't let me see him. I want to see my son."

"Marcia, you won't be able to see him when you're in this state," said Henley. "Why don't we—"

"Get away from me!" Marcia screamed.

"I'm not going to hurt you," Henley said when she saw the fury in Marcia's eyes.

"You. You're the one who's done this. You're the devil!" Marcia screamed. She lunged, her nails digging into Henley's right cheek.

Henley's eye began to water. Her temper flared. Marcia was lucky that Henley was a police officer and not a normal member of the public, or she would have ended up in a hospital bed next to her son.

"Oi, stop that." Henley grabbed Marcia's wrists, spun her around and pushed her against the wall. "What is wrong with you? Calm down. Stop thinking about yourself and consider your son and the other people who are here. You're not helping yourself and you're not helping Brandon."

"You're hurting me," Marcia whimpered as the security guards grabbed her arms.

"I need you to stop." Henley forced herself to speak gently and not add *you stupid cow* to the end of her sentence as the scratch on her cheek began to throb.

"I just want to see him," Marcia said as she began to cry. "I want to hold my baby."

Despite everything, Henley felt a wave of empathy for Marcia at these words. "You can let her go," she said to the security guard.

"We're obligated to call the police and have her arrested," said the guard as he refused to lessen his grip on Marcia. "She threatened staff and she attacked you."

"I know," said Henley, "I know, but I won't make a report if Marcia agrees to let you escort her from the hospital grounds. Marcia, will you agree to that?"

"But... Brandon," Marcia said as her legs gave way.

"Come on. Up you get." The security guards brought her to her feet. "Are you sure that you don't want her arrested?"

"I'm sure," said Henley. "Just make sure that she leaves."

Henley watched the security guards almost carry Marcia out of the ward. She had been all alone. Patrick was nowhere in sight. It was obvious to Henley that Marcia had lied to her husband about seeing Brandon. Henley prayed that Marcia would find the courage to walk away from the confines of her marriage and the coercive behavior of her husband. Patrick Whittaker had very few redeeming qualities.

"That was quite a scene," Ramouter said as Henley approached Brandon's door. "What happened to your face?"

Henley winced as she pulled away the cotton pad soaked with antiseptic. "Marcia happened, but don't worry about it."

Henley took in the sight of Brandon Whittaker. Considering that he had been close to death almost two weeks ago, his recovery so far was impressive. There was still a deathly pallor to his skin, but the bruising on his face had almost disappeared. The head bandages had been removed and his hair was slowly growing back where the surgeons had relieved the pressure on his brain. His sister Amy was sitting in the corner with an unread book.

"My mum?" Amy mouthed as she pointed at her own cheek.

"Yes," Henley replied as she approached Brandon's bed.

"Apparently she made it into his room when Amy wasn't here and the guards were changing shift," Ramouter whispered.

"I don't think that she'll be back," Henley said as she sat

down in a chair and Brandon turned his head toward her. "Hello, Brandon, you certainly look a lot better than the first time I saw you."

"He's been doing really well," said Amy. She reached over and tenderly touched her brother's arm. "He gets tired quickly though."

"My name is Detective Inspector Anjelica Henley. I came to see you a couple of days ago when you first woke up. You probably don't remember. They've had you on a lot of medication."

As if to remind himself that he was indeed on a lot of medication, Brandon raised his right arm, causing the thin plastic tube pumping antibiotics into his body to grow taut.

"I remember," he replied, his words slightly slurred and heavy as though his tongue was weighed down.

"The doctors have said that you should be able to help me with some questions. Do you think that you'll be able to do that?"

"I'll try, but my head hurts sometimes, and things don't... don't make sense."

"That's OK. I'll take it slowly," said Henley. "How are you feeling otherwise? I mean—"

"The voices? The noise?"

Henley nodded.

"Quiet. They've given me medication. I think that it's in this bag." Brandon pointed at the drip on his left arm.

"Do you remember that I told you that we found you in a room in the church?"

"Yeah."

"Can you tell me who brought you there?"

"My dad. My dad took me."

Henley held her tongue when she thought about how Patrick Whittaker had willingly put his son in danger. She was giving serious thought to arresting him for conspiracy to cause grievous bodily harm with intent to his son. She had enough evidence to support the charge but didn't feel comfortable about putting Brandon through any more distress.

"What do you remember?"

"I wasn't well. My stomach was hurting, and I woke up. I couldn't move my arms or my legs."

"Where did you wake up?"

"I don't know. I couldn't see anything, but it wasn't my room. It smelled funny and it was cold."

Amy leaned over with a tissue and wiped away the tears that had begun to fall from her brother's eyes.

"Was anyone else in the room when you woke up?"

"Yes, a black man. He gave me a drink, but the other man said that he was feeding the devil and he pushed it away. There was a woman."

"Can you remember what the other man looked like?"

Brandon slowly shook his head. "I didn't see him."

"What about the woman? Can you describe her?"

"White. Becca," Brandon said. "He called her Becca. She hit me and put the…" Brandon leaned his head back and started to cry again. "She burnt my feet. With the candles."

Amy put a hand to her face as her own tears started to stream down her face. Ramouter looked away and took a step back. Henley knew exactly how he felt. Her anger grew more intense when she remembered how Rebecca Keeler had sat in front of her, at the refuge, talking about her own pain, in full knowledge of what she, Niall and Caleb had done to Brandon and the others.

"She wouldn't stop," Brandon said.

"Brandon, can you remember anyone else's name?"

"No," Brandon shook his head. "I don't know. She let him pour water on my face. Really cold water."

Henley looked at Brandon. She knew that she wouldn't be getting any more out of him today but what she had was enough. She had Rebecca.

"Brandon, I'm going to leave you but I'm going to come and

see you again in a couple of days. The brain is a funny thing. It can surprise us, and you might remember a bit more. Would that be OK?"

"That's OK. Just don't let them hurt me again," Brandon said softly.

74

Henley couldn't quite believe that she was sitting at her desk, on a Sunday night, in a full office. Everyone around her looked exhausted and at a loose end.

"The poor kid," Pellacia said after Henley finished explaining what had happened at the hospital. "Are you sure that you don't want Marcia Whittaker arrested for assaulting a police officer? That scratch looks nasty."

"No, it's fine." Henley brushed away a fleck of dried blood from her cheek. "There's no point. The woman is going through her own personal hell, but her husband, there's enough for an arrest and charge, but I don't know. I'm still mulling it over. So, Stanford and Eastwood, how did it go with the address?"

"Dead end," Stanford and Eastwood said simultaneously.

"Victoria, the doula, gave me an address in Welling, which is where Hadlow had the home birth. The Welling address is the same location that the Cooper Therapy Group had listed as Niall Graff's home," said Stanford.

"The admin assistant for the clinic gave me the details for the local florist that they used to send Graff and Rebecca 'Congratulations' flowers. The florist confirmed that it was the same

Welling address and that when they delivered the flowers, a woman, matching Rebecca's description, answered the door."

"So why was it a dead end?" Pellacia asked.

"They've moved," Eastwood explained.

"We turned up with backup, as ordered," said Stanford, "much to the surprise of the woman who is now living there. Her name is Talia Derry and she's never heard of Rebecca Keeler or Niall Graff. She and her boyfriend only started renting the place on the first of February. Talia gave us the landlord's details and he confirmed that he'd been renting to Niall Graff for the past two years."

"We also checked with the neighbors," Eastwood continued, "and it looks like Rebecca and Niall moved out about five weeks ago."

"Did any of the neighbors see Rebecca and Niall with a baby?" asked Henley.

"A neighbor said that she saw Niall with a car seat in the first week of January, but no one actually saw a baby," said Eastwood.

No one said anything for a while as they all tried to process the current situation of their investigation.

"According to Victoria, the doula, baby Isaac was born on the tenth of January."

"Bloody hell," said Pellacia. "Do you think that it was always their plan to take Alyssa's baby?"

"I wouldn't put anything past them," said Eastwood.

"They can't have just disappeared," Pellacia said after a few minutes had passed.

"Rebecca disappeared after I'd visited her at the hostel," said Henley as a wave of anger surged through her. "But there's nothing that I said that would've spooked her. As far as I was concerned, I was just talking to a victim, not a possible suspect."

"I don't think that it's anything that you said or did, boss," said Ramouter.

"There has to be something." Pellacia stood up and walked

to the murder board. "Where are you with the CCTV with the ATM machines? Those cash withdrawals from Hadlow's bank were made not far from where Kyle Baxter's body was found."

"And the cash withdrawal on Powis Street is literally across the road from where Rebecca Keeler worked," said Henley.

"Nothing so far," said Stanford. "The banks are usually a lot more efficient than the council. There's no point calling them now, it's after seven, but I'll chase them up first thing."

"We should all call it a night," said Pellacia. "We've got alerts out for both Keeler and Graff. There's nothing that we can do unless they slip up overnight."

75

"Serena Annan, aged 42 years old, and Derrick Sullivan, aged 36, both appeared in the dock at Bromley Magistrates' Court this morning, charged with the murder of Serena Annan's husband, Caleb Annan, aged 44 years old, who was the pastor of the Church of Annan the Prophet Pentecostal church and a community leader.

"Caleb Annan was found dead in his church almost two weeks ago and is said to have died from multiple stab wounds.

"Annan and Sullivan initially appeared in the dock together, however, Serena Annan was removed by dock officers after she attacked Sullivan and repeatedly screamed that Sullivan had murdered her husband. Both Serena Annan and Derrick Sullivan spoke to confirm their names, addresses, date of birth and nationality. However, no pleas were entered and both Annan and Sullivan were remanded into custody and their case was adjourned. They will both be appearing at the Old Bailey tomorrow morning, for their first appearance where they will be expected to enter a plea of guilty or not guilty to the charge of murder."

Henley muted the sound on her phone as Pellacia walked into the old canteen on the second floor holding two cups of tea.

"I've just heard from the CPS that both Annan and Sullivan are making bail applications tomorrow."

"I doubt that any judge will give them bail. What are you doing hiding out here?" Pellacia asked. He placed the tea on the table, pulled out a chair and sat opposite Henley.

"I'm not hiding," said Henley. "I just needed somewhere to think, away from everything. I can't help wondering if I may have missed something every time I look at that murder board. That baby is still out there with two murderers."

Henley tried to drink her tea but the lump in her throat was stopping her from swallowing. She could remember how small and vulnerable Emma had been at two months old and how aware she already was of Henley as her mother. Henley could never have harmed her own child and she felt that same feeling of protectiveness toward Isaac and a determination to stop anyone from hurting him.

"Will it make you feel better if I told you that I don't think that baby Isaac is in any danger?" said Pellacia as he sipped his tea. "Infanticide might be pushing it a bit too far. Even murderers have limits."

"No, it doesn't make me feel better that these two have a warped moral code," said Henley. She sipped her tea in a comfortable silence.

"It's nothing serious, you know," Pellacia said after a while. "This thing with Laura. It's not—"

"It's none of my business," said Henley as Pellacia reached out and took hold of her hand.

"You acted as though it was your business. I saw the look on your face in the restaurant. You seem to forget I do know you, Anjelica."

"Don't flatter yourself," Henley said as she pulled her hand away. "My only concern was about the investigation. Laura Halifax was hanging around, poking her nose in, and was too close to Serena Annan for my liking."

"I would never have done anything to compromise the investigation. Do you really think so little of me?" Pellacia asked, a look of hurt flashing on his face.

"Don't say that. You make me sound like an absolute bitch." Henley was trying to compartmentalize the affection that she had for Pellacia from her innate drive to protect everyone on her team. "I don't want you to get hurt. Professionally, I mean."

"Professionally? Is that it?"

"It can't be anything but that. Anyway, I'm sure that there's something about her that you like," Henley said. The lights in the ceiling flickered. "I'm not sure what that is, though. I didn't think that she was your type."

"You're my type," Pellacia said at the same moment Stanford walked into the canteen.

"What are you two doing hiding up here?" he asked, looking at Henley and Pellacia suspiciously.

"I was not hiding. I needed a change of scenery," said Henley and closed her laptop.

"Whatever, you need to get upstairs. The ATM footage from the banks came through and we've got her."

"That is the ATM machine on Jamaica Road," said Stanford as everyone looked up at the smartboard which Ezra had connected to Stanford's computer. "And that is Rebecca Keeler making a cash withdrawal from Alyssa Hadlow's bank account."

Stanford paused the footage and zoomed in on the crystal-clear image of Rebecca.

"That's her," said Henley. She took in the image of Rebecca, her red hair covered by a blue hat as she looked up from the ATM screen.

"I don't think that people realize that there's cameras in most cashpoints," said Ramouter.

"What about the other withdrawals?" asked Henley.

"We've got footage of her making all of the cash withdrawals. We're thinking that she must be living on or have access to property nearby. We've got footage of her walking off in the direction of Nightingale House in the Kirby Estate," Stanford confirmed.

"Kyle Baxter's blood was found on the steps leading into Nightingale House. It wasn't a lot of blood, just droplets," said Ramouter. "CSI didn't find any blood inside the communal area or on the stairwell. We had no evidence to suggest that he'd been inside the block."

"How many flats are in that block?" asked Pellacia. He pulled out his phone and started tapping away. "There are 119 flats."

"We can't just knock on 119 flats and cross our fingers that Keeler and Graff are in one of them," said Henley as she returned to her desk. "And we won't get access to any of them without a warrant."

"We've got no grounds for a mass search warrant, if that's even a thing," said Ramouter. "But I could get onto the local council and see if we can get a tenancy list."

"That estate is going to be a mixture of council and private housing," said Henley, "but it's a good place to start. I keep thinking that I've missed something. Something that Rebecca may have said to me."

"Did she say anything about any friends or family?" asked Ramouter.

"Only that her mum had moved to New Zealand and that her aunt was dead."

"Do we know for sure that her aunt is dead?" asked Ramouter. "It's not as if Rebecca Keeler is the most reliable source of information."

Henley looked up at Ramouter. He'd actually made a point. "No, I don't know that her aunt is actually dead." She picked up the phone and searched around on her desk for the Post-it notes where she'd written Rebecca's mother's number.

"Who are you calling?" Ramouter asked.

"Rebecca's mum, in New Zealand."

"They're thirteen hours ahead. I hope that she doesn't mind being woken up at nearly three in the morning."

Ramouter stopped talking as Henley held up her hand.

"Mrs. Keeler, I am sorry to be calling you at this time. This is Detective Inspector Henley. We spoke a few days ago. No, I haven't heard from Rebecca. Has she been in contact with you? No, right. I just wanted to ask you a question about Rebecca's aunt that took her to the church. Gretta." Henley reached for a pen and urgently began to write. "Your aunt, so Rebecca's great-aunt. When did she die? Were they close? Right. Right. Are you absolutely sure about that? But you don't remember. No, you've been a great help."

"So, the aunt is dead?" said Ramouter as Henley put the phone down and stood up from her desk.

"Very dead. She died in a nursing home three years ago, but she used to live in Bermondsey."

"Don't tell me. Nightingale House on the Kirby Estate."

Henley nodded. "But she can't remember the fucking door number. She said that the aunt didn't have any children and left everything to Rebecca."

"A hundred and nineteen flats though?" said Ramouter.

"I've got the aunt's full name and date of birth. That should be enough for Ezra."

76

Flat 92, Nightingale House, Kirby Estate. Two police cars and a police van were parked downstairs. Six uniformed officers were waiting to be directed. The occupants of flat 91 had confirmed that a man and woman matching the description of Keeler and Graff had moved in recently after the previous tenants had been kicked out and yes, they had heard a baby crying.

Henley made Ramouter turn around and double-checked that his stab vest was secure.

"I'm not taking any chances," Henley said, patting his back.

"I'm fine. We've got backup and I'm pretty sure that Keeler or Graff won't put that baby at risk."

"Do we know that they're definitely in?" Henley asked to PC Waller who had just switched on his bodycam.

"We haven't seen any movement from the flat in the past hour," said PC Waller, "but a light was switched on about twenty minutes ago, but that's not to say that someone didn't leave before we got here."

"OK, let's go up," said Henley.

Henley and Ramouter made their way along the landing and toward the flat. PC Waller and another officer had made their way up the second staircase and had blocked the stairwell in case anyone tried to run.

"Are you OK?" Henley asked Ramouter as she heard him inhale deeply as they approached flat 92.

"Aye, I'm good," Ramouter replied.

"OK," Henley said, and she knocked on the front door twice. She waited as Ramouter moved to the window that faced the landing.

"Can't see anything," Ramouter said. Henley knocked again and there was no answer. "What are we going to do, break it down?"

"Get on the radio and tell them to bring up the enforcer." Henley kneeled down and flicked open the mail slot. She could see floorboards, there was the sound of water running and then a baby started to cry.

"I can see someone moving," said Ramouter once he got off the radio.

"Rebecca Keeler, this is Detective Inspector Henley from the Serial Crime Unit. I need you to open this door right now before I break it down," she shouted.

From inside, Rebecca shouted, "No, you need to leave. You don't understand what you're doing."

Henley opened the letterbox to see Rebecca disappearing down the corridor.

"Shit," Henley said as she pushed against the door, in the wasted hope that it would give way. "Where are they?"

"Look, look," said Ramouter, pointing to two officers who were running along the landing with the red battering ram that was affectionately called the 'enforcer'.

"Step aside, ma'am," the officer said as he approached. Henley joined Ramouter to the side as the officer took a step back and rammed the enforcer against the front door.

"Get back in and don't come out," Henley shouted as the door to number 91 swung open and swiftly closed again.

"We're in," the officer shouted as the door of flat 92 swung back on broken hinges.

Henley and Ramouter walked into the flat as the sounds of a baby's cries grew louder. Ramouter grabbed hold of Henley as she slipped on something wet.

"Fuck." Ramouter looked down at the pool of blood that led into the kitchen, where Niall Graff lay on the floor with a kitchen knife stuck in his neck, blood frothing from his mouth. His leg twitched as his hand weakly scrabbled around his throat.

"Ramouter, stay with him and request an ambulance," Henley said as she made her way along the corridor.

"Be careful," Ramouter shouted out as another officer entered the flat and followed Henley.

Henley followed the cries of a baby that was growing more frantic. She stopped at a closed door.

"Rebecca," Henley called out as she pushed down on the door handle. "I need you to open this door."

"No, you are not coming in," Rebecca shouted back. "All of you are the devil."

"Rebecca, I just want to know if baby Isaac is OK. That's the only reason I'm here," Henley said as she indicated for the officer with the enforcer to come closer.

"His name is Shia. Go away," shouted Rebecca as the baby screamed even louder.

"Do it," Henley said, backing away into the corner. "It doesn't sound as though she's standing by the door."

The officer nodded. The sounds of ambulance sirens grew louder. The door fell apart as the enforcer met the cheap MDF. Henley walked slowly into the bedroom. She stopped when she saw Rebecca standing with her back against a wardrobe, holding on tightly to baby Isaac. Blood covered her face and hands, which had stained the blue Babygro that Isaac was wearing.

"Does any of that blood belong to you or the baby?" Henley asked as she stopped in the middle of the room.

"Get away from me," Rebecca said as she moved toward the window.

"Rebecca, I promise you that I will leave. I just need to know if you and the baby are OK."

"It's not his blood and it's not mine," Rebecca said softly. "It's the devil's."

"OK, OK," Henley said as she gingerly took a step forward. "I need you to hand over Isaac."

"No. No." Rebecca took another step toward the open window. The wind blowing the curtains against her face. "You don't understand. You're just like them."

Henley glanced over at the window. It was too small to jump through, but with Rebecca's state of mind, Henley wasn't sure what she might do.

"Rebecca, please let me take Isaac. If you care about him, then you'll hand him over," Henley said as Isaac started to cry at the sound of paramedics entering the flat.

"Are you crazy?" Rebecca said with surprising clarity. "You can't take my child. He was given to me."

"Rebecca, can't you see that he's upset?" Henley said slowly. "I don't want to take him from you. I just want to look after him for a little while."

"Don't come near me. I know what you're doing. They told me your plan before you came to see me," said Rebecca. "They told me that you was dangerous."

Henley knew that there was no point trying to reason with Rebecca. Niall Graff was choking on his own blood, dying on the kitchen floor. Rebecca pulled Isaac closer and took another step toward the window. Henley's heart raced. She could hear the heavy but steady breathing of the officer behind her and the loud commands of the paramedics working on saving Niall Graff's life in the kitchen.

"Rebecca," Henley said calmly, trying to ignore the smear of blood on Rebecca's face and focus on her wild intense eyes.

"I think that Isaac would like to see his mum. You know how important it is for our babies to smell us, to feel us, to see us."

"His name is Shia," said Rebecca.

"I'm sorry. Shia needs to see you."

"I am his mum," said Rebecca.

"Yes, you are," said Henley. "Why don't you turn him around and let me see if he has his mummy's eyes."

Rebecca slowly peeled the baby away from her chest, and Isaac let out a scream that filled the room.

"He has got my eyes," Rebecca said as she cradled Isaac in her arms.

"Rebecca, why don't you let me hold him?" said Henley as she took a discreet step to the side.

"Why? Why do you want him?" Rebecca looked around in a wild panic.

"I was just thinking that it's a bit chilly in here. I could hold him while you get a jumper or a blanket for him," said Henley.

"No," Rebecca screamed as Isaac cried louder. "You're tainted. Evil. You're not having my child."

"Rebecca, I promise you, that—"

"No! All of you leave. Leave."

"No," Henley screamed out as Rebecca turned quickly toward the window. Henley scrambled around the side of the bed but tripped over the Moses basket that was on the ground. She screamed as her ankle twisted and she felt sharp pains run up her leg. "Rebecca, stop," she shouted as Rebecca banged her head hard against the window to break it, leaving behind a bloody forehead print on the cracked glass. Henley could see Isaac dangling awkwardly from Rebecca's left arm.

"Get her," Henley shouted out to the officer while she reached out and grabbed Isaac from Rebecca's arms right as she threw herself against the glass.

"Shit," said Henley. There was the sound of glass breaking as the officer behind Henley dropped the enforcer, jumped onto the bed and pulled Rebecca away. Henley lay on her back, holding Isaac tightly against her as Rebecca cried hysterically with shards of broken glass in her arm.

"Come on, Isaac, it's OK. It's OK." Henley pushed herself against the wardrobe and gently rocked Isaac, ignoring the pain in her ankle. "I've got you. I've got you."

"Give him back. Give him to me," Rebecca screamed as the officer pushed her against the wall and held her arms.

"Keep still," he said as he reached for his handcuffs.

"Give me back my child," Rebecca wailed. Another officer came into the bedroom.

"Rebecca Keeler," Henley said, handing Isaac over to the second officer and easing herself up from the floor, "I'm arresting you for the murder of Alyssa Hadlow, Charlie Jensen and Kyle Baxter, the attempted murder of Brandon Whittaker and the kidnapping of Isaac Hadlow."

"His name is Shia and he's mine," Rebecca said weakly.

Henley ignored her as she concluded the caution and the adrenaline rushing around her began to subside. The officers led Rebecca Keeler out of the flat.

"Niall Graff is still alive but barely," Ramouter said as Henley limped toward him in the hallway. "They've just taken him downstairs to the ambulance. Hey, do you want the paramedics to take a look at your ankle?"

"I'll be fine," Henley replied as she made her way outside.

"Where are you off to?"

"I'm going downstairs. I need to further arrest Rebecca Keeler for the attempted murder of Niall Graff."

"She's lucky that it's not murder," said Ramouter, taking hold of Henley's arm. "Not that it makes any difference. She won't be coming out of prison anytime soon."

"Is that him? He's so precious," said Stanford as he walked into Ezra's room, which was the warmest in the SCU.

"We're just waiting for social services to get here." Henley leaned back in Ezra's chair holding onto Isaac, who was greedily drinking from a bottle.

"Is he all right?" Stanford asked, sitting down next to Henley.

"The paramedics checked him over and he's absolutely fine. Rebecca may have been as mad as a box of frogs, but she and Niall did a good job of looking after this little one."

"Even if they did kill his mum." Stanford stroked Isaac's hand. "Reminds me of when Emma was that age. I wonder who will look after him now?"

"He actually does have a family. As strange as this sounds, Serena would have been a good option to adopt him."

"If she wasn't charged with murdering his dad."

"God, what a mess," said Henley. "This little one deserves so much more. I can't imagine what Alyssa Hadlow must have gone through," said Henley.

"Ramouter said that Niall Graff is still touch and go."

"I hope that he makes it. Not because I want him to live, but because I want him to talk and tell us exactly what happened with Baxter, Hadlow, Jensen and Whittaker. Isaac deserves to know what happened to his mother."

"I wonder what happened in that flat to make Rebecca want to kill Niall? They've been in this together from day one," said Stanford. "Why did Rebecca switch on him now?"

"Well, I'm not sure if we'll be finding out anytime soon. The custody sergeant just called and said that they're taking Rebecca to hospital. She needs stitches in her arm, and a mental health assessment. She'll probably be kept overnight. I hope that she is. I'm knackered."

"I'm sure that they'll conclude that she's not mentally fit to be interviewed. Take a look at what she's done; how could she be in her right mind?"

"I'm not convinced," Henley replied as she gently removed the empty bottle from Isaac's mouth and handed it to Stanford. "You know the guidance on interviewing detainees who are mentally ill as well as I do."

"It is not the case that someone lacks capacity just because they have a mental disorder," said Stanford.

"Exactly. I'm sure that she knew what she was doing, and I'm not charging her with murder and manslaughter until I find out why."

77

"I'm not happy about Rebecca being interviewed right now. I've already voiced my concerns with the custody sergeant," said Lyndsey Gardner, the appropriate adult allocated to look after Rebecca Keeler while she was being interviewed.

Henley tried to keep her face impassive as she finished her coffee and threw the empty cup in the bin. "Look, Lyndsey, I understand that you want to—"

"Ms. Keeler has been through a lot," Lyndsey interrupted. "I'm sure that you've seen on her custody record that she was sedated at the hospital and that she was given antidepressants by the forensic medical examiner at 8 a.m."

"And if you'd read the custody record then you would have seen that Ms. Keeler was assessed as being fit for interview two hours ago," Henley said firmly as she took a seat next to Ramouter, who was silently completing the paperwork. "And the antidepressant that she was given, more than four hours ago, would not turn her into a bloody zombie."

"It's my job to make sure that *you* treat Rebecca fairly and to make sure that she's able to participate in an interview," Lyndsey said. The door opened and a female police officer escorted Rebecca into the room.

"Sorry about the wait. She wanted a cup of tea," the officer said, ushering Rebecca into her seat.

Henley wondered if there was some validity to Lyndsey's concerns when she looked down and saw that Rebecca was barefooted. Rebecca looked as though she was drowning in the plain gray, police-station issued tracksuit that was two sizes too big for her. Her wild energy had dissipated and left her wilted like a neglected plant. The light in her eyes had dimmed and her red hair hung limply over her shoulder in an unraveling braid that had lost its sheen.

"How are you feeling, Rebecca?" Lyndsey asked as she sat and removed her laptop from her bag.

"I'm fine," Rebecca whispered. She picked up the cup and took a sip of tea that resembled dishwater. "How long will this take?"

"That all depends on you," Henley said, indicating to Ramouter to press the record button.

"Do you want me to tell you everything? I'm not sure if I can do that," Rebecca said as she lowered her head. "No, I don't think that I can."

"Let's just see how we go," Henley replied, ignoring Lyndsey's *I told you so* look. Henley quietly observed Rebecca as Ramouter made the introductions, repeated the caution and explained the role of the appropriate adult. The cuts and bruises on Rebecca's forehead were prominent against her strained, pale skin. She looked younger and vulnerable. Henley chastised herself for feeling some sympathy for her.

"Rebecca. Do you understand that you've been arrested for the murders of Charlie Jensen, Alyssa Hadlow, Kyle Baxter, the attempted murder of Niall Graff and—"

"Niall is still alive?" Rebecca's head jerked up.

"Yes," Henley replied. "He's still in critical condition, but he's still alive."

"Oh. That's a shame."

"Why is that a shame?" Henley asked as Lyndsey pursed her lips and began to type.

"I wanted him gone. I'd had enough of him," said Rebecca. She became more agitated. "He didn't listen to me. He never listened to me. He wanted me to do things his way. He told me what to say, what to wear and how to raise my child."

"Your child? You mean Alyssa Hadlow's child, Isaac Hadlow," said Henley. "Do you remember that I also arrested you for kidnapping him?"

"He was not hers. God gave him to *me*, and he told me to call him Shia. He was, no, he *is* mine. Where is he? I want to see him. I want my baby."

"He's safe," said Henley.

"You have no right to keep him from me."

"You're right. He shouldn't be kept away from his mother," Henley said softly. Rebecca had visibly calmed. "Let's talk about Niall. You said that he never listened to you."

"No, he didn't," Rebecca replied. "He said that I was unreliable and a risk to myself. He changed. He wasn't the same man that I met."

"How did you meet Niall?"

"He came to my house. It was after my dad died. I wasn't coping and Bippy came back."

"And who was Bippy?"

Rebecca let out a laugh. "My bipolar disorder. I was diagnosed when I was seventeen and my therapist said that I should give it a name. So, I called it Bippy."

"You said that you weren't coping after your dad died."

"I missed my daddy," Rebecca said as tears streamed down her face. "It was hard, so hard."

"Did you try and get help?"

Rebecca shook her head. "No. My mum thought that I was looking for attention but then I started hearing voices and she called my aunt."

"Was this your aunt Gretta?"

"Yes." Rebecca wiped her nose with her sleeve. Henley exchanged a look with Ramouter. They had both seen the crisscross of iridescent scars on her left arm and the fresh scratches on her right arm. Henley had no doubt that Rebecca had a history of self-harming and had most likely given herself the scars whilst she'd been waiting in the cells.

"Were you close to your aunt Gretta?" asked Henley.

"She was like my best friend," said Rebecca. "She said that she knew how to make the voices stop. She knew that there were demons inside of me. She said that she had a friend who could help me."

Henley could feel the tension latching onto the small muscles in her back as she listened to Rebecca's story. She wanted to put an end to Rebecca's misery, but Henley couldn't do that. She needed Rebecca to explain to her why she had chosen to kill.

"Rebecca, who was your aunt's friend?" Henley asked as she subtly nudged Ramouter.

"It was Niall."

"The same Niall Graff that was living with you?" Ramouter asked as he opened his folder and pulled out a single sheet of paper.

"Yes. He was so good to me."

"Rebecca, this is a copy of a blog post that we found online," said Ramouter. "We know that you wrote that blog post."

"Niall told me to do that. He said that it would help with my healing."

"OK, in that blog post, you said that your aunt introduced you to a man called Keith, who—"

"Keith was Niall. He told me to write the blog but not to use his real name. He said that writing about the demons in my life would help."

"And did it help?"

"A little, but I didn't like writing for the world to see, so I stopped the blog and wrote everything down in my diaries. I have lot of diaries. Everything is in there."

"What do you mean by everything?" Ramouter asked cautiously.

"Everything. How Niall helped me, and then all the people that we helped together."

"When you say all the people that you helped, how many did you help?"

It was as if the air in the small room had frozen as Henley, Ramouter and Lyndsey watched Rebecca lean back and look up at the ceiling, her lips moving silently as she counted.

There was no mistaking the look of triumph on Rebecca's face as she pulled herself up and gave her answer. "Seventeen."

"You helped seventeen people?" asked Ramouter.

"Yes," Rebecca said proudly.

"Does that seventeen include Brandon, Alyssa, Charlie and Kyle Baxter?"

"Oh no. No. That doesn't include them. I forget to add them."

"That would be a total of twenty-one people that you helped?" Ramouter asked as he looked across at Henley who had closed her eyes as though she didn't want to hear the answer.

"I suppose it does," said Rebecca. "Twenty-one. That's a good number."

"And how did you help them?"

"The same way that we helped Brandon, Alyssa, Charlie and Kyle. We released their demons. You must understand. We never hurt them. We saved them all."

Henley felt her heartbeat quickening as a wave of nausea swept over her. She put her right hand to her temple and tried to massage away the sickening realization that there were, possibly, seventeen more victims out there. It was just a question of whether they were alive or if their dead bodies had been left to rot somewhere. Henley reached for the bottle of water as Ramouter cleared his throat.

"Rebecca, where are your diaries? The diaries that have everything in them?" he asked.

"At home. I hid them in the airing cupboard, behind the

boiler. Away from Niall. They were just for me. I wanted to get better at helping people, so I wrote it all down. Their names, what the demons said when we told them to leave."

Henley scribbled a note to herself. She couldn't recall if any diaries had been found when Rebecca's flat had been searched and she wasn't sure if she wanted to read them if they *were* found. She felt even more sick when she thought about the pain that Rebecca, Niall and Caleb had inflicted on people who were genuinely seeking help.

"Rebecca, what was your relationship like with Niall?" Ramouter asked.

"He told me what to do and I did it. You don't understand, he was nice to me. He took me for walks, he listened to me, he said that he cared; that he loved me."

"And how did you feel about him?"

"He saved me. How could I not love him back?" Rebecca asked as she finished the rest of what was now cold tea. "God gave us a baby. We were a family."

"Rebecca, you said that 'we' helped them," said Henley. She removed a photograph of Caleb Annan from her file and placed it in front of Rebecca. "We found DNA belonging to you, Niall Graff and Caleb Annan under the fingernails of both Brandon Whittaker and Alyssa Hadlow."

"Alyssa." Rebecca tutted and shook her head with annoyance. "She was hard work. She was always asking Caleb to help her. She didn't understand that we were *all* helping to save her, but she was weak. She would have been a terrible mother."

"Is that why you took her baby?" asked Henley. "Because you felt that Alyssa was weak?"

"You need to stop saying that I took him," Rebecca shouted out. She stood up and slammed her hand against the table. "I received a blessing. God told me that I was his mother. I AM HIS MOTHER!"

"Maybe we should have a break and give Rebecca time to

calm down," Lyndsey said, her voice shaking, as she placed her hand on Rebecca's arm.

"Don't touch me," Rebecca hissed. She pulled her arm away. "I don't want to talk anymore. I've had enough. I want to go home. I need to be with Shia."

"Rebecca," Henley said calmly, "why don't you sit back down. I've only got a few more questions to ask you. I promise that I won't be long."

"I don't trust you," said Rebecca as she turned and pointed at Ramouter. "Or you."

"I promise, just a few more questions," Henley reassured her.

Rebecca looked at everyone in the room before turning her head toward the wall and beginning to whisper to herself. Both Henley and Ramouter leaned forward as they both strained to hear what she was saying.

"Fine." Rebecca sat back down. "Ask me."

"I was asking you about Caleb," said Henley as she tried to keep her tone neutral. "How did you meet him?"

"Caleb was too soft. He was always telling us to be careful," said Rebecca. "He didn't understand that they were lying to him."

Henley could hear Dr. Mark Ryan telling the SCU that Caleb Annan may have been the 'moral barometer' that kept Rebecca and Niall from crossing the line. Henley didn't want to accept that as a possible truth but now, after listening to Rebecca, she had to acknowledge Mark may have been right. "But how did you meet Caleb?"

"Niall and my aunt took me to his church in Plaistow," said Rebecca. "He helped me. He healed me. He did have a gift, but he was weak. Very weak around women."

"Did Caleb ever try anything on with you?" asked Ramouter. "To take advantage of you. Sexually, I mean?"

Rebecca released a short burst of laughter. "God no. It was never like that. He knew that I belonged to Niall."

Henley inwardly cringed at the word "belonged." It was becoming increasing clear to her that Niall Graff had seen that Rebecca was susceptible to coercion and had taken both sexual and emotional advantage of her.

"We were a team," Rebecca said matter-of-factly. "We worked together, and we did good."

"Did you send the photos of the baby—"

"My baby."

Henley released a sigh and completed her question. "Did you send the photos of the baby to Caleb Annan?"

"Yes, I did. They're beautiful photos, aren't they? My baby is beautiful."

"Can you tell me how Alyssa Hadlow died?" Henley forced herself to ask.

"I already told you. She was weak. I didn't kill her, if that's what you're thinking."

"And what about Kyle Baxter?" asked Ramouter. "We found him hanging from the bandstand in Southwark Park; not far from where you lived. He'd been stabbed and his throat had been cut."

"Oh. I did that," said Rebecca with a wry smile.

"You killed Kyle Baxter?" Ramouter asked.

"There was too much noise. Too much talking," said Rebecca. "He wouldn't stop screaming for his mum and his dad. He kept waking up my baby. I had to stop him. He needed to be quiet. Are we done now? Yes. I think we're done."

"That was the most bizarre interview that I've ever been involved in," said Ramouter as he and Henley watched Rebecca Keeler being escorted back to her cell.

"I hate to say the word," said Henley. "But the woman is actually mad. I wouldn't be at all surprised if a jury found her not guilty on the grounds of diminished responsibility."

"Even if she didn't have mental health issues, it wouldn't take much for the defense to say that she was under the coercive behavior of Niall Graff and that she simply lost control when she tried to kill him," said Ramouter as his mobile phone began to ring. He looked at the screen quizzically. "Unknown number."

"I'll sign us out on Keeler's custody record, while you deal with your call," said Henley. She made her way to the custody desk and Ramouter took a seat on the bench. She was still reeling from Rebecca's disclosure that there had been seventeen more victims. Henley wondered if her diaries really would tell them not only *who* those victims were but more importantly *where* they were. Henley wasn't looking forward to the revelation. Her instincts told her that none of those victims would be alive.

"That was the Old Bailey," said Ramouter as he joined Henley a minute later. "Derrick Sullivan is refusing to leave the cells until he speaks to you."

"Why on earth would Derrick Sullivan want to speak to me?" Henley asked as she looked up and checked the time on the wall. It was almost three o'clock.

"Apparently they both entered a plea of not guilty to murder," Ramouter explained. "But it all kicked off when the judge refused to grant Sullivan bail, but agreed to give it to Serena Annan."

"She's out? The judge gave Annan bail?"

"Aye. The judge gave Annan conditional bail subject to a £250,000 security which was paid by a member of the church. Annan was released an hour ago."

"I still don't understand why Sullivan wants to see me though," Henley said as she and Ramouter walked out of the custody suite.

"He's refusing to say. He's just adamant that he needs to talk to you, and he needs to talk to you now."

78

Three days of being stripped of his liberty had changed Derrick Sullivan. His left arm was in a blue cast, his right eye was heavily bruised and the cut on his cheek had scabbed over. The cell was freezing, and Derrick had stretched the sleeve of his prison-issue tracksuit over his right hand. Derrick's solicitor, Miles Kelly, was standing just outside the cell door.

"Are you sure that you wouldn't be more comfortable in one of the consultation rooms?" Henley asked Miles as she leaned exhaustedly against the wall next to him. She winced as she felt pain shoot across her ankle.

"Chance would be a fine thing. He's point-blank refusing to leave," said Miles. "It's a good thing that I've known a few jailers since way back when, otherwise I don't know what would have happened to him. Probably drag him back to Belmarsh whether he liked it or not."

"Do you have any idea of the day…actually, scratch that, the weeks that I've had, Miles?" Henley said as she straightened up.

"I'll buy you a drink later and you can tell me." Miles grinned.

"It will take more than one drink," Henley replied. Miles opened the cell door. It was the smell that hit her first. Sour and stale, the result of someone who had sweated profusely through their unwashed clothes and only had access to cheap, prison-issued soap.

"Did Serena give you that black eye?" Henley asked as she reluctantly stepped into the cell and sat down on the wooden bench next to Derrick.

"Yeah," Derrick answered softly. Henley wasn't worried about Derrick attempting to make a run for it. He looked as if he'd had every breath kicked out of him.

"You didn't want to talk to me a few days ago at the station," said Henley. "When Miles told you to give a no-comment interview?"

"Just be careful, Inspector," said Miles. "You know that anything that Derrick and I have discussed is privileged information."

"Forgive me. I've had a very long day, my ankle is killing me and sitting in the cells of the Old Bailey on a Tuesday afternoon is the last place that I want to be. So, what is it?"

"I didn't kill Caleb," said Derrick.

Henley sat back. "Is that what you've dragged me down here for? What do you expect me to do with that? That's something for the jury to decide. Miles, I'm going home."

"I was there..." Derrick said hurriedly.

"We know that already."

"But Serena wasn't. She was never at the church, at least not when I was there. She didn't kill Caleb."

"Did Serena put you up to this?" said Henley.

"No. No. I just can't do this anymore. I can't keep up with the lies. I can't take it. Serena didn't kill Caleb. It was Dalisay."

Henley got up from the bench and stood in front of Derrick, ignoring the pain in her ankle.

"Look at me, Derrick," Henley said. "What are you talking about?"

"Serena didn't kill Caleb. It was Dalisay. I was there. I saw everything."

"And why were you at the church?"

"She told me to come."

"Who told you?"

"Dalisay." Derrick rubbed his forehead with his right hand. "Dalisay and I were… I'm sorry, I'm sorry. We were together."

"Together. In a relationship. An affair?" Henley looked at Miles, who simply raised his eyebrow.

"Just to be clear," said Henley. "We're talking about Dalisay Ocampo? The housekeeper?"

Derrick nodded. "It just happened. I met her at a convention at the church. She was nice to me. Tameka and I, things aren't good. They haven't been good, even with the new baby coming, and Dalisay was there for me. I couldn't help it. I fell for her and then she told me that Caleb had been forcing himself on her."

"Stop right there," Henley said as she pulled out her phone and opened up the voice memo app. "Miles, Code C, section 11, subsection b of the Codes of Practice, an interview must take place at a police station unless it would lead to alerting other people suspected of committing an offense but not yet arrested for it."

"Understood. I'll even sign your notebook," Miles replied, as he took a seat on the right side of Derrick and took out his own notebook.

"Derrick Sullivan, I'm cautioning you," said Henley as she repeated the caution and the relevant law. "This is a police interview that is taking place in the cells at the Central Criminal Court. I'm recording this interview on my phone and making a contemporaneous note. Derrick Sullivan, can you tell me what happened on the night Caleb Annan was murdered?"

"Dalisay Ocampo told me to meet her at the church. I thought that I was just going to pick her up and then we would go to a hotel like we've done before."

"The text messages that you received telling you to go to the church came from Serena's number. Dalisay wasn't the one who called you."

"Dalisay was using Serena's phone," Derrick said as he rubbed away at his temples.

"Why would she be using Serena's phone?" Henley asked. "You're not making any sense and I'm starting to think that you're wasting my time."

"Dalisay's phone was stolen a couple of days before Caleb was killed; at least that's what she told me. Serena had let Dalisay use her phone to make calls until she got a new phone. So when I got the message on Sunday night... I wasn't having an affair with Serena. I thought, no, knew it was Dalisay."

"I thought that Dalisay couldn't leave the house without the Annans' permission."

"That's not true. She was free to do what she wanted. She always said that Serena was very nice to her. I mean, she paid for her ticket to go home at Christmas. She treated Dalisay like family."

Henley inhaled the stale air and tried to stop the spinning wheel of questions in her head. "What time did you arrive at the church?"

"About quarter to twelve."

"What happened in the church, Derrick?"

"I parked my car on Vanguard Street, and I walked to the church."

"This might seem like a stupid question but why didn't you park in the car park?"

"Didn't want to get a ticket. Its private parking and I haven't got a permit."

"So you walked to the church. Did you go to the front entrance or the back?"

"The back. I saw Caleb's car, which was odd because she—"

"Who do you mean by 'she'?" Henley interrupted.

"I mean Dalisay. She'd told me that Caleb wasn't there. I went into the church, and I could hear Dalisay screaming, and I thought that something had happened to her. I thought that Caleb was hurting her, but he was on the church floor and Dalisay was stabbing him over and over again."

"It was definitely Dalisay and not Serena?"

"It was Dalisay but she was wearing Serena's clothes."

"How do you know that they were Serena's clothes?"

"We had a church meeting at the Annans' house, and I remember Serena telling Tameka how expensive her outfit was and that it was a pain getting it dry-cleaned."

"Did you notice anything else about Dalisay?"

"She was wearing gloves. Not winter gloves, but the same gloves that Tameka uses at work in the dental surgery and she was wearing a headscarf. Anyway, I dragged Dalisay off Caleb. I tried to help him, I really did, but he was already dead."

"What happened next?"

"I dragged Dalisay out into the car park. I think that I closed the door."

"Did Dalisay tell you what happened before you came?"

"She said that Caleb had attacked her and that she was defending herself."

"Did you believe her?"

"I, I'm not sure. The entire thing was crazy. I just wanted to get out of there and I wanted to get her out of there, but I should have known something was off. She had Serena's car, the Mercedes, the gloves—" Derrick's voice trailed off. "I'm so stupid," he whispered.

"What happened next?"

"We drove around the corner to another building estate. She had a change of clothes in the boot. She told me that she was going to get rid of everything. I had to take my trainers off because they were covered in his blood. I had to drive home in my socks. I thought that she was going burn everything, but then you found all of that stuff in my garage."

"Why didn't you call the police or at least tell DC Ramouter when he came to see you? You hadn't done anything wrong."

"My wife. She didn't know about the affair. Dalisay threatened to tell her everything. I couldn't have that. I couldn't risk losing my family."

"But being accused of murder and going to prison for life was a better option for you?"

"No, of course not, that's why I'm telling you. I can't go back there, and I'm worried about my family and Serena."

"Why are you now worried about Serena? You didn't give a toss about her before."

"I know. I'm sorry, but Dalisay will be home. I don't know what she's planning but I do know that she wants Serena out of the way. Why else would she have done all of this?"

"Derrick, have you spoken to Dalisay since you've been on remand?" Henley asked, with an instinct of what Derrick was going to say next.

"You need to stop her," Derrick said firmly. "I called Dalisay and told her that I couldn't hack it. That I had to tell the truth."

"And what did Dalisay say?"

"She threatened me. She threatened my family." Derrick started to shake.

"Derrick, Serena Annan wasn't released until after lunch," said Henley. "Have you told Serena any of this?"

"I passed her a note when we were in the dock."

"What did that note say, Derrick?"

"I told her that Dalisay did it. That she killed Caleb," said Derrick. "You need to stop her. You don't know Dalisay. No one does."

79

"The 999 call came in five minutes ago," said Ramouter as Henley turned on the blues and twos. They were only ten minutes from Serena Annan's home, but they could have been an hour away as the traffic ground to a halt on the A2.

"For fuck's sake. Move!" Henley shouted as she banged on the horn. "Bloody roadworks. What exactly did they say?"

"That a neighbor called after hearing shouting when she was putting out the rubbish. She then heard banging and more screaming," said Ramouter, grabbing the door handle as Henley swerved the car.

"I don't understand any of this." Henley rode the pavement and broke every road traffic rule as she pulled onto the heath and overtook the black cab in front of her. "Why didn't Dalisay just leave? The manipulative cow completely set up Serena, but I don't understand why."

"But Serena didn't help herself," said Ramouter. "She was obstructive every inch of the way, and once we had the evidence…"

"Evidence that Dalisay clearly planted," said Henley as she focused on maneuvering through the traffic without actually killing anyone. "Ramouter, can you check that backup is on its way?"

Ramouter relayed the information into his radio. "There's another unit about a minute behind us. If they can get through this bloody traffic."

Henley increased her speed as a gap materialized, but instantly slowed down again as she spotted a woman, her black hair flowing, running barefooted down the road. The high beams of the truck coming in the opposite direction shone briefly on the woman's face.

"Ramouter, to your left," Henley shouted out as she hit the brakes sharply and did a U-turn. "That's Dalisay."

"Stop the car," Ramouter shouted.

"Shit," Henley said as she did her best to avoid a pileup. She drove a little farther along and stopped in front of the gas station that was 100 meters from the Annans' home.

"I've got her," Ramouter said. He unbuckled his seat belt, opened the passenger door and jumped out. Henley grabbed hold of her radio as she spotted the flashing lights of the police cars making their way toward them.

"This is DI Henley, DC Ramouter is on Shooters Hill and in pursuit of a five foot three, IC5 female. The suspect is highly dangerous." Henley watched Ramouter dart across the road in pursuit of Dalisay who had turned away from the traffic and into a residential street. Henley leaned over and pulled the passenger door shut and drove the short distance into the driveway of the Annans' house. The sound of sirens grew louder as she got out of the car and Ramouter's voice screeched from the police radio.

"*I've got her. Stop bloody struggling. The suspect is restrained, I need assistance on Vanbrugh Terrace.*"

The front door was wide open and the security light on the front of the house illuminated Henley as she made her way up the stairs.

"Serena," Henley shouted as she stepped into the hallway. Drops of fresh blood glistened on the freshly varnished floor.

"Serena," Henley shouted again. She ignored the pain in

her ankle and followed the blood up the stairs. The sirens grew louder, and the hallway flashed with blue light as police cars sped into the driveway. As far as Henley was aware, the children were staying with their grandparents. She felt a wave of relief when she saw that the beds were made but the rooms empty. Henley followed the streaks of blood along the white walls.

"Oh my God. Serena."

Henley dropped to her knees as she spotted her lying in a heap on the small landing of the third floor. Serena was still dressed in the blue tracksuit that had been issued to her in the prison. Her face was covered in raw scratches. Henley looked down and saw that the tracksuit was soaked with blood and that Serena was holding on tightly to the handle of a kitchen knife that had pierced her stomach.

"Please be alive," Henley said as she put her fingers to Serena's neck. "Please." She exhaled as she felt the soft rhythm of Serena's pulse under her fingers.

"Inspector Henley. It's DC Duncan. Where are you?"

"We're up here," Henley shouted out. "We're on the top floor. We need an ambulance now."

She looked down as Serena's eyes fluttered open.

"Don't worry," Henley said, cradling Serena's head. "I've got you. I've got you."

80

"Dalisay Ocampo, for the benefit of the tape, it's Wednesday 4 March at 12:45 p.m. and you were arrested last night for the murder of Caleb Annan and the attempted murder of Serena Annan," said Henley as she smoothed out her notes on the table.

"You forgot to add that she's also been arrested for assault on a PC," said Ramouter as he shifted uncomfortably in his seat. "You kicked me in the groin. Twice."

"I had no idea who you were. I thought that you were attacking me," said Dalisay who sat on the other side of the table wearing a gray tracksuit after her clothing had been removed and seized as forensic evidence. She pulled her long hair over her shoulder and started to braid it. "You didn't identify yourself and it was dark. All I did was defend myself."

"I identified myself to you," said Ramouter as he folded his arms.

"Well, I didn't hear you."

"Dalisay," said Henley as Ramouter looked at her and shook his head in disbelief. "You have been arrested for very serious offenses. Are you sure that you don't want a solicitor? Because I have no problem waiting for one to get here."

"I haven't done anything wrong," said Dalisay. "I'm the victim. I've always been the victim. Serena Annan attacked me when she arrived home and I defended myself. This idiot detective didn't identify himself, attacked me and I defended myself."

"And Caleb Annan?" asked Ramouter.

"That has nothing to do with me."

"Not according to the evidence of Derrick Sullivan," said Henley.

"So, you're going to take the word of a man who's already been charged with murder and not the word of a woman who was subject to the controlling and coercive behavior of both Caleb and Serena Annan," Dalisay said confidently.

"There is no evidence of you being subjected to such behavior," said Henley. "You had a legitimate contract of employment with the Annans."

"Mrs. Annan didn't pay me."

"We've got copies of the payments that Mrs. Annan made into a bank account in your name, and we've also got confirmation that Mrs. Annan paid for your Tier 2 visa."

"That doesn't prove anything," said Dalisay. "As I said, I was a victim in this scenario. Mr. Annan took sexual advantage of me just like he did with every other woman who caught his attention."

"Were you aware that Caleb Annan was in a sexual relationship with Nicole Fleming and Uliana Piontek?" asked Henley.

"Caleb Annan slept with anything with a pulse," Dalisay spat out.

"So you were aware?"

"He was always flaunting his affairs in his wife's face. I actually felt sorry for her," Dalisay said with what sounded like sincerity. "Can you imagine sitting down to dinner and your husband takes a phone call from whatever woman is slut of the week, right in front of you?"

"But you were sleeping with him. So, what did that make you?"

Henley enjoyed the small moment of satisfaction as the fake

sincerity disappeared from Dalisay's face. Henley would have sworn that in that moment, Dalisay wanted to kill her as she stared back at Henley with absolute contempt.

"I was a victim," Dalisay said firmly. "Make sure that you make a note of that."

"Did Serena know that you were sleeping with Caleb?"

"I think you meant to ask if she knew that her husband was taking advantage of a vulnerable woman," Dalisay replied smugly. "She probably did, which is why she killed him and why she tried to kill me too."

Henley leaned back as she studied Dalisay's face. "There are no marks on you," she said. "You said that Serena tried to kill you, but—"

"She put her hands around my throat, and she squeezed," Dalisay shouted. She stood, placed her hands on the table and leaned forward. There were mere inches between Henley and Dalisay. Henley could feel the heat from Dalisay's words as she spoke. "She said that she was going to kill me. I couldn't breathe."

"Sit down, before I'm forced to put you down," Henley said calmly.

"I couldn't breathe," Dalisay hissed, but she sat down.

"But you've got no bruises, there's no reddening around your neck. No cuts or scratches. You're almost flawless," said Henley.

"That woman is a killer," Dalisay replied.

"You keep on saying that, but Serena is the one in the hospital with a stab wound in her stomach and cuts to her hands."

Dalisay smiled as she leaned over to her right and spoke into the small microphone on the wall. "I was acting in self-defense," she said.

"OK," Henley replied as Ramouter let out an exasperated sigh. "Let's say that I believe you, that Serena was trying to kill you. Why would Serena perceive you as being such a threat that she would have to get rid of you?"

"Because she was jealous." Dalisay brushed aside a strand of hair and hooked it behind her ear. "Caleb didn't want her. I suppose that she was quite a catch when they first met, but now she's just a tarnished and dented trophy wife. Caleb needed a real woman. He needed someone like…"

"Someone like?" Henley asked as Dalisay sat back with tightly pursed lips. "Someone like me. Is that what you were going to say?"

"You're putting words into my mouth."

"You wanted to be with Caleb, didn't you? You wanted to be more than just *one* of the many women that he was sleeping with?"

"Absolutely not," Dalisay fired back. "How many times do I have to tell you? Caleb took advantage."

"Oh, I agree with you that he took advantage," said Henley. "He took advantage of Uliana, Nicole, Raina Davison and Tameka Sullivan, but with you it was different. You wanted to be with him."

"You're talking rubbish."

"You must have been so angry when you found out that Caleb was pursuing Tameka Sullivan and that he'd set up a love nest with Nicole Fleming."

"No."

"You could have left the Annans at any time," Henley continued. "You had your passport, the funds and plenty of opportunity."

"That's a lie. They kept me prisoner."

"Dalisay, stop wasting our time. The truth is that you didn't like the way that Caleb was treating you. You were angry, vengeful and calculating. You stabbed him forty-eight times and you framed Serena Annan."

"Why would I do that, if Mrs. Annan had been so good to me?" Dalisay smirked.

"Well, only you would know the answer to that," Henley replied.

"Mrs. Annan killed her husband. You have the proof."

"You're right. We have proof that *you* killed Caleb and we'll get to that," Henley said with satisfaction as Dalisay began to fidget with both unease and distrust. "After you viciously murdered Caleb Annan, you stepped in his blood, ripped his wedding ring off his finger and stole his phone; isn't that correct?"

"Oh my God. You're unbelievable." Dalisay ran her hands through her hair and clasped the back of her head.

"You then sent a text to Serena Annan from Caleb's phone that said he wouldn't be home until late and that he had a few things to sort out for tomorrow."

"Can't you shut her up? What sort of a man are you?" Dalisay said to Ramouter.

"A man who listens to his boss, so perhaps you should answer her questions?" Ramouter replied.

"This is an absolute joke. I didn't kill Caleb because I wasn't there," said Dalisay purposefully and with an air of disturbing and chilling clarity. "And you've got no evidence that it was me. As I understand it, Caleb's blood was found on Serena's clothes and her DNA was on the gloves. You've. Got. Nothing. On. Me."

"Wow," said Ramouter as he looked across at Henley and let out a short burst of laughter. "I'm sorry, that was very unprofessional of me."

"Wow indeed," said Henley as she sat back, equally amazed. Dalisay behaved as though she'd been arrested for nothing more than non-payment of a parking fine.

"Here's the thing about evidence," said Henley as she opened the laptop and pressed play on the video player. "You can find it in the strangest of places."

Dalisay straightened up as Henley turned the screen around.

"Did you know that Caleb had installed two dashcams in his car?" asked Henley. "It's very tiny, the size of a car key. He had one in the rearview mirror and another in the back."

Dalisay's face paled as Henley pressed play.

"This is footage taken from the camera on the night that

Caleb was killed," Henley explained. "It turns out that Serena did go to the church that night. This is her car entering the car park at 10:02 p.m."

Dalisay smiled as the footage showed a silver Mercedes entering the car park and parking in front of Caleb's car. Serena could be seen walking in front of the car and entering the church.

"Caleb could control the camera through an app on his phone," said Henley. "It turns out that he never turned the camera off and the footage remains on his phone for thirty days. We didn't find the footage until we found his phone. I'm going to fast-forward to nine minutes past ten and let it play."

One minute later, Uliana Piontek could be seen running across the screen and into the church. One minute and 45 seconds later, Uliana ran out again.

"I don't see the point of this," Dalisay said as the video played on. Eight minutes later Serena reappeared on the screen as she left the church and entered her car. Seventeen seconds later, Caleb left the church and stood in front of Serena's car which then reversed out of the car park.

"Caleb Annan was alive and well when Serena left the church at 10:21 p.m.," said Ramouter. "And if we fast-forward an hour and four minutes. That's footage of you running into the church."

"That must be footage from another day," said Dalisay. "I didn't go out the night that Caleb was killed."

"Well, the footage says otherwise, because twenty minutes later Derrick Sullivan arrives, and fifteen minutes after that..." said Ramouter. "I'm going to pause it right there."

Dalisay didn't say a word as the screen froze on an image of her standing in front of Caleb's car with Derrick holding onto her arm. Her face was softly illuminated by the streetlights that shone into the car park. Her clothing was covered in large dark patches of Caleb's blood which had soaked through the gray cashmere loungewear. Her head was covered with a scarf.

"And if I zoom in right here." Henley moved the cursor to a large knife in Dalisay's hand.

"Is there anything that you would like to say about that?" asked Henley.

"As I said." Dalisay smirked as she shook her head. "I'm the victim and I've got nothing else to say to you. We're done."

81

Henley stepped out of Lewisham police station and breathed the cold winter air into her lungs. She looked up at the few stars that flickered in the city night sky.

"You see more stars in Bradford," Ramouter said as he appeared at Henley's side and looked up.

"Well, this is southeast London, and this is as good as it gets. If you're lucky you might spot a helicopter," said Henley as she pulled on her gloves.

"Yay, I'll get my binoculars out."

"Speaking of Bradford," said Henley, "and you can tell me to mind my own business if you want, and I'm not just thinking about myself, but have you and Michelle made a decision?"

"Are you trying to tell me that you'll miss me if I went back?" asked Ramouter.

"OK, yes. Yes, I would," Henley said with a sigh as she and Ramouter walked back to her car. "I've got used to you."

"Thanks. That makes me feel wanted."

"Good. So have you...ow," Henley said as a red-hot shooting pain ran across her right ankle.

"I don't know why you don't get that looked at," said Ramouter as Henley bent down and gently rubbed it. "You've been limping around like a wounded duck."

"It's just a sprain. I just need to rest and take a couple of painkillers."

"You're so stubborn."

"And you're rude," Henley said. She straightened up with a grimace and they began to walk again, albeit more slowly. "So have you decided?" she asked.

"Aye, we have," said Ramouter. "Michelle wants to be with me, here in London."

"Really?" Henley said, pleased but surprised. "And how do you feel about it?"

"Good. I've got this job and I don't want to give it up. I know that it sounds selfish but that's how I feel. I think that we can make it work."

"We're all here to support you, and Stanford loves to babysit."

"I'll keep that in mind. So, what next?" asked Ramouter.

"We don't have to be in the restaurant until eight, so I was thinking of checking in on Serena Annan and Brandon Whittaker first. I'm happy to go alone. You don't have to tag along."

"I'm more than happy to tag along."

"Good. I just want to make sure that they're OK. This entire thing started with them. It's a bit of a sick thing to say but we may never have found Brandon Whittaker if Caleb hadn't been murdered."

"Hopefully the CPS will come back with a charging decision soon for Dalisay," said Ramouter. "Not that it should be that difficult. Derrick Sullivan has already agreed to give evidence against her. If he's lucky they might drop the murder charge."

"If he's lucky," said Henley. "I don't think that anyone has been lucky in this case, including the ones who have been left behind. Everyone is broken. Including you—how's your groin?"

"It's not funny," Ramouter said as Henley began to laugh. "Don't tell anyone about that."

"Yeah, it might be a bit late for that," said Henley as she

opened the car door. "Stanford already knows and if Stanford knows then that means Eastie knows."

"Great, that means that I'm going to have to listen to his rubbish jokes over dinner."

"Just remind him that he lost a bet that you would leave the SCU in six days," said Henley.

82

"Nice to have you back," said Dr. Isabelle Collins without an ounce of sarcasm.

"I was always going to come back," said Henley. She took off her coat and looked at the armchair where she usually sat before limping over with an air boot on her ankle and sitting down on the small sofa.

"What happened to your foot?" asked Dr. Collins.

"I fractured a bone in my ankle. So, I'm stuck in this thing for six weeks."

"How are things at home?"

"Home is… My husband is not happy with me. He wants things that I can't give him."

"And what are those things?"

Henley shook her head. "No. Not today. Let's leave that for another session."

"OK," Dr. Collins accepted. "We'll park that subject for another day."

"Thank you."

"I saw the news. You found the baby."

"Yes, we did. Thank God. I don't think that I could have lived with myself if something had happened to him."

"And the pastor's murder? I saw that the charges were dropped against his wife?"

"Yeah, they were," Henley said solemnly.

"I suspect that you must have very mixed emotions about the result."

"Not really. I did my job and followed the evidence. It was never a wrongful arrest. I made the right decision based on the information that I had at the time."

Even Henley wasn't convinced by her own words, and she was sure that Dr. Collins would pick up on her uncertainty.

"Then why is there such a strong feeling of resignation around you?" Dr. Collins asked.

Henley felt a tightness in her chest as she thought back to the words that Serena had spat venomously through the wicket after she'd arrested her. "She made me doubt myself," Henley finally said.

"What do you mean?"

"Serena said to me, 'I don't know how you sleep at night, knowing that you're doing this to another black woman. You're a fucking embarrassment to yourself and your family. You should be ashamed of yourself.' She made me feel like a shit."

"She hit a nerve?"

"Of course she did," Henley said. "But I could hardly blame her. It was a horrible situation for her."

Henley didn't tell Dr. Isabelle Collins the rest. How Serena's words had felt like acid on Henley's skin and reignited all her insecurities. Dark memories of how every person of color that she'd encountered, while doing her job as a police officer, had looked at her with either disgust, bewilderment, or, even worse, betrayal.

"Can I ask you a question?" Dr. Collins asked. She removed her glasses and leaned forward in her seat. "Do you want forgiveness from Serena Annan?"

Henley closed her eyes as she thought about her answer. She wondered what it would reveal about her if she admitted the truth of Dr. Collins's words.

"I don't do this job for the thanks or forgiveness," she eventually said. "I can't be wasting my time second-guessing myself or seeking forgiveness from—" Henley sat up as she felt another wave of nausea wash over her. She looked across at the calendar on Dr. Collins's desk. She put a hand to her stomach as she swallowed back the bile and ignored the feel-good message of the day.

"Is everything all right?"

"Yeah. Sorry." Henley winced and inhaled deeply. "Work has just been a lot and I just need some water."

"How are you getting on with DC Ramouter?" Dr. Collins asked as she picked up the jug of water on her table, poured Henley a glass and handed it to her.

Henley took a sip and waited for the nausea to subside. "Ramouter and I are fine," she finally said. "But things are going to change a lot for him and I just think that his life is going to get harder once his family gets here."

"So, you're worried about him?"

"I'm not worried. I'm just…concerned."

"That would be perfectly understandable. You and DC Ramouter have been through a lot together in a very short space of time."

"Trauma," said Henley firmly. "We've shared trauma together and I don't think that I like that, but I'm not talking about that. This isn't about me."

"It's always about you and you need to understand and accept that you and DC Ramouter are bonded by trauma and you're both in a profession that is based on trauma."

Henley sat back. "You make me sound like a sadist."

"That's not my intention and I think that you know perfectly well what I meant."

"No, I don't actually. I don't see why me being concerned about Ramouter is such an issue."

"Why did you keep him on as your partner?"

"Because that is what Pellacia wanted and how would Ramouter have felt if I'd just passed him around to someone else like a regift?"

"You feel responsible for him?"

Henley didn't answer as she focused her attention on the clock on the wall.

"He could have left," she finally said. "No one would have blamed him, but he didn't leave. He's still here."

"Why didn't you leave? And I don't mean six months ago. I mean after the first encounter with Peter Olivier?"

Henley took a breath. "And what would I have done? I mean, I love my daughter, my family, but other than being a mother what would have been the point of me just sitting at home and watching my husband work while Emma jumped headfirst into a sandpit at her nursery?"

"Is that why you kept Ramouter as your partner? To make sure that there was a point to you?"

"A point to me?" said Henley. "You make me sound desperate, as if I'm trying to find a reason to be relevant."

"It's something to think about," Dr. Collins continued. "Trauma, yours and other people's, was always going to be the bond between you and DC Ramouter. It's the nature of your work and whether you like it or not, trauma is the thing that drives you and it's the shared trauma of what took place last year with Peter Olivier that keeps you going."

"I'm going to disagree with you about that."

"OK. If we're not going to talk about what bonds you and DC Ramouter and we're not going to talk about your husband, what *would* you like to talk about?"

Henley leaned back as a second wave of nausea took hold and her forehead prickled with sweat. "Someone close to me."

"Your mum?"

"No. Not my mum. I want to talk to you about my old boss. I need to talk about Rhimes."

★ ★ ★ ★ ★

ACKNOWLEDGMENTS

First things first, there are loads of people that I must thank, and I apologize in advance if I've missed anyone out. Thank you to my brilliant agent, Oli Munson, and the brilliant team at A.M. Heath. I remember when I first pitched the idea of this book to Oli at our very first meeting. I'd been reading about a few court cases where the defendants had been accused of manslaughter or grievous bodily harm because they'd been performing exorcisms on their victims. The idea of exorcisms stuck with me, and my very simple pitch was "a pastor has been murdered and the body of a young man who may have been the victim of an exorcism is found in the church." I'm so pleased that I was able to turn that tiny seed of an idea into *The Binding Room*. As always, I have to thank my brilliant and supportive group of writing friends, especially Jonathan, who was the first person to read the first thirty thousand words of *The Binding Room*. Thank you to my editor, Manpreet Grewal, for her amazingly supportive team at HQ, and John Glynn and his team at Hanover Square Press.

Somehow, and its nothing short of a miracle, I finished this book during a pandemic and the various lockdowns. Like everyone else, there were highs and lows, but I'm so blessed to have had the support of my family and friends. Special thanks and love to my mum, dad, Gavin, Maki, Jason, Sheulee and Gaynor and a special shout out to my nephew, Neo, and my godchildren, Nyra and Zachary, for the video chats (who are far too young for this book and will find out later what their auntie's books are about).

I want to thank my granny, aka the Reverend Priscilda Noel, who is no longer with us but who I know wouldn't have minded one little bit that her granddaughter was writing about murdered church pastors and exorcisms. She would have been the first person to tell the congregation to buy my book.

And finally, thank you to the readers. The best thing about the pandemic was that I was able to meet (virtually) so many readers around the world who received *The Jigsaw Man*, Henley and myself so enthusiastically. You've all been brilliant.